当代英美文学系列教程

总主编 尚必武

当代英国小说教程

主　编　徐　彬

副主编　刘国清

U0360307

上海交通大学出版社
SHANGHAI JIAO TONG UNIVERSITY PRESS

内容提要

  本书包含"当代英国族裔小说""当代英国世界主义小说""当代英国脱欧小说""当代英国战争小说"和"当代英国历史小说"五个板块。教材选取当代英国著名作家的成名作,辅以导读和思考题。在"世界百年未有之大变局"的历史语境下,本书为读者审视当代英国小说的叙事审美机制,对涉及其中的政治经济、文化与心理因素进行较为系统的文学性考察提供了蓝本和依据。本书适合高校英语语言文学专业本科生和研究生使用,也适合对英国小说感兴趣的读者使用。

图书在版编目(CIP)数据

当代英国小说教程/徐彬主编. 一上海:上海交
通大学出版社,2024.5
 当代英美文学系列教程/尚必武总主编
 ISBN 978 - 7 - 313 - 30094 - 2

 Ⅰ.①当… Ⅱ.①徐… Ⅲ.①小说研究-英国-现代
-高等学校-教材 Ⅳ.①I561.074

 中国国家版本馆 CIP 数据核字(2024)第 034437 号

当代英国小说教程
DANGDAI YINGGUO XIAOSHUO JIAOCHENG

主 编:徐 彬
出版发行:上海交通大学出版社   地 址:上海市番禺路 951 号
邮政编码:200030   电 话:021 - 64071208
印 制:苏州市越洋印刷有限公司   经 销:全国新华书店
开 本:889mm×1194mm 1/16   印 张:12
字 数:300 千字
版 次:2024 年 5 月第 1 版   印 次:2024 年 5 月第 1 次印刷
书 号:ISBN 978 - 7 - 313 - 30094 - 2
定 价:58.00 元

　　2012 年，国务院学位委员会第六届学科评议组在外国语言文学一级学科目录下设置了五大方向，即外国文学、语言学与应用语言学、翻译学、国别与区域研究、比较文学与跨文化研究。2020 年起，教育部开始大力推进"新文科"建设，不仅发布了《新文科建设宣言》，还设立了"新文科研究与改革实践项目"，旨在进一步打破学科壁垒，促进学科的交叉融合，提升文科建设的内涵与质量。在这种背景下，外语研究生教育既迎来了机遇，同时又面临新的挑战，这就要求我们的研究生培养模式为适应这些变化而进行必要的改革与创新。在孙益、陈露茜、王晨看来，"研究生教育方针、教育路线的贯彻执行，研究生教育体制改革和教育思想的革新，研究生专业培养方案、培养计划的制定，研究生教学内容和教学方法的改革，最终都会反映和落实到研究生教材的建设上来。重视研究生教材建设工作，是提高高校研究生教学质量和保证教学改革成效的关键所在。"① 从这种意义上说，教材建设是提高外语研究生教育的一个重要抓手。

　　就国内外语专业研究生教材而言，上海外语教育出版社推出的《高等院校英语语言文学专业研究生系列教材》占据了最主要的地位。该系列涵盖语言学、语言教学、文学理论、原著选读等多个领域，为我国的外语研究生培养做出了重要贡献。需要指出的是，同外语专业本科生教材建设相比，外语专业研究生教材建设显得明显滞后。很多高校的外语专业研究生课堂上所使用的教材基本上是原版引进教材或教师自编讲义。我们知道，"教材不仅是教师进行教学的基本工具，而且是学生获取知识、培养能力的重要手段。研究生教材是直接体现高等院校研究生教学内容和教学方法的知识载体，也是反映高等院校教学水平、科研水平及其成果的重要标志，优秀的研究生教材是提高研究生教学质量的重要保证。"② 上海交通大学外国语学院历来重视教材建设，曾主编《研究生英语教程》《多维教程》《新视野大学英语》《21 世纪大学英语》等多套本科和研究生层次的英语教材，在全国范围内产生了较大影响。

---

① 孙益、陈露茜、王晨：《高校研究生教材建设的国际经验与中国路径》，载《学位与研究生教育》2018 年第 2 期，第 72 页。
② 同上。

为进一步加强和推动外语专业,尤其是英语专业英美文学方向的研究生教材建设,助力研究生培养从接受知识到创造知识的模式转变,在上海交通大学出版社的大力支持下,上海交通大学外国语学院发挥优势,携手复旦大学外文学院、上海外国语大学英语学院、北京科技大学外国语学院、东北师范大学外国语学院、中南财经政法大学外国语学院、山东师范大学外国语学院等兄弟单位,主编《当代英美文学系列教程》。本系列教材重点聚焦20世纪80年代以来的英美文学与文论,由《当代英国小说教程》《当代美国小说教程》《当代英国戏剧教程》《当代美国戏剧教程》《当代英国诗歌教程》《当代美国诗歌教程》《当代文学理论教程》《当代叙事理论教程》等8册构成。

本系列教材以问题意识为导向,围绕当代英美文学,尤其是21世纪英美文学的新类型、新材料、新视角、新话题,将文学作为一种直面问题、思考问题、应对问题、解决问题的重要途径和方式,从而发掘和彰显文学的能动性。在每册教材的导论部分,首先重点概述20世纪80年代以来的文学发展态势与特征,由此回答"当代起于何时"的问题,在此基础上简述教材内容所涉及的主要命题、思潮、样式、作家和作品,由此回答"新在哪里"的问题。本系列教材打破按照时间顺序来划分章节的惯例,转而以研究问题或文学样式来安排各章。例如,教材纳入了气候变化、新型战争、族裔流散、世界主义等问题与文学样式。在文学作品的选择标准上,教材以类型和样式的标准来分类,如气候变化文学、新型战争文学等。每个门类下均选取数篇具有典型性的作品,并对其主题特色、历史背景及其相关文学特质进行介绍,凸显对文本性敏锐的分析能力以及对相关文学研究视角及理论知识的掌握。除此之外,教材还有意识地呈现当代英美文学的新的创作手法、文学思潮和文体特征。教材的每章集中一种文学样式、类型、思潮或流派,选择2~3篇代表性作品,单篇选读篇幅在5 000~10 000 词(英文)左右,每篇附有5 000 字(中文)左右的分析导读以及若干思考题。教材对作家或理论家及其著作的选取,不求涵盖全部,而是以权威性、代表性和重要性为首要原则,兼顾年代、流派、思潮等因素。本系列教材适合国内高校外国文学尤其是英美文学专业的博士研究生、硕士研究生、高年级本科生、文学研究者与爱好者使用。

本系列教材在编写过程中得到了上海交通大学外国语学院、上海交通大学出版社以及国内外同行专家学者的关心、帮助与支持,特此谢忱!

尚必武

2023 年 3 月

第二次世界大战后，英国逐渐从一个曾占世界陆地面积 1/4 的庞大帝国回缩至英伦三岛的岛国存在状态。帝国的消逝给当代英国人的生活带来不可估量的深远影响。20 世纪 40 年代末到 60 年代及以后，金融危机和英镑贬值显示出帝国的衰退，与此同时，英国经济和制造业实力大幅下降。如著名历史学家罗伯特·科尔斯在《英格兰的身份》(*Identity of England*, 2002) 中所写，二战后大概 15 年的时间里，"衰退"作为英国独有的特征已嵌入国家政治的中心，成为反思国家政治的关键词。20 世纪 60 年代，苏格兰、威尔士和北爱尔兰部分地区的独立意识愈发强烈。20 世纪 90 年代末，各地自治措施的提出使英国成为一个相对分裂的王国。进入 21 世纪，英国不仅面临以"苏格兰公投"为表征的国家内部的分裂危机，还陷入脱欧后社会发展迟缓的窘境。

20 世纪后半叶，随着英国殖民地相继独立，英国已经开始面临具有其本国特征的"百年未有之大变局"，英国的种族面貌、国内外政治经济和文化状况均发生了翻天覆地的变化。在当代英国社会生活中，英国人和英国性，这两个曾几何时确定无疑的概念变得越发模糊。伴随着大英帝国的衰落，另一个英国逐渐出现：它不再迷恋传统，在观点、生活方式和文化上更加自由和开放。英国社会逐渐出现了新思想和新的自我观念的转型，其中旧思想被淘汰起到了加速转型的作用。英国社会结构的重塑鼓励了一系列新声音的产生；与此同时，英国社会发展的新愿景得以抒发。当代英国小说与英国社会和政治经济之间的共生与互动关系使其成为传播英国新声的有效载体。

标志当代英国"百年未有之大变局"的一系列代表性重大历史事件有：1968 年 4 月 20 日英国保守党国会议员埃诺奇·鲍威尔发表充满种族歧视与迫害色彩的"血河演讲"；"血色星期天"(1972 年 1 月 30 日，英国士兵在北爱尔兰射杀手无寸铁的爱尔兰抗议者)；1973 年 1 月 1 日英国加入欧洲共同体；1979 年玛格丽特·撒切尔成为英国首相；1982 年 4 月到 6 月的英阿马岛海战；1997 年 7 月 1 日香港回归中国；伦敦七七爆炸案(2005 年 7 月 7 日)；苏格兰公投(2014 年 9 月 18 日)；苏格兰筹划举行第二次独立公投；5·22 曼彻斯特恐怖袭

击事件(2017 年 5 月 22 日);英国脱欧(2016 年 6 月英国全民公投决定"脱欧",2020 年 1 月
31 日正式脱欧);2020 年布克奖 13 名入围者中超过半数是有色人种作家;2022 年 9 月 8 日
英国女王伊丽莎白二世驾崩,英国官方称之为"伦敦桥倒塌";2022 年 9 月 6 日伊丽莎白·
特拉斯被任命为英国第 56 任首相,2022 年 10 月 20 日宣布辞职,在任仅 45 天,被称为英国
历史上任期最短的首相;2022 年 10 月 15 日,印裔英国人里希·苏纳克成为英国历史上首
位具有有色族裔身份背景的英国首相,凡此种种不一而足。

编写和使用《当代英国小说教程》的主要目的在于向读者阐明从伊丽莎白一世(1533—
1603)到伊丽莎白二世(1926—2022),英国从帝国到岛国地缘政治收缩状态下所面临的前
所未有的政治经济、种族文化、战争、历史、生态等问题在当代英国小说中的反映。在全球
化语境下,英国不可能独善其身,英国或大英帝国的"过去/历史"同样是作用于英国当下社
会的不可回避的现实。编者希望能从文学批评者而非历史记录者的视角出发,审视当代英
国小说的叙事审美机制,并对其中可能涉及的政治经济、文化与心理因素进行较为系统的
文学性考察。

文学是民族国家意志的表达,是国民集体无意识的抒发。本书编者学习借鉴习近平总
书记"百年未有之大变局"的科学论断,通过对特定文学作品的分析,力图揭示英国已经经
历、正在经历和将要经历的"百年未有之大变局"。以当代英国小说为研究对象,编者详尽
考察了当代英国的变局、乱局、民族国家共同体的危机及其应对策略,这将为我们理解和应
对英国和以英国为代表的欧洲当下及未来一段时间内的政治、经济、文化、意识形态等方面
的问题提供科学判断依据。

《当代英国小说教程》聚焦 20 世纪 70 年代以来英国小说创作的整体状况与文学特征,
共计五章,分别是当代英国族裔小说、当代英国世界主义小说、当代英国脱欧小说、当代英
国战争小说和当代英国历史小说。

一、当代英国族裔小说

在 1968 年 4 月 20 日的"血河演讲"中,为了向伯明翰保守党政治中心的听众以及所有
白皮肤的英国人说明大量有色移民的到来会引发英国"种族纯净"、国家共同体和民族文化
危机,英国保守党议员埃诺奇·鲍威尔引用了一位英国白人工人的话:"在这个国家 15 或
20 年的时间里,黑人将手拿皮鞭控制白人。"英国政府打的"种族牌"不过是一种制造不必
要的异族入侵恐慌的修辞手段。时至今日,在英国现实生活中,"黑人手拿皮鞭控制白人"
的事件尚未发生。有族裔背景的人口从未超过英国人口总数的 8%,英国有色移民及其后

代所创作的文学作品却成为当代英国文坛举足轻重的组成部分。20 世纪 50 年代以来，许多从前殖民地移民到英国的作家和这些移民的子女一直在创作小说，阐明了自身族裔生活的经历以及与之相关的种族、阶级、文化、伦理、身份等问题。

以萨姆·塞尔文（Sam Selvon，1923—1994）、V. S. 奈保尔（V. S. Naipaul，1932—）、萨曼·拉什迪（Salman Rushdie，1947—）、石黑一雄（Kazuo Ishiguro，1954—）、哈尼夫·库雷西（Hanif Kureishi，1954—）、安德里亚·利维（Andrea Levy，1956—）、卡里尔·菲利普斯（Caryl Phillips，1958—）和扎迪·史密斯（Zadie Smith，1975—）为代表的当代英国族裔小说家的创作改变了当代英国文坛的颜色。当代英国作家种族身份与创作主题的多样化使当代英国文学如同朱利安·巴恩斯（Julian Barnes，1946—）在小说《英格兰，英格兰》（*England，England*，1998）中描写的包罗万象的旨在展示"英国性"的主题公园，外部世界与异质元素深切地影响了英格兰主题公园的集体想象。透过小说，巴恩斯探讨了国家刻板印象的流通、国家的商品化以及个人认同与国家认同之间的关系，指出民族认同是文化建构和再生产的产物。

1948 年 6 月，名为"帝国风驰号"的轮船将 492 名来自加勒比的黑人送抵英国，开启了第二次世界大战后有色人种移民英国的高潮。1962 年《英联邦移民法案》（Commonwealth Immigration Act）颁布，英国战后移民潮宣告结束。萨姆·塞尔文、哈尼夫·库雷西、卡里尔·菲利普斯、扎迪·史密斯等族裔作家的小说创作与其自身二战后英国有色移民的生活密不可分。从有色移民及其后代的视角出发，上述作家作品中有关英国的描述可被大致分为两类：一、移民眼中以伦敦为代表的英国是"应许之地""世界上最安全的地方"；二、乔纳森·拉班指出，"污垢"是描写英国城市的作品中经常被提到的唯一特征，污垢似乎被赋予"道德提喻"的功能。当代英国族裔小说承认种族主义的原因是复杂的，殖民主义遗产是其中一个原因。尽管英帝国业已衰落，但在一些白人角色心中仍有种族优越感的残留。第二次世界大战后，世界范围内的去殖民化进程打破了这种思维方式的合理性。

从塞尔文的小说《孤独的伦敦人》（*The Lonely Londoners*，1956）中加勒比移民将伦敦"黑人化"的欲望、库雷西的小说《郊区佛爷》（*The Buddha of Suburbia*，1990）中哈伦的东方文化炒作、史密斯的小说《白牙》（*White Teeth*，2000）中男主人公孟加拉移民萨马德对在儿子所在学校增加穆斯林节日的尝试，到菲利普斯的游记《大西洋之声》（*The Atlantic Sound*，2001）中对利物浦城里非洲奴隶贸易遗迹与遗物的介绍，当代英国族裔小说家试图以其真实的英国生活和创作经历向读者传递如下信息：来自前英国殖民地的有色移民的到来和存在使英国的殖民历史与当下现实、英国本土文化与族裔"他者"文化、英国白人与有色移民之间不可避免地产生了互动关系。"新英国人"（new breed of Englishman）由其外表和杂合身份所决定。上述互动关系共同造就了当代英国的"英联邦"国家属性。与其说英联邦是英国创造的国际政治组织,不如说是以种族和文化杂合为表征的英国国家身份的代名词。霍米·巴巴将"地方世界主义"定义为"从少数主义者的视角出发衡量全球进步"。借用这一定义,可做出如下判断:唤醒英国人对英国"地方世界主义"(从英国有色移民视角出发衡量英国发展)的认知可被视为当代英国族裔流散作家心照不宣的集体创作动机。

二、当代英国世界主义小说

英国首相特雷莎·梅在 2016 年保守党大会上公然驳斥世界主义理想,声称"如果你认为自己是一个世界公民,那你就哪里的公民都不是"。她的宣言引发了明显的仇外心理和反移民暴力情绪的反弹,为当代英国的民族主义和种族主义神话提供了赤裸裸的掩护,这是全球化、全球危机("9·11"恐怖袭击、2008 年全球经济危机、全球生态危机等)与英国国家危机(2014 年苏格兰独立公投和 2016 年英国脱欧公投等)在英国当代历史背景下共同运作的产物。与政治生活中反世界主义情绪不同的是,当代英国小说为世界主义的发展提供了空间。以珍妮特·温特森(Jeanette Winterson,1959—)、大卫·米切尔(David Mitchell,1969—)、阿莉·史密斯(Ali Smith,1962—)、纳迪姆·阿斯拉姆(Nadeem Aslam,1966—)和哈里·昆兹鲁(Hari Kunzru,1969—)为代表的小说家创作的当代英国世界主义小说以全球性的视野和多元文化并存的理念为基点,用文学的虚构形式创造了一个包容、理解和尊重差异的世界,以对抗当代英国狭隘的民族主义、种族主义、分裂主义等霸权话语的潜在威胁。

从温特森的小说《苹果笔记本》(The PowerBook,2000)对父权异性恋霸权话语的颠覆、米切尔的小说《云图》(Cloud Atlas,2004)对非白人和克隆人受奴役遭遇的同情、阿斯拉姆的小说《迷失恋人的地图》(Maps for Lost Lovers,2004)对种族和宗教分裂现象的批判,到昆兹鲁的小说《传播》(Transmission,2004)对第三世界移民生存境况的关注和对精英世界主义的不满,当代英国世界主义小说试图通过对英国社会现状的批判性描写向读者表明,文化的流动与杂糅冲击了以逻各斯为中心的二元对立传统,"他者"与自我、本土与全球、中心与边缘之间的界限逐渐模糊,世界正在形成一个尊重差异与多样性的"全球共同体"。作家们试图以此引导人们正确认识这一过程中多元化英国和人类社会面临的种种挑战。本尼迪克特·安德森在《想象的共同体》一书中指出小说参与"民族共同体"的塑造过程,他将共同体定义为集体想象的结果,超越了地理疆界的限制。在将世界视为一个整体的当代英国世界主义小说中,对共同体的想象完成了从民族到世界的思维范式的转变,小说开始参与"世界共同体"的塑造过程,透过小说,人们能够在一种更大的语境(世界而非民族)中定义自己的身份。

三、当代英国脱欧小说

英国于 2016 年 6 月 23 日举行的脱欧公投活动揭示了英国由来已久的地域分歧、阶级分化、种族主义等问题,造成了脱欧后英国国家分裂的潜在威胁(苏格兰 2022 年的独立公投申请)和社会发展的不确定性,引发了民众对英国未来的忧虑。这在以阿莉·史密斯、阿曼达·克雷格(Amanda Craig, 1959—)、乔纳森·科(Jonathan Coe, 1961—)、伊恩·麦克尤恩(Ian McEwan, 1948—)、萨姆·拜尔斯(Sam Byers, 1979—)和拉切尔·丘彻(Rachel Churcher, 1985—)为代表的作家所创作的脱欧小说中得到了淋漓尽致的体现。脱欧小说是对英国脱欧事件的文学回应,它在想象的文学世界里探讨了英国脱欧的原因、过程以及可能产生的各种结果,主题包括英国国家和民众的身份危机、英国民族主义和种族矛盾的激化、英国民众的怀旧情绪、民众的意见分歧、移民的生存境况等。脱欧小说涉及英国脱欧事件中的政治、经济、文化、历史等各方面因素,对脱欧公投活动进行了全方位文学再现。

从史密斯的小说《秋》(*Autumn*, 2016)对英国社会分裂现状的揭露、科的小说《英格兰中部》(*Middle England*, 2018)对后脱欧时代英国反移民情绪的批判、麦克尤恩的小说《蟑螂》(*The Cockroach*, 2019)对公投中英国政客阴谋手段的讽刺,到丘彻的小说《战场》(*Battle Ground*, 2019)对英国未来走上极权道路的担忧,英国脱欧小说家通过不同的角度和叙述方式展现了英国脱欧事件的多样性和复杂性,让民众有机会在脱欧后以多种视角重新审视英国脱欧事件,并思考英国国家的未来。脱欧小说常常涉及个人的命运和情感故事,呈现了脱欧前后英国社会中个体生存状态的变化,能引发英国民众的情感共鸣,为他们提供认真思考脱欧后遇到的各种困境和挑战的空间。脱欧小说体现出文学作品的社会功能——文学是反映社会现实和探索社会问题的重要媒介,甚至可以成为政治和社会变革的重要推手。

四、当代英国战争小说

纵观英国历史,从 16 世纪英国击败荷兰称霸海上开始,到 18 世纪成为海外殖民地遍布全球的日不落帝国,战争对英国的发展起着至关重要的推动作用。两次世界大战和战后殖民地的相继独立运动使英国丧失了世界霸主的地位。战争夺走了无数生命,造成重大的经济损失,在英国人心中留下挥之不去的创伤。大英帝国的兴衰可谓"成也战争,败也战争",战争成为英国文学家创作的重要主题。作为对战争最生动有效的表现形式的战争小说构成了英国文学的重要组成部分。以杰克·希金斯(Jack Higgins,1929—2022)、弗·福赛斯(Frederick Forsyth,1938—)、帕特·巴克(Pat Barker,1943—)、迈克尔·莫波格(Michael Morpurgo,1943—)、塞巴斯蒂安·福克斯(Sebastian Faulks,1953—)、安迪·麦克纳布(Andy McNab,1959—)、克里斯·瑞安(Chris Ryan,1961—)等为代表的当代英国小说家的战争书写为当代英国文坛添上了浓墨重彩的一笔。

从希金斯的《德国式英雄》(*The Eagle Has Landed*,1975)、巴克的《重生三部曲》(*Regeneration Trilogy*,1996)、福克斯的《鸟鸣》(*Birdsong*,1993)到莫波格的《柑橘与柠檬啊》(*Private Peaceful*,2003)及麦克纳布和瑞安的自传体小说《战火实录》(*Brave Two Zero*,1993)和《逃脱的那个人》(*The One That Got Away*,1995),这些小说无一例外地以普通士兵或军官为主人公,将边缘人物推向叙事中心,让曾经被历史忽略和压制的缄默者发出声音,回首历史,再现战争。当代战争小说几乎没有宏大战争场面的描写,而是侧重从普通军人的视角展现战争的残酷、小人物的无奈等。当代英国战争小说是一种与以往宏大叙事不同的新型战争小说,它的创作不仅展现了生与死的重大母题,也暗含了作家内心深处对"日不落"情结的追寻,同时观照历史,揭露人性,警醒当代人要以史为鉴,反思战争,珍视和平。

从主题上看,当代英国战争小说鲜有对英雄主义的褒扬,而是更多展示战争的残酷,呈现战争带给人们的伤害和灾难,当代英国战争小说具有鲜明的反战色彩。

五、当代英国历史小说

英国历史小说创作传统源远流长。被称为"欧洲历史小说之父"的英国小说家沃尔特·司各特(Walter Scott,1771—1832)以 27 部历史小说绘就了英国社会的宏伟画卷,不仅深刻而长久地影响了英国的历史小说创作,而且对欧洲小说的发展也产生过重大影响。欧洲小说巨匠如巴尔扎克、列夫·托尔斯泰等均有所受益。

尽管英国历史小说历史悠久,但在英国文学发展的洪流中也被推排边岸过,落寞好多岁月。自 20 世纪 60 年代以来,英国历史小说回潮构成了当代文学一道独特亮丽的风景线。当代英国历史小说创作成果丰硕,有英语小说指向标之谓的曼布克奖自 1969 年创设以来,有 1/3 的获奖作品都是英国历史小说即是明证。

当代英国历史小说热堪称英国历史小说的复兴。以保罗·司各特(Paul Scott,1920—

1978)于20世纪60年代初创作的印度历史题材历史小说为起点,当代英国历史小说至今热浪不减。司各特以英国在印度的殖民史为题材的《统治四部曲》(*The Raj Quartet*,1966—1975)和布克奖获奖小说《眷恋》(*Staying On*,1977)在英国文学界奠定了重要地位。詹姆斯·戈登·法雷尔(James Gordon Farrell,1904—1979)、威廉·戈尔丁(William Golding,1911—1993)、波西·纽比(Percy Newby,1918—1997)、约翰·伯格(John Berger,1926—2017)、巴里·昂斯沃斯(Barry Unsworth,1930—2012)、A.S.拜厄特(A.S.Byatt,1936—)、玛格丽特·德拉布尔(Margret Drabble,1939—)、朱利安·巴恩斯(Julian Barnes,1946—)、格雷厄姆·斯威夫特(Graham Swift,1949—)、希拉里·曼特尔(Hilary Mantel,1952—2022)都是当代英国文坛中对当代英国历史小说发展做出过突出贡献的小说家。

当代英国历史小说取材广泛,既有英国本土和欧洲素材,也有英国前殖民地素材。在思想上,当代英国历史小说发出各种声音,不仅钩沉历史、镜鉴当今,而且不乏反思与批判。在艺术上,当代英国历史小说在继承文学传统同时,勇于探索求新,异彩纷呈。当代英国历史小说无论在素材选取、主题承载还是艺术表现上都呈现出多样性、丰富性的特征。

本书是国家社会科学基金重大项目"流散文学与人类命运共同体研究"(21&ZD277)的阶段性成果,是将科研成果向教学资源转化的一次有益尝试。本书的编写离不开东北师范大学外国语学院李春艳博士和王涓涓博士的重要贡献,其中李春艳博士主要参与"当代英国世界主义小说"和"当代英国战争小说"的编写,王涓涓博士主要参与"当代英国战争小说"和"当代英国历史小说"的编写,特此致谢。

徐　彬

2023 年 12 月

于东北师范大学外国语学院

Contents | 目录

第一章
当代英国族裔小说

  "帝国风驰号一代"的到来可被视为当代英国族裔小说创作开始的时代标志。1948 年 6 月,一艘名为"帝国风驰号"的轮船从牙买加等加勒比海国家出发,将 492 名黑人带到英国,开启了第二次世界大战后有色人种移民英国的浪潮。作为对当下社会现实的回应,当代英国族裔小说的创作还与 1958 年诺丁山种族暴力事件和 1968 年英国保守党议员埃诺奇·鲍威尔的"血河演讲"等历史事件密切相关。萨姆·塞尔文、V.S.奈保尔开创了当代英国族裔小说创作的先河。

  进入 20 世纪七八十年代,萨曼·拉什迪、石黑一雄、扎迪·史密斯等作家将当代英国族裔小说创作推向高潮。当代英国族裔小说家已从根本上改变了英国文学乃英国本土白人文学的种族属性。以创作主题和写作方法为分类标准,可将当代英国族裔小说大致分为以下三类:一、以对英国殖民者"我来过,我看见,我征服"的殖民经验的文本再现和新独立国家末世论为主题的帝国遗产小说;二、以英国多元文化和种族主义为主题的批判现实主义小说;三、以互文英国经典文学作品为写作方式的回写帝国的新历史主义小说。

  当代英国族裔小说创作的主旨思想如下:一、争取有色移民的人权和生存权;二、在"帝国"的中心重新审视英国殖民史;三、回写历史,批判英国政治文化领域中的种族歧视与文化霸权思维模式;四、对多元文化生活的幻想和实践失败后的反思;五、试图阐发跨种族命运共同体的构想。在全球化进程与狭隘的民族主义兴起之间矛盾并存的当下,以难民、移民的流散生活和跨种族命运共同体为主题的小说创作更加凸显时代特色,将成为未来英国族裔小说创作的趋势。与此同时,鉴于有色人种在英国社会生活中的身份不确定性和英国政治文化由来已久的排斥"他者"的传统,如何塑造"有色英国人"的政治文化身份仍是未来英国族裔小说创作的焦点所在。

第一节 当代族裔作家旅行写作中殖民遗产的后殖民伦理批判

  V.S.奈保尔和萨曼·拉什迪的小说创作具有较为明显的旅行写作的特征。他们的写作内容与作家个人的旅行经历貌似无关,但两位作家数量众多的文学创作本身就是其由西向东,由英国向(前)英国殖民地旅行的结果。20 世纪末,英国布克奖和英联邦作家奖评委会对以 V.S.奈保尔和萨曼·拉什迪为代表的由前英国殖民地流散至英国的作家的作品情有独钟。他们的作品皆以英国为中心,涵盖对加勒比、印度、非洲等前英国殖民地帝国遗产的描述。上述流散作家创作的帝国遗产文学成为英国文学或英语文学消费市场上的重要组成部分。第二次世界大战后,尽管英国综合国力下降,但英国文化软实力并未减弱;相反,英国因帝国文化遗产而成为众多前殖民地人民的"朝圣地"。

奈保尔和拉什迪的旅行写作中充斥着对昨日殖民历史与今日后殖民现状之间跨越时空的对话关系,其中有对物是人非的帝国怀旧情绪的抒发,更有针对殖民遗产的伦理批判。两位作家的旅行文本在反观历史的同时,深刻揭示了去殖民化后新独立的国家所面临的巨大且近乎难以解决的殖民主义历史遗留问题。揭示问题并非否定国家独立的胜利果实,而是在批判殖民遗产的基础上,为新独立国家的人民提供解决问题的视野宽广的历史参照。

非洲、南美洲、加勒比等前英国或欧洲殖民地是奈保尔旅行写作的目的地。作为受过良好英国教育(牛津大学)的后殖民旅行者,奈保尔具有居高临下审视(前)殖民者和(前)被殖民者特定场所、特定时期内的历史与现实的双重视角。

在游记《重访加勒比》(*The Middle Passage*,1962)中,奈保尔以类似史学家的身份重回加勒比,追溯加勒比地区大西洋奴隶贸易中间航道的殖民历史,阐释当下加勒比地区的殖民遗产与种族关系。在《世间之路》(*A Way in the World*,1994)中,奈保尔更以欧洲殖民政治"知情者"的身份揭露了17世纪以沃尔特·罗利爵士为代表的欧洲探险者和南美革命家们鲜为人知的阴谋与私欲。对他们来说,欺骗乃谋生手段,革命乃成名、致富途径,欧美殖民统治下的南美成为政治投机者和冒险家们的乐园。

在以1975年刚果(旧称扎伊尔)旅行见闻为蓝本写作的小说《河湾》中,奈保尔描写了后殖民语境下非洲腹地生活着的三个典型代表人群的逃避现象,在赋予上述现象丰富政治伦理内涵的同时,奈保尔提出并回答了"非洲为什么没有未来?""非洲如何才能拥有未来?"等有关非洲前途命运的问题。在其21世纪小说《半生》和《魔种》中,奈保尔的故事主人公威利从故乡印度出发的旅行/旅居场所包括英国、莫桑比克和德国。对威利从印度到英国的两次旅行(早期英国求学与后期英国定居)的描写展现出奈保尔对受殖民文化影响、一生一事无成的以威利为代表的印度裔流散者前途命运的担忧。与此同时,奈保尔借助对婚姻主题的描写谴责了西方帝国主义在殖民与后殖民时期对以印度为代表的第三世界国家民族独立运动和民族自尊心、自信心建立过程中的不良影响。小说中,婚姻既是主人公政治牟利和宣泄种族政治、文化焦虑的手段,又是管窥20世纪后半叶以伦敦为缩影的英国社会现实的一面镜子。

在《午夜之子》前言中,拉什迪讲述了该小说创作的时代背景,如1975年印度成为有核国家、撒切尔夫人当选保守党领袖、孟加拉国建国领袖谢赫·穆吉布·拉赫曼惨遭谋杀、美国最后一批士兵从越南撤军等。拉什迪希望以此唤起读者的历史批判意识。在《午夜之子》中,拉什迪宣称要从"过来人"的视角出发,对印度建国前30年和建国后30年的历史加以评判。拉什迪将第一人称叙述者"午夜之子"萨里姆塑造为1915年至1977年间印度历史的演说者,将印度国家与萨里姆个人画上了等号。萨里姆的"死因"即是拉什迪笔下的斯芬克斯之谜。在《午夜之子》中,后殖民语境下的政治伦理悖论以及拉什迪的斯芬克斯之谜的谜底集中表现为三个方面的问题,即"政治伦理乌托邦的幻灭""对帝国'遗产'的政治伦理批判"和"印度政治伦理混乱"。

第二节　互文经典、回写帝国:解构殖民历史与白人种族权威

以卡里尔·菲利普斯为代表的当代英国族裔小说家将互文经典、回写帝国作为写作手段,旨在解构殖民历史与白人种族权威。菲利普斯对英国历史教科书和经典英国文学作品中所讲述的英国历史或殖民地历史持怀疑态度,他认为:"历史即是故事,写故事的人决定了我们(故事/历史人物)的身份;作为故事的历史可被重写。"[1]在"重写历史"和互文经典的创作过程中,菲利普斯实际上担当了霍米·巴巴所说的批评家的角色:"批评家必须试图全面了解,并为那些未被讲述、没有代表的过去/历史肩负责任,那些过去/历史持续不断地与当下历史纠缠在一起。"[2]

菲利普斯对经典英国文学作品、史料和新闻报道的"创造性误读"和改写是回写帝国、重写文学史和消解帝国文化霸权的重要方式,这即是比尔·阿希克洛夫特(Bill Ashcroft)等人所说的"文化解构殖民的过程涉及对欧洲语符的彻底消解以及对支配性欧洲话语的后殖民颠覆和挪用"[3]。

菲利普斯作品中对与黑人流散并发的欧美白人由殖民国前往殖民地的流散,以及由黑人流散引发的欧美社会内部矛盾的描写揭示了以大英帝国为代表的欧洲各殖民帝国引以为荣的殖民史对其人民生活产生的负面和灾难性影响;在此过程中,欧美白人的种族权威理应受到质疑和批判。

菲利普斯的小说《剑桥》(Cambridge,1991)虽以西印度群岛种植园里非洲黑奴剑桥的名字命名,然而就其故事情节而言,该小说的主人公应是第一人称叙述者,即被父亲派往西印度群岛检查种植园情况的英国白人女性艾米莉·卡特赖特。菲利普斯讲述了19世纪初《奴隶贸易法案》(Slave Trade Act of 1807)颁布之后,黑奴与英国白人殖民者在流散西印度群岛的过程中混杂生活的故事,具体表现为:一、艾米莉与黑奴剑桥和黑人女仆斯特拉之间跨种族友谊的建立;二、艾米莉历经磨难后做出的留在西印度与斯特拉生活在一起和从英国人变成克里奥人的决定。通过《剑桥》,菲利普斯阐发了杂合始于流散的观点。

菲利普斯的小说《迷失的孩子》对艾米莉·勃朗特的小说《呼啸山庄》(Wuthering Heights,1847)的改写达到了揭露经典英国文学作品中刻意遮蔽的罪恶殖民史的效果。《迷失的孩子》揭示了《呼啸山庄》中希斯克利夫为恩肖先生与刚果女黑奴私生子的身份及其为母复仇的真实动机。通过对《呼啸山庄》中希斯克利夫身份的互文改写,菲利普斯阐明了18世纪英帝国殖民政治对20世纪英国社会的跨越时空的影响。菲利普斯描述了前殖民者所犯罪行和所承受的家园焦虑与前被殖民者的"复仇"行动之间的因果关系,而这一因果关系可被形象地比喻为"帝国回飞镖"。

在《大西洋之声》中,跨大西洋奴隶贸易这一原已写进教科书中的客观历史事实之所以会变形为幽灵,化为潜意识里袭扰利物浦人和加纳人的梦魇,源自他们对祖辈历史罪责的逃避和对当下物质欲求的抒发。物质欲求的抒发以逃避罪责为前提,引发欲求主体畏罪却不认罪的精神分裂。20世纪

---

① Zhang, H. An Interview with Caryl Phillips. *Foreign Literature Studies*, 2011, Vol. 3, pp. 1 - 7.
② Bhabha, H. Introduction. *The Location of Culture*. London and New York: Routledge.
③ 比尔·阿希克洛夫特、格瑞斯·格里菲斯、海伦·蒂芬:《逆写帝国》,任一鸣(译),北京:北京大学出版社,2014年,第208页。

90 年代末,利物浦人五月天里播放圣诞歌曲的癖好和加纳人"泛非节"空洞无物的商业炒作是菲利普斯笔下利物浦人集体忧郁症和加纳人"被卖者有罪,卖人者无辜"的无罪妄想症等后殖民精神疾病的外现。

《血的本质》中,菲利普斯把威尼斯"血祭"审判、犹太大屠杀、以色列建国、奥赛罗的悲剧等历史事件与文学描述有机融为一体。通过建立与莎士比亚戏剧《威尼斯商人》《奥赛罗》和安妮·弗兰克的《安妮日记》之间互文关系的方式,菲利普斯分别回写并批判了十五六世纪的威尼斯帝国和 20 世纪 40 年代的德意志第三帝国的反犹主义意识形态及其社会表现。由反犹主义论及反黑人的种族主义的同时,菲利普斯巧妙地将"血祭""隔都"和"奥赛罗"设定为欧洲种族主义的政治文化表征并加以批判,对种族主义背后的经济、军事和政治文化动因的揭示实现了解构白人种族权威的目的。

第三节　多元文化与种族杂合、嘉年华与黑色幽默

当代英国族裔小说创作呈现出对多元文化和种族杂合较为强烈的诉求。转基因实验、喜剧表演、拳击运动、男欢女爱等社会和日常活动均被赋予特定的文化与种族意义。当代英国族裔小说具有对跨种族关系的嘉年华式的表层叙事,隐藏其后的是当代英国族裔小说家对英国多元文化与种族杂合现实的无可奈何。究其本质,当代英国族裔小说中多元文化与种族杂合的嘉年华不过是一场又一场的黑色幽默。

借助园艺学和基因科学术语(如"异花传粉"和"基因控制"),扎迪·史密斯在小说《白牙》中揭示了英国多元文化、种族融合的表象之后隐藏着的消除异质文化与种族基因的真实动机。卡里尔·菲利普斯更进一步,将美国黑人喜剧艺术家伯特·威廉姆斯和英国黑人拳王伦道夫·特平的生平事迹融入文学创作,指出以非裔黑人为代表的有色移民及其后代虽然为英美社会的(多元)文化生活做出巨大贡献,然而,其文化贡献者的高大形象却最终被其黑人的种族身份所抵消。

如同菲利普斯在小说《远岸》(A Distant Shore,2003)中所写,尽管非裔黑人加布里埃尔(到英国后改名为"所罗门")与英国白人女性多萝西确有共同生活的现实需求,然而,有体系化种族歧视与种族暴力传统的英国社会却给这一需求打上了违反伦理道德的邪恶的标签。当代英国社会中的多元文化主义转变为上述作家笔下痛苦与欢乐、绝望与希望并存的黑色幽默。在 21 世纪的今天,多元文化和多种族和谐共存的英国仍是可望而不可即的乌托邦式想象。

萨姆·塞尔文、哈尼夫·库雷西和扎迪·史密斯笔下的有色移民均对英国生活抱有"既来之则安之"的态度,他们自我安慰、自我解嘲,试图以一己之力融入英国社会。性、宗教以及有色移民原初国的文化和历史是上述作家作品中主人公与英国社会主流文化和价值观互动、交锋与妥协的场域。

作家诙谐幽默的文字背后隐藏着的多是主人公玩世不恭的心态。有色移民的纵欲、嘉年华般的狂欢和争取少数族裔人群社会文化权利的令人啼笑皆非的斗争是塞尔文、库雷西和史密斯对有色移民英国生活的生动再现,体现出上述作家对建构英国多元文化社会的积极心态;换言之,尽管困难重重,有时会以丧失道德为代价,被同化也罢,维持自我也好,有色移民期盼能在英国谋生,甚至过上相对富裕的

生活。

就出版时间而言,萨姆·塞尔文的小说《孤独的伦敦人》和扎迪·史密斯的小说《白牙》虽相隔近半个世纪,却因对英国有色移民种族危机的诠释而展现出主题上的一致性。以"摩西十诫"和"掉牙"的焦虑为隐喻,塞尔文和史密斯为读者阐释了英国20世纪四五十年代有色移民的生存与道德危机和20世纪八九十年代有色移民种族文化与历史存续危机的社会经济与种族政治成因。

在《孤独的伦敦人》中,加勒比移民在英国的贫苦生活与其嘉年华般的纵欲狂欢交织在一起,痛苦与快乐、道德与邪恶并存。加勒比青年潇洒快活的生理追求与其居无定所、食不果腹的生活现实形成巨大反差;无道德可言的寻欢作乐是其摆脱内心焦虑的唯一途径。他们对英国的迷恋使其无法摆脱夏日里的纵欲与冬日里的贫穷,随季节更替而陷入恶性循环。小说中,"夏"与"冬"两个季节分别象征着英国经济形势和年轻加勒比移民生活状况的好与坏。

在《白牙》中,扎迪·史密斯试图提出所谓"中立空间"(neutral spaces)的观点,即:用中立空间取代纷繁复杂的现在与过去;借助中立空间,摒弃每个人的历史桎梏。从皆大欢喜的结尾可见,史密斯对有色移民抛弃"历史负担"、轻装前进、拥抱英国社会的心态表示赞许。这也反映了新千年之际以史密斯为代表的族裔作家对英国多元文化的美好畅想。

哈尼夫·库雷西对有色人种融入英国社会持积极肯定态度。库雷西的小说《郊区佛爷》中的主人公哈伦似乎从一开始就习得了在英国社会里的生存之道。为赢得英国社会认同,哈伦将穆斯林的身份与印度瑜伽文化和中国道家哲学杂糅在一起,以向英国白人基督徒兜售东方精神的方式成为享誉白人社区的"郊区佛爷"。

不同于扎迪·史密斯的小说《摇摆时光》(Swing Time,2016)中女主人公以投身舞蹈艺术的方式化解本人有色人种身份困惑与文化危机的故事和《郊区佛爷》中库雷西对"郊区佛爷"哈伦成功之道的描述,卡里尔·菲利普斯作品中的非裔黑人主人公如同莎士比亚戏剧《奥赛罗》中受雇于威尼斯帝国的黑人将军奥赛罗一样,虽在白人社会里建功立业,却终究逃不掉受种族歧视与种族暴力的悲惨命运。

在《黑暗中的舞蹈》(Dancing in the Dark,2005)中,菲利普斯再现了1900年代享誉美国第七大道的非裔美国黑人喜剧艺术家伯特·威廉姆斯的故事。威廉姆斯因打破了美国白人社会给黑人喜剧演员规定的舞台形象和行动而被边缘化,后被人遗忘。在小说《外国人》(Foreigners,2007)中,菲利普斯以历史事实和新闻报道为依据,重新讲述了20世纪50年代英国乃至世界拳坛红极一时的英国黑人拳王伦道夫·特平因贫穷杀死自己两岁的小女儿后自杀的悲剧故事。通过对欧美社会中成功黑人"奥赛罗"般悲剧故事的文学再现,菲利普斯意在指出,艺术能改变黑人的社会身份、名气能改变黑人遭受种族歧视与暴力的生活状况的想法是对英美两国所宣称的多元文化社会的一厢情愿的幻想,"成功的"和"被英美社会所接受"的非裔黑人与莎士比亚笔下被利用、遭迫害的"奥赛罗"并无本质差别。

本章选取的作家及其代表作品如下:哈尼夫·库雷西及其小说《郊区佛爷》、卡里尔·菲利普斯及其小说《血的本质》、扎迪·史密斯及其小说《白牙》。

第四节　主要作家介绍与代表作品选读

一、哈尼夫·库雷西

（一）哈尼夫·库雷西简介

哈尼夫·库雷西是英国小说家、剧作家，出生于英格兰布罗姆利，父亲是巴基斯坦人，母亲是英国人。库雷西曾就读于布罗姆利科技学院，1972 年被选为该学院学生会主席。库雷西的半自传小说《郊区佛爷》中的部分人物便取材于这一时期的真实生活。库雷西在兰卡斯特大学学习了一年哲学，此后，进入伦敦国王学院学习并获得哲学学位。

哈尼夫·库雷西的文学创作包括戏剧、小说和电影剧本，英语是其创作语言。库雷西的绝大多数作品在英国和美国出版发行。库雷西的创作生涯始于 20 世纪 70 年代，其早期作品常被归入色情小说之列。1985 年，他写了一部关于在 20 世纪 80 年代在伦敦长大的巴基斯坦裔英国同性恋男孩的电影剧本《年少轻狂》(*My Beautiful Laundrette*)，该剧本获得了纽约市影评人最佳剧本奖和奥斯卡最佳原创剧本提名。他的第一部小说《郊区佛爷》荣获惠特布莱德奖。1991 年，由哈尼夫·库雷西编剧并导演的故事片《伦敦杀了我》(*London Kills Me*)上映。

哈尼夫·库雷西的小说《亲密》(*Intimacy*, 1998)讲述了一个男人在身体和情感上被妻子拒绝后离开妻子和两个年幼的儿子的故事。这部小说引起了一些争议，被认为至少是半自传体的，因为哈尼夫·库雷西当时刚离开自己的女友和两个年幼的儿子。2001 年，这部小说被改编成电影，在柏林电影节上获得了金熊奖最佳影片奖。

哈尼夫·库雷西的戏剧《母亲》(*The Mother*, 2003)被罗杰·米歇尔改编成电影。在戛纳电影节上，该片获得导演双周组的联合一等奖。2001 年，库雷西出版小说《加百列的礼物》(*Gabriel's Gift*)。小说讲述了 15 岁的加百列梦想成为电影制片人，而父母的意外分手让他开始挽救自己的家庭。库雷西为 2006 年的电影《维纳斯》(*Venus*)撰写剧本。2008 年，库雷西出版小说《有件事要告诉你》(*Something to Tell You*)。1995 年，库雷西出版小说《黑色专辑》(*The Black Album*)。2009 年，该小说被改编成戏剧，并于同年 7 月至 8 月在英国国家剧院上演。2008 年，哈尼夫·库雷西被《泰晤士报》评为"1945 年以来英国最伟大的 50 位作家"之一。库雷西是继萨尔曼·拉什迪之后在世界文坛上产生重大影响的亚裔作家。

（二）《郊区佛爷》简介

以对小说人物佛事与性事的描写为主线，库雷西深入伦敦南部郊区 17 岁印裔英国男孩卡里姆·阿米尔的家庭生活，揭示了两代印度穆斯林移民融入英国社会的文化策略，即以卡里姆的父亲哈伦为代表的第一代印度移民凭借对东方文化知识（中国古典哲学思想）的学习和"兜售"成为受英国白人尊重的瑜伽大师/郊区佛爷；以卡里姆为代表的英国出生的第二代印度移民通过性爱、艺术表演等方式参与英国社会活动,进而成为 20 世纪 70 年代英国文化的见证者与代言人。

在《郊区佛爷》中,以卡里姆 17 岁至 20 岁短短 3 年间的成长经历为中心的叙事涉及英国阶级、种族、经济、宗教等方面的问题,展现了库雷西英国文化与种族政治批评的写作动机。通过对佛事与性事的描写,库雷西阐释了在英国特定历史语境下英国白人与印裔有色人种之间共融互动的社会现实。《郊区佛爷》中的佛事与性事背后隐藏着的是英国白人和印裔有色人种在生理与心理层面上的双向欲求,这一欲求自下而上,有效地抵制了英国政府的种族主义政治,并由此引发了读者关于"何谓印裔英国人"和"20 世纪 70 年代英国多元文化"的思考。

在小说中,印裔英国人哈伦顺应英国社会的经济文化欲求,通过将佛教、中国古典哲学和伊斯兰文化结合在一起加以兜售的方式完成了从默默无闻的"英国公务员"到名噪一时的"郊区佛爷"的身份转变。身为"郊区佛爷"的哈伦实际上是身披佛教徒外衣、练习瑜伽术、传播中国古典哲学思想的印裔英国穆斯林。通过对"郊区佛爷"的角色扮演,哈伦成功塑造了自身印裔英国人的高大形象。

《郊区佛爷》以描写哈伦与伊娃间的婚外恋和卡里姆与伊娃的儿子查理之间同性恋关系开篇。库雷西对上述性爱关系的描述超出了单纯性爱主题。由文化与种族差异而引发的异性或同性间的彼此吸引是上述性爱关系的基础。库雷西之所以未对哈伦和卡里姆父子两代人"离经叛道"的性行为进行道德批判,是因为他更看重性行为背后隐藏着的种族文化内涵。

在伦敦南郊,以伊娃的家为活动中心,伊娃帮助哈伦开设了佛教/瑜伽修行班。在被奉为"郊区佛爷"的同时,哈伦凭借对东方文化思想的杂合确立了自己作为英国印裔穆斯林的族裔身份价值。哈伦与伊娃的婚外恋虽有违婚姻道德,却满足了个人精神发展的诉求,伊娃成为哈伦实现其精神追求过程中不可或缺的一环。哈伦与伊娃的婚外恋绝非仅停留在男欢女爱的性爱层面,精神上彼此的归属感是二者婚外恋的基础;小说结尾,哈伦与伊娃的婚姻恰好印证了这一观点。

在与查理、父亲的印裔同乡安华之女杰米拉以及英国姑娘海伦的双性恋中,卡里姆展示出的亚裔男性的阳刚气质惹人注意。卡里姆与伊娃之子查理之间的同性恋关系既是 70 年代英美同性恋运动的缩影,又是卡里姆对英国人身份精神渴望的生理外现。从某种意义上讲,卡里姆已将查理视为英国人的典范;在与查理的同性恋关系中,卡里姆潜意识里已经建立了自己与查理之间的对等关系,等同于查理也就是等同于英国人。查理因此成为卡里姆自我英国人身份认同的有效媒介。

卡里姆与杰米拉之间的性爱是两者英国生活焦虑的一种发泄途径,而卡里姆与英国姑娘海伦之间的性爱与其说是情感的寄托,不如说是卡里姆对怀有种族歧视态度并恶语相加的海伦父亲的报复。卡里姆与杰米拉虽有青梅竹马的成长经历,但二人并未达成婚约,彼此仅是倾诉心声、化解焦虑的对象。库雷西这一情节安排既应和了受 20 世纪 70 年代女权主义影响的杰米拉女性解放的呼声,又符合杰米拉传统保守的穆斯林父亲安华对女儿的婚嫁主张,即杰米拉必须嫁给一个血统纯洁的印度穆斯林,混血儿卡里姆自然不在安华的考虑范围之内。

库雷西巧妙地将盛行于 70 年代英国社会中的诸多文化事件、现象和知名人物(如佛教在英国的勃兴、鲍威尔种族歧视主义、新纳粹主义抬头、英国青年反文化运动、甲壳虫乐队等)编织于小说之中,在凸显英国经济危机和变动不居的社会文化背景的同时,强调了在新经济和新文化语境下英国白人社会与有色移民之间精神与肉体上密不可分的共生关系。

（三）作品选读：《郊区佛爷》①

Dad and Anwar lived next door to each other in Bombay and were best friends from the age of five. Dad's father, the doctor, had built a lovely low wooden house on Juhu beach for himself, his wife and his twelve children. Dad and Anwar would sleep on the veranda and at dawn run down to the sea and swim. They went to school in a horse-drawn rickshaw. At weekends they played cricket, and after school there was tennis on the family court. The servants would be ball-boys. The cricket matches were often against the British, and you had to let them win. There were also constant riots and demonstrations and Hindu-Muslim fighting. You'd find your Hindu friends and neighbours chanting obscenities outside your house.

There were parties to go to, as Bombay was the home of the Indian film industry and one of Dad's elder brothers edited a movie magazine. Dad and Anwar loved to show off about all the film-stars they knew and the actresses they'd kissed. Once, when I was seven or eight, Dad told me he thought I should become an actor; it was a good life, he said, and the proportion of work to money was high. But really he wanted me to be a doctor, and the subject of acting was never mentioned again. At school the careers officer said I should go into Customs and Excise—obviously he thought I had a natural talent for scrutinizing suitcases. And Mum wanted me to go into the Navy, on the grounds, I think, that I liked wearing flared trousers.

Dad had had an idyllic childhood, and as he told me of his adventures with Anwar I often wondered why he'd condemned his own son to a dreary suburb of London of which it was said that when people drowned they saw not their lives but their double-glazing flashing before them.

It was only later, when he came to England, that Dad realized how complicated practical life could be. He'd never cooked before, never washed up, never cleaned his own shoes or made a bed. Servants did that. Dad told us that when he tried to remember the house in Bombay he could never visualize the kitchen: he'd never been in it. He remembered, though, that his favourite servant had been sacked for kitchen misdemeanours; once for making toast by lying on his back and suspending bread from between his toes over a flame, and on a second occasion for cleaning celery with a toothbrush—his own brush, as it happened, not the Master's, but that was no excuse. These incidents had made Dad a socialist, in so far as he was ever a socialist.

If Mum was irritated by Dad's aristocratic uselessness, she was also proud of his family. "They're higher than the Churchills," she said to people. "He went to school in a horse-drawn carriage." This ensured there would be no confusion between Dad and the swarms of Indian peasants who came to Britain in the 1950s and 1960s, and of whom it was said they were not familiar with cutlery and certainly not with toilets, since they squatted on the seats and shat from on high.

---

① Kureishi, H. *The Buddha of Suburbia*. London: Faber and Faber, 2009, pp. 23 – 32.

Unlike them, Dad was sent to England by his family to be educated. His mother knitted him and Anwar several itchy woollen vests and waved them off from Bombay, making them promise never to be pork-eaters. Like Gandhi and Jinnah before him, Dad would return to India a qualified and polished English gentleman lawyer and an accomplished ballroom dancer. But Dad had no idea when he set off that he'd never see his mother's face again. This was the great undiscussed grief of his life, and, I reckon, explained his helpless attachment to women who would take care of him, women he could love as he should have loved the mother to whom he never wrote a single letter.

London, the Old Kent Road, was a freezing shock to both of them. It was wet and foggy; people called you "Sunny Jim"; there was never enough to eat, and Dad never took to dripping on toast. "Nose drippings more like," he'd say, pushing away the staple diet of the working class. "I thought it would be roast beef and Yorkshire pudding all the way." But rationing was still on, and the area was derelict after being bombed to rubble during the war. Dad was amazed and heartened by the sight of the British in England, though. He'd never seen the English in poverty, as roadsweepers, dustmen, shopkeepers and barmen. He'd never seen an Englishman stuffing bread into his mouth with his fingers, and no one had told him the English didn't wash regularly because the water was so cold—if they had water at all. And when Dad tried to discuss Byron in local pubs no one warned him that not every Englishman could read or that they didn't necessarily want tutoring by an Indian on the poetry of a pervert and a madman.

. . .

Anwar was always plumper than Dad, with his podgy gut and round face. No sentence was complete without the flavouring of a few noxious words, and he loved the prostitutes who hung around Hyde Park. They called him Baby Face. He was less suave, too, for as soon as Dad's monthly allowance arrived from India, Dad visited Bond Street to buy bow-ties, bottle-green waistcoats and tartan socks, after which he'd have to borrow money from Baby Face. During the day Anwar studied aeronautical engineering in North London and Dad tried to glue his eyes to his law books. At night they slept in Dr Lal's consulting room among the dental equipment, Anwar sleeping in the chair itself. One night, enraged by the mice running around him, by sexual frustration too, and burning with the itching of his mother's woollen vests, Dad dressed himself in Lal's pale blue smock, picked up the most ferocious drill and attacked Anwar as he slept. Anwar screamed when he awoke to find the future guru of Chislehurst coming at him with a dentist's drill. This playfulness, this refusal to take anything seriously, as if life didn't matter, characterized Dad's attitude to his studies. Dad just couldn't concentrate. He'd never worked before and it didn't suit him now. Anwar started to say of Dad, "Haroon is called to the Bar every day—at twelve o'clock and five-thirty."

Dad defended himself: "I go to the pub to think."

"No, not think—drink," Anwar replied.

On Fridays and Saturdays they went to dances and smooched blissfully to Glenn Miller and Count Basie and Louis Armstrong. That is where Dad first laid eyes and hands on a pretty working-class girl from the suburbs called Margaret. My mother told me that she loved him, her little man, from the first moment she saw him. He was sweet and kind and utterly lost-looking, which made women attempt to make him found-looking.

There was a friend of Mum's whom Baby Face walked out with, and apparently even walked in with, but Anwar was already married, to Jeeta, a princess whose family came on horseback to the wedding held in the old British hill station of Murree, in the north of Pakistan. Jeeta's brothers carried guns, which made Anwar nervous and want to head for England.

Soon Princess Jeeta joined Anwar in England, and she became Auntie Jeeta to me. Auntie Jeeta looked nothing like a princess, and I mocked her because she couldn't speak English properly. She was very shy and they lived in one dirty room in Brixton. It was no palace and it backed on to the railway line. One day Anwar made a serious mistake in the betting shop and won a lot of money. He bought a short lease on a toy shop in South London. It was a miserable failure until Princess Jeeta made him turn it into a grocer's shop. They were set up. Customers flocked.

In contrast, Dad was going nowhere. His family cut off his money when they discovered from a spy—Dr Lal—that he was being called to the Bar only to drink several pints of rough stout and brown ale wearing a silk bow-tie and a green waistcoat.

Dad ended up working as a clerk in the Civil Service for £3 a week. His life, once a cool river of balmy distraction, of beaches and cricket, of mocking the British, and dentists' chairs, was now a cage of umbrellas and steely regularity. It was all trains and shitting sons, and the bursting of frozen pipes in January, and the lighting of coal fires at seven in the morning: the organization of love into suburban family life in a two-up-two-down semi-detached in South London, life was thrashing him for being a child, an innocent who'd never had to do anything for himself. Once when I was left with him all day and I shat myself, he was bewildered. He stood me naked in the bath while he fetched a cup from which, standing on the other side of the bathroom as if I had the plague, he threw water at my legs while holding his nose with his other hand.

I don't know how it all started, but when I was ten or eleven he turned to Lieh Tzu, Lao Tzu and Chuang Tzu as if they'd never been read before, as if they'd been writing exclusively for him.

We continued to visit Baby Face and Princess Jeeta on Sunday afternoons, the only time the shop closed. Dad's friendship with Anwar was still essentially a jokey one, a cricket-, boxing-, athletics-, tennis-watching one. When Dad went there with a library copy of *The Secret of the Golden Flower* Anwar snatched it from him, held it up and laughed.

"What's this bloody-fool thing you're playing with now?"

Dad promptly started up with, "Anwar, yaar, you don't realize the great secrets I'm uncovering! How happy I feel now I'm understanding life at last!"

. . .

Dad was so keen for Anwar to understand that his knees were vibrating. "I don't care about money. There's always money. I must understand these secret things."

Anwar raised his eyes to heaven and looked at Mum, who sat there, bored. They both had sympathy for Dad, and loved him, but in these moods love was mixed with pity, as if he were making some tragic mistake, like joining the Jehovah's Witnesses. The more he talked of the Yin and Yang, cosmic consciousness, Chinese philosophy, and the following of the Way, the more lost Mum became. He seemed to be drifting away into outer space, leaving her behind; she was a suburban woman, quiet and kind, and found life with two children and Dad difficult enough as it was. There was at the same time a good chunk of pride in Dad's Oriental discoveries, which led him to denigrate Anwar's life.

"You're only interested in toilet rolls, sardine tins, sanitary pads and turnips," he told Anwar. "But there are many more things, yaar, in heaven and earth, than you damn well dream of in Penge."

"I haven't got time to dream!" interrupted Anwar. "Nor should you be dreaming. Wake up! What about getting some promotion so Margaret can wear some nice clothes. You know what women are like, yaar."

"The whites will never promote us," Dad said. "Not an Indian while there is a white man left on the earth. You don't have to deal with them—they still think they have an Empire when they don't have two pennies to rub together."

"They don't promote you because you are lazy, Haroon. Barnacles are growing on your balls. You think of some China-thing and not the Queen!"

"To hell with the Queen! Look, Anwar, don't you ever feel you want to know yourself? That you are an enigma to yourself completely?"

"I don't interest anyone else, why should I interest myself?" cried Anwar. "Get on with living!"

On and on these arguments went, above Anwar and Jeeta's shop, until they became so absorbed and hostile that their daughter, Jamila, and I could sneak away and play cricket with a broom handle and a tennis ball in the garden.

Beneath all the Chinese bluster was Dad's loneliness and desire for internal advancement. He needed to talk about the China-things he was learning. I often walked to the commuter station with him in the morning, where he caught the eight-thirty-five to Victoria. On these twenty-minute walks he was joined by other people, usually women, secretaries, clerks and assistants, who also worked in Central London. He wanted to talk of obtaining a quiet mind, of being true to yourself, of self-understanding. I heard them speak of their lives, boyfriends, agitated minds and real selves in a way, I'm sure, they never talked to anyone else. They didn't even notice me and the transistor radio I carried, listening to the Tony Blackburn Show on Radio One. The more Dad didn't try to seduce them, the more he seduced them; often they didn't leave their houses until he was walking by. If he took a different route for fear of having stones and ice-pops full of piss lobbed at him by schoolboys from the secondary modern, they changed their route too. On the train Dad would read his mystical books or concentrate on the tip of his nose, a large target indeed. And he always carried a tiny blue dictionary with him, the size of a matchbox, making sure to learn a new word every day. At the weekends I'd test him on the meaning of analeptic, frutescent, polycephalus and orgulous. He'd look at me and say, "You never know when you might need a heavyweight word to impress an Englishman."

It wasn't until he met Eva that he had someone to share his China-things with, and it surprised him that such mutual interest was possible.

*

Now, I presumed, on this Saturday night, God was going to meet Eva again. He gave me the address on a piece of paper and we caught a bus, this time towards what I considered to be the country. It was dark and icy when we got off in Chislehurst. I led Dad first one way and then, speaking with authority, in the opposite direction. He was so keen to get there he didn't complain for twenty minutes; but at last he became poisonous.

"Where are we, idiot?"

"I don't know."

"Use the brains you've inherited from me, you bastard!" he said, shivering. "It's bloody cold and we're late."

"It's your fault you're cold, Dad," I said.

"My fault?"

It was indeed his fault, for under his car coat my father was wearing what looked like a large pair of pyjamas. On top was a long silk shirt embroidered around the neck with dragons. This fell over his chest and flew out at his stomach for a couple of miles before dropping down to his knees. Under this he had on baggy trousers and sandals. But the real crime, the reason for concealment under the hairy car coat, was the crimson waistcoat with gold and silver patterns that he wore over the shirt. If Mum had caught him going out like that she would have called the police. After all, God was a Civil Servant, he had a briefcase and umbrella, he shouldn't be walking around looking like a midget toreador.

The houses in Chislehurst had greenhouses, grand oaks and sprinklers on the lawn; men came in to do the garden. It was so impressive for people like us that when our families walked these streets on Sunday visits to Auntie Jean we'd treat it as a lower-middle-class equivalent of the theatre. "Ahhh" and "oohh", we'd go, imagining we lived there, what times we'd have, and how we'd decorate the place and organize the garden for cricket, badminton and table tennis. Once I remember Mum looking reproachfully at Dad, as if to say: What husband are you to give me so little when the other men, the Alans and Barrys and Peters and Roys, provide cars, houses, holidays, central heating and jewellery? They can at least put up shelves or fix the fence. What can you do? And Mum would stumble into a pothole, just as we were doing now, since the roads were deliberately left corrugated with stones and pits, to discourage ordinary people from driving up and down.

As we crunched up the drive at last—with a pause for God to put his thumbs together and do a few minutes' trance practice—God told me that the house was owned by Carl and Marianne, friends of Eva, who'd recently been trekking in India. This was immediately obvious from the sandalwood Buddhas, brass ashtrays and striped plaster elephants which decorated every available space. And by the fact that Carl and Marianne stood barefoot at the door as we entered, the palms of their hands together in prayer and their heads bowed as if they were temple servants and not partners in the local TV rental firm of Rumbold & Toedrip.

As soon as I went in I sported Eva, who had been looking out for us. She was wearing a long red dress which fell to the floor and a red turban. She swooped down upon me, and after twelve kisses she pressed three paperbacks into my hand.

"Smell them!" she urged me.

I dipped my nose between the foxed leaves. They smelled of chocolate.

"Second-hand! Real discoveries! And for your dad, this." She gave me a new copy of the Analects of Confucius, translated by Arthur Waley. "Please hold on to it for him. Is he OK?"

"Dead nervous."

She glanced around the room, which contained about twenty people.

"They're a sympathetic lot. Pretty stupid. I can't see he'll have any problems. My dream is to get him to meet with more responsive people—in London. I'm determined to get all of us to London!" she said. "Now, let me introduce you to people."

After shaking a few hands I managed to get comfortably settled on a shiny black sofa, my feet on a furry white rug, with my back to a row of fat books handtooled in plastic—abridged versions (with illustrations) of *Vanity Fair* and *The Woman in White*. In front of me was what seemed to be an illuminated porcupine—some kind of clear bulb with hundreds of different coloured waving quills which stuck out of it and shimmered—an object, I'm sure, designed to be appreciated with the aid of hallucinogenics.

I heard Carl say, "There are two sorts of people in the world—those who have been to India and those who haven't," and was forced to get up and move out of earshot.

Beside the double-glazed french windows, with their view of the long garden and its goldfish pond glowing under purple light, was a bar. Not many people were drinking on this big spiritual occasion, but I could easily have put back a couple of pints. It wouldn't have looked too good, though, even I knew that. Marianne's daughter and an older girl in tight hotpants were serving lassi and hot Indian nibbles, guaranteed, I knew, to make you fart like a geriatric on All-bran. I joined the girl in hotpants behind the bar and found out her name was Helen and she was at the high school.

"Your father looks like a magician," she said. She smiled at me and took two quick sidesteps into the circle of my privacy so she was beside me. Her sudden presence surprised and aroused me. It was only a minor surprise on the Richter surprise scale, a number three and a half, say, but it registered. At that moment my eyes were on God. Did he look like a magician, a wonder-maker?

He was certainly exotic, probably the only man in southern England at that moment (apart, possibly, from George Harrison) wearing a red and gold waistcoat and Indian pyjamas. He was also graceful, a front-room Nureyev beside the other pasty-faced Arbuckles with their tight drip-dry shirts glued to their guts and John Collier grey trousers with the crotch all sagging and creased. Perhaps Daddio really was a magician, having transformed himself by the bootlaces (as he put it) from being an Indian in the Civil Service who was always cleaning his teeth with Monkey Brand black toothpowder manufactured by Nogi & Co. of Bombay, into the wise adviser he now appeared to be. Sexy Sadie! Now he was the centre of the room. If they could see him in Whitehall!

He was talking to Eva, and she had casually laid her hand on his arm. The gesture cried out. Yes, it shouted, we are together, we touch each other without inhibition in front of strangers. Confused, I turned away, to the matter of Helen.

"Well?" she said gently.

She desired me.

I knew this because I had evolved a cast-iron method of determining desire. The method said she desired me because I had no interest in her. Whenever I did find someone attractive it was guaranteed by the corrupt laws which govern the universe that the person would find me repellent, or just too small. This law also guaranteed that when I was with someone like Helen, whom I didn't desire, the chances were they would look at me as she was looking at me now, with a wicked smile and an interest in squeezing my mickey, the thing I wanted most in the world from others, provided I found them attractive, which in her case I didn't.

...

Eva and Marianne were starting to organize the room. The candle industry was stimulated, Venetian blinds were lowered, Indian sandalwood sticks were ignited and put in flowerpots, and a small carpet was put down for the Buddha of suburbia to fly on. Eva bowed to him and handed him a daffodil. God smiled at people recognized from last time. He seemed confident and calm, easier than before, doing less and allowing the admirers to illuminate him with the respect that Eva must have been encouraging in her friends.

Then Uncle Ted and Auntie Jean walked in.

思考与讨论

(1)《郊区佛爷》中所描写的以"父亲"和安华为代表的第一代印度移民的源出生活背景和移民动机分别是什么？

(2) 节选内容中对英国种族问题的反映体现在哪些地方？

(3)"父亲"生活中的东方元素有哪些？

(4)"父亲"如何实现了东方元素的杂合？"父亲"向英国人兜售其东方文化的方式是什么？

(5) 如何看待小说中伊娃这一女性形象？

(6) 如何看待小说中描写的英国人的东方热？

拓展阅读

[1] Hashmi, A. Hanif Kureishi and the Tradition of the Novel. *Critical Survey*. Vol. 5, No. 1 (1993), pp. 25 - 33.

[2] Yousaf, N. Hanif Kureishi and "the Brown Man's Burden". *Critical Survey*. Vol. 8, No. 1, Diverse communities (1996), pp. 14 - 25.

[3] Dharwadker, A. Diaspora, Nation, and the Failure of Home: Two Contemporary Indian Plays. *Theatre Journal*. Vol. 50, No. 1, Theatre, Diaspora, and the Politics of Home (Mar., 1998), pp. 71 - 94.

二、卡里尔·菲利普斯

（一）卡里尔·菲利普斯简介

卡里尔·菲利普斯是英国小说家、纪实文学家、剧作家，出生于西印度群岛的圣基茨，四个月大时随父母移民英国，定居利兹。1976 年至 1979 年就读于牛津大学女王学院学习英国文学，获学士学位。1997 年至 2015 年，菲利普斯先后被利兹城市大学、约克大学、利兹大学、西印度大学、爱丁堡大学和列日大学（比利时）授予名誉博士学位。

卡里尔·菲利普斯曾在加纳、瑞典、新加坡、巴巴多斯、印度和美国的大学里任教。1999 年，菲利普斯获西印度群岛大学人文学科年度学者奖。2002 至 2003 年间，担任纽约公共图书馆学者和作家中心研究员。菲利普斯曾任哥伦比亚大学移民与社会秩序学亨利·R·卢斯教授（Henry R. Luce Professor of Migration and Social Order at Columbia University），现任耶鲁大学英语系教授和牛津大学女王学院荣誉院士。

卡里尔·菲利普斯的文学创作包括戏剧、小说、游记和文集，英语是其创作语言。菲利普斯的绝大多数作品在英国和美国出版发行,其中部分作品已被翻译成十余种语言。通过采用蒙太奇的叙事方法回写英国跨大西洋奴隶贸易史和英国经典文学作品(如《呼啸山庄》《威尼斯商人》《奥赛罗》)的方式,菲利普斯阐释了非裔黑人与英国白人的跨大西洋流散、难民与移民的生活困境、英美国家内部的种族与性别歧视、跨种族团结等主题。透过菲利普斯的作品可以发现:一、始于 16 世纪的跨大西洋黑奴贸易所引发的非裔黑人在欧美范围内的流散已将欧美白人与非裔黑人的命运紧密联系在了一起;二、"我是谁?"不再是黑人流散者对自我身份的单方追问,而已成为黑人与白人、互为"自我"与"他者"的双向度的国家政治经济与文化层面上的道德拷问。菲利普斯的文学创作对第二次世界大战后的英国文坛产生了深远影响,对后殖民政治文化研究和种族关系研究具有重要参考价值。

菲利普斯的创作生涯始于戏剧,代表作有《奇异的果实》(*Strange Fruit*,1980)、《黑暗之地》(*Where There Is Darkness*,1982)和《庇护所》(*The Shelter*,1983)。菲利普斯的广播剧《虚度岁月》(*The Wasted Years*,1984)获"英国广播公司贾尔斯·库珀年度最佳广播剧奖"。菲利普斯为广播公司和电视台撰写了多部戏剧和纪录片。1996 年,菲利普斯将自己的小说《最后的旅程》(*The Final Passage*)改编成长达三小时的电影。菲利普斯曾为电影《客场板球赛》(*Playing Away*,1986)编写剧本。以奈保尔的小说《神秘的按摩师》(*The Mystic Masseur*,2001)为蓝本,菲利普斯为默谦特-艾弗利制作公司改编的剧本获阿根廷马德普拉塔电影节"银树商陆奖"(Silver Ombu)最佳剧本奖。

卡里尔·菲利普斯著有以下小说:《最后的旅程》(1985)、《独立国家》(*A State of Independence*,1986)、《更高的地方》(*Higher Ground*,1989)、《剑桥》(*Cambridge*,1991)、《渡河》(*Crossing the River*,1993)、《血的本质》(*The Nature of Blood*,1997)、《远岸》(*A Distant Shore*,2003)、《黑暗中的舞蹈》(*Dancing in the Dark*,2005)、《外国人》、《在落雪中》(*In the Falling Snow*,2009)、《迷失的孩子》(*The Lost Child*,2015)和《日落时的帝国景色》(*A View of the Empire at Sunset*,2018)。卡里尔·菲利普斯的非虚构作品包括:《欧洲部落》(*The European Tribe*,1987)、《大西洋之声》(*The Atlantic Sound*,2000)、《世界新秩序》(*A New World Order*,2001)和《给我染上英国的颜色》(*Colour Me English*,2011)。1997 年和 1999 年,菲利普斯相继出版了两部文集:《四海为家的异邦人:有关归属的文学》(*Extravagant Strangers:A Literature of Belonging*)和《正确的一局:网球写作文选》(*The Right Set:An Anthology of Writing on Tennis*)。

1992 年,卡里尔·菲利普斯被评为"《星期日泰晤士报》年度最佳青年作家",并入选 1993 年"格兰塔最佳英国青年作家"名单。卡里尔·菲利普斯曾获马丁·路德·金纪念奖、古根海姆奖学金、英国文化协会奖学金、兰南基金会奖学金。小说《渡河》获詹姆斯·泰特·布莱克纪念奖;小说《远岸》入围 2003 年布克奖初选名单,并获 2004 年英联邦作家奖;小说《黑暗中的舞蹈》获 2006 年美国笔会开放图书奖。2013 年,卡里尔·菲利普斯被授予安东尼·萨布加加勒比卓越奖。

(二)《血的本质》简介

在《血的本质》中,以犹太姑娘安妮·弗兰克的《安妮日记》(*The Diary of Anne Frank*,1947)、莎士比亚的戏剧《威尼斯商人》和《奥赛罗》为蓝本,菲利普斯将"以色列建国者史蒂芬·斯特恩的回忆""犹太姑娘伊娃·施特恩对第二次世界大战期间家庭悲剧的自述""1480 年威尼斯犹太血祭审判""奥赛罗的威尼斯爱情故事"等四个跨时空、跨种族的故事拼贴在一起,构建了一个反欧洲种族主义的叙事"迷宫"。

其中,"血祭""隔都""奥赛罗"等特定历史事件、场所和人物形象是菲利普斯笔下以十五六世纪的威尼斯人和20世纪40年代的德国人为代表的欧洲白人基督徒歧视和迫害犹太人与黑人的欧洲种族主义意识形态的政治文化表征。

在《血的本质》中,菲利普斯揭示了1480年威尼斯共和国的犹太"血祭"审判背后的经济动因,建立了20世纪40年代德国反犹主义与1480年威尼斯犹太"血祭"审判之间跨时空的镜像关系。1480年3月25日,威尼斯共和国波托布劳尔小镇上的塞瓦迪奥、摩西和贾科布三名犹太人被指控在安息日的宗教仪式中杀害了基督徒流浪男孩塞巴斯蒂安并饮用了他的鲜血。尽管威尼斯法庭上来自帕多瓦的辩护律师引用犹太《圣经》指出:对犹太人而言,血是世间最肮脏的东西,"摩西十诫"不仅禁止杀人,还禁止犹太人饮食鲜血,但威尼斯法庭并不采信。法庭对塞瓦迪奥、摩西和贾科布死刑判决的证据有二:塞瓦迪奥的仆人多纳托提供的与犹太《圣经》相悖且逻辑混乱的虚假证词和犹太嫌疑人屈打成招后的主动认罪。1480年7月6日,在没有确凿证据的情况下,威尼斯法庭对三名犹太人执行死刑判决。

以1480年犹太"血祭"案为叙事中心,菲利普斯解答了《威尼斯商人》中"夏洛克为何以犹太高利贷者的身份示人并遭到基督徒的憎恶?"以及"基督徒安东尼奥身上尚未流出的鲜血为何具有剥夺夏洛克的财产和宗教信仰的隐性法律效力?"等问题。

在《血的本质》中,"血祭"审判与纳粹犹太人大屠杀背景下伊娃一家的家庭悲剧之间"戏中戏"的套层结构间接揭示了《凡尔赛条约》、希特勒执政和犹太人大屠杀之间种族与政治经济层面上的因果关系,即:与15世纪末威尼斯帝国经济危机引发"血祭"审判的原理相似,20世纪40年代德国犹太人大屠杀与"德意志第三帝国"的经济危机密不可分。

"血祭"审判之后,1516年3月29日,鉴于犹太人在威尼斯数量的增加和地位的提高,威尼斯共和国颁布了迫害和隔离犹太人的法律,以保护犹太人的生命、财产安全为由建立了名为"隔都"(Ghetto)的相对隔离的犹太人聚居区。"隔都"的建立非但未起到保护犹太人的作用,反而为白人基督教徒限制犹太人的社会权力和集中、大规模迫害犹太人提供了便利。《血的本质》中,"隔都"一词具备更为宽泛的指涉功能,除指代十五六世纪威尼斯城里的犹太聚居区外,还是20世纪40年代纳粹集中营的原型。如菲利普斯所说:"威尼斯隔都是最早的隔都,是世界上所有以贫困和迫害为特征的场所的模型。"

对来自非洲的黑人将军奥赛罗而言,威尼斯同样是他的"隔都",奥赛罗的悲剧不仅在于威尼斯基督徒的险恶用心,更在于奥赛罗未能认清的威尼斯城中黑人与犹太人同病相怜的现实。在《血的本质》中,从十五六世纪的威尼斯到20世纪40年代的德国,种族隔离与迫害的"隔都"已成为无处不在的欧洲种族主义的代名词。

在《血的本质》中,奥赛罗的第一人称叙事揭示了奥赛罗杀妻后自杀这一悲剧的种族主义成因。奥赛罗希望通过婚姻获得在威尼斯社会与白人平等的权利,令其意想不到的是以伊阿古为代表的威尼斯种族主义势力对奥赛罗和苔丝狄梦娜展开了恐怖的复仇。如果说奥赛罗杀妻是遗弃神经官能症患者侵略性行动的表现,奥赛罗自杀则可被视为彻底的自我贬低与否定,"被遗弃"的感觉是奥赛罗杀妻后自杀这一极端暴力行动的导火索。奥赛罗并未意识到遗弃他的不是他的妻子,而是威尼斯白人社会。

(三) 作品选读:《血的本质》①

In March of 1480, the people of the small town of Portobuffole, near Venice, were preparing their houses for the much anticipated arrival of relatives. The winter was at an end and the weather had already turned mild, but, more importantly, it appeared that the famine which had troubled the lives of these people for the past three years was now over. There were provisions for everybody, although the poorer members of the community could not afford to indulge themselves with luxuries. However, every household could boast either pork or eggs, or both, and the eager townsfolk now waited for the priest's blessing of house and food before completing their tables with delightful flowers and scented herbs.

The women, in particular, watched the streets in a state of anxiety, for the majority of them were looking for their men. The Most Serene Republic of Venice had recently made a reluctant peace with the infidel Turk and, once again, the Venetian army was being demobilized. Every day, the women expected to see their loved ones, and they contemplated the streets in anticipation of a joyful reunion. There was, however, a further reason why the streets were being scrutinized in such a concentrated manner. After raging for almost a full year, the plague had mercifully ceased, but the old suspicion of strangers remained. So, even as they looked for their men, the women also kept a sharp eye open for those they did not recognize. And then, on one evening, shortly before sunset, a young beggar boy entered the town, but sadly the women did not follow him closely. The boy's hair was blond and unkempt, his tattered linen skirt brushed his bare feet, and he carried a worn sack across one shoulder. One woman did speak to him, for he asked her the name of the town, and the woman remembered that the boy's difficult foreign accent reminded her of her husband's when he had first been recruited to the region by the Venetian army. There was one other woman who saw the boy, but unfortunately she did not speak to him.

The blacksmith claimed he had been busily shoeing a horse at the time that he saw the young vagabond. The boy approached him cautiously and asked him the way to the Jew Servadio's home. It was nearly dusk, and the blacksmith remembered that he simply pointed the wretch in the appropriate direction. The blacksmith then returned to the urgent business of shoeing the horse, in order that he might return it to its impatient owner before nightfall. It was important that the child had also been seen by a man, albeit the temperamental and somewhat unpredictable blacksmith, for in these times nobody would accept the word of a woman unless it had been substantiated by a man. This "male" sighting of the boy became even more important when one considers that the innocent beggar child, who that day entered the small town of Portobuffole, was never seen again. Portobuffole was a small town of less than a thousand people, some living inside and some outside

① Phillips, C. *The Nature of Blood*. New York: Vintage International, 1998, pp. 48 – 59.

the boundary walls. However, despite its small size, it was well known as an important administrative and commercial center which had jurisdiction over fifteen or so neighbouring villages. Upon entering the town, one found a square, and in the town square, between the gates in the boundary wall and the town hall, was the hub of Portobuffole: the warehouse. The building boasted an ugly veranda, but beneath the veranda was a large counter, where one could negotiate for loans and securities. On the stone wall behind this counter was a list which plainly indicated the current taxes for those who wished to borrow. If one entered the town square and looked to the far left, one would see the synagogue and the large and comfortable homes of the principal Jewish moneylenders, Servadio and Moses. These homes were easily distinguishable by the cylindrical containers which held Hebrew scripture written on parchment. By law, these had to be placed to the right of a Jew's front door.

The leader of Portobuffole was Andrea Dolfin, a Venetian aristocrat, chosen by the *Signoria* of Venice. It was understood that he would remain in office for some sixteen months in return for a modest salary, out of which he had to support a deputy, a notary, three pages, three horses and a servant boy. Andrea Dolfin worked together with a local civic body which comprised members of the most important families, but, unlike other towns, these members were not required to be noblemen. The democratic ideals of Portobuffole determined that all men over a certain age could participate in the development of the town and, with some justification, the townspeople of Portobuffole were proud of the manner in which their town was governed.

The Jews had first begun journeying to Portobuffole in 1424, many of them migrating from Colonia in Germany. Back in 1349, the Christian people of that region had suddenly become incensed and irrational from fear of the plague, and the Jews began to suffer as this Christian hysteria manifested itself in violence. Eventually the Jews could take no more and they barricaded themselves into their large synagogue, set fire to it, and recited moribund prayers to each other as they waited for the end. The few Jews that survived this catastrophe remained in the region, but finally they were driven out. And then, a few years later, they were once more readmitted as though nothing had ever occurred. Such is the way of the Germans with their Jews. In 1424, the Jews of Colonia were finally expelled for good, and most decided to travel to the Republic of Venice, where it was rumoured that life was more secure.

Initially, the people of the republic accepted the Jews from Colonia with all the mistrust that is common among people who do not know one another. Sadly, as the years passed, this mistrust did not abate. It became apparent that the Jews wished to speak only among themselves. Further, they chose not to eat or drink with the Christians, and they refused to attend to their heavy German accents. They look different, the average one being between thirty-five and fifty years of age, pale and heavy under the eyes, with a long untidy beard. And even at the height of summer, these men always wore their dark grey, heavy wool coats and their unseemly black hats. Although their women dressed with more propriety, occasionally wearing handkerchiefs on their heads like the Christian women wore in church, even these gentler creatures refused to join in the most innocent female talk about household matters or children. The Jews ate neither pork nor red meat sold from a butcher, preferring instead to slaughter live animals and then drain the blood. They washed their clothes on Sundays and rested on Saturdays, and eight days after a son was born they had huge celebrations in honour of the boy's circumcision. Those who glimpsed the Jewish men praying claimed that they covered their whole bodies, including their heads, with a large shawl that made them appear both animal-like and foolish. These Jews arrived as foreigners, and foreigners they remained.

In Germany they frequently murdered the Jews, because the Christian people claimed (and provided good evidence) that the Jews spread the plague by poisoning the wells with whatever came to hand: spiders' webs, lizards, toads and, most commonly, the severed heads of Christian. Not only had the Jews killed Jesus Christ, but during Holy Weeks it was common practice for them to re-enact this crime and kill a Christian child in order that they might draw out the fresh blood and knead some of it into the unleavened bread which they ate during their own Easter celebration, known as Passover. Their feast was designed to celebrate the moment in their history when they claimed that the Red Sea turned into blood and destroyed the Egyptian army, hence their need for fresh blood. However, this murderous act also demonstrated their hatred of Christianity. At the moment at which they stabbed the innocent Christian child, the Jews were known to recite the words: "Even as we condemned the Christ to a shameful death, so let us also condemn this innocent Christian, so that, uniting the Lord and His servant in a like punishment, we may retort upon them the pain of that reproach which they impute to us." In addition to using this blood in the preparation of bread, it was widely known that the Jews used fresh Christian blood for anointing rabbits, for circumcision, in stopping menstrual and other bleedings, in removing bodily odours, in making love potions and magical powder, and in painting the bodies of their dead.

Although the Venetian *Grand Council* sought to discourage the propagation of false ideas about the Jews (for these people were an important part of the republic's economy), the doge's inner *Council of Ten* nevertheless passed a law according to which the Jews were instructed to distinguish themselves by yellow stitching on their clothes. People detested the Jews for a variety of reasons, but the most often cited referred to their position in society as people who would loan money at an interest, more often than not requiring extravagant security from the borrower. To comprehend fully how shameful a trade this was, one had to understand that Christians were strictly forbidden to give out loans at interest to anyone. In fact, even Jews were forbidden by God Himself, taken from the word of the Scripture, to lend money to their "brothers". However, by interpreting this edict liberally, the Jews discovered that they could give loans to Christians, who were technically not their "brothers", at whatever interest they deemed applicable. By obliging the Jews to lend money in exchange for permission to live in their territory, the Republic of Venice could pretend to be implementing a policy of some tolerance towards the Jews, while serving its own interests and ignoring the fact that it was further exposing the Jews to the multiple dangers of Christian hostility.

The grandparents of Portobuffole's principal Jewish moneylenders, Servadio and Moses, had begun to practise usury in Germany. Jews were unable to practise in either the arts or trades, no matter how skilled, for the various guilds had been deliberately established with religious affiliations to Christianity. Usury, however, because it was forbidden to Christians, remained a professional outlet for the Jews. The work was risky, and therefore profitable, but it was not physically demanding and it left time for both reading and studying. The Jews paid an excessive amount of tax on their profits, but plenty remained for them to live on. There was, however, little for them to invest in, so their money remained liquid, which further drove home the notion of the Jews maintaining a sybaritic lifestyle.

The Jewish moneylender offered to the public an indispensable service. In Portobuffole there was not a single working family who, every now and then, did not have to take out a loan in order to survive periods of poverty. However, a dependency upon the Jews was not confined to any one section of society. After the war with the Turks, the economy of the Mot Serene Republic of Venice began to falter as the opportunity for expansion in the Orient appeared to have been blocked. This led young Venetian aristocrats to begin to explore the commercial and economic prospects inland, but only with the understanding that the Jews would be able to provide large-scale capital investment. However, despite their central role in Venetian society, Jews were ever-mindful that every debtor was a potential enemy, and that the goodwill of the usurer often fed the greediness of the borrower. It remained both easy and convenient for individuals habitually to accuse the Jews of wicked doing, and subsequently to confiscate their profits, but the doge and his *Council of Ten* realized that they could not afford to alienate these Jews completely.

The "Contract of Moses" was the means by which the Jews were allowed "freedom" to practice usury, but under strict controls. Whenever a town such as Portobuffole decided to grant a usurer's licence to a Jew, the contract between them, which was generally valid for five years and was renewable, had to be submitted to the Venetian *Grand Council* for ratification. The contract clearly listed the *rights* of the Jew proprietors and their collaborators:

　- The Jews have usury rights (sometimes exclusively) in the town for the period valid in the contract.

　- The Jews can live the way that they please and erect a synagogue.

　- The Jews are not obliged to keep the banks open on Saturdays, or during other Jewish holidays.

　- The Jews can refuse to lend to foreigners.

　- The Jews can sell securities that have not been claimed for more than one year.

- The Jews are not held responsible for securities that are lost during fire, war, looting or robberies, or for securities that are gnawed by moths or rats (provided they keep cats in their houses).

- The Jews have the right to receive, from the butcher, living animals for the same price paid by Christians.

With as much care and precision, the "Contract of Moses" listed the *duties* of the Jew proprietors and their collaborators:

- The Jews cannot keep banks open on Sundays, or on Christmas, Easter or Corpus Christi Day, or during any of the four feast days set aside for Mary.

- The Jews cannot refuse to lend money on securities with a value of less than ten ducati.

- If the Jews refuse to do this for more than ten consecutive workdays, then they have to pay a fine of ten ducati.

- The interest on their Jewish loans cannot exceed two and a half Venetian lire each month.

- In the case of loans given without securities, or, in other words, written loans, the monthly interest can rise to four lire.

- The Jews have to give loans up to one hundred ducati to the municipal government without interest.

- It is prohibited to take sacred furniture as a security; loans for weapons are given at the discretion of the Jew.

- A half of any fine is to be given to the town council.

For every object received as security, the usurer was obliged to write up a receipt in Italian, which indicated the place and date of the loan, the nature of the object offered as security, the weight of it, and whether it contained any gold or silver. In addition, each usurer generally kept a personal book in which he recorded confidential information. This private record book was usually written in Hebrew characters.

Whereas the state reluctantly admitted their need for the Jews, the church required no such diplomacy. The Franciscans, in particular, preached vehemently against the Jews, and urged that their avaricious monopoly of credit and usury be taken from them and given to a devout Christian group, who might operate without the base objective of profit. One among these Franciscan priests, a seventeen-year-old boy named Martin Tomitano of Fletre, gained much fame for his vigorous rhetoric. He was a small novice of less than one and a half metres, who, when he preached, barely reached the parapet of the pulpit. However, like many small men, he was driven by a desire to achieve great feats in the world. As a young boy, Martin Tomitano had twice witnessed his father travel to Venice to protest in vain to the *Grand Council* against the Jews who wished to open a bank in Feltre. Marin Tomitano was in no doubt as to the primary source of evil in the world in which he lived.

Eventually, the boy took the name of Bernard, after a renowned Franciscan predecessor from Siena, and he began to travel from city to city, preaching in a clear, strong voice. He pronounced the language distinctly, slowing down and speeding up to good effect, accentuating the right words, making comparisons, relating pious anecdotes, techniques that he painstakingly designed, then practised, in order that he might keep the people's attention. He burnt with a love for God, and for God's people, whom he wished to help escape from the influence of the Jews, who were little more than merchants of tears and drinkers of human blood. During Lent, many cities recruited him to preach in town squares, because the churches could never hold all who wished to listen. As soon as he was done he would hurry away, for people would pull at his clothes to try to claim a relic for themselves. After his departure, people would light fires to burn what he had called the "instruments of sin": playing cards, decorative ornaments, and even the emblems of enemy factions, were all cast into the flames. It was only after the feverishly righteous Bernard, formerly known as Martin Tomitano of Feltre, had left that the Jews would dare to show their faces once more, and they always did so cautiously and with the knowledge that the heated passions stirred up by this small man would take some time to die down.

The night of Saturday 25 March 1480 was the occasion of the first full moon of spring. In Portobuffole the atmosphere was merry, as many husbands had now returned from the Venetian army. The recently arrived men were happy in the arms of their loved ones, while those wives who still lived in anxious expectation of their husbands' return eventually tore their eyes from the street and found solace in the company of their children. These highly spirited Christians were joyfully celebrating the Feast of the Annunciation and looking forward to the following day, Palm Sunday.

The Jews of Portobuffole had gathered in the house of Servadio to begin to celebrate the night of the fourteenth day of the month of Nissan in the year 5240 since the creation of their world. In common with all their holidays, this Jewish celebration began after sunset, with the men and children seated around a large table. In front of each person was a large illustrated Hebrew book of stories, which these Jews read from right to left. The men sat with their heads covered and with their elbows leaning against the table, and they read from their history about the night of the fleeing Jews.

At this time of the year, Jewish law called for these people to rid their homes of all fermented foods, and, beginning that night and for the next eight days, these Jews could not eat bread or anything leavened, for they were remembering when they had had to flee Egypt so quickly that their bread did not have time to rise. In place of bread, they ate unleavened crackers that had been carefully sheltered from any fermentation or external contamination. These crackers were placed at the centre of the table on a huge tray that also contained a hard-boiled egg, a thin leg of lamb, herbs, a small cup of vinegar, wine, and various other objects necessary to their Jewish rituals.

For many weeks, Servadio's youngest son had prepared with his tutor to ask in a high and confident voice, and in the Hebrew languages, why this night was different from any other. And then suddenly the moment arrived for the boy to ask his first question, and then three further questions, and his mother, and the other women, left the kitchen with damp eyes and came to listen to this small boy who stood in front of the assembly of men. Servadio responded to his son's questions by reading from the Hebrew book of stories, occasionally interrupting his reading to make comments, and then stopping to listen to statements from those more learned than himself. Eventually everybody had a chance first to read from the books and then chant, "This year, slaves; next year in the land of Israel, free," and the storytelling and chanting continued as the Jewish spirit moved each of them in turn.

For almost three thousand years the Jews had celebrated this holiday by reciting the same prayers, abstaining from the same foods, and reading the same stories as if reading them for the first time. This was the source of their safety, and the basis of their relative confidence and happiness. They repeatedly told each other about how the waters of the Red Sea were opened for the fleeing slaves and how, immediately after, they closed on the ranks of the Egyptians who followed them. Servadio watched his son carefully, and smiled as he recognized himself in the inquisitive young boy. And then Servadio was shaken from his proud contemplation as the hungry children shouted the last words of a prayer, which was the sign for the food and wine to be served. Jewish songs would continue to be sung, and Jewish stories would be joyfully recited, but most would now concentrate upon their feasting, and the eager wolfing of Hebrew food.

The innocent beggar child with blond hair and a sack on his shoulder, who had appeared in Portobuffole at this time of Christian and Jewish festivities, was never seen again. Once Easter had passed, those who thought they had seen him began to talk about him. Those who had definitely not seen him also began to talk about him, and eventually the details of the stories became less conflicting. There was no doubt that the boy had entered the house of Servadio. Someone had noted an unusual number of Jews gathered in the house, and someone else had distinctly heard the sound of a boy sobbing and then suffocating cries, and yet someone else had seen a Jew walking the streets, dragging a sack behind him, at three in the morning. Nearly everyone remembered seeing smoke coming from the chimney of the house of Moses, but no one could remember the name of the boy. The image of the poor boy was clear, but the name was missing, and then one old woman retrieved his name from the corner of her mind. His name was Sebastian. The Jews had killed a beggar boy named Sebastian, and the precise details of this monstrous crime were on everyone's lips. The Jews had killed an innocent Christian boy named Sebastian New. They had dared to make a sacrifice in the Christian town of Portobuffole.

思考与讨论

（1）"1480 年威尼斯犹太血祭审判"的历史背景是什么？

（2）卡里尔·菲利普斯为何如此精确地描述威尼斯政府给犹太人放贷设定的条款？

（3）卡里尔·菲利普斯在小说中穿插讲述"1480 年威尼斯犹太血祭审判"的目的是什么？

（4）在《血的本质》中，卡里尔·菲利普斯对犹太人在威尼斯的生活状况如何评价？

（5）卡里尔·菲利普斯的小说《血的本质》与莎士比亚的戏剧《威尼斯商人》之间的互文关系是什么？

（6）身为黑人作家的卡里尔·菲利普斯为何对犹太人所遭受的种族歧视和迫害深感同情？

 拓展阅读

［1］Dundes, A. *The Blood Libel Legend: A Casebook in Anti-Semitic Folklore*. Madison: The University of Wisconsin Press, 1991.

［2］Ledent, B. *Caryl Phillips*. Manchester: Manchester University Press, 2002.

［3］徐彬. 血祭、隔都、奥赛罗——卡里尔·菲利普斯《血的本质》中欧洲种族主义的政治文化表征［J］. 外国文学评论, 2020(1): 80 - 93.

三、扎迪·史密斯

（一）扎迪·史密斯简介

扎迪·史密斯出生于英国伦敦，母亲是牙买加移民，父亲是英国人。史密斯在伦敦西北部布伦特区的威尔斯登长大，在伦敦国王学院和剑桥大学学习英国文学。她曾在哥伦比亚大学艺术学院教授小说，2010 年入职纽约大学任终身教授。

1994 年至 1997 年在剑桥大学读书期间，扎迪·史密斯开始进行文学创作，曾在名为《梅斯选集》（*The Mays Anthology*）的新学生作品集中发表多篇短篇小说。史密斯的处女作《白牙》完成于她在剑桥大学读书的最后一年，2000 年正式出版。该小说广受国际赞誉，并获得了多个奖项，如詹姆斯·泰特·布莱克纪念奖、贝蒂·特拉斯克奖等。

2002 年，扎迪·史密斯出版第二部小说《签名人》（*The Autograph Man*）。尽管评论家对它的评价不如《白牙》，该小说还是获得了一定的商业成功。《签名人》出版后，扎迪·史密斯作为哈佛大学拉德克利夫高级研究所的研究员访问了美国。2005 年她出版了第三部小说《论美》（*On Beauty*），该小说入围曼布克奖，并获得了 2006 年柑橘奖和阿尼斯菲尔德-沃尔夫图书奖。2009 年，扎迪·史密斯出版小说《玛莎和汉威尔》（*Martha and Hanwell*）。2012 年扎迪·史密斯出版小说《NW》，该小说获皇家文学学会翁达杰奖和女性小说奖提名。2016 年 11 月，扎迪·史密斯的第五部小说《摇摆时间》（*Swing Time*）

出版,该小说入围 2017 年曼布克奖提名。2019 年 10 月,扎迪·史密斯出版短篇小说集《大联盟》(*Grand Union*)。

2004 年,扎迪·史密斯被 BBC 评选为"英国文化中最具影响力的二十位人物"之一。2003 年和 2013 年,史密斯两次入选"格兰塔二十位最佳年轻作家"。《白牙》入选《时代》杂志 1923 年至 2005 年 100 部最佳英文小说。

(二)《白牙》简介

小说《白牙》围绕三个英国家庭的故事展开。三个家庭分别是:英国人阿奇·琼斯、身为牙买加移民后裔的妻子克拉拉·鲍登和女儿伊里埃一家;第二次世界大战后由孟加拉移民到英国的穆斯林萨马德·伊克巴尔、妻子艾尔萨娜和双胞胎儿子马吉德与米拉特一家;基因科学家犹太人马库斯·查尔芬、身为园艺家的妻子乔伊斯和他们的儿子约书亚一家。查尔芬的"未来鼠"项目将三个家庭联系在一起。

萨马德希望通过减少学校非基督教节日如收获节(Harvest Festival),添加穆斯林节日的方式给儿子所在的学校染上穆斯林文化的颜色。尽管萨马德的动议论辩充实可靠,但因家委会成员 11 人赞成、36 人反对未能通过。57 岁的萨马德却"因祸得福"博得儿子所在班级年轻女音乐老师波比·博恩特的喜爱。与波比·博恩特的婚外恋使萨马德陷入道德与文化的双重危机之中。萨马德发现他非但没给英国染上穆斯林文化的颜色,却反被"堕落"的英国文化同化和腐蚀。波比·博恩特被萨马德视为诱惑他道德犯罪的英国"海妖",穆斯林文化传统之根是拯救灵魂的救生绳。

因担心儿子受"堕落"的英国文化的影响,萨马德选择将大儿子马吉德送回孟加拉接受教育。萨马德认为,把大儿子马吉德送回孟加拉接受正统穆斯林教育是实现自我道德救赎和对家族/种族文化传统固本清源的良策。多年后返回英国的马吉德并未如萨马德所愿成为一名虔诚的伊斯兰教徒,却成了一名比英国人还像英国人的无神论者;他立志投身科学研究,担任马库斯的助手。萨马德的小儿子米拉特身陷毒品与种族歧视的双重困境之中,为获得种族自由和解放加入一个名为凯文的激进的原教旨主义兄弟会。查尔芬夫妇自认为是马吉德等人的"庇护者",却忽略了对儿子约书亚的关爱,从而导致他对父亲的反抗。为马库斯工作的伊里埃陷入与马吉德和米拉特兄弟二人的爱情纠葛之中。民族、种族、宗教、家庭和个人的种种矛盾在马库斯召开的"未来鼠"项目发布会上一并爆发,以米拉特刺杀"未来鼠"项目背后主导人德国纳粹医生马克-皮埃尔·佩雷失败宣告结束。

英国历史学家对萨马德祖父潘德兵变英雄身份进行体系化的否定与丑化。二战退伍老兵 J.P.汉密尔顿先生矢口否认第二次世界大战中前英国殖民地人民为英国而战的历史。上述事实令萨马德及其儿子马吉德、米拉特和克莱拉的女儿艾丽倍感英国人种族歧视的敌意与因祖辈历史被抹杀而引发的种族文化与历史存续危机。

在《白牙》中,史密斯借助对 20 世纪 90 年代盛行于英国的科学技术的探讨映射了英国社会的种族文化问题。英国园艺家乔伊斯的"异花传粉论"和基因科学家马库斯的"基因控制论"分别是英国多元文化政策和种族同化政策的缩影。前者旨在创造物种的多样性和更能适应变化了的环境的后代,后者旨在消除偶然性或随机性,如马库斯所说:"消除了偶然性,你就能统治全世界。"在向艾丽介绍如何利用基因技术治疗癌症时,马库斯说:"如你所见,胚胎细胞功能强大,能帮助我们找出诱发癌症的遗传因素,你真正需要弄懂的是肿瘤如何在活体组织上发展。我是说,你不能把这与文化相提并论,两者不是一回事。接下去要将化学致癌物注入靶器官……。"马库斯"科学"与"文化"不可对等的说法貌似公允,却内含借用基因技术的方法消除"文化肿瘤"的动机。对此,马库斯与他人合著的科普书《时间炸弹与身体时钟:基因的未来探险》的年轻读者、亚裔政治学专业女学生一语道破天机:消除"文化肿瘤"意味着用基因控制论的方法实施种族文化的清洗——西方对东方文化与阿拉伯文化的清洗。

20世纪末,有色移民及其后代虽已进入英国社会生活众多领域,却因种族歧视和"认知暴力"而面临失去种族文化与历史传统的焦虑。"掉牙"是小说中该焦虑的文学隐喻。史密斯将萨马德·伊克巴尔与霍坦斯·鲍登[①]两个英国有色移民家族的文化与历史渊源镶嵌于小说现在时的叙事之中。透过这一叙事方式,史密斯实现了对英国有色人种文化传统和家族、种族历史的"变化中的相同"的书写,即:不断"变化"的有色人种英国生活史须以其"相同"(或曰"不变")的种族文化、历史传统和记忆为前提。唯有如此,才能彻底消除有色人种的文化与历史存续危机。

(三) 作品选读:《白牙》[②]

On April Fool's Day, Samad turned up. He was all in white, on his way to the restaurant, crumpled and creased like a disappointed saint. He looked to be on the brink of tears. Irie let him in.

"Hello, Miss Jones," said Samad, bowing ever so slightly. "And how is your father?"

Irie smiled with recognition. "You see him more than we do. How's God?"

"Perfectly fine, thank you. Have you seen my good-for-nothing son recently?"

Before Irie had a chance to give her next line, Samad broke down in front of her and had to be led into the living room, sat in Darcus's chair and brought a cup of tea before he could speak.

"Mr. Iqbal, what's wrong?"

"What is right?"

"Has something happened to Dad?"

"Oh no, no...Archibald is fine. He is like the washing-machine advert. He carries on and on as ever."

"Then what?"

"Millat. He has been missing these three weeks."

"God. Well, have you tried the Chalfens?"

"He is not with them. I know where he is. Out of the frying pan and into the fire. He is on some retreat with these lunatic green-tie people. In a sports centre in Chester."

"Bloody hell."

Irie sat down cross-legged and took out a fag. "I hadn't seen him in school, but I didn't realize how long it had been. But if you know where he is..."

---

① 霍坦斯·鲍登是克拉拉·鲍登的母亲,是牙买加人安布罗西亚的女儿,出生于1907年牙买加金斯顿地震期间。霍坦斯是一个严格的女人,也是一个虔诚的耶和华见证人(Jehovah's Witness),她相信世界末日即将来临。她和克拉拉争论她与阿奇·琼斯的婚姻并指责克拉拉不虔诚。

② Smith, Z. *White Teeth*. London: Penguin Books, 2001, pp.405-410.

"I didn't come here to find him, I came to ask your advice, Irie. What can I do? You know him—how does one get through?"

Irie bit her lip, her mother's old habit. "I mean, I don't know... we're not as close as we were... but I've always thought that maybe it's the Magid thing... missing him... I mean he'd never admit it... but Magid's his twin and maybe if he saw him—"

"No, no. No, no, no. I wish that were the solution. Allah knows how I pinned all my hopes on Magid. And now he says he is coming back to study the English law-paid for by these Chalfen people. He wants to enforce the laws of man rather than the laws of God. He has learnt none of the lessons of Muhammad—peace be upon Him! Of course, his mother is delighted. But he is nothing but a disappointment to me. More English than the English. Believe me, Magid will do Millat no good and Millat will do Magid no good. They have both lost their way. Strayed so far from the life I had intended for them. No doubt they will both marry white women called Sheila and put me in an early grave. All I wanted was two good Muslim boys. Oh, Irie..." Samad took her free hand and patted it with sad affection. "I just don't understand where I have gone wrong. You teach them but they do not listen because they have the 'Public Enemy' music on at full blast. You show them the road and they take the bloody path to the Inns of Court. You guide them and they run from your grasp to a Chester sports centre. You try to plan everything and nothing happens in the way that you expected..."

But if you could begin again, thought Irie, if you could take them back to the source of the river, to the start of the story, to the homeland... But she didn't say that, because he felt it as she felt it and both knew it was as useless as chasing your own shadow. Instead she took her hand from underneath his and placed it on top, returning the stroke. "Oh, Mr. Iqbal. I don't know what to say..."

"There are no words. The one I send home comes out a pukka Englishman, white suited, silly wig lawyer. The one I keep here is fully paid-up green bow-tie-wearing fundamentalist terrorist. I sometimes wonder why I bother," said Samad bitterly, betraying the English inflections of twenty years in the country, "I really do. These days, it feels to me like you make a devil's pact when you walk into this country. You hand over your passport at the check-in, you get stamped, you want to make a little money, get yourself started... but you mean to go back! Who would want to stay? Cold, wet, miserable; terrible food, dreadful newspapers who—would want to stay? In a place where you are never welcomed, only tolerated. Just tolerated. Like you are an animal finally house-trained. Who would want to stay? But you have made a devil's pact... it drags you in and suddenly you are unsuitable to return, your children are unrecognizable, you belong nowhere."

"Oh, that's not true, surely."

"And then you begin to give up the *very idea* of belonging. Suddenly this thing, this *belonging*, it seems like some long, dirty lie... and I begin to believe that birthplaces are accidents, that everything is an *accident*. But if you believe that, where do you go? What do you do? What does anything matter?"

As Samad described this dystopia with a look of horror, Irie was ashamed to find that the land of accidents sounded like *paradise* to her. Sounded like freedom.

"Do you understand, child? I know you understand."

And what he really meant was: do we speak the same language? Are we from the same place? Are we the same?

Irie squeezed his hand and nodded vigorously, trying to ward off his tears. What else could she tell him but what he wanted to hear?

"Yes," she said. "Yes, yes, yes."

When Hortense and Ryan came home that evening after a late-night prayer meeting, both were in a state of high excitement. Tonight was the night. After giving Hortense a flurry of instructions as to the typesetting and layout of his latest *Watchtower* article, Ryan went into the hallway to make his telephone call to Brooklyn to get the news.

"But I thought he was in consultation *with* them."

"Yes, yes, he is... but de final confirmation, you understand, mus' come from Mr Charles Wintry himself in Brooklyn," said Hortense breathlessly. "What a day dis is! What a day! Help me wid liftin' dis typewriter now... I need it on de table."

Irie did as she was told, carrying the enormous old Remington to the kitchen and laying it down in front of Hortense. Hortense passed Irie a bundle of white paper covered in Ryan's tiny script.

"Now you read dat to me, Irie Ambrosia, slowly now... an' I'll get it down in type."

Irie read for half an hour or so, wincing at Ryan's horrible corkscrew prose, passing the whiting fluid when it was required, and gritting her teeth at the author's interruptions as every ten minutes he popped back into the room to adjust his syntax or rephrase a paragraph.

"Mr. Topps, did you get trew yet?"

"Not yet, Mrs. B., not yet. Very busy, Mr. Charles Wintry. I'm going to try again now."

A sentence, Samad's sentence, was passing through Irie's tired brain. *Sometimes I wonder why I bother*. And now that Ryan was out of the way, Irie saw her opportunity to ask it, though she framed it carefully.

Hortense leant back in her chair and placed her hands on her lap. "I bin doin' dis a very long time, Irie Ambrosia. I bin' waitin' ever since I was a pickney in long socks."

"But that's no reason—"

"What d' you know fe reasons? Nuttin' at all. The Witness church is where my roots are. It bin good to me when nobody else has. It was de good ting my mudder gave me, an' I nat going to let it go now we so close to de end."

"But Gran, it's not... you won't ever..."

"Lemme tell you so meting I'm not like dem Witnesses jus' scared of Dyin'. Jus' scared. Dem wan' everybody to die excep' dem. Dat's not a reason to dedicate your life to Jesus Christ. I gat very different aims. I still hope to be one of de Anointed evan if I am a woman. I want it all my life. I want to be dere wid de Lord making de laws and de decisions." Hortense sucked her teeth long and loud. "I gat so tired wid de church always tellin' me I'm a woman or I'm nat heducated enough. Everybody always tryin' to heducate you; heducate you about dis, heducate you about dat... Dat's always bin de problem wid de women in dis family. Somebody always tryin' to heducate them about something, pretendin' it all about learnin' when it all about a battle of de wills. But if I were one of de hundred an' forty-four, no one gwan try to heducate *me*. Dat would be *my* job! I'd make my own laws an' I wouldn't be wanting anybody else's opinions. My mudder was strong-willed deep down, and I'm de same. Lord knows, your mudder was de same. And you de same."

"Tell me about Ambrosia," said Irie, spotting a chink in Hortense's armour that one might squeeze through. "Please."

But Hortense remained solid. "You know enough already. De past is done wid. Nobody learn nuttin' from it. Top of page five please—I tink dat's where we were."

At that moment Ryan returned to the room, face redder than ever.

"What, Mr Topps? Is it? Do you know?"

"God help the heathen, Mrs. B., for the day is indeed at hand! It is as the Lord laid out clearly in his book of Revelation. He never intended a third millennium. Now I'll need that article typed up, and then another one that I'll dictate to you off the cuff—you'll need to telephone all the Lambeth members, and leaflet the—"

"Oh, yes, Mr Topps—but jus' let me tyake it in jus' a minute... It couldn't be any udder date, could it, Mr Topps? I tol' you I felt it in my bones."

"I'm not sure as to how much your bones had to do wiv it, Mrs B. Surely more credit is due to the thorough scriptural study done by myself and my colleagues—"

"And God, presumably," said Irie, cutting him a sharp glare, going over to hold Hortense, who was shaking with sobs. Hortense kissed Irie on both cheeks and Irie smiled at the hot wetness.

"Oh, Irie Ambrosia. I'm so glad you're here to share dis. I live dis century—I came into dis world in an eart-quake at de very beginning and I shall see the hevil and sinful pollution be herased in a mighty rumbling eart-quake once more. Praise de Lord! It is as he promised after all. I knew I'd make it. I got jus' seven years to wait. Ninety-two!" Hortense sucked her teeth contemptuously. "Cho! My grandmudder live to see one hundered-and-tree an de woman could skip rope till de day she keel over and drop col'. Me gwan make it. I make it dis far. My mudder suffer to get me here—but she knew de true church and she make heffort to push me out in de mo' difficult circumstances so I could live to see that glory day."

"Amen!"

"Oh, hamen Mr Topps. Put on de complete suit of armour of God! Now, Irie Ambrosia, witness me as I say it: I'm gwan be dere. An' I'm gwan to be in *Jamaica* to see it. I'm going home that year of our Lord. An' you can come dere too if you learn from me and listen. You wan come Jamaica in de year two thousand?"

Irie let out a little scream and rushed to give her grandmother another hug.

Hortense wiped her tears with her apron. "Lord Jesus, I live dis century! Well and truly I live dis terrible century wid all its troubles and vexations. And tanks to you, Lord, I'm gwan a feel a rumble at both ends."

 ## 思考与讨论

(1) 如何看待萨马德·伊克巴尔的双胞胎儿子马吉德与米拉特之间的差别？

(2) 萨马德·伊克巴尔对英国的消极情绪缘何而来？

(3) 伊里埃的奶奶霍顿斯女士如何看待有色女性的教育问题？

(4) 节选中以萨马德·伊克巴尔和霍顿斯女士为代表的有色英国移民对源出国态度如何？

(5) 身为混血儿的伊里埃是否面临身份困惑？其文本表现是什么？

(6) 扎迪·史密斯对查尔芬一家的描写在情节发展和主题表达上有何种功能？

 ## 拓展阅读

[1] Rogers, K. Affirming Complexity: "White Teeth" and Cosmopolitanism. *Interdisciplinary Literary Studies*. Vol. 9, No. 2 (Spring 2008), pp. 45 – 61.

[2] Trimm, R. After the Century of Strangers: Hospitality and Crashing in Zadie Smith's *White Teeth. Contemporary Literature*. Vol. 56, No. 1 (Spring 2015), pp. 145 – 172.

[3] 徐彬."摩西十诫"与"掉牙"的焦虑——《孤独的伦敦人》与《白牙》中英国有色移民的种族危机 [J].外语与外语教学,2019(1):110 – 118.

第二章
当代英国世界主义小说

世界主义（cosmopolitanism），从词源上看，是由希腊语中的 kosmo（宇宙或世界）和 polis（城市或城邦）两词组合而成，意指世界城邦，即整个宇宙或世界是一个城邦，所有身处这个宇宙中的公民都可被称为世界公民。这类主张和理论教义被称为"世界主义"，信奉这一套理论教义的人便被称为世界主义者。

最早的世界主义者可以追溯至公元前 4 世纪的犬儒派哲人狄奥格尼斯（Diogenes），他常四处游历，认为狭隘的城邦公民身份不足以表明自己的归属，因此当别人问他来自哪里时，他便回答道："我是一个世界公民（kosmopolitês）。"①这一表述为当代世界主义奠定了理论根基，即一个人不论其政治立场为何，总是与他人共享同一个世界，应该对"世界国家"（world-state）②和其他世界公民承担相应的责任和义务。后来的斯多葛学派（the Stoics）将其倡导的世界公民理想推广为对整个人类的博爱，这种博爱论强调对他者的承认和尊重。早期的世界主义追求的是一种乌托邦式的、超越了特定城邦界限的伦理道德与价值体系。

哲学家康德在 1795 年出版的专著《永久的和平：一个哲学计划》中提出了"世界联邦"③的构想。他认为只有人类从国家内部联合起来形成世界联邦，尊重本国和世界公民的权利，履行共同的义务，世界和平才有实现的可能。康德的构想为当代世界主义提供了理论源泉，但他的思想带有明显的种族主义色彩，因为他认为世界联邦只可能出现在欧洲。

19 世纪，经济全球化推动了资本的海外扩张，马克思和恩格斯将世界主义视为资本主义意识形态的反映。他们认为资本主义在本质上是扩张性的，打破了民族国家的地理界限，促进了海外市场的形成与发展，并提出了无差别的社会理想和无产阶级世界革命的设想。

当代世界主义是全球化与全球危机共同作用下的产物，是一种超越民族-国家界限与全人类认同的思想，它被赋予了一种实现全球范围内正义与平等的道德责任。1989 年 11 月 9 日柏林墙的倒塌是当代世界主义兴起的时代标志，这一事件代表了冷战的结束，也为全球化的空前发展提供了条件，人类社会成为一个联系日益紧密的"地球村"。与此同时，全球化的发展危机重重，如"9·11"恐怖袭击引发全球恐慌、2008 年的全球经济危机、2016 年英国脱欧公投的国际影响以及 2019 年全球新冠疫情暴发。全球危机导致当代世界主义随时处于被扼杀的风险之中。然而这些全球危机也证明世界已然形成一个牵

---

① 《斯坦福哲学百科全书》中"Cosmopolitanism"一章中的第 2 页。http://plato. stanford. edu/entries/cosmopolitanism/
② "世界国家"是政治世界主义中的概念，它指的是超越"民族国家"体系的全球国家联盟。参考文献同上，第 11 页。
③ "世界联邦"是一种"国际法律秩序的形式"，它指的是"国家根据'共和'原则在内部组织起来，为了和平而从外部组成的一个自愿的联盟"。参考文献同上，第 7 页。

一发而动全身的"命运共同体",没有个人或国家能在全球危机的影响下独善其身。全球性危机需要全球性的合作与努力去应对,当代世界主义理论话语便是在这种压力下不断发展并自我完善的。

当代世界主义涉猎的领域极其广泛,包括经济世界主义、政治世界主义、文化世界主义、道德世界主义等。当代世界主义之所以重要,"并不是因为其使用的精确性和一致性"①,而是因为其内涵的不断丰富和扩充。要探讨世界主义的多重内涵,有一些关键词无法避免。一、世界公民:世界是一个整体,生活在同一个世界的所有公民享有超越其民族国家政治归属和地理界线的平等权利和义务,正如阿皮亚所言,"我们必须既对本国公民同胞负责,也对世界公民同胞负责"②;二、游牧主义,即跨越民族国家地理界限的位置上的流动,因为"地理上的流动更容易促进不同文化之间的交流、熟悉、理解、洞见甚至是包容"③;三、共情与爱:其基础是不同性别、不同人种、不同文化之间的理解,目的是化解贝克笔下世界主义中存在的矛盾与冲突;四、文化异质化,即强调文化的复杂性与多样性,倡导承认和尊重文化差异性,反对文化同质化,正如克里福德提出的"差异的世界主义"(discrepant cosmopolitanism)④和保罗·吉尔罗伊提出的"世界性欢宴"(cosmopolitan conviviality)⑤;五、想象世界:在现实生活中获知宇宙与人类的全貌是不现实的,那么想象世界便成为一种绝对必要。而文学由于其虚构性特征便成为想象世界和宇宙的最佳领域,世界主义的价值通过想象的虚构空间被挖掘,同时保留其理论本身的伦理维度。文学领域里"元宇宙"(metaverse)概念的诞生便是对当代世界主义中世界是想象的这一主张的回应,该词最早出现于尼尔·斯蒂芬森(Neal Stephenson)于 1992 年出版的科幻小说《雪崩》(Snow Crash)中,指脱胎于现实并与现实世界平行的虚拟世界,人类可以在这个想象的世界里自由驰骋。

置于上述普遍背景之中的当代英国世界主义也有其独特性,这与大英帝国殖民扩张的历史与独特的国家结构密不可分。始于 16 世纪并于 19 世纪达到巅峰的大英帝国的殖民扩张历程使英国与世界上超过四分之三的国家之间保持联系,当时的"日不落帝国"已然成为"世界国家"理想的蓝本。众多前殖民地人民怀着对大英帝国的美好憧憬进入英国首都伦敦,伦敦城成为汇集各色人种的"世界国家"的微缩景观。随着两次世界大战的爆发,大英帝国逐渐失去了世界霸主地位,前殖民地纷纷独立,脱欧公投后的英国正在被边缘化,曾经的帝国正被世界抛弃,世界主义成为英国寻求重新融入世界的理想话语。英国由四个民族(英格兰、威尔士、苏格兰和北爱尔兰)构成,这个多民族国家在脱欧后正面临分崩离析的危机。苏格兰要求于 2023 年举行第二次独立公投,这使英国的统一面临严重挑战,世界主义作为挽救英国分裂的理想频繁出现在公众话语中。

世界主义在当代文学中发挥的影响不断扩大,主要归结于以下三方面原因:一、世界主义本身所具有的矛盾性内涵。一方面它包含杂糅性、流动性和包容性等积极意义,另一方面它又引发寄生性、虚无性和缺乏忠诚的负面联想,这种复杂性和矛盾性使它深受作家的青睐;二、跨国人口流动的不断深入造成了国家公民身份的多重性和不确定性;三、全球危机和矛盾的不断加剧使虚构的文学世界为构建未来图景提供了广阔空间。因此,小说开始想象新的文学世界以应对世界社会的加速发展和公民的身份危

---

① Hannerz, U. *Two Faces of Cosmopolitanism: Culture and Politics*. Barcelona: Cidob, 2006, p.5.
② Appiah, K. A. Kwame Anthony Appiah: Cosmopolitanism. Astra Taylor, ed., *Examined Life: Excursions with Contemporary Thinkers*. New York: The New Press, 2009, pp.87 – 114.
③ Hopper, P. *Living with Globalization*. New York: Berg, 2006, p.54.
④ Clifford, J. *Routes: Travel and Translations in the Late Twentieth Century*. Cambridge: Harvard University Press, 1997.
⑤ "世界性欢宴"是"使多元文化成为英国城区和其他后殖民城市普遍特征的共存和合作的过程"。参见 Gilroy, P. *After Empire: Melancholia or Convivial Culture*? Abington: Routledge, 2004, pp. xi.

机。正如努斯鲍姆所述:"叙事,尤其是小说[……]作为人与读者对话,不只是当地文化中的一个成分;比起宗教和哲学作品,文学作品常常更容易突破文化障碍。"①当代英国小说成为"世界主义的试验场"②,大量世界主义小说纷纷应运而生,诸如珍妮特·温特森的《苹果笔记本》和《石神》(*The Stone Gods* 2007)、阿莉·史密斯的《旅馆世界》(*Hotel World* 2001)、大卫·米切尔的《云图》和纳迪姆·阿斯拉姆的《迷失恋人的地图》等。

珍妮特·温特森聚焦于世界主义理论关照下的同性恋叙事,指出同性恋者处于社会的边缘,被主流话语贴上了他者的标签。为摆脱他者身份、争取平等话语权,同性恋者将主张人人都是享有平等权利的世界公民的世界主义理论观点作为反抗现实压迫的有力武器。《苹果笔记本》中年轻的叙述者阿莉在网络上认识已婚女性郁金香后,踏上了追寻真爱的旅程。旅行经历加深了她对异域文化的理解,她与郁金香之间的同性恋关系也让她开始接受自己,爱的力量治愈了她童年时期被父母遗弃的创伤。同样,佐伊·斯特拉坎(Zoe Strachan)在她的《负空间》(*Negative Space*)中塑造了一个在经历丧亲之痛后,不停地在各个城市之间来回穿梭的年轻女性形象。她在游历途中不停追寻完整的自我和心理上的归属感,最后通过与一位亚洲女性建立同性恋情,走出了丧亲带来的阴霾,找到了自我存在和生活的意义。

阿莉·史密斯的《旅馆世界》是游牧主义的文本再现,游牧主义的核心是地理位置上的人口流动,它有助于加强世界各国之间的联系、沟通与理解,是世界主义的重要内容。史密斯把通过酒店旋转门进出的旅客比喻为全球化的英国社会中形形色色的跨国游牧者。五位性格各异的主人公的命运通过酒店这一媒介在文本的循环结构中交织在一起。随着酒店大门一次次打开,五位主人公的故事逐渐展开,被隐藏的真相也相继浮出水面,这激起了主人公之间的情感共鸣,使她们完成了由彼此厌恶到相互理解的情感转变。

大卫·米切尔的《云图》强调世界是一个整体并通过人类文明的湮灭揭示世界主义理想是拯救人类的良药。《云图》由六个相互独立又彼此联系的故事构成,指涉全球化时代命运相互交织的现实世界。米切尔从历史维度出发,想象了一个充满压迫与斗争的跨时空存在的人类社会,并指出人类毁灭的主要力量是早期的资本主义与殖民扩张。米切尔强调合作与互助是人类社会文化进步的催化剂,同时他还批判白人男性霸权话语对异己力量和文化多样性的压制。

纳迪姆·阿斯拉姆在其《迷失恋人的地图》中指出爱的力量对弥合文化差异、创造和谐世界的重要性。阿斯拉姆详述了当代英国社会中的种族和宗教分裂问题并借此批判文化分裂现象。他指出尽管霸权话语造成了人的差异,但作为人类永恒主题的爱能够创造人类同胞之间的融合与共情,爱的缺乏能够对人类造成毁灭性的打击。和爱的主题一样,阿斯拉姆认为想象力和艺术创造力也是对抗种族分裂和充满威胁的外部世界的有力武器。

当代英国世界主义小说创作的主旨思想主要包括:一、批判二元对立的霸权话语,构建倡导爱与平等的多元文化世界;二、对抗民族主义、分裂主义和保守主义的猖獗力量;三、为社会中被边缘化的"他者"争取权利;四、试图在文学世界中阐释解决现实问题的策略,在满目疮痍的世界里构建一个跨文化、

---

① Nussbaum, M. C. *Love' Knowledge: Essays on Philosophy and Literature.* Oxford and New York: Oxford University Press, 1990, p.391.

② Appiah, K. A. "Cosmopolitan Reading." Vinay Dharwadker. ed., *Cosmopolitan Geographies: New Locations in Literature and Culture.* New York and London: Routledge, 2001, pp.197-227.

跨地理疆界的人类命运共同体的美好愿景;五、解释全球化与民族主义、文化同质化与异质化之间的矛盾与张力。在充满矛盾与冲突的当代英国社会,如何书写英国面临的内部分裂的潜在威胁和缓解英国人欧洲一体化畅想的幻灭焦虑是未来英国世界主义小说创作的主题。

第一节　想象世界:无限流动空间中的杂糅

当代英国世界主义与女性主义和同性恋叙事联系密切。世界主义旨在构建平等自由的话语体系,这一体系应包括所有世界公民的话语,而不只是以男性为中心的霸权话语压抑女性主义的话语。性平等和性别平等是实现世界公民伦理理想的必要前提,将女性从家务中解放出来正如世界主义倡导超越民族国家地理与文化界限一样重要。珍妮特·温特森的《苹果笔记本》想象了一个蔑视父权制传统的酷儿乌托邦,在这个想象的乌托邦中女性同性恋冲破了男权和异性恋社会强加的束缚,获得了发声和书写自我的机会,成为了一名真正具有平等权利的世界公民。

温特森在文中反复强调世界的想象本质,是由语言建构的,而并非男权话语中所描述的存在的实体。通过在小说中构建想象的、复数的、充满差异的世界,温特森批判了男性霸权话语排除异己、追求同质化、抹杀同性恋话语的做法。她写道"这是一个虚构的世界。这是一个自我发明的世界"①,而且并非只存在一个世界,每一滴落下的雨水的水珠中都包含一个不同的世界。世界的虚构性在"网络"一章中表现得尤其淋漓尽致,作者每晚坐在苹果笔记本前给自己素未谋面且永远不会在现实中碰面的读者讲故事,这些故事在不同时空的人之间架起沟通与理解的桥梁,作者幼年被遗弃和童年被束缚的创伤得到了一定程度的缓解。在网络空间中个人的身份与性别无法被定位,可以自由地切换身份而不受父权的控制。网络的发展也使人与人之间的沟通与理解超越了地理的界限,使世界主义的理想不再完全依赖物理空间上的流动。

由于世界的虚构性,"没有什么是可靠的。没有什么是固定的"②,整个世界是流动且不受控制的,因此寻找世界真谛的人也应处于流动状态中。温特森承认"哲学游牧主义是对父权制霸权固定界限的政治挑战"③。《苹果笔记本》中的主人公阿莉在寻爱的途中游历了众多城市,她将生活视为一场必须亲自经历的旅程,穿越未经绘制的荒原以便发现一个新区域实现另一个自我,一个被压抑的自我。她耗尽毕生精力将要追寻的乐土是一个想象中的地方,"那是一个无人可以支配的有序的无政府空间,在那个空间里没有统治者,没有边界,人们都是自由的,可以随意愿想来便来,想走即走"④。尽管阿莉不知这方乐土是否存在,不知该前往何处寻找,但她坚信它一定存在并不会放弃追寻。阿莉坚持追寻的不仅是一方乐土,一种未经定义的、未知的和开放的空间,更是一个完整的自我。

流动状态不仅表现为阿莉不停变动的地理位置,也体现在打破自我-他者二元对立的身份杂糅之中,这与世界主义力图解构以逻各斯为中心的宏大叙事的思想不谋而合。温特森使用元小说叙事技巧

---

① Winterson, J. *The PowerBook*. London: Vintage, 2001, p. 63.
② Ibid., p. 44.
③ McCulloch, F. *Cosmopolitanism in Contemporary British Fiction: Imagined Identities*. Basingstoke: Palgrave, 2012, p. 46.
④ Winterson, J. *The PowerBook*. London: Vintage, 2001, p. 175.

使小说主人公阿莉将读者纳入自己的小说创作中,打破了传统意义上作者与读者的界限,读者也成为了作者。阿莉与她所讲故事中的主人公同名,自己也成为故事的主角,插入自己的叙事话语,使作者、读者和故事主人公的身份完美地融合在一起,这是叙事层面上的身份杂糅。在科学层面上,作者指出人可以通过提取染色体改变其身高、性别、眼睛等生理特征,从而实现"成为其他人的自由"①。作者刻意模糊主人公的性别与姓名,文本中没有了固定的角色,主体变形、难以捉摸,身份也进入一种流动的想象状态之中。作者试图以此建构一个自我和他者你中有我、我中有你的无法区分的乌托邦。

温特森文本的形式与其内容一样,致力于描绘一个无限流动的、想象的而非真实存在的时空。小说打破了传统的线性叙事结构,场景互相穿插,时间来回切换,想象的世界成为一个时空并置的多维空间。在这里,两条平行线甚至可以相交,时间被纵向地堆积在一起,过去、现在和未来之间的严格界限被打破,时间成为一条蜿蜒前进的曲线。作者将童话、传奇、浪漫故事嵌入其他故事之中,所有故事被编织进一个像水一样流动的想象空间,创造了一个混杂的世界,它不能被父权制霸权话语"标记、定义和控制"②。

第二节　批判殖民主义神话与构建差异共存的文本世界

始于 16 世纪并于 19 世纪达到巅峰的大英帝国殖民扩张强化了英国与其殖民地人民之间的依存关系,为世界主义的发展提供了一定的物质基础。殖民者总是打着世界主义的幌子,即推动"世界国家"的发展以使其殖民扩张的动机合理化。但是殖民主义带来的更多的是种族歧视、压迫、剥削和同化,这与世界主义平等、包容、多元化等理念背道而驰。

米切尔以世界主义理论中多元文化并存和平等发展的思想为武器,有力地批判了殖民主义话语建构的种族差异神话。在《云图》里,在亚当·尤因时代,西方帝国通过在太平洋查塔姆岛上设置传教项目为帝国主义的统治提供条件,通过文化同化和压迫的方式推进殖民者的"文明"使命,殖民者披着世界主义救世主的外衣进行掠夺财富和实施文化霸权,就像伪善的亨利医生带着救治尤因的假面具对其下毒而谋夺其财产。岛上信奉没有杀戮、人与人之间应该和平相处的莫里奥人基于包容而建立的彼此联系的和谐的共同体被殖民主义者们所打破,莫里奥人共同体的价值体系被摧毁。米切尔力图解构作为大英帝国殖民扩张遗产的种族主义神话。在尤因时代,所有人被划分等级,黑奴位于最底层。偷渡黑奴奥图瓦出现在尤因所乘船的船舱中,白人公证员尤因出于同情出手相救,当尤因被亨利毒害濒临丧命之际,奥图瓦拼死相救。在被奥图瓦所救后,尤因开始质疑白人的种族优劣论,他的理想开始向世界主义模式靠拢。尤因积极参加废奴运动,希望为全球众多的人创造一个公平和正当的生存条件。世界公民需要成为世界和平进程的推动者,正如尤因所言:"如果我们相信人类可能竭尽全力超越这一切,如果我们相信多样的种族和宗教也能像孤儿和平地分享石栗树一样和平地分享这个世界,[……],这样的世界

---

① Winterson, J. *The PowerBook*. London: Vintage, 2001, p.4.
② McCulloch, F. *Cosmopolitanism in Contemporary British Fiction: Imagined Identities*. Basingstoke: Palgrave, 2012, p.46.

就会实现。"①"这样的世界"不仅是一个所有人平等分享的世界,也是一个人人平等的跨种族团结的世界。

当代世界主义的宇宙观主张各星体并非分散且各自独立,而是相互联系构成一个完整的宇宙,所以人类要承认并允许其他非人类"他者"的存在,接受人类并非宇宙的中心这一事实,这与数千年来西方世界主宰宇宙万物的自大与傲慢心理相背离。米切尔试图从人类对自然的破坏和对克隆人的奴役所造成的恶果解构人类剥削和控制非人类生物的"新型殖民主义"话语。《云图》中从尤因时代对小岛的乱砍滥伐和对海洋生物的过度捕捞,到路易莎·雷时代核污染与泄露的潜在威胁,再到未来的内索国弥漫着下水道的恶臭,几乎每一时期人类都对自然进行着毫无节制的索取和肆无忌惮的践踏,这也导致了人类的灭亡和原始生活状态的回归。原始部落并非伊甸园,人类又开始新一轮的烧杀掳掠和对自然的肆意破坏,这与世界主义中人类与宇宙万物和谐相处的宇宙一体观背道而驰,人类最终只能自食恶果。米切尔对未来内索国的描述有力地抨击了人类对非人类所犯下的恶行,也否定了第一章中尤因对最终会出现一个进步的和充满希望的未来的信念。米切尔塑造了一个跟第一章相呼应的充满奴役与压迫的世界,只不过奴隶主从白人转换成所有纯种人,而奴隶转换成克隆人,且纯种人对克隆人的奴役比起白人对黑人奴隶更是有过之而无不及。克隆人星美被米切尔赋予了一种解放自我、追求平等的世界主义伦理选择。星美在被逮捕之前发表的《宣言》主张废除人类和文化压迫制度,引发了一部分人的觉醒,并可能导致了一场真正的革命。虽然文本中没有明确表明星美所提出的和谐的世界公民的愿望是否得到实现,但是可以肯定的是,她的《宣言》显然在某个历史阶段曾经取得了成功,因为后人类的山谷人将其视为唯一一位仁慈且富有同情心的神。

当代世界主义文本借鉴了后现代的写作方式和叙事结构,打破了传统的时空观,代表世界主义所主张的宇宙处于流动的形成状态中,而非已经形成的静止状态。米切尔以 1-2-3-4-5-6-5-4-3-2-1 的圆形文本结构表达其历史循环观,这个圆形结构与宇宙的形状相似,故事中的每一章节就像宇宙中的一个地方,每一个人物代表一个特定群体,看似毫无关系,却构成一个有机整体和更大的人类社会。若将各个章节视为毫无关系的碎片,就忽略了它们在文本内部的连续性和开放性,既不可能理解这个文本,也不可能理解人类社会。温特森的《苹果笔记本》中的叙事打破了虚拟网络和现实世界、自我和他者这个西方社会所构建的逻各斯中心的二元对立传统。米切尔和温特森致力于在文本中构建一个尊重差异性和多样性的大同世界,践行人类在一个世界中和谐、平等、自由发展的伦理理想。

第三节　全球化语境下文化包容缺失的悲剧

全球化被认为有利于世界主义的发展,因为它加强了世界各国之间的跨国流动,而"地理上的流动更容易促进不同文化之间的交流、熟悉、理解、洞见甚至是包容"②。昆兹鲁在《传播》中探讨了全球化语

---

① Mitchell, D. *Cloud Atlas*. New York: Random House, 2004, p.268.
② Hopper, P. *Living with Globalization*. New York: Berg, 2006, p.54.

境下阿尔琼和盖伊由于文化包容缺失而导致的悲剧命运,借此表明世界主义是一种尊重多元文化差异的立场,包容与理解是前提条件,缺少文化包容的全球化只能给人类社会造成巨大灾难。

莉拉病毒对世界互联网系统的干扰表明在全球化的影响下,世界已然成为一个整体,人们所做的任何事情都有可能对世界产生不可预知的影响。印度移民阿尔琼遭到美国公司解雇时,发布了一种电脑病毒,被这种病毒攻击的计算机上会出现印度女明星莉拉跳舞的视频。他想通过消除这种病毒证明自己的工作能力,从而保住自己的工作。然而,病毒失去了控制,开始繁殖升级,干扰了世界上众多的计算机,最终导致了全球互联网系统的短暂崩溃,阿尔琼也成为被全球通缉的"恐怖分子"。受阿尔琼行为影响最大的是与他没有丝毫联系的英国商人盖伊。盖伊的公司"明天"受到病毒的攻击无法正常运作,他不得不出国寻找合作伙伴并推销自己新的商业计划。在这一过程中,由于电子身份识别系统受到病毒干扰而失效,他被认定为阿尔巴尼亚非法移民而被驱逐并流落境外。起初,阿尔琼和盖伊的故事彼此独立,情节互不相关,甚至会给读者一种不协调的感觉。然而,当电脑病毒将这两个人的故事联系起来时,作者的意图显现出来:一个人看似微不足道的行为深刻影响到了别人的生活。作者借此说明世界的一体性和人类生活的彼此关联性,这就是全球化的表现。阿尔琼和盖伊都是全球化的受害者。

对阿尔琼在美国失败经历的描述表现出昆兹鲁对第三世界移民的关注和对霍米巴巴提出的"本土世界主义"(vernacular cosmopolitanism)愿景的破灭。"本土世界主义"的核心是"家园即世界,世界即家园",这两点在阿尔琼的身上均未实现,阿尔琼的失败归结于他对印度家园的抛弃和世界对他的抛弃。阿尔琼并未表现出对祖国印度的认同和依赖,主要体现在以下两点。其一,他的亲戚们在机场为他送行时,在他的额头上点上点儿,脖子上挂上花环,这是印度文化的象征,而他在分别后立即在机场卫生间将其洗掉,并把花环塞进了包里。阿尔琼急于否认并抹掉自己的印度特征,以便融入美国社会。而就像阿皮亚所认为的,一个不爱自己祖国的人又如何会爱世界。其二,当他被美国公司解雇时,他想过无数种可能性,但唯独没有想回印度。在他被解雇时,他知道因为他是移民,公司一开始就想解雇他,由于"先进先出和外国人"[①]的缘故,他并没有被美国世界所接受。即使阿尔琼抛弃印度家园,也无法融入美国社会,最后成为了一个无家可归的人。

不同于阿尔琼,商人盖伊是全球精英阶层的成员,对他将欧洲打造成富人区计划失败的描写表现出昆兹鲁对精英世界主义的批判。盖伊在全球化世界中可以自由地流动,他有足够的能力支付这些费用。包括盖伊在内的几个欧洲国家的代表讨论全球化社会中边界的性质时一致认为,去疆界化是不可取的,因为各种各样的人在没有严格控制的情况下自由流动会导致欧洲大陆极大的不确定性。所以他们想出了一个计划,要将欧洲打造成世界的贵宾休息室,一个富人区:"一个需要人,但只需要最好的人的大陆"[②]。这项政策针对的显然是非精英人士,这表现出他们极大的排外心理和文化的不包容心态。借助上述情设置,昆兹鲁旨在批判肤浅的、阶级化的、不重视世界联系的精英世界主义。

本章所选取的作家及其代表作品如下:珍妮特·温特森及其代表作《苹果笔记本》、大卫·米切尔及其代表作《云图》、哈里·昆兹鲁及其代表作《传播》。

---

① Kunzru, H. *Transmission*. New York: Penguin, 2005, p.229.
② Ibid., p.242.

第四节　主要作家介绍与代表作品选读

一、珍妮特·温特森

（一）珍妮特·温特森简介

珍妮特·温特森出生于英格兰西北地区的曼彻斯特郡，刚满六周时被生母遗弃至孤儿院，后于五个月大时被信仰五旬节福音教派的工人阶层夫妇收养，在兰开夏州的阿克林顿镇长大。在养父母的教育下，温特森八岁便开始写布道文，但后来父母发现其同性恋倾向与宗教教义和家庭信仰背道而驰。在十六岁时温特森被逐出家门并放弃了宗教信仰。1978 年至 1981 年，温特森就读于牛津大学圣凯瑟琳学院英文系，获学士学位。1981 年至 1987 年，温特森分别于伦敦圆屋剧院、华晨图书和潘多拉出版社工作。1988 年后温特森成为全职作家，专心从事文学创作。

珍妮特·温特森用英语进行创作，其文学创作涉及儿童文学和纪实文学作品。温特森的绝大部分作品出版发行于英国，其中已有部分作品被翻译成十余种语言。温特森擅长使用后现代叙事的碎片性、模糊性、矛盾性等特征建构一个充满差异的、多元化的世界。温特森的创作主题呈现出多维特征，但爱的缺失造成的精神荒原这一主题贯穿其作品始末，寻求爱的治愈成为化解人类精神危机的终极手段。叙述者模棱两可的性别属性和同性恋角色有意颠覆传统性别意识形态中二元对立的父权制异性恋体制，挑战了以男性和异性恋为核心的传统价值观。珍妮特·温特森的文学创作对 21 世纪英国文坛的创新产生了深远影响，对性别研究和叙事学研究具有重要的参考价值。

迄今为止，珍妮特·温特森已发表了十余部小说，包括《橘子不是唯一的水果》（*Oranges Are Not the Only Fruits*，1985）、《激情》（*Passion*，1987）、《给樱桃以性别》（*Sexing the Cherry*，1989）、《写在身体上》（*Written on the Body*，1992）、《艺术与谎言》（*Art & Lies*，1994）、《宇宙的均衡》（*Gut Symmetries*，1997）、《苹果笔记本》、《守望灯塔》（*Lighthousekeeping*，2004）、《重量》（*Weight*，2005）、《石神》（*The Stone Gods*，2007）、《太阳之战》（*The Battle of the Sun*，2009）、《日光之门》（*The Daylight Gate*，2012）、《时间之间》（*The Gap of Time*，2015）和《弗兰基斯坦：一个爱情故事》（*Frankissstein：A Love Story*，2019）。

温特森的非小说包括论文集《艺术的对象》（*Art Objects*，1995），短篇故事集《世界和其他地方》（*The World and Other Places*，1998），四部儿童小说《卡普里国王》（*The King of Capri*，2003）、《混沌残骸》（*Tanglewreck*，2006）、《狮子、独角兽和我》（*The Lion，the Unicorn and Me*，2009）和《十二个圣诞故事》（*Christmas Days*，2016），自传《正常就好，何必快乐？》（*Why Be Happy When You Could Be Normal*，2011）与一部非虚构作品《12 字节》（*12 Bytes*，2021）。

温特森的小说《橘子不是唯一的水果》荣获 1985 年惠特布雷德处女作奖，由她亲自改编的同名 BBC 电视剧获 1992 年英国电影电视艺术学会最佳戏剧奖。小说《激情》获 1987 年约翰·卢埃林·里斯文学奖、布鲁姆伯利奖和美国诺普夫奖。小说《给樱桃以性别》获 1989 年 E. M. 福斯特奖。小说《写在身体上》和自传《正常就好，何必快乐？》分别获 1994 年和 2013 年兰不达文学奖。小说《弗兰基斯坦：一个爱情故事》入围布克奖长名单。温特森还曾获圣·路易斯文学奖并于 2016 年当选皇家文学学会会员。温特森以其突出的文学贡献分别于 2006 年和 2018 年被授予英帝国勋章(OBE)和英帝国高级勋位(CBE)。

(二)《苹果笔记本》简介

《苹果笔记本》中主人公阿莉(有时叫 Ali,有时叫 Alix)被养父母收养后在禁止阅读与写作的"垃圾之屋"长大。成年后的阿莉却成为了一个网络作家,每晚坐在苹果笔记本前给她的读者讲故事:郁金香来到荷兰的故事、《神曲》中保罗和弗兰切西卡的故事、亚瑟王中兰斯洛特与基尼维尔的故事等。阿莉在虚拟网络上认识了一位已婚妇女,她们相约在巴黎相见,在卡普里热恋,最终在伦敦分道扬镳。

在虚拟网络世界中,阿莉讲述了发生在 16 世纪晚期的郁金香的故事。与小说中的作者同名的故事主人公阿莉——一个从小被母亲当成男孩抚养的土耳其女孩被国王选中护送第一批郁金香球茎到荷兰。为保护这两颗经过防腐处理的球茎,阿莉将其隐藏在身着的男装裤裆里。在护送途中,她所乘的船只遭海盗打劫,她被卖给土耳其的意大利特使,被误认为男性送入皇宫成为待嫁的公主的性启蒙师和训练师。这个故事与小说中的女作家和网名为郁金香的已婚女子的同性恋爱情故事遥相呼应。温特森以郁金香替代男人的阴茎,使阿莉获得了"雌雄同体"的身份。身为同性恋者,温特森致力于冲破父权社会对性的束缚与限制,实现同性之间灵与肉的完美结合。

阿莉还讲述了《神曲》中保罗和弗兰切西卡的故事。在《神曲》中,但丁虽然同情保罗和弗兰切西卡的悲惨遭遇,也为他们的悲剧爱情所感动,但还是因为色欲让他们居于地狱的第二层。但温特森却持不同态度,她认为保罗和弗兰切西卡应该上天堂,而不是下地狱,因为他们的爱是如此纯洁、神圣和坚固。温特森笔下的弗兰切西卡坚定地说:"我们的爱坚固无比。没有人能将我们分开,即使是上帝也不行。"[1]温特森将爱视为克服一切困难的动力和治愈所有疾病的良药,只要彼此有爱,人类就是一个坚不可摧的整体。

阿莉在虚拟网络世界中的爱也延续到了现实中。她在网络上认识了郁金香,两人相约在巴黎相见,自此阿莉踏上不断寻爱的旅程,她的每一次寻爱旅行的启程都离不开郁金香的召唤,但是郁金香在每次重逢后均以已婚为借口逃离。阿莉将自己的生活视作一场必须亲自经历的旅程,她不停地穿梭于各国城市中,以便发现未知地区,实现另一个自我。阿莉与郁金香都是英国人,但她们却将约会地点定在法国巴黎和意大利卡普里。她们对异域充满好奇与渴望,甚至在异国他乡感到前所未有的轻松和愉悦。于阿莉而言,对爱的追寻、对外界的理解和对自我解放的渴求是生命的真谛。

小说共有 25 个章节,除第 22 章以外,其他章节均以第一人称叙事为主,与第二人称的"你"即读者对话,将读者引入小说创作中。温特森打破了传统意义上作者与读者的界限,读者也成了作者和故事的一部分,可以将自己的故事加于原有的故事之上,文本成为一个像水一样流动的想象空间。

(三)作品选读:《苹果笔记本》

VIEW

AN ISLAND OF rocks. Sea-bound. Roofed with birds.

---

① Winterson, J. *The PowerBook*. London: Vintage, 2000, p.129.

The island is like an idea lifted out of the sea's brooding.

The island is an idea of itself—an imaginary island and a real one—real and imaginary reflecting together in the mirror of the water.

Look in the mirror. What can you see?

There's Tiberius hiding from the plots of Empire. There he is, ruler of the ancient world, rowed from Naples in a hundred-oared galley, each stroke of the wood to the stroke of the drum, while flutes soothe him to sleep.

He called Capri a sacred place and decorated its wooded slopes with villas and temples and *nymphaea* and shrines. Nowadays, underneath the tourist trade are the remains of the professional gods. The mosaic of the past is a fragment—a bit of coloured glass, a corner of tile—but the present is no more complete. The paint is fresher, that's all.

From an open boat the tourists crane back their necks to stare at the Villa Jovis. The rock face is sheer and unclimbable. Far up, the dot of a human appears.

"Eccola!" *says the guide.* "From that spot Tiberio flung his victims to death. *Morte! Morte! Morte!*"

He spreads his hands expressively, and the party shades its shaded eyes to better imagine the tumbling body twisted through time.

"Women too," says the guide. "*Tiberio cattivo*," and he spits.

Of course, it may well be that spiteful Suetonius was a slandermonger. Perhaps Tiberius never did hurl his enemies into space-time. An imaginary island invents itself. It takes part in its own myth. There is something about this place that suggests more than it reveals. Capri has been thoroughly plundered—its woods, its treasures, its stories. It has been well known for more than two thousand years. Yet it slips through the net of knowing as easily as the small fishes in the harbour.

The Marina Grande was built in the nineteenth century to accommodate the smart steamboats bringing the smart English to the smart hotels. Aquatints of the harbour show luggage being piled on to handcarts, much as it is today, and horse and donkey landaus jostling for custom where the taxi rank is.

The funicular railway, completed in 1906, connects the harbour to the main square, and its sheer, vertiginous ascent is a kind of Tiberio-strategy in miniature. If the tension between the upward car and the downward car were to relax, both cars would crash through the red pantile roofs of the side-by-side houses and, collecting olive trees and grapevines as a memorial, the train and its passengers would career into the sea, nose first, broken backed, to join the other wrecks never recovered.

This does not happen. The upward car brakes the downward car, while the downward car powers the upward car. The passengers are aboard. A bell rings, like the start of an exam. The driver, who was lounging Italian-wise drinking a thimble of coffee, flings it aside, dives into his cab and releases the brake.

It is the moment of action for which there is no preparation.

As I stand in the front car, holding on to the rail, and feeling the train move down through the sunlight towards the tunnel, I feel like I am being born. I find myself gripping the bar, unable to take my eyes off the point where the single track divides as it enters the tunnel. It divides into a curved diamond, a vulva, a dark mouth—one of the many caves on the island where a rite of passage is observed.

Then we are out again, into the sunshine, into the bustle of the harbour, with one glance back at the slow car of souls leaving this life.

Then, as now, the pleasantest way from the Marina Grande to the square is to be driven privately, round and round the impossible bends, the driver with one hand on the wheel, the other glued to the horn. He would sooner let go of the wheel than give up hooting.

Everyone prefers the open-top cars, and those drivers not fortunate enough to own a factory model customise their own. They saw off the roof, sometimes leaving the window pillars, sometimes not. Then they rig up an awning out of bamboo, and fasten it to the windscreen at one end and the boot lid at the other with rusty crocodile clips. The kind you use to jump-start a flat battery.

These bamboo cars will carry anything for you—children, dogs, bags, bikes, boats. I saw a driver strap a dinghy to his bonnet. Off he went, round and round the bends, prow first, both hands on the horn this time. As a safety measure, he said.

The smart hotels are very smart. The oldest, La Palma, reclines in its own tropical garden and offers its guests secluded, shaded tables, from which they may watch the throng of expensive shoppers, glint-eyed over their Cartier and Vuitton.

These shops have always traded expensively. The Medicis used to come here for cameos in the fifteenth century. In the eighteenth century it was antiquities for the English. In the nineteenth century dandies, widows and homosexuals bought silver-backed brushes and gold cigarette cases, stacked beside souvenirs of Pompeii.

Now, day-trippers from Sorrento, on package-holiday outings, clog up the smooth flow of money and goods from trader to shopper. The beautiful ageless women and their slightly sinister iron-haired men have to compete at the luxury windows with red legs and bad haircuts, as the migrant shorts population① wonders out loud how much everything costs before moving on to another ice cream.

At night, Capri partly reclaimed by the rich, the paparazzi hang about the entrance to the Quisisana, waiting to snap a film star or a scandal or, better still, both together.

A young hopeful stands in her evening wear in the doorway. She carries a silk handbag and her hair is dark as the sea. She's nobody. The cameras look the other way.

The Quisisana. The hotel where Oscar Wilde came after his release from prison. Signing himself as Sebastian Melmoth, he sat down wearily to eat his dinner, only to be asked by the manager to leave.

Those waiters in their white coats, those managers in their dark suits, the traders in linen dresses and hand-sewn shirts, know how much everyone is worth, and what something is worth to everyone. The balance between deference and manipulation is as timed to the second as the release brake on the funicular railway. Such tensions allow the system to run smoothly. The island itself is a tension between land and sea, height and depth. Poverty and riches have always lived on either side of the olive tree. The paradox of innocence and knowingness is in the faces of the young boys and the laughter of the girls. For Capri, the secret of success has been found in maintaining these tensions.

Not too slack, not too tight, that's Capri.

I was sitting at a bar in the square. Actually I was sitting in the square itself, so far had the bar extended its territory of bamboo chairs tucked beneath bamboo tables the size of saucers.

I had my laptop on my knee—there was nowhere else to put it—and I was drinking espresso with a slice of *torta Caprese*, when I saw you, just beyond the reach of the bar, crossing the square.

You were wearing a sleeveless dress and sandals, and I realised that you were one of those beautiful ageless women, and that the man with you, slightly sinister, has iron-grey hair. I know what I am—small, disappearing, an outsider—nobody would look at me twice even if they noticed me once. You were used to being looked at, I could see that.

You paused outside a shop selling heavy amethyst jewellery. The assistant appeared like a genie and soon had you bottled inside. That gave me the time I needed to pay my bill, pack my laptop and observe your husband. If it was your husband.

He had his hands in his pockets. Then he checked his watch. Then he put on his sunglasses. Then he went to look down over the harbour. Then he came back and paced outside the shop. Then he went and put a coin in the telescope. I guessed this was a man who went through life with a remote control, constantly flicking the channels. Finding nothing to interest him, he switched off and stared into space.

---

① "migrant shorts population"指的是穿短裤的移民人群,暗指移民的贫穷和着装的随意。

You came out of the shop and smiled like a movie star. You had a package. You took his arm. You talked all the time, pointing out this and that, and he nodded briefly, saw for a second, remembered consciously to enjoy himself.

I followed you both, not far, down to the Quisisana, and hid myself behind a gang of Americans and their tour leader. You were waiting at the lift, when suddenly you turned back and went towards the front desk. This was my chance—not to speak to you but to find out your room number. I got into the lift with your husband, got out with him on the third floor, and walked purposefully past him as he let himself into Room 29.

All right.

Now all I had to do was wait.

It was evening. The air like a kiss.

I was sitting on a low wall opposite the Quisisana. The paparazzi were joking with one another. A man with an accordion was playing on a balcony to a party of Japanese. I had been sitting for a couple of hours, carefully concealed behind my Dolce & Gabbana sunglasses, frames thin as the slit in a burka. I had not intended to be fashionable, merely I had bought my sunglasses in Italy, which amounts to the same thing.

I was typing on my laptop, trying to move this story on, trying to avoid endings, trying to collide the real and the imaginary worlds, trying to be sure which is which.

The more I write, the more I discover that the partition between real and invented is as thin as a wall in a cheap hotel room. I can hear voices on the other side, running water, the clink of bottles, the sound of a door opening and closing. When I get up and go out into the corridor, everything is silent, no one is there. Then, as soon as I reckon I know the geography of what isn't and what is, a chair scrapes in the room beyond the wall and a woman's voice says, "You don't understand, do you?"

When I sit at my computer, I accept that the virtual worlds I find there parallel my own. I talk to people whose identity I cannot prove. I disappear into a web of co-ordinates that we say will change the world. What world? Which world?

It used to be that the real and the invented were parallel lines that never met. Then we discovered that space is curved, and in curved space parallel lines always meet.

The mind is a curved space. What we experience, what we invent, track by track running together, then running into one, the brake lever released. Atom and dream.

It was night.

He sauntered on to the terrace and was shown to a table by a waiter. Yes, I knew what she would be doing. I had seen it before.

I went quickly into the hotel, up to the third floor and along the corridor to Room 29. She was just coming out in a little black dress, scanning her face for the last time, before she snapped the silver mirror shut and slipped it back into her bag.

I stood still, waiting for her to finish.

She suddenly looked up, her face total surprise.

"What are you doing here?"

"Aren't you pleased to see me?"

"Yes. No, listen, I'm busy tonight."

"I saw."

"You've been spying on me."

"Only a little. Is he your husband?"

She nodded.

"How about tomorrow then—lunch?"

She shook her head.

"You choose a time then."

"How about the Middle Ages?"

"The food isn't that good."

She started walking down the corridor towards the lift. I kept up with her, though I didn't put out my hand. She was frowning and she didn't speak as we sped silently down in the moving hall of mirrors. When we got out into the lobby, she paused.

"This isn't a good idea."

"You told me you'd be here."

"I didn't think you'd come after me."

"Think of it as a coincidence."

"I have to go now. Walk out with me and say goodbye."

"Goodbye?"

"I don't want to get into explanations."

"With me or with him?"

"With either of you."

"So you'll just say I was someone you met in the lobby."

"If he notices."

"Depends what channel he's on."

"What?"

"Never mind."

"Don't make a scene, will you?"

"I'm not a playwright."

"Ali?"

"Yes?"

"I'm sorry."

She squeezed my hand and went over to her table. He stood up. There was a glass of champagne waiting.

"*Deux coupes de champagne*," she had said in Paris. Now I suppose it was "Due coppeta de champagne." Champagne, like English, is an international language. She spoke it fluently.

I hesitated, watching them, and then I decided to leave a note at the front desk. I wrote—"Pizza Materita—Anacapri—until 10.30 p.m."

I don't stay in Capri. It's too crowded, too expensive and too noisy for me. I rent a little place in Anacapri, high up on the hillside overlooking the sea. I read, swim, work and feed the stray cats on mince.

When I first came here, I realised from the pitying looks on the faces of the butchers that they thought of me as the Inglesa who only eats mince. This compounded the humiliation of asking every day for "Half a pound of coffee-pot", as I seemed to have been doing. I had mixed up my *macchinetta* and my *macinato*. One is mince, the other is one of those steel coffeepots they heat on the stove.

Anacapri is a small village high on the island. It has a busy square where the bus stops, and where the tourists go to get a chairlift up Monte Solano, followed by "English Toast", as the sign encouragingly offers.

There are some smart shops leading off the square and the usual jostle of tourist stalls, but there is something else too, which I can't quite explain...

About halfway down the Via Orlandini, and for no reason at all that I can tell, an invisible fence rebuffs the tourists. They turn back. Yes, that is exactly what happens, they turn back.

If you continue, you will come to the true heart of Anacapri. There is the church. There is the square in front of it. There are greengrocers and a fishmonger and a bakery and market shops and a bookshop and a chemist and everything you could want. And no tourists.

So why am I not a tourist?

A tourist could be anywhere. The place doesn't matter. It's just another TV channel.

I went to the bus stop in Capri and took my turn with the matrons and off-shift waiters to stand in the tiny, throaty diesel bullet of a bus that fires on all cylinders up the ladder-like road. The cliff face is netted to check falling rocks, and here and there a Madonna cut into the cliff face smiles down under her blue light.

I always cross myself as we reach a particular bend. So does the rest of the bus.

At the Piazza Monumentale out we get, and the women disappear with their string bags, and the men stand together for a moment, jackets slung over their shoulders, lighting cigarettes. I walk down towards the invisible fence and feel a slight tingle as I cross through it. Then I have been admitted. Then I am on the other side.

I know the people at the Pizza Materita, and they always find a table for me on their terrace, which overlooks the church and the square. I don't ask for anything straight away, but still somebody brings a jug of vino rosso and a breadbasket.

I can see Papa, with his long-handled paddle, ladling the pizzas in and out of the wood-fired oven. Nearby, Mama sits at the cash register, her glasses on a string round her neck. The daughter and the son-in-law deal with the customers. She is dark and gorgeous. He is young and good-looking, with his hair tied back like a pirate's.

The food is very good—all done to a secret recipe they say—and they are pleased with their cooking and each other and the new baby. You can taste the pleasure, strong as basil.

And then it happened as I thought it would. You came.

You had taken off the little black dress and you were wearing combat trousers and a hooded sweatshirt. That is, a hooded cashmere sweatshirt. Your hair was in a ponytail and the rings and the jewellery were gone.

You saw me, you came and sat down, your head in your hands for a second, then smiling.

"You bastard."

"They only speak Italian here."

"Very funny."

"So why did you come?"

"Why do you think I came?"

"You are a Gemini and you have to be in two places at once."

"Thanks for the cod astrology."

"All right, here's some cod psychology—you had a row and stormed off."

"I did, as it happens, that's how I'm free to be here, but not why."

"OK. You tell me."

"For this reason."

She kissed me.

While we talked, our food was set before us. We both had bresaola with rocket and transparent slices of parmesan. Then for her there was a fresh fish wrapped in paper and baked in the wood oven. I had a pizza with a base as crisp as lava, bubbled here and there with a black crust and spread with buffalo mozzarella and tomatoes new off the vine.

I looked over into the square. Mothers and grandmothers were sitting chatting, while the men stood in groups. The children were playing some complicated version of hide and seek, using the church door as a touchline.

An Australian in shorts and boots, and a sweat-stained shirt, walked into the square and pulled a frisbee out of his backpack. He was slightly overweight, his girlfriend was tanned and rangy. They started surfing the frisbee to one another, carefully, quietly, she darting about, he standing still, always catching it as though he called it to him.

One by one the Italian children joined in, and then some of the parents, until the whole square was ringed with about twenty people playing frisbee. The Australians couldn't speak Italian and the Italians didn't bother to speak English. The rules, the form, the technique, were all conducted in sign language and body language, with laughter as the interpreter.

Imagine the square.

On one long side is the Pizza Materita. On the short side is the church. On the other long side is a smaller restaurant and a few houses. The fourth side of the square opens on to the street.

The church of Santa Sophia has a great door and niched on the right and left of the door, high up, are two symmetrical statues. One is San Antonio, the patron saint of Anacapri, and the other is the Madonna.

Imagine the square.

Excitement, laughter, the whizz-curve of the frisbee, new people pushing in, tired ones dropping out, then suddenly a boy throws the frisbee too high and too fast, and the purple plastic orb neatly hats the Madonna.

Allora! Mamma mia!

Nobody knows what to do.

Suddenly a matron in black comes forward. She takes the Australian by the hand and stands him below the statue. She crosses herself and gestures to him to do the same. Clumsily, he does it.

Then she shouts to her two sons—big heavy men in short-sleeved shirts. They too cross themselves before the Madonna and stand patiently on either side of the Australian.

The matron fetches her teenage grandchildren, stringy as beans. They cross themselves and are gestured upwards on to the shoulders of the three men, now arms round each other's waists, their feet braced apart.

The matron whistles, and a little kid, about three feet tall, comes running, and climbs, monkey-footed, up the human scaffolding. The base sweats. The teenagers complain, as hair, eyes, mouth and ears are tugged and pulled until the kid is upright. He leans forward to flip the frisbee off the Madonna. There is an imprecation from the ground. He looks down to see the matron shaking her fist at him. Guiltily he nods, crosses himself and tries again.

He has it at a grab and with a cry of pleasure turns round, his feet gripping into the shoulders of his cousins. Their hands clutch his thin ankles. He says something, they let him go and he jumps into space, both hands in the air, holding the frisbee like a parachute. He jumps into the air as if he were a thing of air, weightless, limitless, untroubled by gravity's insistence.

In the second's difference between flying and falling his mother has run forward. She catches him at a swing, taking both of them to the floor.

There she is, scolding and praising at the same time, while everybody gathers round, and wine is fetched from the restaurant, and ice cream in a bowl as big as a font.

Everybody salutes the Madonna. Madonna of the Plastic. Madonna of the Mistake. Madonna who sees all and forgives all. Madonna who can take a joke.

Tonight maybe, when the blinds are drawn and the square is starlit and silent, the Madonna and San Antonio will laugh at the games, and talk over the events of the day, as they always do—watchers and guardians of the invisible life.

There are so many lives packed into one. The one life we think we know is only the window that is open on the screen. The big window full of detail, where the meaning is often lost among the facts. If we can close that window, on purpose or by chance, what we find behind is another view.

This window is emptier. The cross-references are cryptic. As we scroll down it, looking for something familiar, we seem to be scrolling into another self—one we recognise but cannot place. The co-ordinates are missing, or the co-ordinates pinpoint us outside the limits of our existence.

If we move further back, through a smaller window that is really a gateway, there is less and less to measure ourselves by. We are coming into a dark region. A single word might appear. An icon. This icon is a private Madonna, a guide, an understanding. Very often we remember it from our dreams. "Yes," we say. "Yes, this is a world. I have been here." It comes back to us like a scent from childhood.

These lives of ours that press in on us must be heard.

We are our own oral history. A living memoir of time.

Time is downloaded into our bodies. We contain it. Not only time past and time future, but time without end. We think of ourselves as close and finite, when we are multiple and infinite.

This life, the one we know, stands in the sun. It is our daytime and the stars and planets that surround it cannot be seen. The sense of other lives, still our own, is clearer to us in the darkness of night or in our dreams. Sometimes a total eclipse shows us in the day what we cannot usually see for ourselves. As our sun darkens, other brilliancies appear. And there is the strange illusion of looking over our shoulder and seeing the sun racing towards us at two thousand miles an hour.

What is it that follows me wherever I go?

She touched my hand and said, "Will you always follow me?"

"Is life a straight line?"

"Isn't there a straight answer?"

"Not in my universe."

"Which one is that?"

"The one curved by yours."

"I love the curve of your back when you sleep," she said.

"Then why did you get up and disappear that night in Paris?"

"I had to."

"To save your skin?"

"To save my sense of self. You make me wonder who I am."

"Who are you?"

"Someone who wants the best of both worlds."

"So you do believe in more than one reality?"

"No. There's only one reality. The rest is a way of escape."

"Is that what I am? An escape?"

"You said you wouldn't pin me to the facts."

"The fact of your marriage?"

"Why do you keep thinking about it?"

"Because you do."

She said something about life for her parents' generation. How it had been enough to raise a family, make a home, keep a job. Why isn't it enough any more? Why does everyone want to win the lottery or be a film star?

Or have an affair.

I took her hand. I was happy. I couldn't help it. She was here. I was happy.

"Come with me to the showjumping."

"The what!"

"Concorso Ippico. Eleven o'clock tonight. Now."

"You're mad."

"No I'm not. I like horses. Come on."

Looking at me very suspiciously, as intellectuals do when you mention animals, she took my hand and we walked together down the Via Boffe towards the Damacuta. Already we could hear the canned microphone voice of the commentator and see the floodlights of the stadium.

The air was hung with the scent of bougainvillaea, and as we walked past the muddle of houses crushed above the street, broken bars of music dropped through the open windows. A dog barked. Somebody turned up the television. There was the sound of a hosepipe and a trickle of water ran under our feet.

As we turned into the Damacuta, the route to the stadium was lit with flares. Kerosene had been poured into shallow terracotta saucers, each with a wick, and these flares, placed on the ground, lit up the feet of the crowds. We looked like gods with feet of fire. We looked like lovers blazing for each other.

Fire-paced, we found our way to the terraces and squatted right at the front with a load of children shouting excitedly about the horses. The loudspeakers were playing Swan Lake.

Then the riders came out, white jodhpurs, jackets off, to pace the distance between the jumps. This was to be a timed event; fastest time and fewest faults wins.

You said how great it would be if we all got a chance to walk the course before we had to compete.

I said we were walking the course all the time, but when the moment came to jump we still refused.

You glared at me.

Swan Lake was abruptly switched off. The judges assembled in the box, the commentator told us that the first rider was Swiss.

The bell rang. Out came horse and rider and, after a doff at the box, they were off, in a curved canter that sent the sand flying in flurries.

You were sitting right by the first jump, five feet high, and I heard your intake of astonishment at the effort of beauty and the beauty of effort, as the horse cleared the jump.

There's no such thing as effortless beauty—you should know that.

There's no effort which is not beautiful—lifting a heavy stone or loving you.

Loving you is like lifting a heavy stone. It would be easier not to do it and I'm not quite sure why I am doing it. It takes all my strength and all my determination, and I said I wouldn't love someone again like this. Is there any sense in loving someone you can only wake up to by chance?

Mister Archie, the Swiss horse, had a clear round, if a slow one. I was going to speak to you, but you were totally engrossed in the jumping.

The risks are interesting: do you aim for speed and a correspondingly greater risk of knocking off the poles, or do you take it steady and try for no faults?

The best riders manage both, but all riders are subject to the same rule: if a horse refuses to jump, he must be made to take it again. The rider must coax him round and convince him to do it. Horses have sudden fears.

So do I, but in this life you have to take your fences.

Later, walking home through the alleys as thin and black as the cats on every corner, you put your arm around me and asked again.

"Will you always follow me?"

"Who's following whom?"

"That's what I'm beginning to wonder."

"There are two marks on a circle. Which is ahead? Which is behind?"

"Neither."

"Then we're tailing each other."

"Do you believe in fate?" she said, in that nervous way that people say it.

"Ye-es."

"You don't sound so sure."

"Fate isn't an excuse to let go of the reins."

"OK, but what if you find you're riding a completely different horse?"

We were soon back at the place I had rented and I asked her if she was staying the night.

"So this time I don't have to beg?"

"I was the one who was the beggar tonight." She took me in her arms.

"I wish I could explain."

"Explain what?"

"Oh, I know what you think of me."

"What I think of you and what I feel for you are different things."

"Do you usually sleep with people you despise?"

"That's not what I meant."

"I want you to be my lover not my judge."

She's right. I'm the one who's muddling things up. How she lives is her decision. If I don't like it I should stay out of the way. If I don't like it I should say so and close the door.

Her arms were warm and tight.

"What is it you want?" she said.

I want to be able to call you. I want to be able to knock on your door. I want to be able to keep your key and to give you mine. I want to be seen with you in public. I want there to be no gossip. I want to make supper with you. I want to go shopping with you. I want to know that nothing can come between us except each other.

We were lying together in the dark. The candle had burned out. Outside, the wind was whipping the canvas on the deckchairs. I could hear a plastic tumbler blowing round and round.

You were sleeping.

Why does nothing matter as much as this?

How do you seem to write me to myself?

I am a message. You change the meaning.

I am a map that you redraw.

Follow it. The buried treasure is really there. What exists and what might exist are windowed together at the core of reality. All the separations and divisions and blind alleys and impossibilities that seem so central to life are happening at its outer edges. If I could follow the map further and if I could refuse the false endings (the false starts don't matter), I could find the place where time stops. Where death stops. Where love is.

Beyond time, beyond death, love is. Time and death cannot wear it away.

I love you.

In the morning, thunder was rumbling round the island, the waves were white-topped and the birds were quiet.

I like islands because the weather is so changeable. I like the way the morning can be stormy and the afternoon as clear and sparkling as a jewel in the water. Put your hand in the water to reach for a sea urchin or a seashell, and the thing desired never quite lies where you had lined it up to be. The same is true of love. In prospect or in contemplation, love is where it seems to be. Reach in to lift it out and your hand misses. The water is deeper than you had gauged. You reach further, your whole body straining, and then there is nothing for it but to slide in—deeper, much deeper than you had *gauged—and still the thing eludes you.*

 思考与讨论

（1）文本独特的叙事结构与文本内容有何关系？

（2）作者为何刻意模糊主人公的性别与姓名？

（3）如何看待作者对传统故事做出的改编？

（4）文本中反复出现的郁金香有何特殊意义？

（5）阿莉多次提到她写的书是关于"界限与欲望"，这些界限与欲望指的是什么？

（6）如何看待小说中郁金香这一女性形象？

 **拓展阅读**

［1］ Bush，C. Jeanette Winterson. *New Art Publications*. No. 43,（1993）, pp. 54 - 58.

［2］ Hall，E. Nothing Is Solid. Nothing Is Fixed: Participatory Culture and Collaborative Authorship in Jeanette Winterson's *The PowerBook. Reception: Texts, Readers, Audience, History*. Vol. 9,（2017）, pp. 23 - 35.

［3］ Makinen，M. *The Novels of Jeanette Winterson*. New York: Palgrave Macmillan, 2005.

［4］ Onega，S. *Jeanette Winterson*. Manchester: Manchester University Press, 2006.

二、大卫·米切尔

（一）大卫·米切尔简介

大卫·米切尔出生于英国默西塞德郡的绍斯波特,在伍斯特郡度过了平平无奇的童年时光。因其年幼时期说话较晚并有口吃,米切尔较少与人交流,大多数时间沉浸在阅读与想象的世界中。米切尔对文学产生了浓厚的兴趣。他先后于肯特大学获得英美文学学士学位和比较文学硕士学位。米切尔在西西里岛居住一年后,移居日本广岛,在当地担任工程系学生的英文教师,并以写作为生。在广岛居住八年后,米切尔携妻儿回到爱尔兰定居,成为一名职业作家。

大卫·米切尔的文学创作包括小说、短篇小说、歌剧剧本和散文,英语是其创作语言。米切尔的作品大都于英国出版发行,其中绝大部分小说已被翻译至多个国家。通过使用乐高和俄罗斯套娃式的新颖的故事结构、多重叙事视角和叙事场景、相互交织的文本,米切尔建构了一个相互联系的文本网。透过米切尔的作品可以发现,其连续重复的主题包括:一、捕食:不同时期、不同种族之间的相互压迫与残杀是加速人类灭亡的催化剂;二、历史循环与重生:人类历史是一个循环往复的过程,过度贪婪会引发人类向最原始的社会逆向发展;三、文化隔膜与杂糅:语言障碍和文化差异将人类囚困于斗争与分裂的牢笼,对全球异域文化的理解与包容是冲破枷锁的有效方式。米切尔的实验性写作为 21 世纪的英国文坛注入新的活力。

大卫·米切尔的创作生涯始于小说,也以小说而闻名,迄今为止,他已出版八部小说,包括《幽灵代笔》（*Ghostwritten*，1999）、《九号梦》（*Number 9 Dream*，2001）、《云图》、《绿野黑天鹅》（*Black Swan Green*，2006）、《雅各布·德佐特的千秋》（*The Thousand Autumns of Jacob de Zoet*，2010）、《骨钟》（*The Bone Clocks*，2014）、《斯雷德大宅》（*Slade House*，2015）和《乌托邦大道》（*Utopia Avenue*，2020）。他于 2016 年为"未来图书馆"①计划而创作的《你所谓的时光从我身上流过》（*From Me Flows What You Call Time*）将于 2114 年出版发行,米切尔成为继加拿大作家玛格丽特·阿特伍德（Margaret Atwood）后第二位受到该计划发起人邀请的作家。

---

① "未来图书馆"项目是苏格兰视觉艺术家凯蒂·帕特森（Katie Paterson）于 2014 年构思的,它由未来图书馆信托基金管理,并得到挪威奥斯陆市的支持。"未来图书馆"将于 2014 至 2114 年间每年收集一位受欢迎的作家的原创作品,2114 年统一出版发行。

米切尔的小说《幽灵代笔》获得约翰·卢埃林·里斯文学奖和"《卫报》第一本书奖"提名。小说《九号梦》获 2002 年布克奖提名;小说《云图》荣膺英国国家图书奖最佳小说奖和理查与茱蒂读书俱乐部年度选书,并入围布克奖、星云奖和克拉克奖决选,米切尔从此声名大噪,该小说也于 2012 年被改编为同名电影。小说《绿野黑天鹅》入围布克奖;小说《雅各布·德佐特的秋千》问鼎英联邦作家奖;小说《骨钟》入围布克奖长名单。2003 年,米切尔被译为"格兰塔最佳英国青年小说家";2007 年入选《纽约时报》"世界 100 位最具影响力的人物"。

(二)《云图》简介

米切尔运用 1-2-3-4-5-6-5-4-3-2-1 的奇特叙事结构刻画了六位处于不同时空的主人公。美国公证员亚当·尤因以日记的形式记录了 1850 年左右从澳大利亚乘船回旧金山途中的见闻及惨遭虚伪医生古斯毒害险些丧命的故事;1931 年,穷困潦倒的天才作曲家罗伯特·弗罗比舍在比利时被音乐大师埃尔斯污蔑,失去名誉而自杀;1975 年,美国加州的报社记者路易莎·雷为揭露天鹅颈岛上海滨发电公司的巨大阴谋而一次次被谋杀;21 世纪初,英国出版商莫蒂西·卡文迪什遭黑帮威胁谋财,寻求哥哥帮助却被欺骗,软禁于一家养老院痛苦不堪,而后施计逃跑;未来的内索国,宋记餐厅克隆人服务员星美-451 反抗意识觉醒后,与联盟会(恐怖组织)一起反抗纯种人对克隆人的剥削,最终却发现一切只是统一部(政府)自导自演的剧本;世界末日后人类社会回到原始部落的状态,牧羊人扎克里与先知及不同部落的人相互斗争、斗智斗勇。

《云图》是一部书写历史循环与轮回的小说。就其形式而言,小说以第六个故事为轴线,其余五个故事各自折成两半对称地分布在轴线两侧,形成一个闭合的"1-2-3-4-5-6-5-4-3-2-1"的圆形结构。本书首尾呼应,构成一个完整的故事,小说的开始即是结束。整个故事的结束部分则是位于中心位置的第六章,那时候人类已进入后末日时代,回归到了最原始的部落社会,重复着先前已存在过的历史,此前存在的人类文明湮灭,新的历史循环将要重新开始。

米切尔着力刻画了欲望驱使导致的人的异化和世界的荒诞。在 22 世纪的内索国,由于科技的发展,基因序列被随意提取,克隆人被批量制造,成为纯种人的玩物,在服务期满后被屠杀销毁,以提取蛋白质制造供克隆人食用的食品和供纯种人享用的食材。克隆人每天以食用同胞血肉而存活,生活在一个没有基本生存权和人吃人的世界,而纯种人将屠杀克隆人的船建成为一个供其快乐生活的"乐园"。社会贫富差距极大,人被分为三六九等,每一层之间都有难以逾越的鸿沟,人与人之间相互欺骗和残杀,暴力分子、新纳粹分子、阴谋政治家和商人充斥着整个社会。人类生活在一个变态、混乱、道德沦丧、行将就木的世界。作者意在警醒人类,无限扩张的欲望导致人类文明的湮灭和世界的毁灭,正如原始人扎克里好奇先知们拥有无尽的智慧却走向毁灭时,先知向他解释的那样:先知们确实懂的很多,但是他们想要的更多,在欲望的驱动下,人类一步步走向自我毁灭的道路。

生态关怀和反思是米切尔小说关注的另一重点。小说中,人类无论是处在文明达到巅峰的未来社会还是后末日的原始社会,文明与自然永远处于对立状态。小说开始,尤因记录了人类焚烧森林、过度捕捞海豹的恶行和倡导与自然和平共处的莫里奥人。在 22 世纪的内索国,人类科技发展到达顶峰,对生态的破坏也到达顶峰。"内索国正一步步把自己毒死。土壤已被污染,河流毫无生机,空气中充满毒素…。"[1]科技的发展非但不能解决生态破坏危机,反而使其加速,这是导致人类毁灭的重要原因之一。后末日的人类再次重复对生态系统的破坏,播下了人类历史再次循环的种子。米切尔为现世人类敲响了警钟:只有善待自然,遵循自然发展的客观规律,与自然和谐相处,人类才能在自然中生存。

(三) 作品选读:《云图》

Excerpt 1[2]

HôTEL MEMLING, BRUGES

QUARTER PAST FOUR IN THE MORNING, 12TH—XII—1931

Sixsmith,

Shot myself through the roof of my mouth at five A.M. this morning with VA.'s Luger. But I saw you, my dear, dear fellow! How touched I am that you care so much! On the belfry's lookout, yesterday, at sunset. Sheerest fluke you didn't see me first. Had got to that last flight of stairs, when I saw a man in profile leaning on the balcony, gazing at the sea—recognized your natty gabardine coat, your one and only trilby. One more step up, you'd have seen me crouching in the shadows. You strolled to the north side—one turn my way, I would have been rumbled. Watched you for as long as I dared—a minute? —before pulling back and hotfooting it down to Earth. Don't be cross. Thank you ever so for trying to find me. Did you come on the Kentish Queen? Questions rather pointless now, aren't they?

Wasn't the sheerest fluke I saw you first, not really World's a shadow theater, an opera, and such things writ large in its libretto. Don't be too cross at my role. You couldn't understand, no matter how much I explained. You're a brilliant physicist, your Rutherford chap et al. agree you've got a brilliant future, quite sure they're right. But in some fundamentals you're a dunce. The healthy can't understand the emptied, the broken. You'd try to list all the reasons for living, but I left 'em behind at Victoria Station back in early summer. Reason I crept back down from the belvedere was that I can't have you blaming yourself for failing to dissuade me. You may anyway, but don't, Sixsmith, don't be such an ass.

Likewise, hope you weren't too disappointed to find me gone from Le Royal. The manager got wind of M. Verplancke's visit. Obliged to ask me to leave, he said, on account of heavy bookings. Piffle, but I took the fig leaf. Frobisher the Stinker wanted a tantrum, but Frobisher the Composer wanted peace and quiet to finish my sextet. Paid in full—bang went the last Jansch money—and packed my valise. Wandered crooked alleys and crossed icy canals before coming across this deserted-looking caravansary. Reception a rarely manned nook under the stairs. Only ornament in my room a monstrous Laughing Cavalier too ugly to steal and sell. From my filthy window, one sees

---

① Mitchell, D. *Cloud Atlas*. New York: Random House, 2004, p.170.
② Ibid., pp.248-249.

the very same dilapidated old windmill on whose steps I napped on my first morning in Bruges. The very same. Fancy that. Around we go.

Knew I'd never see my twenty-fifth birthday. Am early for once. The lovelorn, the cry-for-helpers, all mawkish tragedians who give suicide a bad name are the idiots who rush it, like amateur conductors. A true suicide is a paced, disciplined certainty. People pontificate, "Suicide is selfishness." Career churchmen like Pater go a step further and call it a cowardly assault on the living. Oafs argue this specious line for varying reasons: to evade fingers of blame, to impress one's audience with one's mental fiber, to vent anger, or just because one lacks the necessary suffering to sympathize. Cowardice is nothing to do with it—suicide takes considerable courage. Japanese have the right idea. No, what's selfish is to demand another to endure an intolerable existence, just to spare families, friends, and enemies a bit of soul-searching. The only selfishness lies in ruining strangers' days by forcing 'em to witness a grotesque-ness. So I'll make a thick turban from several towels to muffle the shot and soak up the blood, and do it in the bathtub, so it shouldn't stain any carpets. Last night I left a letter under the manager's day-office door—he'll find it at eight A. M. tomorrow—informing him of the change in my existential status, so with luck an innocent chambermaid will be spared an unpleasant surprise. See, I do think of the little people. Don't let 'em say I killed myself for love, Sixsmith, that would be too ridiculous. Was infatuated by Eva Crommelynck for a blink of an eye, but we both know in our hearts who is the sole love of my short, bright life.

Along with this letter and the rest of the Ewing book, I've made arrangements for a folder containing my completed manuscript to find you at Le Royal. Use the Jansch money to defray publishing costs, send copies to everyone on the enclosed list. Don't let my family get hold of either of the originals, whatever you do. Pater'll sigh, "It's no Eroica, is it?" and stuff it into a drawer; but it's an incomparable creation. Echoes of Scriabin's White Mass, Stravinsky's lost footprints, chromatics of the more lunar Debussy, but truth is I don't know where it came from. Waking dream. Will never write anything one-hundredth as good. Wish I were being immodest, but I'm not. Cloud Atlas Sextet holds my life, is my life, now I'm a spent firework; but at least I've been a firework.

People are obscenities. Would rather be music than be a mass of tubes squeezing semisolids around itself for a few decades before becoming so dribblesome it'll no longer function.

Luger here. Thirteen minutes to go. Feel trepidation, naturally, but my love of this coda is stronger. An electrical thrill that, like Adrian, I know I am to die. Pride, that I shall see it through. Certainties. Strip back the beliefs pasted on by governesses, schools, and states, you find indelible truths at one's core. Rome'll decline and fall again, Cortés'll lay Tenochtitlán to waste again, and later, Ewing will sail again, Adrian'll be blown to pieces again, you and I'll sleep under Corsican stars again, I'll come to Bruges again, fall in and out of love with Eva again, you'll read this letter again, the sun'll grow cold again. Nietzsche's gramophone record. When it ends, the Old One plays it again, for an eternity of eternities.

Time cannot permeate this sabbatical. We do not stay dead long. Once my Luger lets me go, my birth, next time around, will be upon me in a heartbeat. Thirteen years from now we'll meet again at Gresham, ten years later I'll be back in this same room, holding this same gun, composing this same letter, my resolution as perfect as my many-headed sextet. Such elegant certainties comfort me at this quiet hour.

Sunt lacrimæ rerum.

Excerpt 2[①]

Monday, 13th January—

Sitting under the candlenut tree in the courtyard is pleasant in the afternoon. Laced shadows, frangipani & coral hibiscus ward away the memory of recent evil. The sisters go about their duties, Sister Martinique tends her vegetables, the cats enact their feline comedies & tragedies. I am making acquaintances amongst the local avifauna. The pallia has a head & tail of burnished gold, the *akohekohe* is a handsome crested honeycreeper.

Over the wall is a poorhouse for foundlings, also administered by the sisters. I hear the children chanting their classes (just as my schoolmates and I used to before Mr. & Mrs. Channing's philanthropy elevated my prospects). After their studies are done, the children conduct their play in a beguiling babel. Sometimes, the more daring of their number brave the nuns' displeasure by scaling the wall & conduct a grand tour above the hospice garden by means of the candlenut's obliging branches. If the "coast is clear," the pioneers beckon their more timid playmates onto this human aviary & white faces, brown faces, *kandka* faces, Chinese faces, mulatto faces appear in the arboreal overworld. Some are Rafael's age & when I remember him a bile of remorse rises in my throat, but the orphans grin down at me, imitate monkeys, poke out their tongues, or try to drop *kukui* nuts into the mouths of snoring convalescents & do not let me stay mournful for very long. They beg me for a cent or two. I toss up a coin for dextrous fingers to pluck, unerringly, from the air.

My recent adventures have made me quite the philosopher, especially at night, when I hear naught but the stream grinding boulders into pebbles through an unhurried eternity. My thoughts flow thus. Scholars discern motions in history & formulate these motions into rules that govern the rises & falls of civilizations. My belief runs contrary, however. To wit: history admits no rules; only outcomes.

What precipitates outcomes? Vicious acts & virtuous acts.

---

① Mitchell, D. *Cloud Atlas*. New York: Random House, 2004, pp. 267 – 268.

What precipitates acts? Belief.

Belief is both prize & battlefield, within the mind & in the mind's mirror, the world. If we believe humanity is a ladder of tribes, a colosseum of confrontation, exploitation & bestiality, such a humanity is surely brought into being, & history's Horroxes, Boer-haaves & Gooses shall prevail. You & I, the moneyed, the privileged, the fortunate, shall not fare so badly in this world, provided our luck holds. What of it if our consciences itch? Why undermine the dominance of our race, our gunships, our heritage & our legacy? Why fight the "natural" (oh, weaselly word!) 268 order of things?

Why? Because of this:—one fine day, a purely predatory world *shall* consume itself. Yes, the Devil shall take the hindmost until the foremost is the hindmost. In an individual, selfishness uglifies the soul; for the human species, selfishness is extinction.

Is this the doom written within our nature?

If we *believe* that humanity may transcend tooth & claw, if we *believe* divers, races & creeds can share this world as peaceably as the orphans share their candlenut tree, if we believe leaders must be just, violence muzzled, power accountable & the riches of the Earth & its Oceans shared equitably, such a world will come to pass. I am not deceived. It is the hardest of worlds to make real. Torturous advances won over generations can be lost by a single stroke of a myopic president's pen or a vainglorious general's sword.

A life spent shaping a world I *want* Jackson to inherit, not one I *fear* Jackson shall inherit, this strikes me as a life worth the living. Upon my return to San Francisco, I shall pledge myself to the Abolitionist cause, because I owe my life to a self-freed slave & because I must begin somewhere. I hear my father-in-law's response: "Oho, fine, *Whiggish* sentiments, Adam. But don't tell *me* about justice! Ride to Tennessee on an ass & convince the rednecks that they are merely whitewashed negroes & their negroes are black-washed Whites! Sail to the Old World, tell 'em their imperial slaves' rights are as inalienable as the Queen of Belgium's! Oh, you'll grow hoarse, poor & gray in caucuses! You'll be spat on, shot at, lynched, pacified with medals, spurned by backwoodsmen! Crucified! Naïve, dreaming Adam. He who would do battle with the manyheaded hydra of human nature must pay a world of pain & his family must pay it along with him! & only as you gasp your dying breath shall you understand, your life amounted to no more than one drop in a limitless ocean!" Yet what is any ocean but a multitude of drops?

 思考与讨论

(1) 1-2-3-4-5-6-5-4-3-2-1 的叙事结构意在表达什么？

(2) 处于不同时空的几位主人公身上的彗星状胎记有何意义？

(3) 作者对生态危机进行了何种批判与反思，对未来生态图景做出了何种预测？

（4）为何每位主人公都深陷谎言与阴谋的圈套？

（5）节选中弗罗比舍创作的曲子《云图六重奏》与书名《云图》之间有何联系？

（6）小说中多次出现"6"这一数字的特殊含义是什么？

 拓展阅读

［1］Harris，P. A. David Mitchell in the Laboratory of Time: An Interview with the Author. *Substance*. Vol. 44，No. 1(2015)，pp. 8 - 17.

［2］Mezey，J. H. A. "A Multitude of Drops": Recursion and Globalization in David Mitchell's *Cloud Atlas*. *Modern Language Studies*. Vol. 40，No. 2(2011)，pp. 10 - 37.

［3］Selisker，S. The Cult and the World System: The Topoi of David Mitchell's Global Novels. *Novels: A Forum on Fiction*. Vol. 47，No. 3(2014)，pp. 443 - 459.

［4］高扬. 论米切尔《云图》中的历史观[J]. 外国文学研究动态，2017(5):42 - 52.

三、哈里·昆兹鲁

（一）哈里·昆兹鲁简介

哈里·昆兹鲁出生于伦敦，父亲是印度外交官，母亲是英国人。昆兹鲁在埃塞克斯长大，在家中受到了印度和英国双重文化的熏陶。昆兹鲁曾在牛津大学瓦德汉学院学习英语，并于华威大学取得了哲学和文学硕士学位。

哈里·昆兹鲁的文学创作以小说为主。昆兹鲁用英语写作，他的小说大都出版发行于英国和美国，并被翻译成20种语言在多个国家出版。通过使用多重叙事视角和虚实穿插，昆兹鲁试图呈现一个复杂、多元和包容的世界。透过昆兹鲁的作品可以发现，贯穿其作品始终的创作主题包括：一、移民和少数族裔人群在多元文化社会中的文化碰撞与身份认同；二、对现实和政治问题的批判以及对历史事件的探索和重塑；三、探讨全球化和科技进步对人类社会的影响和挑战；四、个体和群体对不公和权威的抵制和反抗。昆兹鲁的作品关注社会中的边缘群体，强调人类的共性和共同面临的问题，以此体现全球化进程中人类团结合作的重要性。

昆兹鲁新闻记者的身份和经历为他的小说创作奠定了基础。迄今为止，他已出版六部小说，包括《印象主义者》(*The Impressionist*，2002)、《传播》、《我的革命》(*My Revolutions*，2007)、《没有人类的神祇》(*Gods Without Men*，2011)、《白泪》(*White Tears*，2017)和《红药丸》(*Red Pill*，2020)；短篇小说集《噪音》(*Noise*，2005)。

昆兹鲁的小说《印象主义者》获2002年贝蒂特拉斯克文学奖和2003年毛姆文学奖；小说《传播》获评《纽约时报》2005年度瞩目好书。2003年昆兹鲁被评为"格兰塔最佳英国青年小说家"；2008年成为纽约公共图书馆会员；2014年成为约翰·西蒙·古根海姆纪念基金会成员；2016年成为柏林美国学院院士。

(二)《传播》简介

《传播》围绕着年轻印度程序员阿尔琼·梅塔的生活故事展开。阿尔琼在毕业后的一次面试中得到了去美国工作的机会。带着发财的梦想和家人的骄傲来到美国后,他发现自己仅是一名合同工。经过几个月令人烦恼的面试后,阿尔琼进入了华盛顿州一家计算机病毒检测公司工作。好景不长,不久他便被告知自己将被解雇。在多次央求经理让其继续留在公司无果后,为保住工作,他故意暗中发送了含有病毒的邮件,想要通过清除这种病毒证明自己对公司的价值,这无意中造成了全球范围内的计算机的瘫痪。结果是,阿尔琼不仅失去了工作,而且被贴上了"恐怖分子"的标签,受到通缉,最终他在从美国逃往墨西哥的途中失踪,从此下落不明。

贯穿小说始末的主题是人类对科技的过度依赖造成的自身伤害与损失,主要体现在社会和个人两个层面。首先,阿尔琼制造的莉拉病毒经过一代又一代的升级后,造成了全球网络系统的短暂瘫痪,这对整个人类社会的政治和经济造成了沉重的打击和无法估量的损失,这段时间被称作"灰色之日"。期间,家用电脑、系统网络和移动电话都受到了不同程度的损害,"骇人听闻的损失、辍学、崩溃和各种缺席……[这]是一场信息灾难,一场比特大屠杀"①。人类的一切活动都依赖于科技的存在,所以"信息灾难"的发生似乎让整个世界的发展停滞了下来,没有科技支撑,人类社会发展举步维艰。"灰色之日"的效果早已超出了阿尔琼能够控制的范围。阿尔琼、莉拉和盖伊的生活发生了翻天覆地的变化。阿尔琼成为国际逃犯,再也无法回到自己的祖国;印度知名女星莉拉因为病毒使用了自己的视频而成为全球计算机病毒的代名词,在一众记者的围堵中出逃,自此杳无音信;著名白人商人盖伊因为病毒对身份识别系统的入侵,导致身份识别出错,因此在境外流落数月。科技已成为人类生活中不可分割的一部分。当科技突然失效时,人类才能意识到对它的依赖程度已然超出我们的想象。

小说的背景涉及美国、英国、印度等多个国家,国与国之间的文化差异导致了难以克服的沟通障碍和误解,对小说人物的社交、工作和生活产生了重大影响,这主要体现在盖伊和阿尔琼两个人的身上。盖伊由于对阿拉伯文化知识的缺乏而无法成功地向其合作伙伴推销他的商业计划,这是他生意受挫的主要原因之一。阿尔琼对双性恋的误解造成了他和克里斯廷的争吵和他们友谊的短暂破裂。

莉拉、阿尔琼和盖伊三人的失败命运与其相似的家庭教育有着密不可分的关系。莉拉的母亲强迫她成为一名演员,做自己的赚钱工具,所以在她非常年轻时就被迫参加各种聚会并与年长的男人一起出去玩儿,从而获得各种资源,而不是上学,这给莉拉带来了非常大的压力。她渴望过上没有母亲影响的正常生活,因而选择在一个漆黑的夜晚从苏格兰郊区独自出逃,放弃自己拥有的一切。盖伊从小被父亲教导生活中不允许有失败。他在工作上的成功导致了他以自我为中心的性格,所以经常忽略女友的感受,最终两人不欢而散。阿尔琼的父母虽从未强迫他,也没有直接表达出对他的期待,但在阿尔琼决定前往美国时,他们的欣喜和骄傲使他意识到他的父母希望他在美国成为百万富翁。因此当他得知自己即将被解雇的消息,不得不面临身无分文地返回印度的窘境时,感觉到了前所未有的压力。但他始终未向父母透露过自己在美国的真实经历,反而谎称自己过得非常好。父母的过高期待让他在面对短暂职业生涯的终结时棋走险招,成为被追捕的"恐怖分子"。

---

① Kunzru, H. *Transmission*. New York: Penguin, 2005, p.258.

（三）作品选读

Excerpt 1[①]

The border between the United States and Mexico is one of the most tightly controlled in the world. From Brownsville, Texas, to the California coast it runs for 2,000 miles, monitored by armed patrols equipped with thermal-imaging cameras and remote-movement sensors, portable X-ray devices, GPS optics, satellite maps and other technologies intended to prevent (or at least minimize) the unauthorized crossing of goods, vehicles and people. At San Ysidro, just south of San Diego, twenty-four lanes of traffic funnel into an artful system of concrete barriers designed to prevent vehicles turning or reversing as their details are checked against databases and trained dogs are encouraged by their handlers to sniff their wheel arches.

On the north side of the border is an outlet mall, where, under red-tiled roofs with fake adobe façades, piles of discount jeans and sports shoes are sold by sleepy staff who look out all day over the parking lot, hoping and dreaming about whatever you hope and dream about if you are administrating the disposal of surplus clothing and footwear at the very edge of America.

Arjun arrived on the morning shoppers' shuttle, which made the journey from downtown San Diego in twenty minutes. It felt too quick. He needed more time to prepare. He stood for a while on a road bridge over the freeway, watching the vehicles inch forward towards the barriers, then meandered back into the mall, stopping to look in the window of a shoe store. Was it safe just to stroll out of America? That's what all the other people were doing. They were just walking into Mexico. Surely that was too easy. Shouldn't he take precautions?

He decided on a disguise. The unit next to the shoe store sold sunglasses, so he bought a pair and put them on. A few minutes later, catching sight of himself in the plate glass of Laura Ashley, he stopped to bite off the tag. Then he carried on, aimlessly wandering from Nautica to Levis to Banana Republic.

His first sight of Mexico had scared him. Beyond the parking lots and freight yards on the US side was a wide concrete river channel. Beyond that was a range of low hills clustered with flat-roofed cinderblock buildings. The air was hazy, scented with oil fumes and sewage. Over the sullen-looking city on the far side of the river, a giant Mexican flag hung limply on a tall pole. When Arjun saw the flag, the forlorn droop of it against the yellow-grey sky, he found he no longer knew which frightened him more: the possibility that he would be captured or the possibility he would not. For days the border had acted as the outer limit of his imagination. Beyond it were abstractions: Escape, Freedom, The Future. Now the future had a landscape, a mess of flat roofs strung with telephone and electrical wires, the store signs and billboards written in a language he did

---

① Kunzru, H. *Transmission*. New York: Penguin, 2005, pp. 251 – 253.

not understand. What kind of a life could he have over there?

The place on the other side of the river had a hopeless quality, not at all like the Mexico portrayed in cowboy movies. Where were the cacti, the white-clad peasants with the big hats? He browsed neurotically through racks of souvenir t-shirts. Their humorous slogans (one tequila, two tequila, three tequila, floor!) passed through his mind without leaving a trace. As he picked up snow globes and methodically sorted through postcards he had no intention of buying, his body started to send out contradictory signals, most of them related in some way to physical distress. He felt hot and cold simultaneously. Under the arms of his pink polo shirt (the one he had been wearing for the previous seventy-two hours) there were large circles of sweat. He decided to drink coffee. Coffee, in his experience, was a drink with negen-tropic properties.

Slang terms for coffee: java, a cup of joe. In his first weeks in America, he had said these words to the mirror. Later he had carried his plastic beaker to work like a runner with the Olympic torch. He wished he still had that cup. As he stood outside Starbucks, a paper cup heating his hand, he conjured up a soothing image of a darkened room and a TV set. A TV not tuned to a news channel. A TV showing an easy-to-follow narrative fiction in which he was not the central character. Preferably with romance and songs. And a happy ending.

A block behind the San Ysidro Factory Outlet Center was the Riverside Motel. Carrying his coffee in one hand and his bag in the other, Arjun crossed the road and checked in, taking a room on the second floor with a south-facing balcony. The two teenage boys who had followed him all the way from San Diego watched from the parking lot as he briefly walked out on to it to look at the view. He took a sip of coffee, then went back inside, closed the curtains and stepped into legend.

Excerpt 2[①]

Noise

"We want to abolish the unknown," writes one Leela researcher. It is a common enough desire. As humans, we want to know what is lurking outside our perimeter, beyond our flickering circle of firelight. We have built lenses and Geiger counters and mass spectrometers and solar probes and listening stations on remote Antarctic islands. We have drenched the world in information in the hope that the unknown will finally and definitively go away. But information is not the same as knowledge. To extract one from the other, you must, as the word suggests, inform. You must transmit. Perfect information is sometimes defined as a signal transmitted from a sender to a receiver without loss, without the introduction of the smallest uncertainty or confusion.

In the real world, however, there is always noise.

Since 1965 the Russian Academy of Sciences has published a journal called *Problems of*

---

① Kunzru, H. *Transmission*. New York: Penguin, 2005, pp. 257 - 261.

Information Transmission. It is, insofar as it is possible for a scientific publication (even a Russian one) to convey an emotional tone, a melancholy read. Threaded through recondite papers on Markov Chains and Hamming Spaces and binary Goppa codes and multivariate Poisson flow is a vocabulary of imperfection, of error correction and density estimation, of signals with unknown appearance and disappearance times, of indefinite knowledge and losses due to entropy. Sparse vectors are glimpsed through a haze of Gaussian white noise. Certainty backslides into probability. Information transmission, it emerges, is about doing the best you can.

In media dissections of the impact of the Leela variant viruses, the period when there was most noise in the global system has come to be known as Greyday. Greyday certainly lasted more than a day and was only grey in the most inexact and metaphorical sense, which means the person who invented the term was probably not an engineer. Nevertheless, the name captures a certain cybernetic gloom that hung about the time, the communal depression of network administrators yearning for perfection while faced with appalling losses, drop-outs, crashes and absences of every kind.

Greyday was an informational disaster, a holocaust of bits. A number of major networks went down simultaneously, dealing with such things as mobile telephony, airline reservations, transatlantic email traffic and automated-teller machines. The details of those events are in the public domain. Other systems were undoubtedly affected, but their military, corporate or governmental owners have been unwilling to discuss in public what may or may not have happened. As for the number of smaller cases, the problem becomes one of counting. Home computers? Individuals? Do you know anyone whom Leela did not touch in some way?

Leela's noise passed effortlessly out of the networks into the world of things. Objects got lost: a van carrying armaments from a depot in Belgrade; a newly authenticated Rembrandt. Money in all sorts of physical forms dropped out of sight, but also money in its essence, which is to say that on Greyday a certain amount of money simply ceased to exist. This is a complicated claim. Money tends to virtuality. It hovers about in the form of promises and conditionalities, lying latent in the minds of market technicians until actualized through confidence, central bank fiat or a particularly long lunch. It is hard, in the end, to judge whether some of the money which did not exist after Greyday actually existed before it. Had Greyday not happened, perhaps a certain amount of unborn money might have come into the world. We cannot be certain. We do know that money disappeared, but how much and where it went are questions to which the market makers don't really want an answer. Better, they say, to forget about it. Better to move on, dream up more.

So Greyday names a moment of maximal uncertainty, a time of peaking doubt. We have records of events which may not have taken place. Other events took place but left no record. All that can be said with honesty is that afterwards there were absences, gaps which have never been filled.

Empty hotel rooms, for example. Three rooms whose occupants are no longer there. When a person disappears, the objects they leave behind can be almost unbearable in their muteness. The more personal they are, the more they seem to underline the absence of their owner. The chambermaid at the four-star Hotel Ascension in Brussels turns down the bed, leaves on the pillow a chocolate and a voucher for a complimentary shoe-shine. On the dressing table is a litter of British coins, taxi receipts and other small items. Walkman headphones. An electrical adaptor. She hangs the suit-carrier in the cupboard and moves the washbag from the top of the television into the bathroom. The passport on the bedside table she does not touch. The maid working the morning shift receives no response to her knock. She enters to find everything exactly as her colleague left it. The bed has not been slept in. The toothbrush is dry. At lunchtime, the management take a call from a business associate of the occupier. He has failed to keep an appointment. Ten minutes later he calls again. At two, the hotel bills the absent businessman for an extra night. The police are not called until the following morning, by which time it is clear that something untoward has happened to Guy Swift.

A room upstairs at the Clansman's Lodge Hotel in Scotland. One of the better ones, with a view over the garden and the loch. A mess of chintz and lace and rose-patterned wallpaper. A bowl of pot-pourri on the nightstand and a white plastic drinks-maker on the dresser, next to a little basket containing filters, creamer and vacuum-packed sachets of coffee. Most of her things are there, the expensive Banarsi saris, the make-up bags, the rows of spray cans and bottles in the bathroom. She has left a little portable DVD player and a stack of unwatched discs, still in a duty-free bag. She has left the giant stuffed monkey someone bought her as a get-well present. Under the bed is an empty cigarette packet and a torn-up copy of the shooting script, but Leela Zahir herself is not there. Her mother, sedated and incoherent, manages to communicate that she thinks some clothes have gone. Also her daughter's laptop. Iqbal is holding Leela's passport, but it is possible she has another. The police are reassuring. In rural Scotland, an Indian girl will not be able to travel far without attracting attention.

Events at the Riverside Motel in San Ysidro are more violent. Acting on information provided by a member of the public, the FBI has traced a man on their most-wanted list to a room on one of the upper floors. Though the suspect is not believed to be armed, he has known militant connections and the team assembled at the FBI field office in San Diego includes staff from the Joint Terrorism Task Force. Written orders have been received confirming the authorization of maximum force. Weapons specialists from the police, the FBI and the Bureau of Alcohol, Tobacco and Firearms draw equipment from stores and under the direction of a senior officer from the San Diego Police the team proceeds at speed to the named location. A command post is established in a nearby parking lot, and a discreet perimeter is set up around the motel, a priority being not to cause panic among shoppers at the outlet mall. Staff are evacuated from the area before the team moves in.

Access to Room 206 is swift and brutal. The door gives way immediately under the impact of a 35-pound close-quarter battle ram. Agents shout a warning to the occupant, who does not respond.

Shots are fired. The occupant goes down. An ambulance is called and arrives quickly, but the victim is pronounced dead at the scene. Later the corpse is transferred to a morgue in San Diego. Unfortunately for the arresting team, when examined it turns out to be not Arjun Mehta, suspected terrorist and subject of a federal warrant, but an unidentified South-East Asian teenager. The dead boy is found to be carrying a cheap. 22 handgun.

Within minutes local news media is on the scene. The officer who fired is taken back to the field office for debriefing and psychological assessment, while the Riverside Motel is cordoned off and a series of photographs of the room are taken, photographs which will rapidly leak out on to the internet and spawn detailed speculation about (among other things) the brands of packaging in the waste-paper basket, the crumpled Oakland Raiders shirt in the bathroom. Some information trickles out to the media. The boy's name was Kim Sun Hong, a high-school student from San Diego. The gun was of a type sold for $7.98 in certain out-of-state gun stores. What he was doing in Arjun Mehta's room remains, for the moment, a mystery.

 思考与讨论

(1) 阿尔琼的人物形象经历了什么样的转变？原因是什么？

(2) 阿尔琼和莉拉销声匿迹的命运安排有何意义？

(3) 电脑病毒的象征意义是什么？

(4) 阿尔琼美国梦破灭的原因是什么？

(5) 阿尔琼和莉拉为何会被贴上"恐怖分子"的标签？

 拓展阅读

[1] Chung, H. "Viral Cosmopolitanism" and the Politics of Identity Production/Destruction in Hari Kunzru's *Transmission*. *English & American Cultural Studies*. Vol.14, No.1(2014), pp.219 - 240.

[2] Johansen, E. Becoming the virus: Responsibility and cosmopolitan labor in Hari Kunzru's *Transmission*. *Journal of Postcolonial Writing*. Vol.49, No.1(2013), pp.419 - 431.

[3] Shelden, A. T. Cosmopolitan Love: The One and the World in Hari Kunzru's *Transmission*. *Contemporary Literature*. Vol.53, No.2(2012), pp.348 - 373.

第三章

当代英国脱欧小说

英国于 2016 年 6 月 23 日宣布脱离欧盟这一事件对英国的政治和经济产生了深远的影响,如:英国经济发展的不确定性、政党内部矛盾的尖锐化,国家内部分裂的风险加剧。脱欧也影响到了英国文化领域。脱欧公投结束后,英国作家用文学作品揭示英国脱欧带来的诸多问题,这催生了一种新兴的文学类型,即脱欧文学(BrexLit)的诞生。脱欧文学一词由脱欧(Brexit)和文学(Literature)两词组合而成。克里斯蒂安·肖(Kristian Shaw)将脱欧文学定义为以小说为代表的"直接回应或间接影射英国退出欧盟"或"探讨英国脱欧后产生的社会文化、经济、种族或世界主义发展问题"[①]的文学。

脱欧小说分为两类:前脱欧(pre-Brexit)小说和后脱欧(post-Brexit)小说。前脱欧小说指出版于脱欧公投前的、直接预示脱欧事件的发生或描写公投前英国政治、经济、社会环境变化的小说。前脱欧小说是英国疑欧主义的产物,最早的前脱欧小说可以追溯至达芙妮·杜穆里埃(Daphne du Maurier)于 1972 年发表的《统治吧,不列颠》(*Rule Britannia*)。这部小说描写了英国在多年以后因为经济困境选择退出欧盟,转而与美国结盟的故事。后脱欧小说集中出现于 2016 年公投之后,是对公投活动的记录和反思,主要探讨英国脱欧的原因或脱欧产生的真实的或想象的结果。第一部后脱欧小说是阿莉·史密斯于公投结束后三个月出版的小说《秋》,它记录了脱欧公投后英国社会的分裂状况。前、后脱欧小说都描写了英国脱欧后的混乱局面,并想象英国未来的发展方向,但由于后脱欧小说创作建立在脱欧公投已然发生的历史事实之上,且创作时间集中,因而受到了更多关注。具有代表性的后脱欧小说包括:道格拉斯·博德(Douglas Board)的《谎言时刻》(*Time of Lies*,2017)、阿曼达·克雷格的《这片土地的谎言》(*The Lie of the Land*,2017)、乔纳森·科的《英格兰中部》、伊恩·麦克尤恩的《蟑螂》、萨姆·拜尔斯的《背信弃义的奥尔滨》(*Perfidious Albion*,2019)、拉切尔·丘彻的《战场》和安东尼·卡特莱特(Anthony Cartwright)的《切割》(*The Cut*,2017)等。

脱欧小说较少涉及英国与欧盟之间的关系,多聚焦于英国社会内部的矛盾和问题,这些小说表达的主题包括:一、不确定性:脱欧后的英国政治、经济和社会文化领域充满了不确定性,这种不确定性常常伴随着一种对未来的担忧和焦虑情绪;二、国家分裂:脱欧暴露了英国存在已久的分裂问题,主要包括地域分歧、阶级分歧以及对移民政策和边境控制的分歧等;三、身份危机:脱欧后的英国国家和民众都面临着身份转变和归属感丧失的危机;四、历史怀旧:脱欧后英国国家的衰落和社会的混乱局面引起了民众

[①] Shaw, K. *"BrexLit": Brexit and Literature: Critical and Cultural Response*. Robert Eaglestone Ed. London and New York: Routledge, 2018, pp. 15 – 30.

对大英帝国辉煌历史的怀旧情绪。脱欧小说普遍流露出一种消极情绪，多表达对英国脱欧的不满，将脱欧后的英国描绘成一个充满歧视、危机和混乱的国家。如何在文学的世界里积极应对脱欧产生的种种危机并思考英国国家的未来是脱欧小说未来的发展方向。

第一节　国家分裂与公民身份危机

英国国家的分裂是以阿莉·史密斯和乔纳森·科为代表的小说家后脱欧小说的创作基调，在此基础上描写了英国民众的身份危机，阐释了脱欧带给国家和民众的不可逆转的伤害。

史密斯的小说《秋》真实地反映了后脱欧时代英国的分裂现状，正如克里斯蒂安·肖所指出的那样："脱欧并没有分裂（英国）国家，它只是揭示了社会内部的固有分歧。"①在英国脱欧公投中，脱欧派虽然最终胜出，但是其百分之五十二的票比优势相当微弱，留欧派与脱欧派人数相差不大，两者间存在巨大分歧，这在《秋》中得到了真实再现。《秋》揭示了脱欧公投前后民众分裂矛盾的心理状态，史密斯写道："在整个国家，人们感觉这事儿不对，在整个国家，人们感觉这事儿没错，在整个国家，人们感觉到挫败，在整个国家，人们体会着胜利。在整个国家，人们觉得他们的选择是正确的，而其他人的选择是错误的。"②在《秋》的开篇，史密斯借狄更斯在《双城记》中的表达方式写道："这是最坏的时代，这是最坏的时代。历史在重演。"③19世纪的工业化将英国分裂成贫富两个"国家"的历史再次上演，但脱欧时英国所面临的境况似乎更加糟糕，它被对与错、胜利与挫败等情绪分裂得更加七零八落。正如史密斯所指出的那样，"全国各地，鸿沟遍野，这儿一道围栏，那儿一堵墙"④。在史密斯看来，这对任何人都是"最坏的时代"，而狄更斯笔下那个"最好的时代"早已不复存在。

国家的分裂状态通过《秋》中围栏的意象表现得淋漓尽致，围栏造成了英国各地居民彼此之间地理和心理上的双重隔绝。伊丽莎白的母亲居住在英格兰东部的一个小村庄里，村庄周围被当地政府用三米多高的带电铁丝网围了起来，不许外人靠近。这些铁丝围栏阻断了当地村民与外界的接触。有形的围栏成为英国分裂的象征。伊丽莎白的母亲发出感叹，"在这个时代，人们仍然彼此交谈，却无法形成对话。对话终结了"⑤，人们之间的相互理解与包容随之消失。

史密斯描写了脱欧后在英国的分裂状态下，英国本土居民伊丽莎白所遭遇的身份危机。女主人公伊丽莎白在英国脱欧后去更新唯一能证明其身份的护照，却遇到了诸多阻碍：如相关部门以证件照上脸部尺寸不符合要求或眼部间距太小等诸多理由拒绝帮助她办理新护照，而这一切的起源只因为伊丽莎白名字的英文拼写是Elisabeth，而非英国书写传统中的Elizabeth。工作人员因她名字的拼写方式更符合法国书写传统便对其百般刁难，这导致伊丽莎白的许多正常要求因无法自证身份而遭到拒绝。身为

---

① Shaw, K. *"BrexLit"*: *Brexit and Literature: Critical and Cultural Response*. Robert Eaglestone Ed. London and New York: Routledge, 2018, pp.15-30, p.16.
② Smith, Ali. *Autumn*. London: Penguin Books, 2017, p.59.
③ ibid., p.3.
④ ibid., p.61.
⑤ ibid., p.112.

本土居民的伊丽莎白在自己的国家里都沦为不被接受的"他者",英国脱欧后移民的生活困境可见一斑。

第二节 "政治正确"失效与反移民情绪升级

科的《英格兰中部》描写了脱欧前后移民在英国生存境况的变化,这与"政治正确"立场的变化有重要关系。英国的"政治正确"是指避免使用种族、性别、宗教、性取向等方面的冒犯性语言或行为的伦理道德规约,其目的是促进尊重、包容和理解边缘化人群,如移民和同性恋者。因为"政治正确"对英国本土居民的约束和对移民的庇护,脱欧前的本土居民与移民之间保持着表面上的和谐,而脱欧后"政治正确"失效,英国民众的反移民情绪到达顶点,对移民的歧视与迫害成为一种常态。

《英格兰中部》描述了英国本土居民对"政治正确"的不满,其中最具代表性的人物是伊恩的母亲海伦娜和威尔科克斯先生。当威尔科克斯得知伊恩和另外一名亚洲女性纳希德是升职竞争对手,而最后的升职机会给了纳希德时,他认为这是"政治正确"运作的产物,对白人来说是不公平的。科指出英国本土居民认为移民的涌入剥夺了本该属于他们的权利,"如果你来自一个少数群体——那好。排到队伍的前面去。黑人、亚洲人、穆斯林、同性恋:我们为他们做多少都是不够的。"[1]这无形中加强了英国本土居民对移民的恨意,只是碍于"政治正确",这种恨意无法被表达和发泄。对于"政治正确",海伦娜愤慨地说道,"英国并不是一个自由的国家,而是一个专制的国家。"[2]这种专制指的是对英国公民无法公开表达对移民仇恨的言论自由的压制。海伦娜和威尔科克斯代表了英国本土居民极度的排外情绪,这是英国脱欧的原因之一,也表明所谓的英国多元文化融合不过是政治强制手段施行的结果,并未获得英国民众的认可。

脱欧后英国的"政治正确"失效,本土居民被压制许久的反移民情绪达到了顶峰,将对移民的仇恨付诸行动。在《英格兰中部》中,波兰移民格雷特被英国白人小青年辱骂的遭遇是后脱欧时代英国移民经历的缩影。2018年2月的一个周六下午,格雷特去村庄小商店购物,结账时恰巧接到了妹妹的电话,她便用母语跟妹妹聊了起来。不料这时一位刚和收银员吵完架的白人小青年走上前抓住了格雷特的胳膊,并说"在这个国家我们都说英语",辱骂她,朝她吐口水。格雷特感到惊诧又恐惧,她是第一次遭受这样直接的暴力行为,所以她和丈夫决定去报警。然而当他们邀请目击者——她的前雇主海伦娜为她作证时,却遭到了海伦娜的拒绝,并被告知:"我认为,也许,你和你的丈夫回家会更好。"[3]"回家"是脱欧后移民经常听到的话,这在史密斯的《秋》中也有类似的描写,移民居住房屋的墙上被喷上了"滚回家"的涂鸦,[4]意思是让他们滚回自己的国家,如若继续呆在英国,那么类似的各种暴力遭遇则无法避免。反移民情绪不仅伤害了移民,也让那些真正尊重多元文化的本土居民对英国失去了希望,主人公本杰明和格雷特夫妇一样,最后也选择了离开英国,定居国外。

---

① Coe, J. *Middle England*. London: Penguin Books, 2019, p.166.
② Ibid., p.212.
③ Coe, J. *Middle England*. London: Penguin Books, 2019, p.383.
④ Smith, A. *Autumn*. London: Penguin Books, 2016, p.53.

第三节　逆转主义与政治阴谋

不同于《秋》和《英格兰中部》从社会生活层面描写脱欧对英国国家和民众的影响,麦克尤思的小说《蟑螂》聚焦脱欧政治事件,用名为"逆转主义"的运动影射英国脱欧公投,指出脱欧完全是政客们精心策划的政治阴谋与骗局。

《蟑螂》自始至终虽未直接提及英国脱欧公投,但小说中众多细节表明逆转主义是脱欧公投的映射,麦克尤恩以此种方式描述了公投期间发生的事情。逆转主义起初是一项由占据英国首相吉姆·萨姆斯身体的蟑螂提出的经济计划,它的主旨是与资本市场资金运行方式相反的资金的逆向流转,即人们为他们的工作支付费用,通过消费得到报酬,这一经济计划在实施的过程中逐步转变为一项政治制度,并就是否要施行这一制度举行了公投。逆转主义运动中的"逆转派"(Reversalist)和"顺时派"(Clockwiser)分别对应脱欧公投事件中的"脱欧派"和"留欧派"。逆转派的目的是使英国的政治、经济和文化倒退,顺时派由遵循事物本身发展规律的人组成,这表明麦克尤恩认为英国留在欧盟是符合历史发展潮流的,体现了他留欧派的文学创作主张。保证首相的成功竞选和平息党内纷争是逆转主义兴起的原因。《蟑螂》指出"在那些关心逆转主义的人中,逆转主义的起源是很模糊的"[1]。与之类似,脱欧公投中,民众已经不再思考和深究脱欧的原因究竟是什么,他们只是在媒体的煽动下盲目地跟着其他人投票,这就像科在《英格兰中部》中所描写的,"就像其他人那样,跟着感觉投"[2]。虽然逆转主义的起源很模糊,但麦克尤恩明确地指出了逆转主义公投能够成功实施的原因:"为了获得选举支持和安抚逆转派,保守派承诺在2015年的选举宣言中就逆转资金流动举行公投。"[3]这完美地映射了时任首相的卡梅伦为了获得英国独立党的选票所做出的如他能再次当选,便就英国是否脱离欧盟的问题进行公投的承诺。脱欧派与逆转派之间的口号极为相似,逆转派的口号是"把钱转过来"(Turn the Money Around)[4],脱欧派的口号则是"夺回控制权"(Take Back Control)。

逆转主义起初是一项经济计划,它的目的是解决英国国家当下的现实问题,但在实施的过程中,麦克尤恩慢慢揭露了该经济计划的真实目的。计划开始时,吉姆指出"这个国家的所有问题,包括财富和机会的不平等、南北差异和工资的停滞不前,都是因为资金流动的方向所引起的"[5],所以他要逆转资金流向以解决这些问题。这难免让读者感觉吉姆是一个尽职尽责、为国为民,却不懂金融市场运行规则的荒唐可笑的人。实则不然,吉姆深知逆转主义将给英国带来毁灭性打击,而他的目的也正是在此:让英国堕落腐败,自己的蟑螂种族才能在污秽和肮脏中发展壮大。麦克尤恩借此批判脱欧公投是政客们组织的一场有预谋的颠覆英国的计划。这场政治阴谋主要表现在议会投票的非公正性和逆转派在内阁排除异己时使用的卑劣手段。尽管逆转主义是由全民公投通过的,但最终实施的权力取决于议会的内部投票,而这场投票根本就毫无公平性可言。投票开始前,当吉姆的一些支持者被派往美国参加一次活动

①　McEwan, I. *The Cockroach*. London: Jonathan Cape, 2019, p.25.
②　Coe, J. *Middle England*. London: Penguin Books, 2018, p.307.
③　McEwan, I. *The Cockroach*. London: Jonathan Cape, 2019, p.28.
④　Ibid., p.29.
⑤　同上。

时,他要求反对派成员以相同的人数配比一同前往,这样就能保证在法案表决期间,反对派和支持派的人数相同,从而不会造成不利于他的投票人数上的差异。吉姆在投票期间打破了这一协议,他迅速从美国召回了他的支持者,并要求他们投票支持逆转主义法案,从而赢得多数投票,保证了逆向主义法案的顺利实施。麦克尤恩借此讽刺脱欧公投中政治领域的暗箱操作并质疑公投的合理性和公平性。吉姆还使用恶意诋毁竞争对手的方式排除异己。内阁中的大部分部长都是吉姆的同类,是人类形态的蟑螂,他们都同意吉姆的逆转主义计划。只有外交部长本尼迪克特·圣约翰是个人类,他忠于自己的工作,出于对国家和人民利益的考虑反对逆转主义计划。圣约翰对吉姆的计划构成了威胁。所以吉姆和交通部长简·菲什合谋散布谣言,制造政治丑闻,最终导致圣约翰辞职。欺骗和谎言是吉姆为了达到目的而经常使用的手段,麦克尤恩批判了政客们为了自己的利益,置国家利益于不顾的丑恶嘴脸。小说最后,麦克尤恩揭示了蟑螂们用逆转主义颠覆英国,使英国一贫如洗,从而为蟑螂种族的发展铺路的企图,再次达到影射脱欧是一场导致英国贫苦和堕落的政治阴谋的目的。

本章所选取的作家及其代表作如下:阿莉·史密斯及其代表作《秋》、乔纳森·科及其代表作《英格兰中部》、伊恩·麦克尤恩及其代表作《蟑螂》。

第四节　主要作家介绍与代表作品选读

一、阿莉·史密斯

(一) 阿莉·史密斯简介

阿莉·史密斯出生在苏格兰因弗内斯的一个工人阶级家庭,1980 年至 1985 年在阿伯丁大学学习英语语言文学,获学士和硕士学位。1985 年至 1990 年间在剑桥大学纽纳姆学院进修美国和爱尔兰现实主义文学,并开始戏剧创作,最终未能取得博士学位。

史密斯于 1990 年离开剑桥,移居爱丁堡,在斯特拉斯克莱德大学担任讲师,教授苏格兰、英格兰和美国文学。史密斯于 1992 年由于慢性痨症被迫放弃教职返回剑桥休养,成为一名职业作家。

史密斯的文学创作包括小说、短篇故事集、戏剧和纪实文学,英语为其创作语言。史密斯的绝大部分作品出版发行于英国,其中多部作品被翻译成十多种语言。史密斯擅于运用开放式结局、嵌套式叙事的元小说叙事技巧解构男性霸权话语,致力于建构开放包容的话语体系。透过史密斯的作品可以发现,生活在"后真理"时代的史密斯质疑真理的可靠性和唯一性,合理化真理的虚无性和复杂性。作为女性同性恋作家的史密斯关注社会边缘人物遭受的压迫和面临的生存焦虑,批判严格的社会等级制度和异性恋父权制对女性和同性恋群体的束缚。史密斯的文学创作作为处于世纪之交的英国文学的创新注入了活力,为英国的性别研究和脱欧文学研究提供了重要的参考。

史密斯的创作生涯始于戏剧,其中大部分是她在攻读博士学位期间为爱丁堡艺术节而创作的,但并未发表,包括《僵局》(*Stalemate*,1986)、《舞蹈》(*The Dance*,1988)、《英格兰之女》(*Daughters of*

England，1989—1990)、《亚马逊》(*Amazons*，1990)、《预言家》(*The Seer*，2001)等。

史密斯出版了五部短篇故事集，包括《自由的爱和其他故事》(*Free Love and Other Stories*，1995)、《其他故事和其他故事》(*Other Stories and Other Stories*，1999)、《完整故事和其他故事》(*The Whole Story and Other Stories*，2003)、《第一人称和其他故事》(*The First Person and Other Stories*，2008)和《公共图书馆和其他故事》(*Public Library and Other Stories*，2015)。

史密斯创作了 12 部小说，包括《相像》(*Like*，1997)、《旅馆世界》、《迷》(*The Accidental*，2005)、《女孩与男孩相遇》(*Girl Meets Boy*，2007)、《纵横交错的世界》(*There But For The*，2011)、《巧妙》(*Artful*，2012)、《如何双全》(*How to Be Both*，2014)、"季节四部曲"[《秋》、《冬》(*Winter*，2017)、《春》(*Spring*，2019)和《夏》(*Summer*，2020)]和《姊妹篇》(*Companion Piece*，2022)。史密斯还创作了一部纪实文学作品《郡》(*Shire*，2013)。

史密斯的小说《旅馆世界》获安可奖、苏格兰艺术理事会奖、橘子小说奖和布克小说奖的提名。小说《迷》获 2005 年度布克奖的提名、橘子小说奖和 2005 年度惠特布雷德小说奖；小说《女孩与男孩相遇》获 2007 年苏格兰艺术理事会小说奖，并入选 *Diva* 杂志读者年度好书；小说《纵横交错的世界》被《卫报》评为年度最佳小说之一；小说《如何双全》获 2014 年布克奖提名、金史密斯奖、2015 年贝利女性小说奖和福里奥文学奖；小说《秋》获 2017 年度布克奖的提名；小说《夏》获 2021 年奥威尔政治小说奖。纪实文学《巧妙》入围 2013 年金史密斯奖。史密斯于 2007 年入选皇家文学学会会员，2015 年以其杰出的文学成就被授予英帝国高级勋位(CBE)，2018 年被《泰晤士报文学增刊》评选为英格兰和爱尔兰当今最佳小说家。

(二)《秋》简介

《秋》出版于 2016 年 10 月，是评论界公认的第一部严肃的脱欧小说。该书将故事背景设置于英国脱欧公投一个月后，32 岁的单身大学女讲师伊丽莎白回到母亲居住的村庄陪她过周末，却目睹往日宁静美丽的村庄在脱欧后变得面目全非。移民居住的房屋墙面被喷上了"滚回家"的涂鸦；西班牙游客在出租车等待站点遭人谩骂；街上的移民处处受到歧视与威胁；排外情绪达到顶点，国家内部分裂严重，整个国家被冷漠的情绪所笼罩，人与人之间缺乏交流，对话已经失去了交流和沟通的功能。史密斯将此刻混乱的英国比喻为逐渐失去生机的秋季，即将接受寒冬的摧残，这是脱欧后英国不得不面对的残酷现实。英文中秋季的另一个表述为 fall，含堕落之意，作者暗指脱欧后的英国像亚当和夏娃离开伊甸园后一样开始堕落并遭受苦难。该书的标题暗示了史密斯对英国脱欧后的现状深感痛心，对英国的未来充满了怀疑与不安。

故事以昏睡在照料中心的 101 岁老人丹尼尔的梦境开始。在梦里，丹尼尔发现自己被冲到了一个沙滩上，这里遍地都是冰冷的尸体。这些尸体暗指脱欧后遭受迫害的移民，死亡成为他们最终的命运。在梦里，虚弱的老人丹尼尔奇迹般地变成了一个身强力壮的年轻小伙，这表达出史密斯梦想回到脱欧前英国生机勃勃的状态。现实中的丹尼尔躺在疗养院里，虽然还有呼吸，但是其呼吸间隔之久让人误以为他没有能力进行下一次呼吸。史密斯用丹尼尔指涉脱欧后在垂死边缘挣扎的英国。

小说值得关注的另一重点是伊丽莎白与丹尼尔之间的关系。文中伊丽莎白经常会说"我爱他"并且因为多次在梦中呼唤丹尼尔的名字导致交往已久的男朋友和她分手，所以将伊丽莎白对丹尼尔的爱理解为柏拉图式的爱情确有其道理,但伊丽莎白对丹尼尔的爱更多地可以被理解为对缺失父爱的转移。童年时期的伊丽莎白缺少父亲的陪伴,但她一直极其渴望父爱。此时,伊丽莎白和母亲刚好搬家住在丹尼尔的隔壁,丹尼尔扮演了伊丽莎白所描述的非官方保姆的角色,虽然这一点遭到了她母亲的否认。尽管如此,丹尼尔对伊丽莎白的照顾、陪伴和保护是毋庸置疑的,这也是长大后伊丽莎白能够原谅二十多年来素未谋面的父亲的原因之一。然而史密斯想要表达的却远不止如此,她将具有德国和法国血统的英国移民丹尼尔刻画为古老欧洲的化身,将伊丽莎白作为英国的象征,是丹尼尔的教导激起了伊丽莎白对艺术(故事、拼贴画和绘画)的兴趣。史密斯借此表达英国对欧洲的文化依附。丹尼尔的昏睡似乎表明欧洲价值观在英国的终结。在丹尼尔昏睡期间,伊丽莎白常来给他读书以期能唤醒他,而伊丽莎白的努力也并没有白费,丹尼尔最终虚弱地睁开了眼睛,这一情节设置表明史密斯对未来英国与欧洲的关系仍然抱有一丝希望。

　　小说中的身份危机与其应对策略也是一个研究重点。脱欧后的英国公民陷入了"我是谁"和"未来的我如何自处"的焦虑之中,他们通过观看英国历史节目等行为表达其对历史的眷恋,缓解强烈的身份焦虑,然而这些做法并未能帮助伊丽莎白重构英国公民身份。史密斯有意塑造了伊丽莎白和丹尼尔之间的和谐关系,以此表达她对本土居民和移民友好相处的美好希冀。值得注意的是,伊丽莎白的姓氏Demand 源自法语词 de 和 monde,意为"世界的"。在脱欧后的英国社会,成为世界公民是解决身份危机的重要策略。

(三) 作品选读:《秋》①

It is just over a week since the vote. The bunting in the village where Elisabeth's mother now lives is up across the High Street for its summer festival, plastic reds and whites and blues against a sky that's all threats, and though it's not actually raining right now and the pavements are dry, the wind rattling the plastic triangles against themselves means it sounds all along the High Street like rain is hammering down.

The village is in a sullen state. Elisabeth passes a cottage not far from the bus stop whose front, from the door to across above the window, has been painted over with black paint and the words GO and HOME.

People either look down, look away or stare her out. People in the shops, when she buys some fruit, some ibuprofen and a newspaper for her mother, speak with a new kind of detachment. People she passes on the streets on the way from the bus stop to her mother's house regard her, and each other, with a new kind of loftiness.

Her mother, who tells her when she gets there that half the village isn't speaking to the other half of the village, and that this makes almost no difference to her since no one in the village speaks to her anyway or ever has though she's lived here nearly a decade now (in this her mother is being a touch melodramatic), is doing some hammering herself, nailing to the kitchen wall an old Ordnance

---

① Smith, A. *Autumn*. London: Penguin Books, 2017, pp.53 – 66.

Survey map of where she now lives, which she bought yesterday in a shop that used to be the local electrician's business and electrical appliances store and is now a place selling plastic starfish, pottery looking things, artisan gardening tools and canvas gardening gloves that look like they've been modelled on a 1950s utilitarian utopia.

The kind of shop with the kinds of things that look nice, cost more than they should and persuade you that if you buy them you'll be living the right kind of life, her mother says between lips still holding two little nails.

The map is from 1962. Her mother has drawn a red line with a Sharpie all round the coast marking where the new coast is.

She points to a spot quite far inland, on the new red line.

That's where the World War II pillbox fell into the sea ten days ago, she says.

She points to the other side of the map, furthest from the coast. That's where the new fence has gone up, she says. Look.

She is pointing to the word common in the phrase common land.

Apparently a fence three metres high with a roll of razorwire along the top of it has been erected across a stretch of land not far from the village. It has security cameras on posts all along it. It encloses a piece of land that's got nothing in it but furze, sandy flats, tufts of long grass, scrappy trees, little clumps of wildflower.

Go and see it, her mother says. I want you to do something about it.

What can I do about it? Elisabeth says. I'm a lecturer in history of art.

Her mother shakes her head.

You'll know what to do, she says. You're young. Come on. We'll both go.

They walk along the single-track road. The grass is high on either side of them.

Can't believe he's still alive, your Mr Gluck, her mother is saying.

That's what everybody in The Maltings Care Providers plc pretty much says too, Elisabeth says.

He was so old back then, her mother says. He must be more than a hundred. He must be. He was eighty back in the 90s. He used to walk up the street, remember, all bowed with age.

I don't remember that at all, Elisabeth says.

Like he carried the weight of the world on his back, her mother says.

You always said he was like a dancer, Elisabeth says. An old dancer, her mother says. He was all bent over. You used to say he was lithe, Elisabeth says.

Then she says,

oh dear God.

In front of them, slicing straight across a path Elisabeth's walked several times since her mother came to live here, and blocking the way as far as the eye can see no matter which way she turns her head, is a mass of chainlink metal.

Her mother sits down on the churned-up ground near the fence. I'm tired, she says.

It's only two miles, Elisabeth says.

That's not what I mean, she says. I'm tired of the news. I'm tired of the way it makes things spectacular that aren't, and deals so simplistically with what's truly appalling. I'm tired of the vitriol. I'm tired of the anger. I'm tired of the meanness. I'm tired of the selfishness. I'm tired of how we're doing nothing to stop it. I'm tired of how we're encouraging it. I'm tired of the violence there is and I'm tired of the violence that's on its way, that's coming, that hasn't happened yet. I'm tired of liars. I'm tired of sanctified liars. I'm tired of how those liars have let this happen. I'm tired of having to wonder whether they did it out of stupidity or did it on purpose. I'm tired of lying governments. I'm tired of people not caring whether they're being lied to any more. I'm tired of being made to feel this fearful. I'm tired of animosity. I'm tired of pusillanimosity.

I don't think that's actually a word, Elisabeth says.

I'm tired of not knowing the right words, her mother says.

Elisabeth thinks of the bricks of the old broken-up pillbox under the water, the air bubbles rising from their pores when the tide covers them.

I'm a brick under water, she thinks.

Her mother, sensing her daughter's attention wandering, sags momentarily towards the fence.

Elisabeth, who is tired of her mother (already, and she's only an hour and a half into the visit) points to the little clips placed at different positions along the wire.

Careful, she says. I think it's electrified.

All across the country, there was misery and rejoicing.

All across the country, what had happened whipped about by itself as if a live electric wire had snapped off a pylon in a storm and was whipping about in the air above the trees, the roofs, the traffic.

All across the country, people felt it was the wrong thing. All across the country, people felt it was the right thing. All across the country, people felt they'd really lost. All across the country, people felt they'd really won. All across the country, people felt they'd done the right thing and other people had done the wrong thing. All across the country, people looked up Google: what is EU? All across the country, people looked up Google: move to Scotland. All across the country, people looked up Google: Irish passport applications. All across the country, people called each other cunts. All across the country, people felt unsafe. All across the country, people were laughing their heads off. All across the country, people felt legitimized. All across the country, people felt bereaved and shocked. All across the country, people felt righteous. All across the country, people felt sick. All across the country, people felt history at their shoulder. All across the country, people felt history meant nothing. All across the country, people felt like they counted for nothing. All across the country, people had pinned their hopes on it. All across the country, people waved flags in the rain. All across the country, people drew swastika graffiti. All across the country, people threatened other people. All across the country, people told people to leave. All across the country, the media was insane. All across the country, politicians lied. All across the country, politicians fell apart. All across the country, politicians vanished. All across the country, promises vanished. All across the country, money vanished. All across the country, social media did the job. All across the country, things got nasty. All across the country, nobody spoke about it. All across the country, nobody spoke about anything else. All across the country, racist bile was general. All across the country, people said it wasn't that they didn't like immigrants. All across the country, people said it was about control. All across the country, everything changed overnight. All across the country, the haves and the have nots stayed the same. All across the country, the usual tiny per cent of the people made their money out of the usual huge per cent of the people. All across the country, money money money money. All across the country, no money no money no money no money.

All across the country, the country split in pieces. All across the country, the countries cut adrift.

All across the country, the country was divided, a fence here, a wall there, a line drawn here, a line crossed there,

a line you don't cross here,

a line you better not cross there,

a line of beauty here,

a line dance there,

a line you don't even know exists here, a line you can't afford there,

a whole new line of fire,

line of battle,

end of the line,

here/there.

It was a typically warm Monday in late September 2015, in Nice, in the south of France. People out on the street were staring at the exterior of the Palais de la Prefecture where a long red banner with a swastika at the top of it had just coursed down the length of the front of the building and was settling itself against the balconies. Some people screamed. There was a flurry of shouting and pointing.

It was just a film production unit filming an adaptation of a memoir, using the Palais to recreate the Hotel Excelsior, where Alois Brunner, the SS officer, had had his office and living quarters after the Italians surrendered to the Allies and the Gestapo had taken over in their place.

The Daily Telegraph reported next day on how the local authorities were apologizing for not having given enough notice about the film unit's plans to people who lived in the city, and how public confusion and offence had soon shifted to a mass taking of selfies.

It ran an online survey at the end of the news story. Were locals right to be angry about the banner: Yes or No?

Nearly four thousand people voted. Seventy percent said no.

It was a typically warm Friday in late September 1943, in Nice, in the south of France. Hannah Gluck, who was twenty two years old (and whose real name wasn't on her identity papers, which stated that her name was Adrienne Albert), was sitting on the floor in the back of a truck. They'd picked up nine so far, all women, Hannah didn't know any of them. She and the woman opposite her exchanged looks. The woman looked down, then she looked back up, exchanged the look with Hannah one more time. Then they both lowered their eyes and looked down at the metal floor of the truck.

There were no accompanying vehicles. There were, in total, a driver plus a guard and a single quite young officer up front, and the two at the back, both even younger. The truck was part-open, part-roofed with canvas. The people on the streets could see their heads and the guards as they went past. Hannah had heard the officer saying to one of the men at the back as she climbed into the truck, keep it calm.

But the people on the street were oblivious, or made themselves it. They looked and looked away. They looked. But they weren't looking.

The streets were bright and splendid. The sun sent shockingly beautiful light off the buildings into the back of the truck.

When they stopped up a sidestreet to pick up two more, Hannah's eyes met again the eyes of the woman opposite. The woman moved her head with near-invisible assent.

The truck jolted to a stop. Traffic snarl-up. They'd taken the stupidest route. Good, and her sense of smell told her, the Friday fishmarket, busy.

Hannah stood up.

One of the guards told her to sit down.

The woman opposite stood up. One by one all the other women in the truck took their cue and stood up. The guard yelled at them to sit down. Both guards yelled. One waved a gun in the air at them.

This city isn't used to it yet, Hannah thought.

Get out of the way, the woman who'd nodded to Hannah said to the men. You can't kill us all. Where are you taking them?

A woman had come over to the side of the truck and was looking in. A small gathering of women from the market, elegant women, headscarfed fish-seller girls and older women, formed behind her.

Then the officer got out of the truck and pushed the woman who'd asked where they were taking the women in the face. She fell and hit her head against a stone bollard. Her elegant hat fell off.

The women in that small gathering on the side of the road moved closer together. Their hush was audible. It spread back across the market like shadow, like cloud-cover.

It was a hush, Hannah thought, related to the quiet that comes over wildlife, happens to the birdsong, in an eclipse of the sun when something like night happens but it's the middle of the day.

Excuse me, ladies, Hann ah said. This is where I get off.

The body of women on the truck huddled aside, let her through, let her go first.

思考与讨论

(1) 小说如何书写个人和国家层面的危机？作者提出的危机应对策略是什么？

(2) 文本中反复提及的拼贴画与英国国家身份有何种内在联系？

(3) 伊丽莎白多次阅读《美丽新世界》的原因是什么？

(4) Elisabeth 的名字有何特殊含义（为何是 Elisabeth 而不是英国传统书写中的 Elizabeth）？

(5) 文本叙事为何不停地在过去与现在、梦境与现实之间来回切换？

(6) 伊丽莎白的母亲对待英国脱欧的态度经历了什么样的变化？原因是什么？

拓展阅读

[1] Pittel, H. Fiction in Dark Times: The Brexit Novel and Ali Smith. *Hard Times*. Vol. 101, No. 1(2018), pp. 58 – 67.

[2] Ranger, H. Ali Smith and Ovid. *International Journal of the Classical Tradition*. Vol. 26, No. 4(2019), pp. 397 – 416.

[3] 秋瑾. 英国当代作家阿莉·史密斯[J]. 外国文学, 2007(4): 20 – 25.

二、乔纳森·科

（一）乔纳森·科简介

乔纳森·科出生于伍斯特郡的布罗姆斯格罗夫，于剑桥大学三一学院取得学士学位，随后在沃里克大学任教，并在此获得英语文学硕士和博士学位。

科的创作包括小说、儿童文学、纪实文学和名人传记，英语是其创作语言。科的作品多在英国出版，并已被翻译成30多种语言在各国家出版。科善于运用反讽和幽默的写作手法、多重叙事视角、错综复杂的人物关系和时间线以及多种文体的交叉使用，探索当代社会的诸多问题以及人类错综复杂的社会关系。科的作品探讨的主题主要包括：一、当代社会的种种矛盾和弊病，如政治腐败、阶级差异、种族歧视等；二、不同历史和文化背景下英国人的生活状态以及他们对自身身份和国家身份的认同；三、人类的孤独、沟通障碍等情感问题以及人类社会关系的复杂性和多样性；四、描写和批判当代生活中的各种文化现象，如流行文化、消费文化、媒体文化等；五、家庭关系的复杂性及其与政治生活的相互关联。科的作品涵盖英国社会、政治、历史、文化等多个领域，绘制了一幅当代英国社会生活的全景图。

迄今为止，科已出版 14 部小说，包括《意外的女人》(*The Accidental Woman*，1987)、《一点点爱》(*A Touch of Love*，1989)、《死亡小矮人》(*The Dwarves of Death*，1990)、《瓜分殆尽》(*What a Carve Up*，1994)、《睡眠之屋》(*The House of Sleep*，1997)、《恶人俱乐部》(*The Rotter's Club*，2001)、《封闭的圈子》(*The Closed Circle*，2004)、《落下之前的雨》(*The Rain Before It Falls*，2007)、《麦克斯韦·西姆的可怕隐私》(*The Terrible Privacy of Maxwell Sim*，2010)、《58 届世博会》(*Expo 58*，2013)、《11 号》(*Number 11*，2015)、《英格兰中部》(*Middle England*，2018)、《怀尔德先生与我》(*Mr. Wilder and Me*，2020)、《伯恩维尔》(*Bournville*，2022)。

科的其他作品还包括儿童文学《格列佛的故事》(*La storia di Gulliver*，2011)和《你看起来很好》(*Lo specchio dei Desideri*，2012)；纪实文学《亨弗莱·鲍嘉》(*Humphrey Bogart: Take It and Like It*，1991)、《詹姆斯·史都华》(*James Stewart: Leading Man*，1994)、《宛如怒象》(*Like a Fiery Elephant: The Story of B.S.Johnson*，2004)

科的小说《瓜分殆尽》获得 1994 年约翰·卢埃林·里斯文学奖；小说《睡眠之屋》获得 1998 年法国梅迪西斯最佳外国小说奖；小说《恶人俱乐部》获得波灵格大众伍德豪斯奖；纪实文学《宛如怒象》获得 2005 年塞缪尔·约翰逊奖；小说《英格兰中部》荣获 2019 年欧洲图书奖和科斯塔图书奖。科于 2012 年被授予英国皇家文学学会会员的荣誉称号。

(二)《英格兰中部》简介

《英格兰中部》是科"恶人俱乐部"三部曲中的第三部，其中的人物和部分故事情节取自前两部《恶人俱乐部》和《封闭的圈子》。《英格兰中部》是一部探讨脱欧前后英国社会变化的小说。小说内部时间线长达九年，故事始于 2010 年的联合政府选举，涉及 2011 年的伦敦动乱、2012 年伦敦奥林匹克运动会、2016 年的脱欧公投，以对 2018 年脱欧动乱的描述结尾。小说主人公半退休状态的本杰明搬家到什普罗郡居住，在那里他沉溺于小说《无刺玫瑰》的创作，历经多次删减和修改后，他的小说得以出版并入围布克奖，这为他赢得了一定的声誉。但是脱欧后英国社会的巨大变化让本杰明感到不适，他最终移居欧洲大陆生活。

怀旧是小说的主题之一。怀旧情绪在主人公本杰明的身上表现得尤为明显，他被禁锢在历史记忆的牢笼里，成为过去的囚徒，无法活在当下。首先体现为他对塞西莉亚始终无法释怀的爱与思念，这是他创作《无刺玫瑰》的初衷，也是他的生活信念。其次，他对英国过去统一美好景象的记忆不容半分质疑，所以当他的妹妹对 20 世纪 70 年代电视频道匮乏发表评论时，他感到非常气愤和恼火，因为"这破坏了（可能是她没有意识到）他最珍视的早期记忆之一。在他的童年时代，英国一直是一个团结、统一、协商一致的地方，这仍然是他信仰体系的基石"[①]。最后，本杰明和朋友们回到童年学校时的各种回忆既

---

① Coe, J. 2018. *Middle England*. London: Penguin, p.49.

是怀旧的个人情感的体现,也是民族怀旧情感的体现。时隔多年,本杰明的朋友们竟然能够回忆起如此多过去的细节,这让道格感到非常震惊,他感叹道"你们这些家伙痴迷于过去",并认为"怀旧是英国病"①,是英国民众共有的问题,然而本杰明却坚持认为回首往事并非坏事。怀旧的另一个代表人物是本杰明的父亲科林,他是英国工业化时代的一员,他曾经工作过的英国利兰汽车厂的巨大变化令其深感诧异。他认为英国的历史和集体记忆被埋葬了,他对未来产生了深深的忧虑,他疑惑地说道:"我们怎么能继续这样下去。我们不制作任何东西。如果我们什么都不做,那我们就没有东西可卖,那么……我们怎么才能生存下去呢?"②科林渴望回到过去英国制造业繁荣发达的工业时代,而不是现在这个销售业占主导的英国社会。

《英格兰中部》在展现脱欧前后英国社会的矛盾和问题的同时,科也描述了短暂的英国人团结一致的时刻,这主要体现在他对 2012 年伦敦奥林匹克运动会开幕式的描写。小说开篇将开幕式描绘为一场庆祝英国历史和文化的盛宴,虽然许多人坐在他们各自的电视机前,但是他们都在共同关注这一事件,这是一个难得的团结时刻。即使是满不在乎的本杰明也被卷入其中,一边听着电视里开幕式的声音,一边修改着他的小说,像其他人一样,他被这共同的热情所吸引,感受到了国家团结和英国人的自豪感。

(三)作品选读:《英格兰中部》

Excerpt 1③

The publication of these latest immigration figures had a galvanizing effect on the referendum campaign as it entered its final phase. The debate shifted. There was less discussion of economic forecasts and sovereignty and the political benefits of EU membership: now, everything seemed to hinge upon immigration and border control. The tone changed too. It became more bitter, more personal, more rancorous. One half of the country seemed to have become fiercely hostile towards the other. More and more people began to wish, like Benjamin, that the whole wearying, nasty, divisive business could be finished and forgotten as soon as possible.

Meanwhile, Lois put her house in York on the market and moved down to Birmingham. On the evening of 13 June 2016, ten days after her return, she invited Sophie and Ian round for dinner. She baked a lasagne and they drank plenty of Montepulciano and it was all very jolly but after the meal Lois seemed to disappear from the table while they were still drinking coffee, and a few minutes later Sophie found her in the sitting room all alone, listening to Classic FM and finishing off the last of the wine.

"You all right, Mum?" she asked.

Lois looked up and smiled.

"Yes, I'm fine."

"Didn't you want to stay and talk?"

---

① Coe, J. 2018. *Middle England*. London: Penguin, p.391.
② Ibid., p.261.
③ Coe, J. *Middle England*. London: Penguin Books, 2019, pp.299 – 301.

"Not really."

Sophie sat down beside her. On the coffee table next to the sofa was a pile of newspapers and other odds and ends. Four sheets of A4 on top of the pile caught Sophie's eye. She picked them up and glanced through them.

"What are these?"

"What do they look like?"

"They look like adverts for houses in France."

"Then that's what they are."

"You're thinking of buying somewhere in France?"

"Your father is."

Sophie looked at the brochures more closely. The properties, all priced at around 300,000 euros, seemed to boast the kinds of idyllic settings and generous proportions that would set the purchaser back twice as much if they were located somewhere in England.

"Well, aren't you keen?" she said. "You've always wanted a place in France. You've been talking about it for ages. And Dad'll be retiring in a couple of years. It could be great—for both of you."

Lois nodded. "Yes, it could." But she didn't sound over-enthusiastic.

Sophie said, nervously: "You are intending to spend your retirement with Dad, aren't you?"

"Well, I don't have anyone else to spend it with," said Lois, sipping her wine. "And I don't want to spend it in this bloody city, that's for sure."

Sophie laid a hand on her mother's arm. Lois turned to look at her. Her eyes were brimming.

"It's forty-three years, since that bomb went off," she said. "Forty-one years, six months and twenty-three days. Every night, I still hear it. That bomb going off is the last thing I hear, before I go to sleep. If I go to sleep. I daren't watch the news on television, in case there's something that reminds me. I can't even go to the cinema or watch a DVD in case there's anything in it—anything at all—any blood, any violence, any noise. Anything that reminds me what human beings can do to each other. Politics can make people do terrible things. . ." She looked at Sophie closely now, and her voice became more urgent. "You and Ian are in trouble, aren't you?"

"Not really," said Sophie, after a brief hesitation. "We'll get through it. We'll sort it out."

"Politics can tear people apart," said Lois. "Stupid, isn't it? But true. That's what happened to my Malcolm. That's what killed him. Politics."

There was a noise behind them—the creaking of a floorboard—and both women turned around. It was Ian, standing in the doorway with his coffee mug in his hand.

"Everything OK in here?" he asked.

"Come in," said Lois, moving up to make room for him on the sofa. "Sit down, and tell me what you think of these houses."

Excerpt 2[①]

Afterwards, in a reflective frame of mind, she strolled down to the river and began to walk eastwards in the direction of Fulham. The Thames was full, its brown-grey waters slapping turgidly against the embankment walls. Seagulls whirled and cried out. Lazy river traffic chugged by. She had no real idea where she was heading, or what she would do when she got there. This aimlessness appeared to be a new but recurrent feature of her life.

Sophie thought back to the moment when her conversation with Emily had been cut off. What she had said was true: from every rational point of view, the trigger for her separation from Ian looked crazy. A couple might decide to separate for all sorts of reasons: adultery, cruelty, domestic abuse, lack of sex. But a difference of opinion over whether Britain should be a member of the European Union or not? It seemed absurd. It was absurd. And yet Sophie knew, deep down, that it had not so much been a reason as a tipping point. Ian had reacted (to her mind) so bizarrely to the referendum result, with such gleeful, infantile triumphalism (he kept using the word 'freedom' as if he were the citizen of a tiny African country that had finally won independence from its colonial oppressor) that, for the first time, she genuinely realized that she no longer understood why her husband thought and felt the way that he did. At the same time, she herself had been possessed by the immediate sense, that morning, that a small but important part of her own identity—her modern, layered, multiple identity-had been taken away from her.

During their first session a few weeks later, their relationship counsellor, Lorna, told them that many of the couples she was seeing at the moment had mentioned Brexit as a key factor in their growing estrangement.

"I usually start by asking each of you the same question," she said. "Sophie, why are you so angry that Ian voted Leave? And Ian, why are you so angry that Sophie voted Remain?"

Sophie had thought for a long time before answering:

"I suppose because it made me think that, as a person, he's not as open as I thought he was. That his basic model for relationships comes down to antagonism and competition, not cooperation."

Lorna had nodded, and turned to Ian, who had answered:

"It makes me think that she's very naive, that she lives in a bubble and can't see how other people around her might have a different opinion to hers. And this gives her a certain attitude. An attitude of moral superiority."

To which Lorna had said:

"What's interesting about both of those answers is that neither of you mentioned politics. As if

---

① Coe, J. *Middle England*. London: Penguin Books, 2019, pp. 326 - 327.

the referendum wasn't about Europe at all. Maybe something much more fundamental and personal was going on. Which is why this might be a difficult problem to resolve."

She had suggested a course of six sessions, but it turned out that she was being optimistic. In fact they attended nine, before admitting defeat, and calling it a day.

Excerpt 3[①]

Gail's duties in Westminster required her to spend four days of each week in London while parliament was sitting. Her son Edward was away at university, but her daughter Sarah was still at school in Coventry, and so Sarah would typically spend those four days at her father's house. This week, however, he happened to be away on business. In these circumstances Doug (as had occasionally happened before) volunteered to move into the house in Earlsdon and assume the role of carer.

It was a role he took on with mixed feelings. Having failed, fairly comprehensively, to build a satisfactory relationship with his own daughter, he had been sceptical at first of his chances with another fourteen-year-old. But over time he had started to grow fond of Sarah, even though it was hard to tell whether she felt the same way. She had none of Coriander's self-assurance or sense of entitlement. She was quiet, obedient, studious and a little bit dowdy. She wore braces on her teeth and horn-rimmed glasses that gave her the look of a tomboy. She had no boyfriend and showed little interest in acquiring one, appearing happy instead to live a life of quiet domestic contentment with her mother (and Doug, if he was around). A few years earlier he might have been concerned by her lack of rebellious spirit; now he was simply relieved to be spending time with someone who gave him so little trouble.

On the morning of Wednesday, 15 November, shortly after seven o'clock, he was busy in the kitchen, preparing Sarah's breakfast and packed lunch. It was still dark outside and Sarah, although she was awake, had not yet managed to drag herself out of bed. Doug was in the middle of mixing some salad and cold pasta together in a tupperware box when his phone rang. It was Gail, calling from London.

"Have you seen it?" she said. Her voice was strained and unsteady.

"No. Seen what?"

"The paper."

"What about it?"

"I'm on the front page."

"Really? What do they—?"

"I should just go out and get one."

① Coe, J. *Middle England*. London: Penguin Books, 2019, pp. 354 – 359.

The newsagent was only thirty seconds' walk away. After shouting up the stairs to tell Sarah her cereal was on the table, Dough hurried around the corner of the street. He quickly saw what Gail was talking about. Word of her meeting with the whips had leaked out and one of the papers had decided to make a front-page splash of it. Hers was one of sixteen faces pictured under the banner headline: "THE BREXIT MUTINEERS".

The headline was nasty. The publication of each MP's photograph was done with a clear intent to point the finger, to identify. In the fevered, polarized atmosphere that still pervaded the country more than a year after the referendum, it was a dangerous thing to do.

Hugely irresponsible, in fact: that was Doug's first thought, as he walked back to the house with a copy folded under his arm.

Sarah was in the kitchen. She had finished her cereal and was spreading Nutella on a slice of toast. Doug called Gail from the sitting room and spoke in a low voice.

"Well, that's pretty horrible. Any fallout yet?"

"I'll say. My Twitter feed's gone berserk. Emails too."

"Bad?"

"I've forwarded the worst on to the office and they reckon four or five of them should be passed on to the police. Do you want to hear them?"

"Not really. But go on."

"OK, so we've got... *Ransom you bitch—that's Ransome without an 'e', of course—you will burn in hell for this. Look over ur shoulder when ur walking home tonight. You attack the people the people will attack you.* Oh, and this is a nice one: *Remember Jo Cox it could happen again.*"

"Jesus Christ. Are you OK? Do you... I don't know, do you want me to come down?"

Gail sighed. "I don't think so. Life has to go on, doesn't it? I don't suppose anyone'll come round to the house, or anything like that. Just make sure that Sarah's OK."

"Sure." He looked at the headline again, with the newspaper spread out in front of him on the coffee table. "I can't believe they'd do something like that."

"I know," said Gail. "I mean, I never liked its politics, but that used to be a respectable paper. What's going on, do you think?"

"I don't know. This country's gone mad."

"I hope Sarah's all right at school. I hope nobody says anything horrid to her."

"Don't worry," Doug said. "I've got my eye on her."

It was tempting to think, at times like this, that some bizarre hysteria had gripped the British people; that the pitch of collective madness to which everyone had risen during the campaign of 2016 had simply not abated yet. But Doug was not entirely satisfied with this explanation. He knew that a headline like that was calculated. He knew that the outrage it was designed to foment was being stoked because it was valuable to someone: not to any one individual, of course, or even to any one clearly identifiable movement or political party, but to a disparate, amorphous coalition of vested interests who were being careful not to declare themselves too openly. The first thing he did, after walking Sarah to school, was to settle down at his desk upstairs and reach for a Manila envelope containing forty or fifty pages of A4 which had arrived in the post, anonymously, three days after his meeting with Nigel Ives.

There had been no note accompanying them: no written farewell message from the eccentric informant with whom he'd shared so many bizarre, circular conversations over the last few years. Doug had simply been presented with the papers, and expected to make what he could of them. Briefing notes; draft press releases; minutes of confidential meetings; reports marked "Classified" and "Not for Publication". Many of them bore the initials "R. C." or the signature "Ronald Culpepper". Most of them were printed on the headed notepaper of the Imperium Foundation.

He had read through these documents many times, and knew exactly where to find the one that seemed most germane to today's events. It was a paper of some two and a half thousand words, jointly authored by an academic and a well-known journalist and commentator. The title was: Keeping the Fires Burning: Media Strategies for Sustaining and Harnessing the Energies behind the Referendum Result.

Doug flipped to the first page. The paper began:

The EU referendum result of 23 June 2016 presents a great, and unexpected, opportunity to further the aims that Imperium has always supported.

The narrow victory for the Leave campaign represented a coalition of different groups, all of whom wanted something different from Brexit. Some voted to restore sovereignty and to repatriate laws, some to reduce immigration and to increase border controls, some were hoping to restore Britain's sense of self-worth as an independent nation, while some (a small minority, perhaps, but the group with which Imperium is itself most closely aligned) voted to liberate Britain from the EU's oppressive tax and other regulations and allow it to become a genuine free-trading country with its principal endeavours directed towards Asian and US markets.

Thus we have an opportunity for radical and permanent change. However, the window of opportunity is small. It must not be allowed to close altogether.

A complete, immediate, root-and-branch break from the EU would have been the ideal outcome, but given the smallness of the Leave majority, arguing that a mandate for this exists is problematic. The government has embarked upon a protracted period of negotiations and, while we have had some success in arguing for the imposition of a deadline to leave (currently set at 29 – 03 – 2019) this will be followed by a transitional period of two years or more. The grave danger regarding such a gradual and incremental process of departing the EU is that public enthusiasm for

Brexit might wane if negative economic effects start to become apparent.

This paper will set out the steps we can take to minimize this danger, with specific emphasis on the role played by the building of friendships and informal alliances with the print and broadcast media, thereby putting the Foundation in a position to influence editorial direction and tone. (A separate paper will be prepared on social media strategy.) Imperium already has excellent and close relationships with a number of broadsheet and tabloid newspaper editors: these contacts must be renewed regularly and exploited to the full.

Our central argument is that the various and disparate forms of discontent which led 51.9% of voters to vote Leave must not be allowed to fade away until the Brexit process is complete. This discontent is the energy which will power our programmes. If Brexit was fuelled, first and foremost, by a sense on the part of many of the British people that the political class had betrayed them, that sense of betrayal must be sustained. Indeed, it can now be focused more accurately since, with the reframing of Leave's narrow majority as the 'will of the people', public anger will be turned most effectively on those members of the political and media establishment who can be portrayed as frustrating that will...

 ## 思考与讨论

(1) 本杰明移居欧洲大陆生活的原因和意义是什么？
(2) 索菲与伊恩离婚和复婚的原因和政治文化内涵是什么？
(3) "脱欧宝贝"的象征意义是什么？
(4) "再见了，古老的英格兰"，古老的英格兰指的是什么？
(5) 作者为何要写"Brexit"与"Brixit"两词使用之间的争议？
(6) 本杰明创作小说《动荡》的原因是什么？

 ## 拓展阅读

[1] Tew, P. *Jonathan Coe: Contemporary British Satire*. London: Bloomsbury Publishing, 2018.

[2] Linder, E. Brexit-Tales from a Divided Country: Fragmented Nationalism in Anthony Cartwright's *The Cut*, Amanda Craig's *The Lie of the Land*, and Jonathan Coe's *Middle England*. Leiden: University of Leiden, 2020.

[3] 乔修峰."再见了，古老的英格兰":〈英格兰中部〉与后脱欧时代英国的排外情绪[J].外国文学动态研究,2021(6):5-15.

三、伊恩·麦克尤恩

（一）伊恩·麦克尤恩简介

伊恩·麦克尤恩出生于英国汉普郡的奥尔德肖特，在利比亚、德国、新加坡等地度过童年时光，12岁时被父母送入英国萨福克郡名为沃尔夫斯通·霍尔的公立学校学习，随后分别于萨塞克斯大学获得英语学士学位，于东英吉利大学获得文学硕士学位。

麦克尤恩的文学创作包括长篇小说、短篇小说集、儿童小说、剧本和纪实文学。麦克尤恩用英语写作，他的作品多于英国出版发行，并被翻译成 30 多种语言在多个国家出版。麦克尤恩通过使用重复、拼贴、意识流、黑色幽默、讽刺等叙事手法刻画了一个异化的、恐怖的文本世界，向读者展示人类行为和心理的复杂性，引发读者对当代社会弊病和人类情感、道德问题的关注和思考。麦克尤恩的创作主题包括：一、科技和人工智能带给人类社会的机遇与挑战及其对人类感知和理解世界方式的影响；二、人性的阴暗和扭曲，包括叛逆、暴力、俄狄浦斯情节等；三、友谊、爱情、家庭等亲密关系的反复无常和不可靠；四、不同历史时刻英国社会的混乱状态，如二战、冷战、爱尔兰恐怖活动、英国脱欧等。麦克尤恩对人类内心世界深入而透彻的洞察、对当代英国社会问题关注以及复杂的叙事技巧使他成为当代英国文学史上最受关注的作家之一。

麦克尤恩的创作生涯始于短篇小说。迄今为止，他已出版四部短篇小说集，包括《最初的爱情，最后的仪式》(*First Love，Last Rites*，1975)、《床笫之间》(*In Between the Sheets*，1978)、《短篇故事》(*The Short Stories*，1995)和《我的紫色芳香小说》(*My Purple Scented Novel*，2016)；十七部小说，包括《水泥花园》(*The Cement Garden*，1978)、《只爱陌生人》(*The Comfort of Strangers*，1981)、《时间中的孩子》(*The Child in Time*，1987)、《无辜者》(*The Innocent*，1990)、《黑犬》(*Black Dog*，1992)、《爱无可忍》(*Enduring Love*，1997)、《阿姆斯特丹》(*Amsterdam*，1998)、《赎罪》(*Atonement*，2001)、《星期六》(*Saturday*，2005)、《在切瑟尔海滩上》(*On Chesil Beach*，2007)、《追日》(*Solar*，2010)、《甜牙》(*Sweet Tooth*，2012)、《儿童法案》(*The Children Act*，2015)、《坚果壳》(*Nutshell*，2016)、《像我一样的机器》(*Machines Like Me*，2019)、《蟑螂》和《课程》(*Lessons*，2022)。

麦克尤恩的其他作品还包括电视剧本《杰克·弗利的生日礼物》(*Jack Flea's Birthday Celebration*，1976)和《模仿游戏》(*The Imitation Game*，1981)；电影剧本《庄稼汉的午餐》(*The Ploughman's Lunch*，1983)、《酸甜》(*Soursweet*，1988)和《好儿子》(*The Good Son*，1993)；儿童小说《罗斯·布兰奇》(*Rose Blanche*，1985)和《空想家》(*The Daydreamer*，1994)以及纪实文学《科学》(*Science*，2019)。

麦克尤恩的短篇小说集《最初的爱情，最后的仪式》获 1976 年毛姆奖；小说《只爱陌生人》获 1981 年布克奖提名；小说《黑犬》获 1992 年布克奖提名；小说《阿姆斯特丹》荣获布克文学奖；小说《赎罪》获 2001 年布克奖提名；小说《星期六》获詹姆斯·泰特·布莱克纪念奖；2000 年麦克尤恩被授予"大英帝国勋章"；2011 年获以色列耶路撒冷奖，被《泰晤士报》评为"1945 年以来最著名的英国作家"。

（二）《蟑螂》简介

《蟑螂》是一部政治讽刺小说，它是对卡夫卡《变形记》的创造性模仿。故事主人公是一只蟑螂，某一天夜晚它占据了英国首相吉姆·萨姆斯的身体。在与自己的新身体进行了一番斗争和适应之后，蟑螂/吉姆开始实施逆转主义运动计划。这场运动旨在实现货币流向的逆转，即人们为自己的工作付钱，却能在购物消费时获得报酬。这场看似荒谬无比的计划最终被成功实施，其中不可忽略的原因是除外交大臣以外的所有内阁成员都是人类形态的蟑螂。他们的目的是使人类贫困堕落，以此实现蟑螂一族的幸福。在逆转主义运动成功后，蟑螂离开寄居的人类身体，回到了自己的蟑螂形态。

小说中吉姆能够成功实施逆转主义计划的一个重要原因是他对新闻媒体的利用，麦克尤恩借此表明新闻媒体对政治事件的重要影响。英国"拉金"号渔船在法国海域非法捕捞时，由于大雾天气被法国军舰无意撞毁。吉姆杜撰了法国蓄意挑衅的假新闻，宣称死去的六位渔民是为国牺牲的伟大英雄，并通过媒体大肆宣传来激起英国民众的爱国情绪和愤怒情绪，将这场偶然性的悲剧变成一桩举国关注的政治事件。吉姆成功地利用了公众舆论，通过引发一场外交丑闻，转移了公众对逆转主义必然给英国经济带来毁灭性打击的注意力，推动了逆转主义计划的实施。

在政客和媒体的煽动下，英国民众的投票行为已不是理性思考的结果，而是一种"盲目的集体服从"[1]。公投结果看似由英国民众自主投票产生，但其实只是意识形态国家机器操控下的产物，正如吉姆所说，他们"盲目地跟随我们进入未来"[2]，但是根本不知道他们即将面对的是什么。

除了对英国内部逆转主义运动的讽刺，麦克尤恩也对英国实施这一计划时的国际反应进行了描写，以此批判其他国家对英国脱欧的态度。首先，麦克尤恩把美国总统塔珀刻画成一个支持逆转主义运动的反复无常的人物。在一次口误中，他将英国即将实施的逆转主义一词说成了"复仇主义"（Revengelism），暗示整个逆转主义计划是英国对欧盟的报复，塔珀鼓励吉姆完成这一计划并让欧盟去承受由此引发的"黑暗时刻"[3]。不同于塔珀，德国总统对英国的逆转主义计划提出了质疑并觉得难以接受，他质疑吉姆"为什么，为了什么目的，你要分裂你的国家[……]，还假装我们是你的敌人?"[4]。作为欧盟成员国的德国对英国脱欧的行为难以理解，认为这不仅分裂了英国，损害了英国国家的利益，也让他们从盟友变成敌人，损害了整个欧盟的利益。

整个小说的讽刺基调在结尾时蟑螂们蚕食同类的情节描写中得到了进一步强化。蟑螂们最后回归了自己的原始形态，它们在马路上过红灯时，同伴兰开斯特被一辆汽车碾死在了柏油路上，"从他的壳下挤出一堆浓稠的乳白色物质，一种非常受欢迎的美味"[5]。此时的蟑螂们并没有感到悲伤，反而是从同伴的尸体中嗅出了食物的美味。因此它们抬起它的尸体，准备以它为食。麦克尤恩借此批判政客们为了自己的利益，不惜残害同胞，毫无人性可言。

（三）作品选读：《蟑螂》

Excerpt 1[6]

The origins of Reversalism are obscure and much in dispute, among those who care. For most

---

① McEwan, I. *The Cockroach*. London: Jonathan Cape, 2019, p.32.
② Ibid. p.84.
③ Ibid. p.29.
④ Ibid. p.29.
⑤ Ibid. p.100.
⑥ Ibid. pp.25 – 31.

of its history, it was considered a thought experiment, an after-dinner game, a joke. It was the preserve of eccentrics, of lonely men who wrote compulsively to the newspapers in green ink. Of the sort who might trap you in a pub and bore you for an hour. But the idea, once embraced, presented itself to some as beautiful and simple. Let the money flow be reversed and the entire economic system, even the nation itself, will be purified, purged of absurdities, waste and injustice. At the end of a working week, an employee hands over money to the company for all the hours that she has toiled. But when she goes to the shops, she is generously compensated at retail rates for every item she carries away. She is forbidden by law to hoard cash. The money she deposits in her bank at the end of a hard day in the shopping mall attracts high negative interest rates. Before her savings are whittled away to nothing, she is therefore wise to go out and find, or train for, a more expensive job. The better, and therefore more costly, the job she finds for herself, the harder she must shop to pay for it. The economy is stimulated, there are more skilled workers, everyone gains. The landlord must tirelessly purchase manufactured goods to pay for his tenants. The government acquires nuclear power stations and expands its space programme in order to send out tax gifts to workers. Hotel managers bring in the best champagne, the softest sheets, rare orchids and the best trumpet player in the best orchestra in town, so that the hotel can afford its guests. The next day, after a successful gig at the dance floor, the trumpeter will have to shop intensely in order to pay for his next appearance. Full employment is the result.

Two significant seventeenth-century economists, Joseph Mun and Josiah Child, made passing references to the reverse circulation of money, but dismissed the idea without giving it much attention. At least, we know the theory was in circulation. There is nothing in Adam Smith's seminal The Wealth of Nations, nor in Malthus or Marx. In the late nineteenth century, the American economist Francis Amasa Walker expressed some interest in redirecting the flow of money, but he did so, apparently, in conversation rather than in his considerable writings. At the crucial Bretton Woods conference in 1944, which framed the post-war economic order and founded the International Monetary Fund, there occurred in one of the sub-committees a fully minuted, impassioned plea for Reversalism by the Paraguayan representative Jesus X. Velasquez. He gained no supporters, but he is generally credited with being the first to use the term in public.

The idea was occasionally attractive in Western Europe to groups on the right or far right, because it appeared to limit the power and reach of the state. In Britain, for example, while the top rate of tax was still eighty-three per cent, the government would have had to hand out billions to the most dedicated shoppers. Keith Joseph was rumoured to have made an attempt to interest Margaret Thatcher in "reverse-flow economics" but she had no time for it. And in a BBC interview in April 1980, Sir Keith insisted that the rumour was entirely false. Through the nineties, and into the noughties, Reversalism kept a modest profile among various private discussion groups and lesser-known right-of-centre think tanks.

When the Reversalist Party arrived spectacularly on the scene with its populist, anti-elitist message, there were many, even among its opponents, who were already familiar with the "counter-flow" thesis. After the Reversalists won the approval of the American president, Archie Tupper, and even more so when it began to lure voters away, the Conservative Party began, in reaction, a slow drift to the right and beyond. But to the Conservative mainstream, Reversalism remained, in the ex-chancellor George Osborne's words, "the world's daftest idea". No one knows which economist or journalist came up with the term "Clockwisers" for those who preferred money to go round in the old and tested manner. Many claimed to have been first.

On the left, especially the "old left", there was always a handful who were soft on Reversalism. One reason was that they believed it would empower the unemployed. With no jobs to pay for and plenty of time for shopping, the jobless could become seriously rich, if not in hoarded money, then in goods. Meanwhile, the established rich would be able to do nothing with their wealth other than spend it on gainful employment. When working-class Labour voters grasped how much they could earn by getting a son into Eton or a daughter into Cheltenham Ladies' College, they too began to raise their aspirations and defect to the cause.

In order to shore up its electoral support and placate the Reversalist wing of the party, the Conservatives promised in their 2015 election manifesto a referendum on reversing the money flow. The result was the unexpected one, largely due to an unacknowledged alliance between the working poor and the old of all classes. The former had no stake in the status quo and nothing to lose, and they looked forward to bringing home essential goods as well as luxuries, and to being cash rich, however briefly. The old, by way of cognitive dimming, were nostalgically drawn to what they understood to be a proposal to turn back the clock. Both groups, poor and old, were animated to varying degrees by nationalist zeal. In a brilliant coup, the Reversalist press managed to present their cause as a patriotic duty and a promise of national revival and purification: everything that was wrong with the country, including inequalities of wealth and opportunity, the north—south divide and stagnating wages, was caused by the direction of financial flow. If you loved your country and its people, you should upend the existing order. The old flow had merely served the interests of a contemptuous ruling elite. "Turn the Money Around" became one of many irresistible slogans.

The Prime Minister who had called the referendum resigned immediately and was never heard of again. In his place there emerged a compromise candidate, the lukewarm Clockwiser James Sams. Fresh from his visit to Buckingham Palace, he promised on the steps of Downing Street to honour the wish of the people. The money would be turned around. But, as many economists and other commentators had predicted in the low circulation press and unregarded, specialist journals, it was not so easy. The first and overwhelming question concerned overseas trade. The Germans would surely be happy to receive our goods along with our hefty payments. But they would surely not reciprocate by sending their cars to us stuffed with cash. Since we ran a trade deficit, we would soon be broke.

So how was a Reversalist economy to flourish in a Clockwise world? Negotiations with our most important trading partners, the Europeans, stalled. Three years went by. A mostly Clockwise parliament, torn between common sense and bending to the people's will, could offer no practical solutions. Sams had inherited a slim majority and flailed about between passionate factions in his party. Despite that, he was known to some newspapers as Lucky Jim, for it could have been far worse: Horace Crabbe, the leader of the opposition, was himself an elderly Reversalist of the post-Leninist left.

While Sams dithered, and his Cabinet remained divided along several lines of dissent, a purist faction on the Conservative backbenches was hardening its position. Britain must go it alone and convert the rest of the world by example. If the world failed to follow, so much the worse for it. This was ROC. Reversalism in One Country. Then the song and the graffiti were everywhere—Roc around the Clock. We had stood alone before, in 1940, after the fall of France, when German Nazi terror was engulfing Europe. Why bother with their automobiles now? But Sams held back, promising everything to all sides. Most economists, City journalists, business leaders and the entire financial sector predicted economic catastrophe if Sams went the way of the hard Reversalists. Banks, clearing houses, insurance brokers and international corporations were already relocating abroad. Eminent scientists, Nobel laureates, despaired in high-profile letters to the press. But on the street, the popular cry was lusty and heartfelt: get on with it! There was a mood of growing anger, a reasonable suspicion of having been betrayed. A newspaper cartoon depicted Jim Sams as Shakespeare's Gloucester, blinded, teetering on the chalk cliff's edge while Edgar, a tough John Bull Reversalist, urged him to jump.

Then, without warning and to general amazement, Sams and his wavering Cabinet seemed to find their courage. They were about to leap.

Excerpt 2[①]

From *Hansard*, 19 September, Vol. 663 Priorities for Government

The Prime Minister (James Sams)

With permission, Mr Speaker, I shall make a statement on the mission of what is, in effect, a new Conservative government. When the bill returns to this house, Mr Speaker, our mission will be to deliver Reversalism for the purpose of uniting and re-energising our great country and not only making it great again, but making it the greatest place on earth. By 2050 it is more than possible, and less than impossible, that the UK will be the greatest and most prosperous economy in Europe. We will lie at the centre of a new network of reverse-flow trade deals. We will be the best on the

---

① McEwan, I. *The Cockroach*. London: Jonathan Cape, 2019, pp. 45 – 48.

planet in all fields. We will be the earth's home of the electric airplane. We will lead the world in not wrecking our precious planet. That same world will follow our shining example and every nation will reverse its money flow in order not to be left behind—*[Interruption.]*

Mr Speaker

Order. There is far too much noise in this Chamber. Too many members think it is all right for them to shout out their opinions at the prime minister. Let us be clear: it is not.

The Prime Minister

Mr Speaker, I applaud your intervention. This government is no longer divided. Myself and all the ministers are one body and we speak with one mind. We are formidable in our unity. The Bill will therefore pass. Nothing will stand in our way. We are turbocharging the civil service to prepare for the transition. We will move swiftly to accelerate and extend our trade deals beyond brave St Kitts and Nevis. Until that time, we proclaim Reversalism in One Country. We will stand alone just as we have stood alone in the past. A lot of negativity about Reversalism has been wildly overdone. This is no time for faint Clockwise thinking. Let no one doubt it, the money flow is about to change direction—and about time, too. On day one, on R-Day, the beneficial effects will be felt on both macro and micro levels. On R-Day, for example, our newly empowered police might pull over a recklessly speeding motorist and hand through the window two fifty-pound notes. It will be that driver's responsibility, in the face of possible criminal charges, to use that money to work and pay for more overtime, or find a slightly better job. This is just one example, Mr Speaker, of how Reversalism will stimulate the economy, incentivise our brilliant citizens, and render our democracy more robust.

Reversalism will bless our future—clean, green, prosperous, united, confident and ambitious. When, together, we bend our sinews to the task, the dead hand of Clockwise economics and its vast bureaucracy of enterprise-denying rules and Health and Safety impediments will be lifted from us, all of us, one by one. And very soon, it will be lifted from all the nations on earth. We stand at the beginning of a golden age. Mr Speaker, I commend this future to the house just as much as I commend this statement.

Several hon. Members rose—

Mr Speaker

Order.

[Continues.]

Excerpt 3[①]

In the afternoon, before the last Cabinet meeting, the PM sent all the staff home and arranged for the policeman on the front door to keep it ajar. All Cabinet members were to leave their

---

① McEwan, I. *The Cockroach*. London: Jonathan Cape, 2019, pp. 95 – 100.

borrowed bodies tidily at their ministry desks, ready for the return of their rightful owners. Jim left his own body on the bed upstairs. Thus, for the meeting itself, he imposed a strict dress code: exoskeletons. He had thought it would be fitting to convene on the Cabinet room table, but once they had assembled in the room, it looked an awfully long way up and rather tricky, since the table legs were highly polished. So they gathered in a corner of the room behind a wastepaper bin and stood in a proud circle. The PM was about to launch on his opening remarks but was cut off by a rendition of "Happy Birthday", sung in lusty unharmonious chirrups. Afterwards they looked nervously towards the door. The duty policeman had not heard them.

The Cabinet meeting was conducted in pheromone, which runs at ten times the speed of standard English. Before Jim could speak, Jane Fish proposed a vote of thanks. She praised the PM's "single-mindedness coupled, unusually, with rambunctious charm and humour." Britain now stood alone. The people had spoken. The genius of our party leader had got them over the line. Their destiny was in their hands. Reversalism was delivered! No more dithering and delay! Britain stood alone!

As she called out the beloved slogans she was overcome with emotion and could not go on, but it did not matter. Rising applause, an earnest susurration of carapaces and vestigial wings greeted her words. Then each Cabinet minister added a few words, ending with the new foreign secretary, Humphrey Batton, recently promoted from the Ministry of Defence. He led everybody in a round of "For He's a Jolly Good Fellow".

To give his speech, the PM stepped into the centre of the circle. As he spoke, his antennae quivered with passion and he rotated slowly on the spot to catch everyone's attention.

"My dear colleagues, thank you for these kind thoughts. They touch me deeply. In these closing moments of our mission, our duty is to the truth. There is one that we have never concealed from our brilliant citizens. For the mighty engines of our industry, finance and trade to go into reverse, they must first slow and stop. There will be hardship. It might be punishing in the extreme. I don't doubt that enduring it will harden the people of this great country. But that is no longer our concern. Now that we have cast off our temporary, uncongenial forms, there are deeper truths that we may permit ourselves to celebrate."

"Our kind is at least three hundred million years old. Merely forty years ago, in this city, we were a marginalised group, despised, objects of scorn or derision. At best, we were ignored. At worst, loathed. But we kept to our principles, and very slowly at first, but with gathering momentum, our ideas have taken hold. Our core belief remained steadfast: we always acted in our own best interests. As our Latin name, blattodea, suggests, we are creatures that shun the light. We understand and love the dark. In recent times, these past two hundred thousand years, we have lived alongside humans and have learned their particular taste for that darkness, to which they are not as fully committed as we are. But whenever it is predominant in them, so we have flourished.

Where they have embraced poverty, filth, squalor, we have grown in strength. And by tortuous means, and much experiment and failure, we have come to know the preconditions for such human ruin. War and global warming certainly and, in peacetime, immoveable hierarchies, concentrations of wealth, deep superstition, rumour, division, distrust of science, of intellect, of strangers and of social cooperation. You know the list. In the past we have lived through great adversity, including the construction of sewers, the repulsive taste for clean water, the elaboration of the germ theory of disease, peaceful accord between nations. We have indeed been diminished by these and many other depredations. But we have fought back. And now, I hope and believe that we have set in train the conditions of a renaissance. When that peculiar madness, Reversalism, makes the general human population poorer, which it must, we are bound to thrive. If decent, good-hearted, ordinary people have been duped and must suffer, they will be much consoled to know that other decent, good-hearted, ordinary types like ourselves will enjoy greater happiness even as our numbers grow. The net sum of universal wellbeing will not be reduced. Justice remains a constant."

"You have worked hard on our mission these past months. I congratulate and thank you. As you have discovered, it is not easy to be Homo sapiens sapiens. Their desires are so often in contention with their intelligence. Unlike us who are whole. You have each put a human shoulder to the wheel of populism. You have seen the fruits of your labour, for that wheel is beginning to turn. Now, my friends, it is time to make our journey south. To our beloved home! Single file please. Remember to turn left as you go out the door."

He did not mention it, but he knew that every minister in his Cabinet understood the perils that lay ahead. It was just after 4 p.m. on a cloudy afternoon when they slipped through the open door and past the duty policeman. They welcomed the winter gloom. Because of it, they did not see the little creature scurrying towards Number Ten to resume its life. Within half an hour Jim's group was passing under the gates of Downing Street into Whitehall. They crossed the pavement and climbed down into the gutter. The mountain of horse dung had long gone. The moving forest of rush-hour feet thundered above them. It took ninety minutes to reach Parliament Square and it was here that tragedy struck. They were waiting for the lights to change and were preparing to make their dash across the road. But Trevor Gott, the chancellor of the Duchy of Lancaster, got ahead of himself, as he sometimes did, and ran out too soon and disappeared under the wheel of a rubbish truck. When the traffic stopped the entire Cabinet ran out into the road to help him. He lay on his back, truly two-dimensional. From under his shell, there was extruded a thick, off-white creamy substance, a much-loved delicacy. There would be a heroes' banquet that night and what fun it would be, with so many extraordinary stories to tell. Before the lights changed again, his colleagues had just enough time to pick him up and place the extrusion reverently on his underbelly. Then, with six ministers each taking a leg, they bore him away to the Palace of Westminster.

思考与讨论

(1) 麦克尤恩为什么把吉姆·萨姆斯比作莎士比亚《李尔王》中的葛罗斯特？

(2) 吉姆如何平衡自己的人类身体与昆虫身份？

(3) 如何看待吉姆这一人物形象？

(4) 吉姆要实现的最终目标是什么？

(5) 吉姆在小说结尾时的演讲有何意义？

(6) "变形"叙事的作用是什么？

 拓展阅读

［1］ Head, D. Ed. *The Cambridge Companion to Ian McEwan*. Cambridge: Cambridge University Press, 2019.

［2］ Leith, S. *The Cockroach* by Ian McEwan Review—Bug's Eye View of Brexit. *The Guardian*. Sep. 26, 2019. ［https://amp. theguardian. com/books/2019/sep/26/the-cockroach-ian-mcewan-review-sam-leith］

［3］ 陈丽."变形"的多重阐释:论麦克尤恩〈蟑螂〉的"脱欧"叙事［J］.当代外国文学,2021(3): 155－161.

第四章
当代英国战争小说

对英国而言,兴也战争,衰也战争。昔日的大英帝国辉煌无比,皇家海军所向披靡,海外殖民地无数,可谓战无不胜,但经历了一战和二战后,英国国力迅速衰落,国际霸主已悄然易主,留给英国人无尽的惆怅和今非昔比的感慨。

第二次世界大战后,美国和苏联迅速崛起成为世界超级大国,英国的霸主地位一去不返。随着英国前殖民地国家纷纷独立,英国版图逐渐缩小,英国人不得不面对帝国不再的现实。

二战后不久,冷战开启,以美国为首的北约和以苏联为首的华约关系紧张,战争危机令人担忧。文学界关注、反思战争,英国战争小说繁盛不息,不仅写二战,还有关于一战、马岛战争、海湾战争,甚至印度兵变的小说。不仅专于战争题材的小说家书写战争,甚至连长期专事其他题材的小说家,如詹姆斯·格雷厄姆·巴拉德(James Graham Ballard, 1930—2009)和莫·海德(Mo Hayder, 1962—2021)也投笔书写战争。

当代英国战争小说既避开传统战争小说的宏大叙事,也缺少英雄形象,多以普通人,甚至边缘人物为叙事中心,主人公从以往的缄默者变成叙述者,小说以普通士兵、普通平民的视角展示战争景象。当代英国战争小说不仅描述战争造成的灾难,展现战争带给人们的创伤,揭示战争的残酷性,还承载着描写爱情、亲情与人性的善与恶,并以战争为背景怀恋与反思大英帝国的责任。小说家笔下不仅有欧洲的战场,还有亚洲等东方战场,在书写东方时抛却不掉英国人的傲慢与偏见。当代英国战争小说并非清一色以现实主义手法叙述战争,而是凭借主题的多元性和形式的多样性展现出爱情小说、成长小说、日记体小说、历史小说、间谍小说、自传体小说等诸多文类的特征。叙事并不总是线性展开,非线性叙述颇受青睐。

概而言之,当代英国战争小说在主题和艺术上主要有以下特点:主题的多元性、东方主义情节、文类混杂、非线性叙事。

第一节　当代英国战争小说主题的多元性

当代英国战争小说不仅呈现战争的残酷性,承载爱情、亲情与人性,还以战争为线索反思大英帝国。

战争是残酷的,无论是士兵还是平民都会受到战争的伤害,因而战争灾难是战争文学最常见的主题。

塞巴斯蒂安·福克斯的小说《鸟鸣》通过主人公斯蒂芬的战友们写给家人的信件,从侧面展现战争的苦难。前线士兵遭受随时失去生命的威胁,后方的平民饱受战争的摧残,战争灾难随时可能发生在他们身上,食物短缺,生病得不到有效的医治,只能忍受疾病的折磨。士兵和平民都无助无奈地活着,唯一的希冀就是尽早停战。

帕特·巴克的《重生三部曲》将战争前线的残酷场面和军人遭受的严重战争创伤呈现给读者。小说聚焦饱受战时神经官能症困扰的普通士兵。残酷的战争场面对参战士兵如梦魇般无时不在。不仅军人遭受身体和精神摧残,平民百姓同样遭受战争的苦难。巴克在小说中描写了战时平民的艰难生活。城里的女性为了生计在军工厂生产枪弹等战争必需品,不仅工作时间过长,而且工作环境对人的身体和皮肤造成伤害。但在战争时期,这样的工作却成了一份因报酬较高而难得的好工作。乡村百姓的生活同样举步维艰,养鸡场因战时物资短缺、饲料价格上涨,入不敷出难以为继。

爱情是当代英国战争小说的另一常见主题。塞巴斯蒂安·福克斯的《鸟鸣》虽然聚焦主人公斯蒂芬·雷斯福德一战的作战经历,但也讲述了斯蒂芬与法国女子伊莎贝拉相遇、相爱、分离的爱情故事。斯蒂芬与伊莎贝拉在战前相识相爱,因战争而分开。怀孕的伊莎贝拉担心斯蒂芬无法承担起家庭的责任,于是决定离开他回到家乡。战争爆发后,斯蒂芬成为一名士兵,在战场上经历了许多痛苦和恐怖的时刻。伊莎贝拉是斯蒂芬的精神支柱。战争结束后,伊莎贝拉已经离世,留下了一个女儿。斯蒂芬决定照顾女儿。《鸟鸣》通过斯蒂芬和伊莎贝拉的爱情故事,展现了战争对人们生活的影响以及人们在战争的阴影下对爱情和希望的追寻。

迈克尔·莫波格的《柑橘与柠檬啊》是一部以一战为背景的小说。故事的主人公是一位名叫托马斯(他的家人称其为“小托”)的年轻士兵,他在战场上回忆起了自己的爱情经历。小托的爱情故事始于他的童年时光,他一直暗恋着一个名叫莫莉的女孩。然而,这段感情并非一帆风顺。随着时间的推移,小托发现自己一直崇拜的哥哥查理也爱着莫莉,这使得三人之间的关系变得微妙。最终,查理与莫莉结为夫妻。战争爆发后,小托和查理应征入伍。在战场上,查理为保护弟弟小托违抗军令,被判处死刑。在查理被处决的前一天晚上,小托陪伴着他度过了最后的时光。他们回忆起了一起度过的快乐童年以及与莫莉相处的美好时光。《柑橘与柠檬啊》中的爱情故事充满了悲伤,展示了人们在战争中对爱情和亲情的渴望和坚守。

当代英国战争小说通过对战争的残酷、对生命的摧残和对人性的挑战等方面的描写,表达对战争的反思和批判,使读者能够更加深刻地认识到战争的后果,引发人们对和平的诉求和对战争的抵制。在战争中,人们可能会丧失理智,变得冷酷无情,甚至犯下残忍的罪行。战争扭曲人性,使人丧失道德底线。安迪·麦克纳布的《战火实录》中安迪等人在伊拉克被俘后惨遭羞辱,不仅遭受严刑拷打,还被剥夺了衣服和食物,甚至被迫舔尝粪便。

战争是残酷的,它考验着人性。当代英国战争小说中闪烁着人性的光辉。在杰克·希金斯的二战小说《德国式英雄》中,施泰因纳等人组成的突击小队虽是德国军人,却有善良的一面,他们对军人这一身份有着无限的忠诚和荣誉感。虽然他们与英国的战争立场不同,但因其英勇救人、不滥杀无辜而受到英国村民的尊重。这些德国军人牺牲后,这些普通村民不惜冒着生命危险为其秘密立碑并加以守护。

当代英国战争小说也是怀古思今的平台。J. G. 法瑞尔(J. G. Farrell，1935—1979)的《克里希纳普尔之围》(*The Siege of Krishnapur*，1973)就是一部怀恋和反思帝国的小说。小说借助印度反抗英国的历史事件，重新讲述了发生在 1857 年的印度士兵将英国殖民者围困在克里希纳普尔的故事。该小说获得 1973 年布克奖。借助这部小说，法瑞尔表达了对此次兵变原因的思考和对大英帝国衰落的反思。

1857 年英印军队的涂油子弹事件是印度民族起义的导火索。英国殖民高压政治导致印度爆发了民族大起义。虽然这次起义以失败告终，但埋下了印度人民仇恨英国殖民者的种子。印度长期作为英国殖民地，直到 1947 年才脱离英国获得独立。印度独立的道路曲折漫长，1857 年的印度民族起义是印度争取独立的先声。

法瑞尔以细腻的笔触揭示了当时的殖民者心态。英国殖民者虽被印度士兵围困在克里希纳普尔长达十个月之久，但他们始终对英国的道德传统和军事优势自鸣得意，始终保持着宗主国殖民者高高在上的姿态。

法瑞尔在英印历史事件发生近一百年后书写这段历史，以文学的形式再现战争场面，对大英帝国的衰落进行了反思。但小说刻意淡化英国对印度的殖民统治，将涂油子弹事件描述为英国军官对印度文化无知而酿成的大错，既无反省意识，更无批判效果。

第二节　当代英国战争小说东方书写中的东方主义

英国是对外发动战争最多的国家之一，也是在一战和二战中参与世界各地战事最多的国家之一。当代英国战争小说中，不仅有对欧洲的描述，也有对东方的描述，在东方书写中存在着或多或少的东方主义色彩。

詹姆斯·格雷厄姆·巴拉德于 1985 年创作的自传体小说《太阳帝国》(*Empire of the Sun*)的故事背景是二战时期的上海。巴拉德本人童年在上海的生活经历促发了《太阳帝国》的创作，但小说并未客观地呈现二战时期真实的上海。小说以一位天真而茫然的少年视角揭开了战争残酷的一面，在巴拉德淡定的文字叙述之下却隐藏着西方的帝国与殖民意识。小说以少年主人公的视角和经历，片面地构造了 20 世纪三四十年代的上海，文字中充斥着对东方他者的丑化与贬低。

莫·海德于 2004 年创作的以南京大屠杀为主题的作品《南京的恶魔》(*The Evil of Nanking*)是另一部具有东方主义意蕴的当代英国战争小说。小说揭露了日本士兵令人发指的罪行，再现了当时南京如同地狱般的血腥恐怖场景。虽然海德对日军暴行的记叙符合史实，但对小说主要人物——中国人史重明及其妻子的刻画存在明显的东方主义倾向，充满对东方人形象的扭曲和贬低。小说将中国人形象刻意丑化，尽显人物言谈举止的怪异、荒诞。

法瑞尔的《克里希纳普尔之围》同样是一部充满东方主义色彩的战争小说。作为殖民者的英国人从未真正去了解印度人和印度文明，在他们眼中，印度人野蛮低劣，印度文明仍处于低级阶段。这种狂妄自大的民族心理势必导致英国殖民者与印度人之间的对立与冲突并最终导致英国殖民统治的终结。法瑞尔通过小说主人公的言行展现了英国人自视甚高的心理：他们不仅自诩为世界文明的传播者，而且以怜悯的心态对待这些处于"蛮夷"地区的印度人。英国殖民者认为英国的殖民给印度带来了文明的福音,使"愚昧"的印度人民沐浴到了知识的甘霖,英国对印度的统治是"文明"对"野蛮"的救赎,印度人民理应理解和感激英国人。

正如萨伊德所言,"对东方事物富于想象的审察或多或少建立在高高在上的西方意识"[①]之内,"东方主义是一种思维方式,其核心思想是西方优秀、东方低劣,其实质是西方对东方的傲慢与偏见"[②]。被扭曲和被妖魔化了的东方形象已经深深根植于西方人的集体无意识中。当代英国战争小说家们的东方书写中难免存在东方主义的成分,究其根本,是作者的东方主义意识形态的无意识流露。

第三节　当代英国战争小说的文类混杂

当代英国战争小说的特点之一是文类的混杂,其中包括爱情小说、成长小说、日记体小说、历史小说、间谍小说、自传体小说等文类。文类混杂的创作方式为战争小说带来了多元化的审美效果,增加了对读者的吸引力,提高了读者的阅读和探索兴趣。

塞巴斯蒂安·福克斯的《鸟鸣》以一战为背景,聚焦主人公斯蒂芬·雷斯福德的一战的经历。其间,小说还讲述了斯蒂芬与法国女子伊莎贝拉之间曲折的爱情故事,所以《鸟鸣》也是一部爱情小说。除了战争与爱情外,《鸟鸣》的故事从 1910 年主人公斯蒂芬前往法国遇见伊莎贝拉开始,一直延续到 20 世纪 70 年代两人的外孙女伊丽莎白发现斯蒂芬的战时日记。伊丽莎白通过外祖父的日记了解了过去,重新认识了自己,因而《鸟鸣》带有成长小说的色彩。小说中有大量日记,记述了众多事件,《鸟鸣》也具有明显的日记体小说痕迹。

当代英国战争小说除了对前线战场的描述外,还有对后方战场的描写,杰克·希金斯的《德国式英雄》和《无路可退的士兵》(*Night of the Fox*,1986)就属于此类作品。两部小说叙述了二战战场背后的故事,再现了战争中的"灰色地带"——鲜为人知的间谍战,因此两部作品也可被看作间谍小说。弗·福赛斯的《上帝的拳头》(*The Fist of God*,1994)也属于此类作品。福赛斯将小说的主要叙事时间和地点定为海湾战争中的伊拉克。在高科技和信息化的时代,战争各方势力为获得战争的最终胜利,除了在主要战场剑拔弩张外,还在主战场外展开间谍行动。间谍行动成功与否是决定信息化战争胜负的关键。

亲历战争的将士也书写战争。安迪·麦克纳布和克里斯·瑞安曾是英国空军特种部队成员,曾一起参加海湾战争中代码为"B20"的特别军事行动,退役后都成为作家。以海湾战争的参战经历为蓝本,他们分别创作了《战火实录》(*Brave Two Zero*,1993)和《逃脱的那个人》(*The One That Got Away*,1995)。两部小说均带有浓重的自传色彩,因而也可将其归入自传体小说之列。

---

①　爱德华·W·萨伊德:《东方学》,王宇根(译),北京:生活·读书·新知三联书店,1999 年,第 10 页。
②　刘国清:《漠视、蔑视与凝视——南京大屠杀英语小说中的东方主义》,载《当代外国文学》2018 年第 2 期,第 28 页。

第四节　当代英国战争小说的非线性叙事

当代英国战争小说呈现叙事多元化趋势,倒叙、插叙、复调、嵌套等非线性叙事方式不一而足,为作品增色添彩。

巴克的《重生三部曲》大量使用倒叙、插叙和复调结构。在《重生》中,小说主要人物之一的英国军官萨松因创作反战诗歌而被送到战时医院接受治疗,在与心理医生瑞夫斯的谈话中,萨松通过倒叙讲述了战场上的经历。巴克对战争残酷现实的描写,使读者对萨松的反战行为有了更深刻的理解。在《门中眼》中,倒叙被用来展示主人公普莱尔的童年经历和他的战争回忆。这些回忆揭示了普莱尔的心理创伤和他恐怖的战争经历。在《幽灵之路》中,倒叙同样被用来展示人物的内心世界。瑞弗斯以倒叙的方式回忆过去,描写战争对自己的影响,这些回忆有助于读者理解瑞弗斯对战争受害者产生强烈同情心的原因。

除了倒叙,《重生三部曲》还频繁使用插叙的手法。插叙被用来展示人物的回忆、梦境和幻觉。插叙片段揭示了人物在战争中所经历的创伤,以及他们应对创伤的心理机制。《重生》中,主人公萨松的诗歌被用作插叙,展示了他对战争的看法和感受。在《幽灵之路》中,以插叙形式出现的普莱尔的梦境和幻觉揭示了他在战场上的经历以及与家人的关系。在《门中眼》中,插叙被用来展示主人公普莱尔在战争中的道德困境及其身份危机。插叙的写作手法使故事丰富多彩,作品的主题更加鲜明深刻,使读者对战争的残酷和人性的复杂有了更深刻的认识。

复调在《重生三部曲》中表现为多个角色的交织、多种叙事手法的并用和多个主题的并置。不同的经历和观点相互交织,展现出战争对人们的心理、道德和社会的复杂影响。在《门中眼》中,巴克通过比利·普赖尔的经历探讨了战争对个人身份的影响,以及战争中道德的模糊界限。在《幽灵之路》中,瑞弗斯的回忆和他在南太平洋的经历揭示了战争与殖民主义之间的联系。

嵌套结构在当代英国战争小说中被用来展示不同时间线和人物之间的联系,呈现这些人物在战争与和平时期的不同经历。福克斯的小说《鸟鸣》内含主人公斯蒂芬在三个不同时间段里的故事,分别是:20世纪前十年的法国生活、第一次世界大战参战经历和20世纪70年代的英国生活。在这三个时间段中,福克斯通过嵌套结构展现主要人物斯蒂芬的生活以及他与其他人物的关系。在20世纪前十年的法国部分,小说主要围绕斯蒂芬与法国女子伊莎贝拉的爱情故事展开。爱情故事被嵌套在第一次世界大战的战争故事中,使读者在战争背景下更加深刻地理解了斯蒂芬与伊莎贝拉之间的爱情。在第一次世界大战期间的部分,故事主要关注斯蒂芬在战场上的经历,以及他与战友的友谊。这段时间的故事被嵌套在20世纪70年代的英国故事中。嵌套结构展现了战争对家庭和后代的影响,以及人们如何在战争中寻找希望和勇气。在20世纪70年代的英国故事部分,斯蒂芬的孙女伊丽莎白,她试图了解祖父的过去以及第一次世界大战对家庭生活的影响。这段时间的故事将前两个时间段的故事嵌套其中,读者在不同代际的视角下理解战争、爱情、家庭等主题。

本章选取的作家及其代表作品如下:詹姆斯·法瑞尔及其代表作《克里希纳普之围》、J.G.巴拉德及其代表作《太阳帝国》、帕特·巴克及其代表作《鬼魂之路》。

第五节　主要作家介绍与代表作品选读

一、詹姆斯·法瑞尔

（一）詹姆斯·法瑞尔简介

詹姆斯·法瑞尔是二战后英国杰出小说家，1935 年出生于英格兰默西赛德郡首府利物浦，父亲是英格兰人，母亲是爱尔兰人。法瑞尔早年随全家移居爱尔兰，在当地接受几年学校教育后，进入英格兰的一所寄宿学校，就读期间展现出一定的写作才能。1956 年，法瑞尔进入牛津大学布拉兹诺斯学院法律专业学习，在一次橄榄球比赛中受伤后被确诊为小儿麻痹症，康复之后他的右臂落下了残疾。牛津大学毕业后，法瑞尔先后在法国和美国工作学习，1969 年结束了耶鲁大学的研究生课程，最终定居伦敦并在那里完成他的大部分文学创作。1979 年法瑞尔在爱尔兰溺水身亡。

詹姆斯·法瑞尔以历史小说见长，他的作品既有恢宏的历史叙事，又兼具幽默的笔触和细腻的描写，具有独特的魅力。法瑞尔的创作生涯开始于他在法国教书两年后，他的第一部小说《从别处来的人》（*A Man From Elsewhere*，1963）围绕法国文艺复兴、华沙起义等历史事件，以忧郁的笔调描写了对二者的哲学思考。1970 年，法瑞尔的第四部小说，也是他的成名作《困境》（*Troubles*）问世。这部作品后来成为他的《帝国三部曲》（*Empire Trilogy*）的首卷，因其对 1919 年至 1921 年间爱尔兰反英民族解放运动的深刻描写赢得当年的乔法纳瑞·法伯纪念奖。他用这笔奖金前往印度旅行，在参观著名的"英国总督府遗址"时获得了创作《帝国三部曲》第二部《克里希纳普之围》的灵感，该作品于 1973 年出版后获布克奖。1978 年，法瑞尔出版了小说《新加坡争夺战》（*The Singapore Grip*）。作为帝国三部曲的最后一部，该作品讲述了 1942 年的新加坡沦陷。之后法瑞尔又着手创作另一部关于印度的小说《山中避暑地》（*The Hill Station*），但最终并未完成。

法瑞尔的历史小说通过描写英国殖民地人民和殖民者的殖民地生活，体现出当代英国人的怀旧情绪和对昔日大英帝国盛况的追思，其作品打破了纯文学小说与通俗小说之间的界限，以严谨客观又不失风趣幽默的叙述独树一帜。

（二）《克里希纳普之围》简介

《克里希纳普之围》再现了 1857 年印度士兵反对英国殖民统治的斗争，讲述了英国维多利亚时期发生在印度次大陆一个孤立的殖民地上的印度雇佣兵哗变的故事。

1857 年至 1858 年印度北部和中部发生了英国雇佣军中的印度士兵反抗英国殖民统治的民族起义。1857 年初，英印殖民当局采用的 1852 式恩菲尔德来福枪膛使用动物脂肪作为润滑剂，这种油脂由猪油和牛油混合而成。由于在打开枪膛装填子弹前，士兵需先用嘴咬破涂有牛油和猪油的弹筒包装纸，这一做法违背了雇佣兵中印度教徒和伊斯兰教徒的宗教信仰，士兵们拒绝使用这种步枪。在印度士兵中还流传着一种说法,即使用新式涂油子弹是英国当局强迫印度士兵改信基督教的阴谋,印度士兵和英国指挥官矛盾激化,爆发起义,史上将之视为印度第一次独立战争。

《克里希纳普之围》以突然出现在税务官霍普金斯先生公文箱中的印度薄饼开篇,随后印度雇佣兵爆乱的谣言从远处传来,然而英国殖民者仍然对他们的军事和道德优势充满信心。但当他们发现被围困时,他们身上殖民者的劣根性——残暴、浮躁和占有欲便显露无遗。被围困的英国殖民者失去了作为所谓帝国文明代表的权威,他们用以粉饰文明的殖民文化和生活方式的表象被揭穿。

小说中处处可见大英帝国和殖民地文化、殖民者和殖民地人民之间的冲突。克里希纳普的外科医生邓斯特普尔与内科医生麦克纳布虽然一起负责治疗伤员,但他们在疗法上存在分歧。当麦克纳布医生带着伤员回来时,邓斯特普尔取笑麦克纳布医生打算尝试用布顿加蚂蚁对伤口进行治疗,而这是他从印度当地人那里学来的方法。霍普金斯先生始终坚持英国的文明是优势文明,正如他认为其一直挂在嘴边的"科学"优于殖民地文明那样,而弗勒利则辩驳称谈论优势文明是错误的,根本没有那么回事。他认为任何文明都是坏的,它腐蚀人们内心高贵而自然的本能。小说深刻批判了大英帝国殖民者傲慢自大的心态,通过戏仿的手法将殖民行径去神秘化,颠覆了"优等种族""优势文明"的帝国神话。

《克里希纳普之围》于1973年出版后不久便获得了第五届布克奖。凭借其对人物性格丰满的刻画、对维多利亚殖民文化的质疑与反思,以及其文字蕴含的冒险精神和优秀的文学品质,《克里希纳普之围》被广泛认为是一部现代经典之作,并被评为近50年来最优秀的英语小说之一。

(三) 作品选读:《克里希纳普之围》①

From the beginning of the siege the Union Jack had floated from the highest point of the Residency roof and had constantly drawn the fire of the sepoy sharpshooters. Passing into the shadow of the Residency on his way to Cutter's battery, the Collector looked up and saw that the flag was once again in difficulties.

The halyards had been severed and great splinters of wood had been struck off the shaft so that it looked as if a strong wind might well bring it down altogether. On one occasion, indeed, the staff had been completely shattered and a great cheer had gone up from the sepoys... but as soon as darkness permitted, another staff and new halyards had been erected in its place. The flag was crucial to the morale of the garrison; it reminded one that one was fighting for something more important than one's own skin; that's what it reminded the Collector of, anyway. And somewhere up there, too, in the most perilous position of all within the enclave, there was an officer crouching all day behind the low brick wall of the tower, watching the movements of the sepoys with a telescope.

While the Collector's eyes had been lifted to the sky a loathsome creature had approached him along the ground; it was the hideous pariah dog, looking for Fleury. Since the Collector had last set eyes on the animal a ricocheting musket ball had taken off part of its rat-like tail, which now

---

① Farrell, J. G. *The Siege of Krishnapur*. London: George Weidenfeld & Nicolson Ltd, 1993, pp. 198 - 215.

terminated in a repulsive running sore. The Collector launched a kick at it and it hopped away yelping.

As the Collector raised his eyes again for a last, inspirational glance at the flag before moving on, a dreadful smell of putrefaction was borne to his nostrils and he thought: "I must have something done about that tonight before we have an epidemic." This smell was no longer coming from the bodies of men and horses rotting outside the ramparts as it had done for the first few days; these, thank Heaven, had now been cleaned by the kites, vultures and jackals; it came from the dead horses and artillery bullocks that lay scattered over the Residency lawns and gardens, hit by the random shot and shells that unceasingly poured into the compound. But there was also a powerful and atrocious smell from behind the wall he had built to shield the croquet court, which lay between the Residency and Dunstaple's house. Here it was that Mr Rayne, aided by Eurasians from the opium agency, conducted the slaughter and butchery of the Commissariat sheep, commandeered at the outbreak of the mutiny from the Krishnapur Mutton Club on the Collector's instructions.

The smell, which was so atrocious that the butchers had to work with cloths tied over their noses, came from rejected offal which they were in the habit of throwing over the wall in the hope that the vultures would deal with it. But the truth was that the scavengers of the district, both birds and animals, were already thoroughly bloated from the results of the first attack...the birds were so heavy with meat that they could hardly launch themselves into the air, the jackals could hardly drag themselves back to their lairs. And so, out of the garrison's sight, but not out of range of their noses, a mountain of corruption had steadily built up.

Combined with the animals scattered on the lawns, the smells from the hospital and from the privies, and from the human beings living in too close contact with insufficient water for frequent bathing, an olfactory background, silent but terrible, was unrolling itself behind the siege.

The back wall of Dr Dunstaple's house, which like the Residency was built of wafer-like red bricks, had been amazingly pocked by the shot which dashed against it; hardly a square foot of smooth surface remained now to be seen. In some places round shot had smashed through one wall after another so that if you had been unwise enough to raise your head to the appropriate angle you could have followed their passage through a series of rooms. After one such journey, the Collector had been told, a shot had finally burst through the wall into the Doctor's drawing-room on the other side of the building, scattering candlesticks and dropping them to roll along the carpet, right up to where Mrs Dunstaple and a group of disobedient ladies playing truant from the suffocating air of the cellar were cowering under the piano. From these larger holes in the wall Enfield rifles bristled and occasionally orange flowers blossomed from their muzzles; the wall in the room behind them had been painted black so that no movement could be seen against them.

From the house a shallow trench had been dug out towards the crescent of earthworks behind which the cannons had been placed. Here, too, there was a pit about fourteen feet deep with a ladder against the side, down which the Collector now stiffly climbed. Lieutenant Cutter was standing at the bottom with his finger to his lips.

"Are they mining?"

"Yes. We're digging a listening gallery." Cutter described in a whisper what was happening: at the head of the gallery a man sat and worked with a short-handled pick or crowbar to loosen the earth; just behind him sat another man with an empty wine case to fill up with the loose earth; when full, this was drawn back by a rope.

The sepoys here were very close and it was thought inevitable that sooner or later they would begin mining, given the number of men at their disposal. For several nights the Collector had stayed up until dawn reading his military manuals by the light of an oil-lamp in his study to instruct himself in the art of military mining; only Cutter of the officers, two Cornish privates from Captainganj, and one or two Sikhs, had had any experience of mining before. What an advantage that knowledge can be stored in books! The knowledge lies there like hermetically sealed provisions waiting for the day when you may need a meal. Surely what the Collector was doing as he pored over his military manuals, was proving the superiority of the European way of doing things, of European culture itself. This was a culture so flexible that whatever he needed was there in a book at his elbow. An ordinary sort of man, he could, with the help of an oil-lamp, turn himself into a great military engineer, a bishop, an explorer or a General overnight, if the fancy took him. As the Collector pored over his manuals, from time to time rubbing his tired eyes, he knew that he was using science and progress to help him out of his difficulties and he was pleased. The inventions on his desk, the carriage which supplied its own track and the effervescent drinking vessel, watched him in silent admiration as he worked.

The Collector had learned that there are two cardinal rules of defensive mining...One is that your branch galleries (whose purpose is for listening to the approaching enemy miners) should run obliquely forward in order not to present their sides to the action of enemy mines...The other is that the distance between the ends of the branch galleries should be such that the enemy cannot burrow between them unheard (a distance which varies with the nature of the soil but which can be roughly taken as twenty yards).

The trouble with these cardinal rules, though wonderful in their way, was that they required a great deal of digging. No doubt they would have served perfectly if there had been enough men in the garrison to dig listening galleries in the approved manner, reaching towards the enemy like the spread fingers of a hand.

But Cutter lacked men. The best he and the Collector had been able to devise was a single lateral tunnel, slightly crescent-shaped to follow the contour of the ramparts, and which more resembled the hook of a man whose hand had been amputated.

The Collector, at the head of the gallery, strained his ears despondently for the scrape of the sepoy picks, but the only sound that came to them was the ghostly echo of a phrase of Vauban he had read: Place assiégée, place prise! For the Collector knew the truth of the matter: the sepoys did not even have to resort to mining. By using their artillery to make a breach in the defences and then digging a properly directed series of saps to approach it, they would be able to take the Residency in a matter of days. It was a commonplace of siegecraft that there was no way of countering such a methodical attack except by making sorties to harass the enemy and destroy his works... But where could he find the men to make sorties without hopelessly denuding the ramparts in several places?

Meanwhile Cutter, in a whisper, was explaining that he wanted to run an offensive gallery under the enemy lines and explode a mine of his own to breach their defences. With a sudden attack they might succeed in spiking or capturing the Sepoy cannons, in particular the eighteen-pounder which was slowly but surely reducing Dr Dunstaple's house to rubble. The Collector hesitated to agree to this... There was another difficulty: the shortage of powder. Anything less than, say, two hundred pounds of powder at a depth of twelve feet underground would be insufficient to make the required breach. Yet with two hundred pounds of powder you could fire a cannon a hundred times! And the slightest error of length or direction would mean that all this valuable powder would be thrown away fruitlessly.

"Very well," he said at length, "but make sure it does what it's supposed to."

Later, as he walked away, he recalled a work by another French military engineer, Cormontaingne, who had described in his imaginary Journal of the Attack of a Fortress the inevitable progress of a siege through its various stages up to the thirty-fifth day, ending with the words: "It is now time to surrender." That, at least, was one option not open to the Collector.

The Collector, conscious of himself gently floating in the blue prism of his daughters' telescope like a snake in a bottle of alcohol, now had to cross the most dangerous piece of ground within the enclave. He strode out firmly, pulling down the peak of his pith helmet and lowering his head as if walking into a blizzard. It was here on this lawn, green and wellwatered during the magnificent Indian winter, that he had been host to many enjoyable garden parties. Over there, beneath that group of now shattered eucalyptus trees, had stood the band of one of the infantry regiments. Once he had looked out from the upper verandah of the Residency as the bandsmen were assembling; it was evening and somehow the deep scarlet of their uniforms against the dark green of the grass had stained his mind with a serious joy... so that even now, in spite of everything, those two colours, scarlet and dark green, still seemed to him the indelible colours of the rightness of the world, and of his place in it. Looking towards the river as he skirted a shell crater, across a parched brown desert dotted with festering animals, he had to make an effort of imagination to perceive that this was indeed the same place where he and his guests had sat drinking tea.

From his pocket the Collector produced the last of his clean, white handkerchiefs (soon he, too, would be in the power of the dhobi who had been terrorizing the ladies with his new prices) and held it to his nose while he considered a new and disagreeable problem. By now so many gentlemen had been killed that a large quantity of stores and other belongings had been collected. What he had to decide was whether to allow them to be auctioned, as they would have been in normal times, or to confiscate them for the good of the community. Ultimately, it seemed to him, the question boiled down to this: was it right that only those who had money to buy these provisions in the event of a famine should survive? The Magistrate was not the ideal person to ask for his view on such a matter. As the Collector had feared he had been unable to restrain his sarcasm.

"In the outside world people perish or survive depending on whether they have money, so why should they not here?"

"This is a different situation," the Collector had replied, scowling. "We must all help each other and depend on each other."

"And must we not outside?"

"People have more resources in normal times."

"Yet many perish even so, simply because they lack money."

The Collector's sigh was muffled by the handkerchief as he reached the fiercely humming rib-cage, head and flanks of a horse which had collapsed there with the saddle still strapped ludicrously to what was now only a rim of bones. Further on there was the carcass of a water buffalo, its eyes seething, its head and long neck looking as if they had literally been run into the ground. The Collector was fond of water buffaloes, which he found to have a friendly and apologetic air, but he could not think why there should have been one on his lawn.

By the time he had paid a visit to the banqueting hall the light was beginning to fade; on his way back, the Collector removed his pith helmet to air his scalp. It was his belief, based as yet on no scientific evidence, that lack of air to the scalp caused premature baldness; for this reason he had taken a particular interest in the hat shown at the Great Exhibition which had had a special ventilation valve in the crown; moreover, when the present troubles had started he had been considering the most delicate and interesting experiment to evaluate this suspicion and which would have involved hiring natives in large numbers to keep their heads covered and submit to certain statistical investigations.

At the thought of statistics, the Collector, walking through the chaotic Residency garden, felt his heart quicken with joy... For what were statistics but the ordering of a chaotic universe? Statistics were the leg-irons to be clapped on the thugs of ignorance and superstition which strangled Truth in lonely byways. Nothing was able to resist statistics, not even Death itself, for the Collector, armed with statistics, could pick up Death, sniff it, dissect it, pour acid on it, or see if it was soluble. The Collector knew, for example, that in London during the second quarter of 1855 among 3,870 men of the age of 20 and upwards who had succumbed, there had been 2 peers of the realm, 82 civil servants, 2S policemen, 209 officers, soldiers and pensioners, 103 members of the learned professions including 9 clergymen, 4 barristers, 23 solicitors, 3 physicians, 12 surgeons, 43 men of letters, men of science or artists, and twelve eating- and coffee-house keepers... and so much more the Collector knew. He knew that out of 20,257 tailors 108 had passed to a better world; that 139 shoemakers had gone to their reward out of 26,639... and that was still only a fraction of what the Collector could have told you about Death. If mankind was ever to climb up out of its present uncertainties, disputations and self-doubtings, it would only be on such a ladder of objective facts.

Suddenly, a shadow swooped at him out of a thin grove of peepul trees he was passing through. He raised a hand to defend himself as something tried to claw and bite him, then swooped away again. In the twilight he saw two green pebbles gazing down at him from beneath a sailor cap. It was the pet monkey he had seen before in the shadow of the Church; the animal had managed to bite and tear itself free of its jacket but the sailor hat had defied all its efforts. Again and again, in a frenzy of irritation it had clutched at that hat on which was written HMS John Company... but it had remained in place. The string beneath its jaw was too strong.

Near the trees the Collector could see some dogs slumbering beside a well used by gardeners in normal times for the complicated system of irrigation which brought water to the Residency flower beds. He could recognize certain of these dogs from having seen them in the station bobbery pack on their way to hunt jackals with noisy, carefree young officers; they included mongrels and terriers of many shapes and sizes but also dogs of purer breed... setters and spaniels, among them Chloë, and even one or two lap-dogs. What a sad spectacle they made! The faithful creatures were daily sinking into a more desperate state. While jackals and pariah dogs grew fat, they grew thin; their soft and luxurious upbringing had not fitted them for this harsh reality. If they dared approach the carcass of a horse or bullock, or the fuming mountain of offal beside the croquet wall, orange eyes, bristling hair and snapping teeth would drive them away.

It was dark by the time the Collector's tour was over and the night was brilliantly starlit. Tonight, as always, in the darkness around the enclave he could see bonfires burning. Were they signals? Nobody knew. But every night they reappeared. Other, more distant bonfires could be seen from the roof, burning mysteriously by themselves out there on the empty plain where in normal times there was nothing but darkness.

During the daytime it had become the custom for a vast crowd of onlookers to assemble on the hillslope above the melon beds to witness the destruction of the Residency. They came from all over the district, as to a fair or festival; there was music and dancing; beyond the noise of the guns the garrison could hear the incessant sighing of native instruments, of flutes and sitars accompanied by finger-drums; there were merchants and vendors of food and drink, nuts, sherbets and sugarcane... sometimes a caprice of the wind would torment the garrison with a spicy smell of cooking chicken as a relief from the relentless smell of putrefaction (at intervals the Collector would stop and curse himself for having so ignorantly ordered the offal to be jettisoned to windward); in addition there were the *ryots* from the indigo plantations and those from the opium fields in bullock-carts or on foot, there were the peasants from the villages, the travelling holy men, the cargoes of veiled Mohammedan women, the crowds from the Krishnapur bazaars and even one or two elephants carrying local *zemindars*, surrounded like Renaissance princes with livened retainers. This cheerful and multifarious crowd assembled every day beneath awnings, tents and umbrellas to watch the *feringhees* fighting for their lives. At first the Collector had found this crowd of spectators a bitter humiliation, but now he seldom gave it a thought. He had issued orders that no powder was to be wasted on dispersing them, even though they were well within range.

The Collector still had one more call to make; this was to a shed with open, barred windows which formed the very last of the long row of stables, now converted into the hospital. It was here, in the days when life in Krishnapur had been on a grander scale, that a former Resident, anxious to emulate the local rajahs, had kept a pair of tigers. Now, where once the tigers had lived, Hari strode endlessly back and forth behind the bars, while the Prime Minister, sitting on a pile of straw, followed his movements with expressionless eyes.

Hari had been moved here "for the good of the community", causing the Collector another severe inflammation of conscience. It had been noticed that the one part of the enclave which the sepoys had been careful to avoid hitting with their cannons was precisely the spot where Hari was quartered. Word of his whereabouts had no doubt filtered out to the sepoy lines by way of the native servants who continued to defect one by one as the plight of the garrison became more desperate. Once this unfortunate discovery had been made, the Collector found himself morally obliged (it was his duty) to make use of it. So Hari had been turned out of the relative comfort and safety of the Residency and lodged in the tiger house which conveniently happened to be adjacent to the hospital.

Hari had not taken well to this change. Watching him as the days went by, the guilty Collector had noticed signs of physical and moral decline. His fat cheeks, always pale, had taken on a greyish tinge. He had complained, first that he could not eat, then that the food he was given was not fit for a human being...It was true that the food was not very good, but what could one expect during a siege? And food was not the only trouble. Always inclined to petulance, Hari had now taken on a permanent look of discontent.

"You should go outside, visit people, talk with them, perhaps even do a spot of fighting," the Collector had counselled him, increasingly disturbed by the change which was taking place in Hari's character. Hari had been so full of enthusiasm, so interested in every new and progressive idea. And now he was so listless!

"You give permission to going outside camp, perhaps?"

"Well, no, not outside the ramparts, of course."

"Ha!"

"But you must occupy yourself. You can't remain here in this room for ever. Who knows how long the siege will go on?"

"Correct! You keep me prisoner but you pretend to yourself that you do not keeping prisoner myself and Prime Minister. You want me to kill for British perhaps my own little brothers and sisters who plead with me for lives, raising little hands very piteously? I will not do it, Mr Hopkin, I will rather die than do it, I can assure you. It is no good. You torture me first. I still not killing little brother and sister."

"Oh, I say, look here... no one is asking you to kill your brother and sister. You mustn't exaggerate."

"Yes, you asking me to killing brother and sister and you asking Prime Minister to sticking with bayonet his very old widow mother lady!"

"Oh, what rubbish!"

"Oh, what rubbish, you say, but I knowing very different. All is not well that end well if I killing little babies for Queen, I assure you. I die rather than do that. Prime Minister also, to my way of thinking!"

The Prime Minister, sitting on his heap of straw, his eyes as expressionless as ever, had shown no sign of being partial either to killing babies or not killing them, or to anything whatsoever.

"If only the poor lad could have brought someone a bit more stimulating as a companion," the Collector had thought miserably. "He's pining away for lack of something to occupy his mind."

Once again the Collector had to take out his handkerchief and hold it to his nose, this time because he was passing the open doors and windows of the hospital. He could not shut his ears, though, to the cries and groans; he even believed he could hear the monotonous chanting of the Crimean veteran as he hurried by, but he already had enough to think about with Hari. As he approached the tiger house he braced himself for the inevitable reproaches. But today, for some reason, Hari's interest in the world seemed to have revived.

As usual he was striding up and down behind the bars while the Prime Minister sat passively on his heap of straw. There was a significant change, however. Hari was looking excited, indeed feverishly so... but something else had changed, too, and for a while the Collector could not think what it was. Then it came to him: the Prime Minister's head was bare. It was not simply that he had removed his French military cap, he had removed his hair as well. His skull was shaved and oiled, and it gleamed in the lamplight. For some reason it was covered by a hair net with a large mesh.

The Collector assumed that this shaving of the Prime Minister's skull had some religious significance; he knew that Hindus are always shaving their heads for one reason or another; but then he noticed that Hari's eyes kept returning to the gleaming cranium as to a work of art. Looking a little closer, he noticed that what he had taken for the strings of a net were, in fact, ritual lines drawn in ink on the Prime Minister's scalp.

"I become devotee of Frenloudji!" exclaimed Hari.

"Frenloudji?"

"Frenla-ji! Correct? Science of head!"

"Oh, phrenology! I see what you mean!"

"Correct! Let me explain you about phrenology... Most interesting science and exceedingly useful for getting the measure of your man... I have got measure of Prime Minister without least difficulties. You see, head is furnished with vast apparatus of mental organ and each organs extend from the gentleman's medulla oblongata, or top of spinal marrow, to surface of brain or cerebellum. Every gentleman possess all organ to greater or lesser degree. Let us say, he possess big organ of Wit, if he say very amusing things then organ of Wit is very big and powerful and we see large bump on right and left of forehead here..." and Hari pointed to a spot somewhat above each of the Prime Minister's eyebrows.

"This organ is very big in Mr F. Rabelais and Mr J. Swift. In Prime Minister not so big. In you, Mr Hopkin, not so big. In me, not so big." The Prime Minister fingered his sacred thread but offered no comment.

"The man who discovered this science, Dr Gall of Vienna, remove many skulls from people he had known in life. He found brain which is covered by dura mater..." (Hari pronounced this with relief, as if it were the name of an Indian dish) "has same shape as skull having during life. So that's why we see bump or no bump on Prime Minister's head."

"I see," said the Collector, who felt that his understanding of phrenology might be vulnerable to any further explanations from Hari.

"There are certain parts at base of brain, in middle and posterior regions, size of which cannot be discover during life and whose function therefore remain unknown. But some bumps we seen even though in difficult position. You see, for example... *Amativeness*..." Hari snatched up a book lent him by the Magistrate, and read: "Amativeness. The cerebellum is the organ of this propensity, and it is situated between the mastoid processes on each side... and so on and so forth... The size is indicated during life by the thickness of the neck at these parts. The faculty gives rise to the sexual feeling. In newborn children the cerebellum is the least developed of all the cerebral parts. It is to the brain as one to twenty and in adults as one to six. The organ attains its full size from the age of eighteen to twenty-six. It is less in females, in general, than in males. In old age it frequently diminishes."

Hari put the book down and beckoned the Collector to come and examine the Prime Minister.

"Amativeness is not very powerful organ in Prime Minister. In me, very powerful. In Father it is fearfully, fearfully powerful so that all other organ wither away, I'm thinking..." Hari laughed heartily and then suddenly clutched his organ of Wit.

"Well, I must be on my way, Hari," said the Collector sadly. How distressed he felt to see this young man's open mind tainted by the Magistrate! But before Hari allowed him to leave he insisted on staring indiscreetly for a long time at the back of the Collector's neck and even prodding it with a muttered, "Excuse liberty, please." His only verdict, however, was a cough and modestly lowered eyes.

As he was returning to the Residency he thought he heard a voice calling from the far side of the hospital, beyond the churchyard wall. He went to investigate and saw the faint silhouette of the Padre, digging wearily with a spade and muttering to himself as he worked. Beside the path the Collector dimly perceived three long forms sewn up in bedding.

"Padre, is there no one to help you?"

But the Padre made no reply, perhaps had not even heard. He went on digging and muttering to himself. The Collector could just hear his words: "...Man that is born of woman hath but a short time to live. He cometh up, and is cut down, like a flower; he fleeth as it were a shadow, and never continueth in one stay..."

The Collector spoke to him again, but still the Padre paid no attention. So in the end the Collector took the spade himself and made the Padre lie down on the path beside the corpses.

Then, for an hour or more the Collector dug steadily by himself. At first he thought: "This is easy. The working classes make a lot of fuss about nothing." But he had never used a spade in his life before and soon his hands became blistered and painful. He was invaded by a great sadness, then. The sadness emanated from the three silent figures sewn up in bedding and he thought again of his death statistics, but was not comforted...And as he dug, he wept. He saw Hari's animated face, and numberless dead men, and the hatred on the faces of the sepoys...and it suddenly seemed to him that he could see clearly the basis of all conflict and misery, something mysterious which grows in men at the same time as hair and teeth and brains and which reveals its presence by the utter and atrocious inflexibility of all human habits and beliefs, even including his own. Presently, he heard the Padre's voice whispering over the bodies in the darkness: "They shall hunger no more, neither thirst any more; neither shall the sun light on them, nor any heat. For the Lamb which is in the midst of the throne shall feed them, and shall lead them unto living fountains of waters: and God shall wipe away all tears from their eyes." When the Collector had finished digging two of the graves he helped the Padre carry the bodies over and bury them, and then set to work on the third grave. By the time a fatigue party came out of the darkness to relieve him he had composed himself again, which was just as well in the circumstances, for no garrison is encouraged by the sight of its commander in tears.

Now at last the Collector's long day was over. A lamp was burning in his study and in the glass of the bookcases he saw his own image, shadowy in detail, wearing an already rather tattered morning coat, the face also in shadow, anonymous, the face of a man like other men, who in a few years would be lost to history, whose personality would be no more individual than this shadowy reflection in the glass. "How alike we all are, really... There's so little difference between one man and another when one comes to think of it."

As he moved to turn out the lamp before going upstairs he thought how normal everything still was here. It might have been any evening of the years he had spent in Krishnapur. Only his ragged coat, his boots soiled from digging graves, his poorly trimmed whiskers, and his exhausted appearance would have given one to suspect that there was anything amiss. That and the sound of gunfire from the compound.

On his way upstairs he passed Miriam in the hall and without particularly meaning to he put his arm around her. She was on her hands and knees when this happened, searching the floor with a candle for some pearls she had dropped when the string she was wearing had broken; in spite of their increasingly ragged appearance it had become the habit for the ladies to wear all the jewellery they possessed for safe-keeping. They should have been quite easy to find but some had rolled away into the forest of dusty, carved legs of tables and chairs which here comprised the lumber of "possessions". When the Collector touched her she did not faint or seem offended; she returned the pressure quite firmly and then sat back on her heels, brushing a lock of hair out of her eyes with her knuckles because her hands were dirty. She looked at him for a long time but did not say anything. After a while she went on looking for her pearls and he went on his way upstairs. He did not know what had made him do that. It had been discouragement more than anything. At that moment he had been feeling the need for some kind of comfort... perhaps any kind would have done... a good bottle of claret, for example, instead. Still, Mrs Lang was a sensible woman and he did not think she would mind. "Funny creatures, women, all the same," he mused. "One never knows quite what goes on in their minds."

Later, while he was drinking tea at the table in his bedroom with three young subalterns from Captainganj a succession of musket balls came through the window, attracted by the oil lamp... one, two, three, and then a fourth, one after another. The officers dived smartly under the table, leaving the Collector to drink his tea alone. After a while they re-emerged smiling sheepishly, deeply impressed by the Collector's sangfroid. Realizing that he had forgotten to sweeten his tea, the Collector dipped a teaspoon into the sugar bowl. But then he found that he was unable to keep the sugar on the spoon: as quickly as he scooped it up, it danced off again. It was clear that he would never get it from the sugar-bowl to his cup without scattering it over the table, so in the end he was obliged to push the sugar away and drink his tea unsweetened. Luckily, none of the officers had noticed.

That night, as soon as he closed his eyes the bed on which he lay began to spin round and round; within a few seconds, it seemed, he had been drawn down into a sleep where shattering events raged back and forth over his unconscious mind. Gradually, however, they receded and he fell into a more calm, profound sleep... but not so profound that he could not hear, though at a great distance, the heart-rending screams of Mrs Scott giving birth a few rooms away on the next floor. Once, he suddenly started up in bed, thinking: "The poor mite! What a world to be born into!" but perhaps that was merely part of a long, sad, ineffably sad dream he had before dawn.

But as it turned out, the baby was not born alive and Mrs Scott herself, in spite of everything that was done to save her, sank rapidly and died before morning. In the first light Dr McNab, who had not slept at all, sat at a table by the window in the room where Mrs Scott had died (which formed part of the flagstaff tower), writing in his notebook the brief details of what had happened. He wrote: "Caesarean section. Felt head of child, which had come low down, suddenly recede; symptoms of ruptured uterus followed... The foetus could easily be felt through the abdominal walls and was apparently quite loose, while it could not be reached by the vagina; it was evident that the uterus had given way. The patient not yet in a very collapsed state, but declining rapidly. Proceeded to remove the foetus by gastrotomy... an incision about six inches in breadth was made in the median line between the umbilicus and pubes; the foetus was easily reached and, as expected was found loose in the peritoneal cavity; it was removed (dead) together with the whole of the cord and the placenta; not much haemorrh age occurred, nor was much blood found in the abdomen. Stimulants, opiates, etc. were liberally employed afterwards, but in spite of them the woman sank, and died in about three hours..."

Dr McNab paused for a moment in his writing and turned round in his chair to stare at the bed, which was now empty for Mrs Scott, sewn in her bedding, had been carried to the Church where she would lie until darkness came and it was safe to bury her. He frowned thoughtfully, as if trying to concentrate, then he went on writing.

In this room where throughout the night the most terrible shrieks of pain had echoed, there was now no sound to break the silence except the scratching of Dr McNab's pen-nib as he wrote and an occasional clink of china as he dipped it into the inkwell. Outside, the gunfire continued steadily.

 思考与讨论

（1）节选中为何多次提到科学和文明？税务官所想到的死亡统计数据体现了什么？

（2）节选中对克里希纳普附近的旁观者的描写有何用意？

（3）小说中对克里希纳普行政区的欧洲殖民者居住环境和该行政区所处的广大印度北部地区原住民生活环境的描写分别有何作用？

（4）小说中对英国殖民问题的反映体现在哪些地方？

（5）小说中女性角色的塑造是否具有维多利亚时代的女性风范？

（6）作者的帝国情结体现在哪里？

 **拓展阅读**

［1］Binns，R. *J. G. Farrell*. London：Methuen，1986.

［2］Ferrie，J. *The Siege of Krishnapur* by J. G. Farrell. *International Journal of Epidemiology*，Vol. 42，No. 2(2013)，pp. 371 - 378.

［3］Greacen，L. *J. G. Farrell：the Making of a Writer*. Cork：Cork University Press，2012.

［4］张金凤. 从疾病隐喻到帝国神话的破灭——解读法瑞尔的《克里希纳普之围》［J］. 国外文学，2012(2)：117 - 124.

二、J. G. 巴拉德

（一）J. G. 巴拉德简介

J. G. 巴拉德 1930 年生于中国上海，父亲就职于曼彻斯特纺织品公司，后被派往上海分公司。巴拉德的少年时期在上海度过，就读于教会学校，他熟悉上海的生活环境并在西式家庭和西方教育的影响下长大。珍珠港事件爆发后，巴拉德曾被关入日军在上海的龙华集中营，饱受苦难。二战结束后，巴拉德及其家人离开上海返回英国，那时巴拉德已经 16 岁。回到英国后，巴拉德进入剑桥大学国王学院攻读了两年医学。之后，他尝试了很多职业，也曾服役于英国皇家空军。从巴拉德的作品创作和写作风格中能够窥见其特殊的成长经历对他产生的巨大影响。年少时的战争记忆和丰富的人生经历为巴拉德的文学创作提供了丰富的养料。他的战争小说《太阳帝国》(*Empire of the Sun*，1984)就是关于他年少时战争经历的佳作。

巴拉德以科幻小说著称，是英国科幻小说新浪潮的代表。20 世纪科学技术飞速发展所带来的人类生活剧变引发了巴拉德对科幻小说的浓厚兴趣，促使他创作了一系列优秀科幻作品。人类生存与生态环境危机、科技时代人类的道德危机以及对人类与人类社会未来的焦虑是巴拉德科幻作品的主题。

在巴拉德 1962 年创作的小说《淹没了的世界》(*The Drowned World*)中，遭到破坏的大气电离层让全人类陷入巨大的生态和生存危机之中，失去大气层保护的地球成了一片汪洋，末日的阴影笼罩着整个人类社会。巴拉德聚焦末日危机与生态危机的作品深刻反映了作者对科技和社会发展所带来的负面问题的担忧与焦虑。

巴拉德笔下的未来世界中科技的发展并没有给人类文明带来曙光，反而造成了人类的异化。在小说《摩天楼》(*High-Rise*，1975)中，生活在具有先进设施的高楼中的居民变成充满原始本能的野蛮动物。小说中充斥着与道德和文明背道而驰的混乱、暴力与冲突，反映了人类文明、精神和道德的脆弱性以及人类社会未来潜在的危机。该小说由英国导演本·维特利改编为同名电影并于 2016 年上映。

巴拉德的另一部小说《撞车》(*Crash*)于 1973 年出版。加拿大导演大卫·柯南伯格将作品搬上电影银幕。该影片于 1996 年上映并一举斩获同年戛纳电影节评审团特别大奖。《撞车》《摩天楼》和出版于1974 年的《混凝土岛屿》三部小说组成了巴拉德著名的"都市灾难三部曲"(*Urban Disaster Trilogy*)。

在科幻小说上的杰出成就和对科幻小说的不懈创作使巴拉德获得"科幻小说之王"的美誉。

虽然巴拉德创作了大量的科幻小说,但他最为人知的还是其战争小说《太阳帝国》。

(二)《太阳帝国》简介

《太阳帝国》被视为巴拉德的自传体小说,其灵感来源于巴拉德同家人和上海租界中的其他白人在珍珠港事件后被日军关押进龙华集中营的遭遇。该小说讲述了居住在上海英租界的主人公吉姆在第二次世界大战期间与父母失散并被关入日军集中营,在残酷的生存条件下艰难求存的故事。小说从主人公吉姆的视角出发,让读者从落入战争旋涡中的孩童的角度重新审视战争,见证吉姆所代表的饱受战争摧残的儿童和普通人如何在战争时期畸形的生存环境中被改变和重塑,揭示了战争之下严酷的生存环境和无休止的暴力与死亡。

《太阳帝国》的主人公吉姆出生于中国上海租界中生活富足的外籍家庭。主人公和租界中其他外籍家庭的生活与同时期上海平民的生活形成了鲜明的对照。租界中外籍家庭所生活的五光十色、充满吸引力的上海与随处可见乞丐、艰难讨生活的劳动者与难民的上海奇异地交融在一起。珍珠港事件后,日军开始袭击租界中的白人,意外与父母失散的吉姆在寻找父母的过程中被友人家的保姆狠狠扇了耳光,隐藏在貌似平静的上海生活表面下深刻的阶级与民族矛盾可见一斑。

战争未将吉姆卷入其中之前,吉姆对于战争、飞机有着极其浓厚的兴趣,特别是在见识到日本轰炸机的威力后,吉姆对日本飞机充满兴趣,这种着迷甚至在吉姆被关进日军集中营后仍然存在。但日本人于1937年起对中国的全面侵略还是让吉姆亲眼见到了累累白骨、成千上万的难民和血流成河的战争的残酷。小说中,暴力与死亡描写随处可见,动荡的社会、疾病和贫穷所造成的灾难和死亡皆是在中国土地上日本人战争罪恶的体现。然而小说所展现的呆板、脸谱化甚至扭曲的中国人形象和吉姆对中国人个体与群体的单方面揣测也让作者难逃刻板化、丑化中国的嫌疑。

《太阳帝国》以很大篇幅记述了主人公吉姆被关进集中营后的遭遇。在第一章中提到了吉姆对真实战争的认识,在他看来,在真实战争里没人知道自己站在哪一边,没有胜利者,也没有敌人。集中营中的生活对人的改变验证了他的看法。在朝不保夕的生活中,生存是最大的问题,真正的敌人不再重要,威胁生存的一切才是真正的敌人。为了生存,在龙华的大多数俘虏都不得不同日本人合作。尽管吉姆潜意识中并不完全赞同,但三年集中营生活的捶打与消磨让他们中的大多数为求生存可以做任何事。随着物资的日益稀缺,他人的死亡不再令人悲伤,反而成了好事,因为这意味着能省下更多的资源。在日军节节败退后,为了能始终得到日本人的照顾,得到更多食物,吉姆甚至想要将自己算出的对美军飞机射程的事告诉日本人。尽管最终战争结束,吉姆平安获救,但局势并不乐观,这让吉姆陷入对第三次世界大战的焦虑之中。作为一部优秀的战争小说,《太阳帝国》曾入围英国布克奖,被誉为"关于二战的最佳英国小说",并在1987年被导演史蒂芬·斯皮尔伯格搬上电影荧幕,获得广泛关注。

(三)作品选读:《太阳帝国》[①]

On his way to the hospital, Jim paused to do his homework at the ruined assembly hall. From

---

① Ballard, J.G. *Empire of the Sun*. London: Grafton Books, 1985, pp.186-194.

the balcony of the upper circle he could not only keep an eye on the pheasant traps across the wire, but also bring himself up to date on any fresh activity at Lunghua Airfield. The stairway to the circle was partly blocked by pieces of masonry that had fallen from the roof, but Jim squeezed himself through a narrow crevice worn smooth by the camp's children. He climbed the stairway, and took his seat on the cement step that formed the first row of the balcony.

The Kennedy propped on his knees, Jim made a leisurely meal of the second potato. Below him, the proscenium arch of the assembly hall had been bombed into a heap of rubble and steel girders, but the landscape now exposed in many ways resembled a panorama displayed on a cinema screen. To the north were the apartment houses of the French Concession, their facades reflected in the flooded paddy fields. To Jim's right, the Whangpoo River emerged from the Nantao district of Shanghai and bent its immense way across the abandoned land.

In front of him was Lunghua Airfield. The concrete runway moved diagonally across its grassy table to the foot of the pagoda. Jim could see the barrels of the anti-aircraft guns mounted on its ancient stone decks, and the powerful landing lights and radio antennae fixed to the tiled roof. Below the pagoda were the hangars and engineering shops, each guarded by sandbag emplacements. A few elderly reconnaissance planes and converted bombers sat on the concrete apron, all that was left of the once invincible air wing that had flown from Lunghua.

Around the edges of the field, in the deep grass by the perimeter road, lay the wreckage of what seemed to Jim to be the entire Japanese Air Force. Scores of rusting aircraft sat on their flattened undercarriages among the trees, or lay in the banks of nettles where they had swerved after crashlanding with their injured crews. For months crippled Japanese aircraft had fallen from the sky on to the graveyard of Lunghua Airfield, as if a titanic aerial battle was taking place far above the clouds.

Already gangs of Chinese scrap-dealers were at work among the derelict planes. With the tireless ability of the Chinese to transform one set of refuse into another, they stripped the metal skins from the wings and retrieved the tyres and fuel tanks. Within days they would be on sale in Shanghai as roofing panels, cisterns and rubber-soled sandals. Whether this scavenging took place with the permission of the Japanese base commander Jim could never decide. Every few hours a party of soldiers would ride out in a truck and drive some of the Chinese away. Jim watched them running across the flooded paddies to the west of the airfield as the Japanese hurled the tyres and metal plates from the salvage carts. But the Chinese always returned to their work, ignored by the anti-aircraft gun-crews in the sandbag emplacements along the perimeter road.

Jim sucked his fingers, drawing the last taste of the sweet potato from his scuffed nails. The warmth of the potato eased the nagging pain in his teeth. He watched the Chinese scavengers at work, tempted to slip through the wire and join them. There were so many new marques of Japanese aircraft. Only four hundred yards from the pheasant traps was the crashed hulk of a

Hayate, one of the powerful high altitude fighters that the Japanese were sending up to destroy the Super fortress bombers on fire-raids over Tokyo.

The long grass between the camp and the southern edge of the airfield was rarely patrolled. Jim's practised eye searched the dips and gullies in the banks of nettles and wild sugar-cane, following the course of a forgotten canal.

A second gang of Chinese coolies was at work in the centre of the airfield, repairing the concrete runway. The men carried baskets of stones from the trucks parked among the bomb craters. A steamroller moved to and fro, manned by a Japanese soldier.

The sharp whistle of its valve-gear held Jim to his seat. The gang of coolies reminded him that he too had once worked on the runway. During the past three years, whenever he watched the Japanese aircraft take off from Lunghua, Jim felt an uneasy pride as their wheels left the concrete surface. He and Basie and Dr Ransome, along with those Chinese prisoners being worked to death, had helped to lay the runway that carried the Zeros and Hayates into the air war against the Americans. Jim was well aware that his commitment to the Japanese Air Force stemmed from the still fearful knowledge that he had nearly given his life to build the runway, like the Chinese soldiers buried in their untraceable lime pit beneath the waving sugar-cane. If he had died, his bones and those of Basie and Dr Ransome would have borne the Japanese pilots taking off from Lunghua to hurl themselves at the American picket ships around Iwo Jima and Okinawa. If the Japanese triumphed, that small part of his mind that lay forever within the runway would be appeased. But if they were defeated, all his fears would have been worth nothing.

Jim remembered those pilots of the dusk who had ordered him from the work gang. Whenever he watched the Japanese moving around their aircraft he thought of the three young pilots with their ground crew who had walked through the evening light to inspect the runway. But for the English boy wandering towards the parked aircraft the Japanese would not even have noticed the work gang.

The fliers fascinated Jim, far more than Private Kimura and his kendo armour. Every day, as he sat on the balcony of the assembly hall or helped Dr Ransome in the vegetable garden of the hospital, he watched the pilots in their baggy flying suits carrying out the external checks before climbing into the cockpits. Above all, Jim admired the kamikaze pilots. In the past month more than a dozen special attack units had arrived at Lunghua Airfield, which they used as their base for suicide missions against the American carriers in the East China Sea. Neither Private Kimura nor the other guards in the camp paid the least attention to the suicide pilots, and Basie and the American seamen in E Block referred to them as "hashi-crashies" or "screwy-siders".

But Jim identified himself with these kamikaze pilots, and was always moved by the threadbare ceremonies that took place beside the runway. The previous morning, as he worked in the hospital garden, he left his sewage pail and ran to the barbed-wire fence in order to see them leave. The three pilots in their white headbands were little older than Jim, with childlike cheeks and boneless noses. They stood by their planes in the hot sunlight, nervously brushing the flies from their mouths, faces pinched as the squad leader saluted. Even when they cheered the Emperor, shouting hoarsely at the audience of flies, none of the anti-aircraft gunners noticed them, and Private Kimura, striding across the tomato plots to call Jim from the wire, seemed baffled by his concern.

Jim opened his Latin primer and began the homework which Dr Ransome had set him: the entire passive tenses of the verb *amo*. He enjoyed Latin; in many ways its strict formality and its families of nouns and verbs resembled the science of chemistry, his father's favourite subject. The Japanese had closed the camp school as a cunning reprisal against the parents, who were trapped all day with their offspring, but Dr Ransome still set Jim a wide range of tasks. There were poems to memorize, simultaneous equations to be solved, general science (where, thanks to his father, Jim often had a surprise for Dr Ransome), and French, which he loathed. There seemed a remarkable amount of schoolwork, Jim reflected, bearing in mind that the war was about to end. But perhaps this was Dr Ransome's way of keeping him quiet for an hour each day. In a sense, too, the homework helped the physician to sustain the illusion that even in Lunghua Camp the values of a vanished England still survived. Misguided though this was, Jim was keen to help Dr Ransome in any way.

"Amatus sum, amatus es, amatus est..." As he recited the perfect tense, Jim noticed that the Chinese scavengers were running from the derelict aircraft. The work gang of coolies had scattered, throwing their baskets of stones to the ground. The Japanese soldier leapt from the steamroller and ran bare-chested towards the anti-aircraft emplacements, whose guns were searching the sky. Already a flicker of light came from Lunghua Pagoda, as if the Japanese were setting off a devotional firecracker. The sound of this lone machine-gun crossed the airfield, soon drowned by the complaining drone of an air-raid siren. The klaxon above the guardhouse in Lunghua Camp took up the call, a harsh rattle that drilled through Jim's head.

Excited by the prospect of an air raid, Jim peered at the sky through the open roof of the assembly hall. All over the camp the internees were running along the cinder paths. The men and women dozing like asylum inmates on the steps of the huts scrambled through the doors, mothers leaned from ground-floor windows and lifted their children to safety. Within a minute the camp was deserted, leaving Jim to conduct the air raid alone from the balcony of the assembly hall.

He listened keenly, already suspecting a false alarm. The air raids came earlier each day, as the Americans moved their bases forward across the Pacific and the Chinese mainland. The Japanese were now so nervous that they jumped at every cloud in the sky. A twin-engined transport plane flew across the paddy fields, its pilots unaware of the panic below.

Jim returned to his Latin primer. At that moment an immense shadow crossed the assembly hall and raced along the ground towards the perimeter fence. A tornado of noise filled the air, from which emerged a single-engined fighter with silver fuselage and the Stars-and-Bars insignia of the US

Air Force. Only thirty feet above Jim's head, the Mustang's wings were broader than the assembly hall. The fuselage was stained with rust and oil, but its powerful engine had the smooth drive of his father's Packard. The Mustang crossed the perimeter fence and hurtled along the concrete runway of the airfield, the height of a man's head above the deck. In its wake a whirlwind of leaves and dust boiled from the ground.

Around the airfield the anti-aircraft guns turned towards the camp. The tiers of Lunghua Pagoda crackled with light like the Christmas tree display outside the Sincere Company department store in Shanghai. Undeterred, the Mustang flew straight towards the flak tower, the noise of its guns drowned in the blare of another Mustang that swept across the paddy fields to the west of the camp. A third plane came in behind it, so low that Jim was looking down at the cockpit. He could see the pilots, and the insignia on their fuselages blackened by oil spraying from the engine exhausts. Two more Mustangs overflew the camp, and the wash from their engines tore the corrugated iron sheets from the roof of the barrack hut beside G Block. Half a mile to the east, between Lunghua Camp and the river, a second wing of American fighters swept in from the sea, so close to their own shadows on the empty paddy fields that they were hidden behind the lines of grave mounds. They rose as they crossed the perimeter of the airfield, then dived again to fire at the Japanese aircraft parked beside the hangars.

Anti-aircraft shells burst above the camp, their shadows pulsing like heartbeats on the white earth. A shell exploded in a searing flash above the assembly hall, stunning the air. Dust cascaded from the concrete roof and poured onto Jim's shoulders. Waving his Latin primer, Jim counted the dozens of shellbursts. Did the Mustang pilots realize that Basie and the American merchant seamen were imprisoned at Lunghua Camp? Whenever they attacked the airfield the fighter pilots hid until the last moment behind the three-storey dormitory blocks, even though this drew Japanese fire on to the camp and had killed several of the prisoners.

But Jim was glad that the Mustangs were so close. His eyes feasted on every rivet in their fuselages, on the gun ports in their wings, on the huge ventral radiators that Jim was sure had been put there for reasons of style alone. Jim admired the Hayates and Zeros of the Japanese, but the Mustang fighters were the Cadillacs of air combat. He was too breathless to shout to the pilots, but he waved his primer at them as they soared past under the canopy of anti-aircraft shells.

The first flights of attacking planes had swept across the airfield. Clearly visible against the apartment houses of the French Concession, they flew towards Shanghai, ready to strafe the dockyards and the Nantao seaplane base. But the anti-aircraft batteries around the runway were still firing into the air. Cat's cradles of tracer stitched the sky, threads of phosphorus knit and reknit themselves. At their centre was the great pagoda of Lunghua, rising through the smoke that lifted from the burning hangars, its guns throwing out an unbroken flak ceiling.

Jim had never before seen an air attack of such scale. A second wave of Mustangs crossed the paddy fields between Lunghua Camp and the river, followed by a squadron of two-engined fighter-bombers. Three hundred yards to the west of the camp one of the Mustangs dipped its starboard wing towards the ground. Out of control, it slid across the air, and its wing-tip sheared the embankment of a disused canal. The plane cartwheeled across the paddy fields and fell apart in the air. It exploded in a curtain wall of flaming gasoline through which Jim could see the burning figure of the American pilot still strapped to his seat. Riding the incandescent debris of his aircraft, he tore through the trees beyond the perimeter of the camp, a fragment of the sun whose light continued to flare across the surrounding fields.

A second crippled Mustang pulled away from the others in its flight. Trailing a plume of oily smoke, it rose through the anti-aircraft bursts and climbed into the sky. The pilot was trying to escape from the airfield, but as his Mustang began to lose height he rolled the craft on to its back and fell safely from the cockpit. His parachute opened and he dropped steeply to the ground. His burning plane righted itself, towed its black plume in a wavering arc above the empty fields, and then plunged into the river.

The pilot hung alone in the silent sky. His companions sped on towards Shanghai, their silver fuselages lost in the sun-filled windows of the French Concession. The hammering noise of their engines had gone, and the anti-aircraft fire had ceased. A second parachutist was coming down among the canals to the west of the airfield. A stench of burnt oil and engine coolant filled the disturbed air. All over the camp, miniature tornadoes of leaves and dead insects subsided and then whirled along the pathways again as they hunted for the slipstreams of the vanished Mustangs.

The two parachutes fell towards the burial mounds. Already a squad of Japanese soldiers in a truck with a steaming radiator sped along the perimeter road, on their way to kill the pilots. Jim wiped the dust from his Latin primer and waited for the rifle shots. The halo of light which had emerged from the burning Mustang still lay over the creeks and paddies. For a few minutes the sun had drawn nearer to the earth, as if to scorch the death from its fields.

Jim grieved for these American pilots, who died in a tangle of their harnesses, within sight of a Japanese corporal with a Mauser and a single English boy hidden on the balcony of this ruined building. Yet their end reminded Jim of his own, about which he had thought in a clandestine way ever since his arrival at Lunghua. He welcomed the air raids, the noise of the Mustangs as they swept over the camp, the smell of oil and cordite, the deaths of the pilots, and even the likelihood of his own death. Despite everything, he knew he was worth nothing. He twisted his Latin primer, trembling with a secret hunger that the war would so eagerly satisfy.

 思考与讨论

(1) 在选段中,作者从何种视角切入对战争进行了书写? 这一视角有何意义或独特之处?

（2）从选段中可以体现出主人公吉姆对战争抱有怎样的态度和立场？是什么造成了他对战争的态度？

（3）作者在文中刻画了一些中国人形象，这些中国人形象有何特点？如何看待作者对中国人的刻画？

（4）选段中塑造了怎样的日本人形象？如何看待主人公眼中的日本军人形象？

（5）伦塞姆医生给吉姆布置课业的原因是什么？医生和吉姆对此的不同观点说明了什么？两者在集中营中对民族身份的不同坚持和认知是怎样造成的？

（6）吉姆在战争中对生命产生了怎样的认知？如何看待这种观点？

 拓展阅读

［1］ Baxter, J. *J. G. Ballard*: *Contemporary Critical Perspectives*. London; New York: Continuum, 2008.

［2］ Francis, S. T. *The Psychological Fictions of J. G. Ballard*. London; New York: Continuum, 2011.

［3］ Kong, B. Shanghai Biopolitans: Wartime Colonial Cosmopolis in Eileen Chang's *Love in a Fallen City* and J. G. Ballard's *Empire of the Sun*. *Journal of Narrative Theory*. Vol. 39, No. 3 (2009), pp. 280 - 304.

三、帕特·巴克

（一）帕特·巴克简介

帕特·巴克是一位英国女小说家，生于英国约克郡索纳比。巴克自幼在外祖父母身边长大，深受外祖父的影响（她的外祖父是一战老兵，饱受战争创伤之苦），和"战争"结下了不解之缘。其代表作"战争三部曲"皆以一战为背景。1965 年巴克从伦敦政治经济学院毕业，之后进行了长达 16 年的历史和政治教学工作。1982 年巴克开始专心小说创作，并得到英国著名作家安吉拉·卡特（Angela Carter，1940—1992）的指导。2000 年，因其在文学上的卓越表现，巴克获得大英帝国指挥官勋章（CBE）。

帕特·巴克的小说创作始于 20 世纪 80 年代中期，早期作品反响平平。90 年代初，巴克发表第一部战争题材小说《重生》（*Regeneration*，1991），获英美两国文学评论界一致认可。巴克于 1993 年发表小说《门后的眼睛》（*The Eye in the Door*），获当年的英国卫报小说奖；1995 年发表《鬼魂之路》（*The Ghost Road*），获当年的布克奖。因皆涉及战争，且相互联系，《重生》《门后的眼睛》以及《鬼魂之路》被合称为"战争三部曲"。"三部曲"之后，巴克笔耕不辍，坚持创作，发表了心理小说《越界》（*Border Crossing*，2001）、宗教小说《双重视野》（*Double Vision*，2003）、战争小说《写生课》（*Life Class*，2007）等。

《重生》以历史人物神经科医生威廉·瑞弗思和英国作家西格弗里德·萨松为主人公，虚构了一场理智与感情的斗争。萨松参军后发现了战争的残酷和无情,因此不愿继续在部队服役。由于被认为精神异常,萨松被送到战地医院接受治疗,遇到了主治医师瑞弗思。一方面,瑞弗思竭尽全力想要"治愈"萨松,送他重回战地;另一方面,萨松绞尽脑汁想要说服瑞弗思,让他看清战争的残酷与无益。1997年,《重生》被改编成电影,由英国和加拿大两家电影公司联合推出。

《门后的眼睛》同样以一战为背景,聚焦男同性恋群体,呈现了英国在战争期间的一系列社会问题。一战期间,尤其是英国即将战败的时候,同性恋在当时的英国社会中会受到警方的缉捕,在英国军队中也不被允许。因此,英国的许多同性恋者终日惶惶不安,生活在恐惧之中。《门后的眼睛》关注社会非主流人群在一战期间的生存状态,拓展了欧洲文学对第一次世界大战的叙事主题。

(二)《鬼魂之路》简介

在《鬼魂之路》中,作者以主人公比利·普莱尔和威廉·瑞弗思医生的战时生活为主线,涉及战争、伦理、创伤等主题。通过对主要人物内心世界的描写,小说揭示了战争中人与人之间的复杂矛盾关系。

小说中,比利·普莱尔是一位热血青年,一心要为祖国参战。为了能重返战场,他不顾自己的身体状态,小心翼翼地隐瞒自己的哮喘病和缄默症。在被批准重回战场后,普莱尔满心欢喜。通过描写普莱尔对战场的向往,巴克揭示了英国社会中的一个独特现象:也许是源于英国中世纪的骑士精神,更多的是为了改变自己的阶级地位,许多热血青年选择上战场成为英雄。

因为满心都是对战场的向往,普莱尔虽与萨拉同居,却没娶她为妻的打算。当萨拉嘱咐普莱尔把他们的婚事告知他的母亲时,普莱尔保持沉默。普莱尔和街头妓女、军中战友都有亲密行为,而毫不知情的萨拉依然痴情地等待着他。普莱尔在拜访他的朋友瑞弗思时,也显得心不在焉。瑞弗思是普莱尔在战地医院住院期间的主治医生,两人因此成为了很好的朋友。当瑞弗思从医生的角度给普莱尔提出建议的时候,普莱尔只是频频看手表,害怕会赶不上回前线的火车;当瑞弗思从心理学方面提建议的时候,普莱尔只是付之一笑,便匆匆告辞。通过描写参军路上普莱尔对待恋人和朋友的态度,巴克展现了在战争的裹挟下,人与人之间淡薄的情感和混乱的伦理道德观。

回到战场上,普莱尔被指派负责毒气防护。当亲眼看到自己的副官被子弹打死时,普莱尔才想起瑞弗思的忠告,感到战争的恐怖。虽承认战争的可怕,普莱尔依然坚信打仗是他唯一要做的事情。然而,普莱尔还想到如果他战死沙场,无法回到祖国,那么他确实是一个愚蠢的人。在目睹了一个个战友阵亡之后,普莱尔也中弹身亡。巴克通过对普莱尔在战事中的心理描写,展示了普莱尔既向往战争,又向往生命的两难困境。

《鬼魂之路》的另一条叙事线围绕战地医生和人类学家威廉·瑞弗思的战地工作和文化考察回忆展开。在战地医院里,瑞弗思既救治身体伤残的哈里特,也医治战争创伤人员,包括患缄默症的普莱尔、患幻想症的杰弗里·万斯贝克、患恐战症的伊恩·莫菲特,以及饱受梦魇折磨的萨松和哈林顿。巴克透过瑞弗思的视角,让读者见证了战争带给人们的身体伤害和心理创伤。

在细心治疗病患的同时,瑞弗思自己不幸染疾,陷入高烧和梦魇的折磨之中。在瑞弗思的梦魇中,他开始了回忆自己在西南太平洋的小岛埃迪斯通上所见所闻。在埃迪斯通小岛的文化中,如果部落酋长去世,需要用人头献祭,称为"猎首"。如果酋长死去后很久都没有成功"猎首",那么酋长的遗孀只能一直蜷缩在一个狭小的空间中,不吃不喝,也没有自由。"猎首"是小岛女性选择配偶的标准,是小岛男性扬名立威的壮举。瑞弗思虽然惊讶于小岛的"猎首"文化,但作为一个外来访客,他自知无权干涉小岛事务。巴克通过瑞弗思的回忆,为读者介绍了远离欧洲的小岛文化;揭示了不同的时间和空间中,人类的杀戮行为异曲同工,并无本质差别。

小说结尾,瑞弗思辗转反侧,无法入睡,陷入对战争和死亡的思考。威廉·瑞弗思是 20 世纪英国著名的人类学家和精神科医生。巴克在《鬼魂之路》中借真实的历史人物,辅以虚构的故事情节,巧妙融合时间与空间、历史与文本、或然性与必然性,多角度呈现了战争中人类所经受的创伤、文化与伦理道德危机。

(三) 作品选读:《鬼魂之路》[①]

Brown fog enveloped the hospital. Coils of sulphurous vapour hung in the entrance hall, static, whirled into different patterns whenever somebody entered or left the building. He'd gone out himself earlier in the evening to buy a paper from the stand outside Victoria Station, a brisk ten-minute walk there and back, a chance to get some air into his lungs, though air these days scorched the throat. The news was good. At any moment now, one felt, the guns would stop and they would all be released into their private lives. They all felt it—and yet it almost seemed not to matter. The end that everybody had longed for was overshadowed by the Spanish influenza epidemic that had the hospital in its grip. If somebody had rushed along the corridor now opening doors and shouting, "The war's over," he'd have said, "Oh, really?" and gone back to writing up notes.

He looked at his watch and stood up. Time to go up to the ward.

Marsden was trying to catch his eye. He'd had the impression that morning, during his ward round, that Marsden wanted ask something, but had been deterred by the formality of the occasion. Rivers had a quick word with Sister Roberts—the staffing situation for this duty was particularly bad—and then went and sat by Marsden's bed, chatting about this and that while he worked himself up to say whatever it was he wanted to say. It was quite simple. He'd overheard a junior doctor talking to a colleague at the foot of his bed and had caught the phrase "elicited the coital reflex". Did this mean, Marsden wanted to know, that he would *eventually*, he stressed, hedging his bets, not *now* obviously, *eventually*, be able to have sex again? "Have sex" was produced in a flat, no nonsense, all-chaps-together tone. He meant "make love". He meant "have children". His wife's photograph stood on his locker. Rivers's neck muscles tensed with the effort of not looking at it. No, he said slowly, it didn't mean that. He explained what it meant. Marsden wasn't listening, but he needed a smoke-screen of words behind which to prepare his reaction. He was pleating the hem of the sheet between his fingertips. "Well," he said casually, when Rivers had finished. "I didn't really think it meant that. Just thought I'd ask."

One incident; one day.

---

① Barker, P. *The Ghost Road*. London: Penguin Books, 2008, pp. 259 - 276.

Faces shadowed by steel helmets, they would hardly have recognized each other, even if the faint starlight had enabled them to see clearly. Prior, crouching in a ditch beside the crossroad, kept looking at the inside of his left wrist where normally his watch would have been. It had been taken away from him twenty minutes ago to be synchronized. The usual symptoms: dry mouth, sweaty palms, pounding heart, irritable bladder, cold feet. What a brutally accurate term "cold feet" was. Though "shitting yourself"—the other brutally accurate term—did *not* apply. He'd been glugging Tincture of Opium all day, as had several others of the old hands. He'd be shitting bricks for a fortnight when this was over, but at least he wouldn't be shitting himself tonight.

He looked again at his wrist, caught Owen doing the same, smiled with shared irritation, said nothing. He stared at the stars, trying to locate the plough, but couldn't concentrate. Rain clouds were massing. All we need. A few minutes later a runner came back with his watch and with a tremendous sense—delusional, of course—of being in control again he strapped it on.

Then they were moving forward, hundreds of men eerily quiet, starlit shadows barely darkening the grass. And no dogs barked.

The clock at the end of the ward blurred, then moved into focus again. He was finding it difficult to keep awake now that the rounds were done, the reports written and his task was simply to *be there*, ready for whatever emergencies the night might throw his way. Sister Roberts put a mug of orange-coloured tea, syrupy with sugar, in front of him, and he took a gulp. They sat together at the night nurses' station—there were no night nurses, they were all off with flu—drinking the too strong, too sweet tea, watching the other end of the ward, where the green screens had been placed round Hallet's bed. A single lamp shone above his bed so the green curtains glowed against the darkness of the rest of the ward. Through a gap between the screens Rivers could see one of the family, a young boy, fourteen, fifteen years old perhaps, Hallet's younger brother, wriggling about on his chair, bored with the long hours of waiting and knowing it was unforgivable to be bored.

"I wish the mother would go home and lie down," Sister Roberts said. "She's absolutely at the end of her tether." A sniff. "And that girl looks the hysterical type to me."

She never liked the girls. "Is she his sister?"

"Fiancée."

A muttering from behind the screen, but no discernible words. Rivers stood up. "I'd better have a look."

"Do you want the relatives out?"

"Please. It'll only take a minute."

The family looked up as he pushed the screens aside. They had been sitting round this bed off and on for nearly thirty-six hours, ever since Hattet's condition had begun to deteriorate. Mrs Hallet, the mother, was on Hallet's right, he suspected because the family had decided she should be spared, as far as possible, seeing the left side of Hallet's face. The worst was hidden by the dressing over the eye, but still enough was visible. The father sat on the bad side, a middle-aged man, very erect, retired professional army, in uniform for the duration of the war. He had a way of straightening his shoulders, bracing himself that suggested chronic back pain rather than a reaction to the present situation. And then the girl, whose name was... Susan, was it? She sat, twisting a handkerchief between her fingers, often with a polite, meaningless smile on her face, in the middle of the family she had been going to join and must now surely realize she would not be joining. And the boy, who was almost the most touching of all, gauche, graceless, angry with everything, his voice sometimes squeaking humiliatingly so that he blushed, at other times braying down the ward, difficult, rebellious, demanding attention, because he was afraid if he stopped behaving like this he would cry.

They stood up when he came in, looking at him in a way familiar from his earliest days in hospital medicine. They expected him to *do* something. Although they'd been told Hallet was critically ill, they were still hoping he'd "make him better".

Sister Roberts asked them to wait outside and they retreated to the waiting-room at the end of the main corridor.

He looked at Hallet. The whole of the left side of his face drooped. The exposed eye was sunk deep in his skull, open, though he didn't seem to be fully conscious. His hair had been shaved off, preparatory to whatever operation had left the horseshoe-shaped scar, now healing ironically well, above the suppurating wound left by the rifle bullet. The hernia cerebripulsated, looking like some strange submarine form of life, the mouth of a sea anemone perhaps. The whole of the left side of his body was useless. Even when he was conscious enough to speak the drooping of the mouth and the damage to the lower jaw made his speech impossible to follow. This, more than anything else, horrified his family. You saw them straining to understand, but they couldn't grasp a word he said. His voice came in a whisper because he lacked the strength to project it. He seemed to be whispering now. Rivers bent over him, listened, then straightened up, deciding he must have imagined the sound. Hallet had not stirred, beyond the usual twitching below the coverlet, the constant clonus to which his right ankle joint was subject.

Why are you alive? Rivers thought, looking down into the gargoyled face.

Mate, would have been Njiru's word for this: the state of which death is the appropriate and therefore the desirable outcome. He would have seen Hallet as being, in every meaningful way, dead already, and his sole purpose would have been to hasten the moment of actual death: *mate ndapu*, die finish. Rivers fingered his lapel badge, his unimpaired nerves transmitting the shape of the caduceus to his undamaged brain, his allegiance to a different set of beliefs confirmed without the conflict ever breaking the surface of consciousness.

He took Hallet's pulse. "All right," he said to Sister Roberts. "You can let them back in."

He watched her walk off, then thought it was cowardice not to face them, and followed her down the corridor, passing Mrs Hallet on the way. She hesitated when she saw him, but the drive to get back to her son was too strong. Susan and the younger brother followed on behind. He found Major Hallet lingering by an open window, smoking furiously. A breath of muggy, damp, foggy air came into the room, a reminder that there was an outside world.

"Pathetic, isn't it?" Major Hallet said, raising the cigarette. "Well?"

Rivers hesitated.

"Not long now, eh?"

"No, not long."

In spite of his terseness, tears immediately welled up in Major Hallet's eyes. He turned away, his voice shaking. "He's been so brave. He's been so bloody brave." A moment during which he struggled for control. "How long exactly do you think?"

"I don't know. Hours."

"Oh God."

"Keep talking to him. He *does* recognize your voices and he can understand."

"But we can't understand him. It's terrible, he's obviously expecting an answer and we can't say anything."

They went back to the ward together, Major Hallet pausing outside the screen for a moment, bracing his back. A muttering from the bed. "You see?" Major Hallet said helplessly.

Rivers followed him through the gap in the screens and leant over to listen to Hallet. His voice was a slurred whisper. "Shotvarfet."

At first Rivers could only be sure of the initial consonant and thought he might be trying to say "Susan", but the phrase was longer than that. He straightened and shook his head. "Keep talking to him, Mrs Hallet. He does recognize your voice."

She bent forward and shyly, covered with the social embarrassment that crops up so agonizingly on these occasions, tried to talk, telling him news of home, Auntie Ethel sent her love, Madeleine was getting married in April...

Susan had that smile on her lips again, fixed, meaningless, a baboon rictus of sheer terror. And the boy's face, a mask of fear and fury because he knew that any moment now the tears would start, and he'd be shamed in front of some merciless tribunal in his own mind.

Rivers left them to it. Sister Roberts and the one orderly were busy with Adams who had to be turned every hour. He sat in the night station's circle of light, looking up and down the ward, forcing himself to name and recall the details of every patient, his tired mind waiting for the next jerk of the clock.

The glowing green screens round Hallet's bed reminded him of the tent on Eddystone, on the nights when the insects were really bad and they had to take the lamp inside. You'd go out into the bush and come back and there'd be this great glow of light, and Hocart's shadow huge on the canvas. Safety, or as close to it as you could get on the edge of the dark.

On their last evening he sat outside the tent, packing cases full of clothes and equipment ranged around him, typing up his final notes. Hocart was away on the other side of the island and not due back for hours. Working so close to the light his eyes grew tired, and he sat back rubbing the inner corners; he opened them again to find Njiru a few feet away watching him, having approached silently on his bare feet.

Rivers took the lamp from the table and set it on the ground, squatting down beside it, since he knew Njiru was more comfortable on the ground. The bush exuded blackness. The big moths that loved a particular flowering bush that grew all round the tent bumped furrily against the glass, so that he and Njiru sat in a cloud of pale wings.

They chatted for a while about some of the more than four hundred acquaintances they now had in common, then a long easy silence fell.

"Kundaite says you know Ave," Rivers said very quietly, almost as if the bush itself had spoken, and Njiru were being asked to do no more than think aloud.

Njiru said, almost exactly as he'd said at the beginning, "Kundaite he no speak true, he savvy *gammon* 'long *nanasa*'," but now he spoke with a faint growl of laughter in his voice, adding in English, "He is a liar."

"He *is* a liar, but I think you do know Ave."

He was reminded suddenly of an incident in the Torres Straits when Haddon had been trying to get skulls to measure. One man had said, with immense dignity, "Be patient. You will have all our skulls in time." It was not a comfortable memory. He was not asking for skulls but he was asking for something at least equally sacred. He leant forward and their shadows leapt and grappled against the bush. "Tell me about Ave."

Ave lives in Ysabel. He is both one spirit and many spirits. His mouth is long and filled with the blood of the men he devours. Kita and Mateana are nothing beside him because they destroy only the individual, but Ave kills "all people' long house". The broken rainbow belongs to him, and presages both epidemic disease and war. Ave is the destroyer of peoples.

And the words of exorcism? He told him even that, the last bubbles rising from the mouth of a drowning man. Not only told him, but, with that blend of scholarly exactitude and intellectual impatience for which he was remarkable, insisted on Rivers learning the words in Melanesian, in the "high speech", until he had the inflection on every syllable perfect. This was the basis, Rivers thought, toiling and stumbling over the words, of Njiru's power, the reason why on meeting him even the greatest chiefs stepped off the path.

"And now," Njiru said, lifting his head in a mixture of pride and contempt, "now you will put it in your book."

I never have, Rivers thought. His and Hocart's book on Eddystone had been one of the casualties of the war, though hardly—he glanced up and down the ward with its rows of brain-damaged and paralysed young men—the most significant.

He had spoken them, though, during the course of a lecture to the Royal Society, and had been delighted to find that he didn't need to consult his notes as he spoke. He was still word-perfect.

A commotion from behind the screens. Hallet had begun to cry out and his family was trying to soothe him. A muttering all along the ward as the other patients stirred and grumbled in their sleep, dragged reluctantly back into consciousness. But the grumbling stopped as they realized where the cries were coming from. A silence fell. Faces turned towards the screens as if the battle being waged behind them was every man's battle.

Rivers walked quietly across. The family stood up again as he came in. "No, it's all right." he said. "No need to move."

He took Hallet's pulse. He felt the parents' gaze on him, the father's red-veined, unblinking eyes and the mother's pale fierce face with its working mouth.

"This is it, isn't it?" Major Hallet said in a whisper.

Rivers looked down at Hallet, who was now fully conscious. Oh God, he thought, it's going to be one of those. He shook his head. "Not long."

The barrage was due to start in fifteen minutes' time. Prior shared a bar of chocolate with Robson, sitting hunched up together against the damp cold mist. Then they started crawling forward. The sappers, who were burdened by materials for the construction of the pontoon bridge, were taking the lane, so the Manchesters had to advance over the waterlogged fields. The rain had stopped, but the already marshy ground had flooded in places, and over each stretch of water lay a thick blanket of mist. Concentrate on nothing but the moment, Prior told himself, moving forward on knees and elbows like a frog or a lizard or like—like anything except a man. First the right knee, then the left, then the right, then the left again, and again, and again, slithering through fleshy green grass that smelled incredibly sharp as scrabbling boots cut it. Even with all this mist there was now a perceptible thinning of the light, a gleam from the canal where it ran between spindly, dead trees.

There is to be no retirement under any circumstances. That was the order. They have tied us to the stake. We cannot fly, but bear-like we must fight the course. The men were silent, staring straight ahead into the mist. Talk, even in whispers, was forbidden. Prior looked at his watch, licked dry lips, watched the second hand crawl to the quarter hour. All around him was a tension of held breath. 5:43. Two more minutes. He crouched further down, whistle clenched between his teeth.

Prompt as ever, hell erupted. Shells whined over, flashes of light, plumes of water from the drainage ditches, tons of mud and earth flung into the air. A shell fell short. The ground shook beneath them and a shower of pebbles and clods of earth peppered their steel helmets. Five minutes of this, five minutes of the air bursting in waves against your face, men with dazed faces braced against it, as they picked up the light bridges meant for fording the flooded drainage ditches, and carried them out to the front. Then abruptly, silence. A gasp for air, then noise again, but further back, as the barrage lifted and drummed down on to the empty fields.

Prior blew the whistle, couldn't hear it, was on his feet and running anyway, urging the men on with wordless cries. They rushed forward, making for the line of trees. Prior kept shouting, "Steady, steady! Not too fast on the left!" It was important there should be no bunching when they reached the bridges. "Keep it straight!" Though the men were stumbling into quagmires or tripping over clumps of grass. A shell whizzing over from the German side exploded in a shower of mud and water. And another. He saw several little figures topple over, it didn't look serious, somehow, they didn't look like beings who could be hurt.

Bridges laid down, quickly, efficiently, no bunching at the crossings, just the clump of boots on wood, and then they emerged from beneath the shelter of the trees and out into the terrifying openness of the bank. As bare as an eyeball, no cover anywhere, and the machine-gunners on the other side were alive and well. They dropped down, firing to cover the sappers as they struggled to assemble the bridge, but nothing covered *them*. Bullets fell like rain, puckering the surface of the canal, and the men started to fall. Prior saw the man next to him, a silent, surprised face, no sound, as he twirled and fell, a slash of scarlet like a huge flower bursting open on his chest. Crawling forward, he fired at the bank opposite though he could hardly see it for the clouds of smoke that drifted across. The sappers were still struggling with the bridge, binding pontoon sections together with wire that sparked in their hands as bullets struck it. And still the terrible rain fell. Only two sappers left, and then the Manchesters took over the building of the bridge. Kirk paddled out in a crate to give covering fire, was hit, hit again, this time in the face, went on firing directly at the machine-gunners who crouched in their defended holes only a few yards away. Prior was about to start across the water with ammunition when he was himself hit, though it didn't feel like a bullet, more like a blow form something big and hard, a truncheon or a cricket bat, only it knocked him off his feet and he fell, one arm trailing over the edge of the canal.

He tried to turn to crawl back beyond the drainage ditches, knowing it was only a matter of time before he was hit again, but the gas was thick here and he couldn't reach his mask. Banal, simple, repetitive thoughts ran round and round his mind. *Balls up. Bloody mad. Oh Christ.* There was no pain, more a spreading numbness that left his brain clear. He saw Kirk die. He saw Owen die, his body lifted off the ground by bullets, describing a slow arc in the air as it fell. It seemed to take for ever to fall, and Prior's consciousness fluttered down with it. He gazed at his reflection in the water, which broke and reformed and broke again as bullets hit the surface and then, gradually, as the numbness spread, he ceased to see it.

The light was growing now, the subdued, brownish light of a November dawn. At the far end of the ward, Simpson, too far gone himself to have any understanding of what was happening, jargoned and gobbled away, but all the other faces were turned towards the screens, each man lending the little strength he had to support Hallet in his struggle.

So far, except for the twice repeated whisper and the wordless cries, Hallet had been silent, but now the whisper began again, only more loudly. *Shotvarfet. Shotvarfet.* Again and again, increasing in volume as he directed all his strength into the cry. His mother tried to soothe him, but he didn't hear her. *Shotvarfet. Shotvarfet.* Again and again, each time louder, ringing across the ward. He opened his one eye and gazed directly at Rivers, who had come from behind the screens and was standing at the foot of his bed.

"What's he saying?" Major Hallet asked.

Rivers opened his mouth to say he didn't know and then realized he did. "He's saying, 'It's not worth it.'"

"Oh, it is worth it, it *is*," Major Hallet said, gripping his son's hand. The man was in agony. He hardly knew what he was saying.

"*Shotvarfet.*"

The cry rose again as if he hadn't spoken, and now the other patients were growing restless. A buzz of protest not against the cry, but in support of it, a wordless murmur from damaged brains and drooping mouths.

"*Shotvarfet. Shotvarfet.*"

"I can't stand much more of this," Major Hallet said. The mother's eyes never left her son's face. Her lips were moving though she made no sound. Rivers was aware of a pressure building in his own throat as that single cry from the patients went on and on. He could not afterwards be sure that he had succeeded in keeping silent, or whether he too had joined in. All he could remember later was gripping the metal rail at the end of the bed till his hands hurt.

And then suddenly it was over. The mangled words faded into silence, and a moment or two later, with an odd movement of the chest and stomach muscles like somebody taking off a too tight jumper, Hallet died.

Rivers reached the bedside before the family realized he was gone, closed the one eye, and from sheer force of habit looked at his watch.

"6:25," he said, addressing Sister Roberts.

He raised the sheet as far as Hallet's chin, arranged his arms by his sides and withdrew silently, leaving the family alone with their grief, wishing, as he pulled the screens more closely together, that he had not seen the young girl turn aside to hide her expression of relief.

On the edge of the canal the Manchesters lie, eyes still open, limbs not yet decently arranged, for the stretcher-bearers have departed with the last of the wounded, and the dead are left alone. The battle has withdrawn from them; the bridge they succeeded in building was destroyed by a single shell. Further down the canal another and more successful crossing is being attempted, but the cries and shouts come faintly here.

The sun has risen. The first shaft strikes the water and creeps towards them along the bank, discovering here the back of a hand, there the side of a neck, lending a rosy glow to skin from which the blood has fled, and then, finding nothing here that can respond to it, the shaft of light passes over them and begins to probe the distant fields.

Grey light tinged with rosy pink seeps in through the tall windows. Rivers, slumped at the night nurses' station, struggles to stay awake. On the edge of sleep he hears Njiru's voice, repeating the words of the exorcism of Ave.

O Sumbi! O Gesese! O Palapoke! O Gorepoko! O you Ngengere at the root of the sky. Go down, depart ye.

And there, suddenly, not separate from the ward, not in any way ghostly, not in *fashion blong tomate*, but himself in every particular, advancing down the ward of the Empire Hospital, attended by his shadowy retinue, as Rivers had so often seen him on the coastal path on Eddystone, came Njiru.

There is an end of men, an end of chiefs, an end of chieftains' wives, an end of chiefs' children— then go down and depart. Do not yearn for us, the fingerless, the crippled, the broken. Go down and depart, oh, oh, oh.

He bent over Rivers, staring into his face with those piercing hooded eyes. A long moment, and then the brown face, with its streaks of lime, faded into the light of the daytime ward.

 思考与讨论

(1) 以节选内容为例,总结《鬼魂之路》的叙事特点有哪些?

(2) 如何理解节选内容中普莱尔和瑞弗思看表的习惯?

(3) 节选内容中瑞弗思的回忆是什么,回忆是如何被触发的?

(4) 节选内容中的战争创伤表现有哪些,与小说的主题有什么关系?

(5) 如何理解小说中埃迪斯通小岛文化中的鬼神"阿委"?

(6)《鬼魂之路》的主要人物普莱尔是一个怎样的人,具体体现在哪里?

 拓展阅读

[1] Shaddock, J. "Dreams of Melanesia: Masculinity and the Exorcism of War in Pat Barker's 'The Ghost Road'". *Modern Fiction Studies*. Vol. 52, No. 3(2015), pp. 656 – 674.

[2] Smethurst, T. & Craps, S. Phantasms of War and Empire in Pat Barker's *The Ghost Road*. *Ariel*. Vol. 44, No. 2 – 3(2013), pp. 141 – 167.

[3] 刘建梅.帕特·巴克战争小说的创伤叙事[M].北京:社会科学文献出版社,2020.

第五章
当代英国历史小说

"欧洲历史小说之父"沃尔特·司各特(Walter Scott，1771—1832)对英国的历史小说与英国小说中的历史书写影响深远。遗憾的是，在相当长的时间里，由于历史小说被视为通俗文学，加之其他小说文类荣兴，历史小说渐失辉煌。20世纪60年代起，历史小说在世界文坛渐次复苏，逐步发展与繁荣，颇有异军突起之势。

20世纪60年代，结构主义、后结构主义哲学思潮在欧美盛行并开始向世界各处传播。上述思潮引发人们对约定俗成的传统思想进行反思。在米歇尔·福柯、海登·怀特等新历史主义领袖人物看来，传统意义上的"历史"已不再是一种过去的客观存在，而是一种"历史文本"，其中含有人为的叙述或杜撰成分。他们认为，历史学家不可能客观描述过去。他们将历史的深层结构视为是诗性的，历史从本质上不能脱离想象，历史的表现方式是文本的，在语言上不能脱离虚构。伴随新历史主义对历史文本中的历史的怀疑，20世纪60年代中期英美文坛出现了一批具有新历史主义特征的历史小说。

英国作家保罗·司各特于20世纪60年代初就以印度的历史题材创作历史小说。他以关涉英国在印度的殖民史为题材的《统治四部曲》和获布克奖的小说《眷恋》在英国文学界赢得声誉。《皇冠上的宝石》(*The Jewel in the Crown*)出版于1966年，是《统治四部曲》中最早面世的一部小说。在《统治四部曲》之前，司各特在1962年出版了具有浓重象征色彩的历史小说《天堂之鸟》(*The Birds of Paradise*)。作品以"天堂鸟"隐喻即将崩溃犹做困兽之斗的大英帝国。《天堂之鸟》奠定了司各特之后的印度题材历史小说的隐喻功能，是其印度题材历史小说系列的发轫之作。

20世纪60年代初英国历史小说创作开始活跃，佳作频出，英国历史小说作品屡获布克奖等文学大奖。20世纪90年代以来英国历史小说发展更为迅猛，至今繁盛不衰。在当今全球历史小说创作热潮中英国的历史小说令人瞩目。当代英国历史小说纷繁芜杂，五彩纷呈，具有如下特征：帝国情节、传达理念、历史人物重塑与历史重写、小说艺术实验。

第一节　帝国情结与历史回眸及反思

经过长期对外侵略、殖民扩张和经济掠夺，英国成为有史以来世界上最强大的帝国，殖民地遍布五大洲,成了名副其实的"日不落帝国"。盛极必衰。第一次世界大战之后,大英帝国逐渐衰落。英国虽赢得了战争,但元气大伤。饱受欺压剥削的殖民地人民掀起摆脱英国殖民统治的民族独立解放运动。第二次世界大战的爆发给岌岌可危的大英帝国致命一击。原殖民地民族解放运动蓬勃发展,殖民地人民纷纷要求独立,大英帝国迅速瓦解。大英帝国往日辉煌虽已不再,但深受帝国政治文化影响的英国人对帝国却有着深深的眷恋。当代英国历史小说中有浓重的挥之不去的忆往昔式的帝国情结也就不足为奇了。

　　第一次世界大战后爱尔兰的独立是大英帝国大厦崩塌的前兆。詹姆斯·戈登·法雷尔的《麻烦》(Troubles,1970)是记述这一历史时刻最有影响力的历史小说。《麻烦》将故事发生地设定在 1919 到 1921 年的南爱尔兰东南海岸边一处乡村小镇基纳洛。小镇中有一家名为"帝王"的宾馆。"帝王"宾馆装饰豪华,外观富丽堂皇,但内部已朽裂破损,摇摇欲坠,象征着大英帝国金玉其外败絮其中的现状。小说通过在情节中插入书信和报纸报道的方式把读者带回 1919 到 1921 年间爱尔兰的重要历史时刻。个人记忆与官方报道形成对照,凸显了英国帝国意识形态,反思了帝国主义者的傲慢与偏见,旨在探寻英国作为宗主国与各殖民地最终分道扬镳的深层次原因,即:英国殖民者从未将殖民地当作平等的伙伴,而是以拯救者和征服者的姿态歧视、掠夺与剥削殖民地人民,因而随着英国国力衰微,各殖民地纷纷寻求独立便是情理之中的事情。

　　印度是英国海外最大的殖民地,是英国最大的市场和原料产地,在大英帝国具有极为重要的地位,有"失去印度就失去大英帝国"的说法。印度的独立加速了大英帝国的衰败。保罗·司各特的《统治四部曲》聚焦于从 1942 年 8 月到 1947 年 8 月五年间在印度发生的历史事件。小说自印度民族解放运动开始写起,一直写到英国结束在印度的殖民统治,以全景图的方式展示了英国殖民统治在印度衰落的过程。

　　虽然英国在 1947 年撤出印度结束了对印度的殖民统治,但仍有一些英国人及其后裔定居印度。保罗·司各特的小说《眷恋》讲述了塔斯克·斯莫里上校不顾夫人露西反对留在印度生活的种种际遇。由于肤色、服饰、语言和文化的差异,斯莫里一家无法与印度人很好地沟通与交流,成了在印度被边缘化的英印人①代表。独立后的印度有强烈的抹去英国殖民者影响的民族主义情绪,在印度的英印人普遍遭到排斥。《眷恋》揭示了殖民时期的英印关系对于后殖民时代英印关系的深刻影响,"在《眷恋》中,一部分滞留印度的英国人不仅感受到印度独立带给西方人的心理冲击,还一如既往地感受到那种处处存在的文化隔膜。"②虽然《统治四部曲》和《眷恋》对英国殖民统治进行了一定程度的批判性反思,但囿于帝国意识形态、世界观和历史观,不仅对殖民统治的本质缺少深刻认识,对殖民统治充满溢美之词,还大量使用了妖魔化印度人的词语。

　　第二次世界大战后英国的海外控制力急剧萎缩。苏伊士运河是继英军从印度、希腊、土耳其、巴勒斯坦等地撤军后在全球为数不多的基地之一。号称"日不落帝国"的大英帝国在繁盛期其殖民地遍布全球,虽然今不如昔,但还是想放手一搏,尽力挽回一点颜面。战后英国想尽办法维持其在埃及的影响。波西·纽比的布克奖小说《给某事一个交代》(Something to Answer for,1969)以苏伊士运河事件为背

---

①　英印人对应的英语词汇是"Anglo-Indian"。"Anglo-Indian"的第一个用法是描述所有居住在印度的英国人。混合了英国和印度血统的人则被称为"欧亚人"(Eurasians)。

②　Gupta, S. & Bhatt, P. *Contemporary British Fiction: History and Present*. Jaipur, New Delhi, Bangalore: Rawat Publications, 2007, p.47.

景讲述了来自英国的主人公唐罗在埃及的经历,展现了当年的政治风云,揭示了大英帝国的衰亡命运。

《给某事一个交代》的主人公唐罗在伦敦收到了好友艾利·库里遗孀的来信,想请他去开罗帮忙料理已故丈夫的后事,并帮助她查清丈夫的死因。唐罗刚到达目的地,就被人打得头晕目眩,被脱光衣服,赤身裸体地躺在大街上。他并不清楚到底发生了什么,不知道是谁打了他,为什么打他。不仅如此,他连自己的身份也不记得了,不知道自己为什么会来到这里。小说以苏伊士运河危机为历史背景,以隐喻的方式通过对唐罗在埃及经历的叙述,展示了苟延残喘的大英帝国衰败无助的窘境。

第二节　作为理念承载平台的历史

当代英国历史小说不乏在历史叙事中传达理念之作。威廉·戈尔丁的《启蒙之旅》(*Rites of Passage*,1980)讲述了 19 世纪早期拿破仑战争期间在一艘驶往澳洲殖民地的船上发生的故事,传达出人性亦善亦恶的思想观念。玛格丽特·德拉布尔的小说《红王妃》(*The Red Queen*,2004)传达了东西方文化需要沟通理解的理念。朱利安·巴恩斯的《福楼拜的鹦鹉》(*Flaubert's Parrot*,1984)借古寻今探究感情的谜团,他的《十又二分之一章世界史》(*A History of the World in 10$^{1/2}$ Chapters*,1989)展现了作者的爱情观与历史观。

威廉·戈尔丁善于探索人性,他认为"人性的缺陷是导致社会缺陷的主要原因,而他身为作家的使命是揭示人对自我本性的惊人无知,让人去正视人自身的残酷和贪欲的可悲事实"[①]。其布克奖小说《启蒙之旅》揭示了人性中的恶,人性的阴暗面、道德沦丧、信仰缺失和社会腐败。

小说《启蒙之旅》以埃德蒙·塔尔波特的书信和牧师科利的日记为主要内容。年轻的塔尔波特登上了一艘前往澳大利亚的航船,在那里教父为他安排了政府要员一职。在船上他先后遇到了侍从、军官、安德森船长以及科利牧师。牧师科利在水手们举行的"海神袋"仪式中遭到凌辱,他原打算向船长安德森讨回公道,却在一次醉酒中发生了不正当性行为。此后他便闭门不出,水米不进,最后死于船舱内。

船长安德森是这条船上飞扬跋扈的专制者和暴君。他规定任何人未经他允许不能进入后甲板。他专制而虚伪,对手下人极为残暴,对有权有势之人奴颜婢膝。他因父亲为了金钱放弃神职把职位让给自己妻子的情夫,内心充满对神职人员的憎恨。在船上他处处为难科利,也助长了船上水手们对待科利牧师的嚣张气焰。科利本以为自己作为船上唯一的牧师能够得到人们的尊重,却遭到人们的冷眼和漠视。在一次水手们安排的酒会上,水手们把脏东西往他嘴里塞,在他脸上抹脏东西。他还被强行浸入盛满尿液的污水盆中。在"海神袋"仪式中,科利被水手们戏弄,遭受凌辱,给他带来致命的心理伤害。总督大人的教子塔尔波特也曾沦陷于人性堕落的漩涡。在船上塔尔波特遇到妓女季诺碧亚,没能忍住内心的欲望给她写了一封暗示性的情书。趁全船人员观看为穿越赤道举行的"海神袋"仪式之机,塔尔波特将季诺碧亚约到了自己的船舱。当塔尔波特的信件被发现后,为不让事情传开,他收买惠勒[②]保守秘密。就连牧师科利也被人性之恶左右。科利内心充满着兽性的欲望,这种兽性的欲望使他在醉酒后发生了

---

① 威廉·戈尔丁:《启蒙之旅》,陈绍鹏(译),北京:北京燕山出版社,2016 年,第 10 页。
② 惠勒是船上的服务员,是一位跛脚的老头。

不当性行为。科利无颜面对自己的丑事,最后自杀身亡。

虽然小说更多展现人性之恶,但也揭示了人性向善的一面。塔尔波特为掩盖自己的丑行,想把信件丢在科利的船舱嫁祸于人,好在他良心未泯,未将此念头付诸实施。在科利自杀后,塔尔波特悔恨没有向他伸出援手,而是和船上的人们一起合伙欺负科利,成了科利死亡的帮凶。

德拉布尔的历史小说《红王妃》聚焦东西方文化间的误解与困惑,凸显了东西方文化间沟通与理解的重要性[①]。

威廉·戈尔丁等很多当代英国小说家都曾创作历史小说,但多偶尔为之,朱利安·巴恩斯则是一位专于历史小说、以历史书写传达理念的作家。他的《福楼拜的鹦鹉》阐释了爱情是无法参透的谜团的主题,他的《十又二分之一章世界史》虽仍认为爱情神秘像个谜,但坚信爱情能给人以力量,给人带来幸福。

第三节　历史人物重塑与历史重写

20世纪60年代末以来,重写历史的思潮席卷世界。一些历史事件得到重新审视与书写,一些在过去历史文献中鲜有涉及的人物有机会从边缘走向中心。在英国小说界也出现了重塑历史人物和重写历史的潮流。巴里·昂斯沃斯的《神圣的渴望》(*Sacred Hunger*,1992)、朱利安·巴恩斯的《亚瑟与乔治》(*Arthur and George*,2005)和希拉里·曼特尔的《狼厅》(*Wolf Hall*,2009)是其中最具代表性的三部历史小说。

巴里·昂斯沃斯的小说《神圣的渴望》写下了黑奴的血泪史,对奴隶贸易进行了重新审视与深刻反思。该小说由两部分构成,第一卷的故事背景设定在1752至1753年,主要讲了马修·帕里斯在担任一艘充满粗俗语言、血汗泪水的贩奴船上的外科医生时的所见所闻。第二卷的故事发生在1765年,主要讲的是在目睹和经历了船长令人发指的残暴统治后,马修带领船员奋起反抗,和奴隶们一起逃往佛罗里达州的一座荒岛,在那里建立了一个村落,黑人和白人和谐生活的故事。

小说以小见大,把奴隶贸易对非洲人民的迫害淋漓尽致地展现给读者。在奴隶贩子眼中,黑人是与牲畜无异的动物。《神圣的渴望》多处显示了奴隶贩子对非洲人所进行的言语上的侮辱,他们认为非洲人是"未开化的人""野蛮的黑人""乞丐""流氓""叫花子";认为他们"没比野兽好多少,他们对艺术和科学一无所知,没有宗教的慰藉,缺乏健全的法律……"[②]小说构建了一个种族平等、共享未来的乌托邦:"无论白人黑人,大家都是自由人,都是兄弟,共同居住在这个地方,都是同一条船上的人。"在这个乌托邦世界,人们秉持善念,互助互爱,"真实世界永远不会是这样的画面——人与人之间互相帮助,倾其一生行善事。"[③]

朱利安·巴恩斯的《亚瑟与乔治》则对历史记载的冤案进行回溯重写,探寻种族主义的隐秘根源。小说的题材取自英国19世纪历史上真实的大沃利伤马案。乔治是一位印英混血的律师,在证据不足的

①　王桃花.论《红王妃》中的异文化书写及其"理解"主题[J].当代外国文学,2012(1):65.
②　Unsworth, B. *Sacred Hunger*. London: Penguin Books, 1992, p.262.
③　Ibid., p.583.

情况下被指控为大沃利一系列伤马事件的元凶,被判 7 年劳役。该小说以解构历史事件的方式重写历史,将大沃利伤马案定性为种族歧视所造成的冤案。小说以此事件映射当代的种族主义问题。正如巴恩斯所言:"这故事反映了当代的问题。"[①]小说凭借一百年前的种族歧视事件反思当代社会的种族问题,展示了社会中潜在的种族主义倾向,一种"不明言"的种族主义[②],提醒人们对此保持警惕。

希拉里·曼特尔的历史小说《狼厅》重塑了英国重要历史人物托马斯·克伦威尔。这位英国近代社会转型时期杰出的政治家,一直被认为是乱臣贼子、奸佞小人,在历史著作与文学作品中长期以来处于边缘地位。小说彻底颠覆了克伦威尔的反面形象,他不仅被刻画为忠心报国、恪尽职守的好臣子,还是知恩图报、悲天悯人、豁达宽厚、仁慈和善的人文主义者。

第四节　历史小说的艺术实验

曾几何时,"文学之死""小说之死"甚嚣尘上。无论是"文学之死"还是"小说之死",死的不是其自身,而是其原有的形式。英国当代小说一直在进行艺术探索,英国当代历史小说也在不断进行着艺术实验。

A. S. 拜厄特被称为"魔书"的历史小说《占有》(Possession,1990)是一部杂糅之作。维多利亚英国社会与英国现代社会时空交错,相隔百年的爱情故事并置,小说中穿插大量的童话和神话,诗歌、书信和日记等非小说题材,爱情传奇、侦探故事、荒诞神话、校园喜剧、历险故事、哥特小说等文学体。

朱利安·巴恩斯坚持不懈地进行历史小说艺术实验。他善于使用戏仿、反讽、拼贴或文体杂糅等后现代写作技巧打破不同文类之间的界限。巴恩斯的《福楼拜的鹦鹉》是众多文本的大融合。小说包括经济文本、地理文本、逻辑文本、医学文本、传记文本、道德文本、心理学文本、集邮文本、语言学文本、戏剧文本、历史文本、占星术文本等。他的《十又二分之一章世界史》是对"宏大叙事"的颠覆与抵制。巴恩斯将宗教故事、传说、历史记载、个人叙述拼贴于小说之中,从多元视角出发探寻历史的不确定性,表达了对世界历史的怀疑态度。巴恩斯打破传统线性叙事,历史小说《福楼拜的鹦鹉》的叙述中单一的线条被多条线索取代,单一的时间向度不复存在,读者跟着叙述者从一个空间越到另一空间或者从一个时间跳转到另一时间的人物叙事上。这打破了传统线性叙事的顺序性、完整性、时空的统一性、因果关系和叙事连贯性。

专注于历史小说创作的格雷厄姆·斯威夫特也在叙事上进行探索。他的小说《水之乡》(Waterland,1983)中,当汤姆以讲故事的方式回忆过去时,小说使用过去时,而当他叙述创伤经验时,即他所谓的"此处现在"时,小说改用现在时。时态的变更旨在打破"内在"与"外在"时间的界限,瓦解线性连续的时间感,营造历史循环发生的效果[③]。

历史元小说是英国当代历史小说的艺术实验成果之一。元小说被认为是关于小说的小说,是揭示小说的身份及其创作过程的小说。所谓历史元小说,就是在历史小说中加入评论,引导或邀请读者参与

---

①　Guignery, V. & Roberts, R. *Conversations with Julian Barnes*. Jackson: University Press of Mississippi, 2009, p.135.
②　塔吉耶夫:《种族主义源流》,高凌瀚(译),北京:生活·读书·新知三联书店,2005 年,第 6 页。
③　苏忱:《再现创伤的历史:格雷厄姆·斯威夫特小说研究》,苏州:苏州大学出版社,2009 年,第 131—132 页。

到与小说创作相关的艺术、美学或哲学等的讨论中来。

约翰·伯格的《G》是一部历史元小说。主人公大谈特谈其作为作家的责任与义务,以及他在故事叙述、情节安排、人物刻画上所遇到的技术难题。这一切无疑是在与读者进行交流和切磋,具有明显的历史元小说特征。

玛格丽特·德拉布尔的《红王妃》除正文的三部分外,有序,有跋,还有致谢、资料来源说明,甚至还列出了参考书目。小说正文外的这种安排使小说显得特别另类,读者似乎感到这不是一部小说,而是一部学术著作,但这些均是小说《红王妃》的有机组成部分,这些部分揭示了作者小说《红王妃》的创作过程。

本章选取的作家及其代表作品如下:朱利安·巴恩斯及其代表作《终结的感觉》、格雷厄姆·斯威夫特及其代表作《水之乡》、希拉里·曼特尔及其代表作《狼厅》。

第五节　主要作家介绍与代表作品选读

一、朱利安·巴恩斯

(一)朱利安·巴恩斯简介

朱利安·巴恩斯出生于英格兰列斯特市,后随父母移居伦敦郊区,父母皆为法语教师。1968 年巴恩斯毕业于牛津大学,专修现代语言。大学毕业后,巴恩斯曾参与《牛津大词典》增补本的编纂工作。之后,出任《新政治家》(*New Statesman*)和《新评论》(*New Review*)的评论员和编辑。

朱利安·巴恩斯的文学创作包括侦探小说、长篇小说与短篇小说集。巴恩斯的创作生涯始于 20 世纪 80 年代。1980 年,巴恩斯以丹·卡瓦纳(Dan Kavanaugh)的笔名发表侦探小说《达菲》(*Duffy*, 1980);同年,又发表了第一部具有半自传体特征的长篇小说《伦敦郊区》(*Metroland*, 1980)。之后,他陆续出版了长篇小说《她遇见我之前》(*Before She Met Me*, 1982)、《福楼拜的鹦鹉》、《盯住太阳》(*Staring at the Sun*, 1986)、《十又二分之一章世界史》、《尚待商榷的爱情》(*Talking It Over*, 1991)、《豪猪》(*The Porcupine*, 1992)、《英格兰,英格兰》(*England, England*, 1998)、《爱,以及其他》(*Love, Etc*, 2000)、《亚瑟与乔治》(*Arthur & George*, 2005)、《终结的感觉》(*The Sense of an Ending*, 2011)、《生命的层级》(*Levels of Life*, 2013)、《时间的噪音》(*The Noise of Time*, 2016)、《惟一的故事》(*The Only Story*, 2018)、《穿红衣服的男人》(*The Man in the Red Coat*, 2021)。巴恩斯出版了短篇小说集《穿越海峡》(*Cross Channel*, 1996)、《柠檬桌》(*The Lemon Table*, 2004)、《脉搏》(*Pulse*, 2011)。巴恩斯以诙谐幽默的语言、新奇多变的形式和富含哲理的笔调,探讨了诸多人生问题,涵盖历史、记忆、死亡、爱情、婚姻、友谊、信仰、道德和身份等日常生活的各个层面。

朱利安·巴恩斯与伊恩·麦克尤恩、马丁·艾米斯(Martin Amis)一起被认为是当代英国文坛的三剑客。1983 年巴恩斯被列入权威文学杂志《格兰塔》(*Granta*)最有潜力新晋小说家榜单。其后,巴恩斯相继赢得了 E.M.福斯特文学奖、莎士比亚文学奖和大卫·科恩终身成就奖。巴恩斯获得了法国费米娜文学奖和普利美迪斯奖,并被授予法国文学艺术骑士勋章。他还是德国古登堡文学奖和奥地利欧洲文学国家奖获得者。在先后四次被提名布克奖最终遴选短名单之后,巴恩斯终于在 2011 年凭借《终结的感觉》获布克奖。

(二)《终结的感觉》简介

小说借托尼的个人记忆,描写了真实史料外没有文献记载的史实,阐发了各种历史故事都难免受写作者个人立场与情感影响的主张。巴恩斯试图回答:历史是什么的问题。他认为,小说传达对历史的理解,历史既不是胜利者的谎言,也不是失败者的自欺欺人,不可靠的记忆和不充分的材料的集合所产生的确定事实就是历史。

在《终结的感觉》中,历史不再是关于社会或民族的宏大叙事,而是微观、琐碎的个人故事。正如托尼所言:"想到自己站在未来的某一点回望过去,去体会岁月带给你的新的情感。"这种"新的情感"便是对过往的自我的一种全新的,甚至颠覆性的认知与阐释。巴恩斯清楚地表达了记忆对个人历史阐释的媒介作用。记忆并不固定,记忆的形成受各种不确定因素的影响,例如时间的流逝、情感的变化等。记忆的主观性使得记忆的内容模糊、扭曲。

小说分为两个部分。第一部分以看似毫无联系且"次序不定"的六个记忆片段开始,是托尼对学生时代的回顾,聚焦他的中学与大学生活。回忆中,托尼展现出一副温和的、无害的、没有多少过错的普通人形象。女友维罗妮卡则是魅惑迷人、神秘莫测、吹毛求疵并企图操控他的感情的满腹心机的女人。她最后抛弃了托尼,与自己的好友艾德里安相爱。这使得托尼在与维罗妮卡的爱恋中成为无辜的受害者。托尼的记忆赋予艾德里安一副智力超群、超凡脱俗的哲学家形象。他是他们"铁三角"中最较真、最有哲学思想的。他的历史观非常新颖,他的自杀更是其哲学思考的结果。在遗书里艾德里安写明:自杀完全是其个人的选择,与周围的人毫不相关。这顺理成章地免除了托尼在这一事件中可能负有的责任。艾德里安的自杀也因看似确定的事实、未被深究而被托尼抛之脑后。隐藏在对维罗妮卡妖魔化、对艾德里安崇高化背后的,是托尼对自我责任的逃避。

小说第二部分是托尼退休之后的故事。托尼平淡的生活被维罗妮卡的母亲的遗嘱打破,托尼开始重新审视自己的过往历史,寻回被记忆修饰、扭曲、剔除的片段,托尼重新认识自己,也更多地了解了艾德里安和其他人。在向前女友维罗妮卡追索她母亲福特夫人遗嘱中留给他的艾德里安日记被维罗妮卡反复拒绝的过程中,托尼了解了大部分真相,知道了艾德里安和前女友一家发生的诸多变故。托尼曾出于嫉妒和仇恨给艾德里安写了一封信,信中以恶毒的语言诅咒艾德里安和维罗妮卡一生不顺,而且他们的后代也将凄惨无比。当维罗妮卡把托尼写给艾德里安的那封诅咒信以复印件的方式寄给他时,托尼震惊于自己曾写过如此恶毒的一封信。在托尼的记忆中,他当时写给艾德里安的是一封祝福信。托尼一直自认为是宽厚平和之人,却发现自己恶毒刻薄的行为。因为这封恶毒的诅咒信,不仅艾德里安和维罗妮卡没有走在一起,而且艾德里安与福特夫人发生了不伦之情,生下了一个智障男孩。知道真相后的托尼深感悔恨,他向维罗妮卡真诚致歉,并试图搜寻记忆深处的点滴来建构一个新的自我,也部分修正了对艾德里安等人的认知。

（三）作品选读：《终结的感觉》①

I remember, in no particular order:

- a shiny inner wrist;

- steam rising from a wet sink as a hot frying pan is laughingly tossed into it;

- gouts of sperm circling a plughole, before being sluiced down the full length of a tall

house;

- a river rushing nonsensically upstream, its wave and wash lit by half a dozen chasing

torchbeams;

- another river, broad and grey, the direction of its flow disguised by a stiff wind exciting the

surface;

- bathwater long gone cold behind a locked door.

This last isn't something I actually saw, but what you end up remembering isn't always the same as what you have witnessed.

We live in time—it holds us and moulds us—but I've never felt I understood it very well. And I'm not referring to theories about how it bends and doubles back, or may exist elsewhere in parallel versions. No, I mean ordinary, everyday time, which clocks and watches assure us passes regularly: tick-tock, click-clock. Is there anything more plausible than a second hand? And yet it takes only the smallest pleasure or pain to teach us time's malleability. Some emotions speed it up, others slow it down; occasionally, it seems to go missing—until the eventual point when it really does go missing, never to return. I'm not very interested in my schooldays, and don't feel any nostalgia for them. But school is where it all began, so I need to return briefly to a few incidents that have grown into anecdotes, to some approximate memories which time has deformed into certainty. If I can't be sure of the actual events any more, I can at least be true to the impressions those facts left. That's the best I can manage.

There were three of us, and he now made the fourth. We hadn't expected to add to our tight number: cliques and pairings had happened long before, and we were already beginning to imagine our escape from school into life. His name was Adrian Finn, a tall, shy boy who initially kept his eyes down and his mind to himself. For the first day or two, we took little notice of him: at our school there was no welcoming ceremony, let alone its opposite, the punitive induction. We just registered his presence and waited.

The masters were more interested in him than we were. They had to work out his intelligence and sense of discipline, calculate how well he'd previously been taught, and if he might prove "scholarship material". On the third morning of that autumn term, we had a history class with Old

---

① Julian, B. *The Sense of an Ending*. London: Jonathan Cape Random House, 2011, pp. 4 – 19.

Joe Hunt, wryly affable in his three-piece suit, a teacher whose system of control depended on maintaining sufficient but not excessive boredom.

"Now, you'll remember that I asked you to do some preliminary reading about the reign of Henry VIII." Colin, Alex and I squinted at one another, hoping that the question wouldn't be flicked, like an angler's fly, to land on one of our heads. "Who might like to offer a characterisation of the age?" He drew his own conclusion from our averted eyes. "Well, Marshall, perhaps. How would you describe Henry VIII's reign?" Our relief was greater than our curiosity, because Marshall was a cautious know-nothing who lacked the inventiveness of true ignorance. He searched for possible hidden complexities in the question before eventually locating a response.

"There was unrest, sir." An outbreak of barely controlled smirking; Hunt himself almost smiled.

"Would you, perhaps, care to elaborate?" Marshall nodded slow assent, thought a little longer, and decided it was no time for caution. "I'd say there was great unrest, sir." "Finn, then. Are you up in this period?" The new boy was sitting a row ahead and to my left. He had shown no evident reaction to Marshall's idiocies.

"Not really, sir, I'm afraid. But there is one line of thought according to which all you can truly say of any historical event—even the outbreak of the First World War, for example—is that 'something happened'" "Is there, indeed? Well, that would put me out of a job, wouldn't it?" After some sycophantic laughter, Old Joe Hunt pardoned our holiday idleness and filled us in on the polygamous royal butcher.

At the next break, I sought out Finn. "I'm Tony Webster." He looked at me warily. "Great line to Hunt." He seemed not to know what I was referring to. "About something happening." "Oh. Yes. I was rather disappointed he didn't take it up." That wasn't what he was supposed to say.

Another detail I remember: the three of us, as a symbol of our bond, used to wear our watches with the face on the inside of the wrist. It was an affectation, of course but perhaps something more. It made time feel like a personal, even a secret, thing. We expected Adrian to note the gesture, and follow suit; but he didn't.

Later that day—or perhaps another day—we had a double English period with Phil Dixon, a young master just down from Cambridge. He liked to use contemporary texts, and would throw out sudden challenges. "'Birth, and Copulation, and Death'—that's what T. S. Eliot says it's all about. Any comments?" He once compared a Shakespearean hero to Kirk Douglas in *Spartacus*. And I remember how, when we were discussing Ted Hughes's poetry, he put his head at a donnish slant and murmured, "Of course, we're all wondering what will happen when he runs out of animals." Sometimes, he addressed us as "Gentlemen". Naturally, we adored him.

That afternoon, he handed out a poem with no title, date or author's name, gave us ten minutes to study it, then asked for our responses.

"Shall we start with you, Finn? Put simply, what would you say this poem is *about*?" Adrian looked up from his desk. "Eros and Thanatos, sir." "Hmm. Go on." "Sex and death," Finn continued, as if it might not just be the thickies in the back row who didn't understand Greek. "Or love and death, if you prefer. The erotic principle, in any case, coming into conflict with the death principle. And what ensues from that conflict. Sir." I was probably looking more impressed than Dixon thought healthy.

"Webster, enlighten us further." "I just thought it was a poem about a barn owl, sir." This was one of the differences between the three of us and our new friend. We were essentially taking the piss, except when we were serious. He was essentially serious, except when he was taking the piss. It took us a while to work this out.

Adrian allowed himself to be absorbed into our group, without acknowledging that it was something he sought. Perhaps he didn't. Nor did he alter his views to accord with ours. At morning prayers he could be heard joining in the responses while Alex and I merely mimed the words, and Colin preferred the satirical ploy of the pseudo-zealot's enthusiastic bellow. The three of us considered school sports a crypto-fascist plan for repressing our sex-drive; Adrian joined the fencing club and did the high jump. We were belligerently tone-deaf; he came to school with his clarinet. When Colin denounced the family, I mocked the political system, and Alex made philosophical objections to the perceived nature of reality, Adrian kept his counsel—at first, anyway. He gave the impression that he believed in things. We did too—it was just that we wanted to believe in our own things, rather than what had been decided for us. Hence what we thought of as our cleansing scepticism.

The school was in central London, and each day we travelled up to it from our separate boroughs, passing from one system of control to another. Back then, things were plainer: less money, no electronic devices, little fashion tyranny, no girlfriends. There was nothing to distract us from our human and filial duty which was to study, pass exams, use those qualifications to find a job, and then put together a way of life unthreateningly fuller than that of our parents, who would approve, while privately comparing it to their own earlier lives, which had been simpler, and therefore superior. None of this, of course, was ever stated: the genteel social Darwinism of the English middle classes always remained implicit.

"Fucking bastards, parents," Colin complained one Monday lunchtime. "You think they're OK when you're little, then you realise they're just like..." "Henry VIII, Col?" Adrian suggested. We were beginning to get used to his sense of irony; also to the fact that it might be turned against us as well. When teasing, or calling us to seriousness, he would address me as Anthony; Alex would become Alexander, and the unlengthenable Colin shortened to Col.

"Wouldn't mind if my dad had half a dozen wives." "And was incredibly rich." "And painted by Holbein." "And told the Pope to sod off." "Any particular reason why they're FBs?" Alex asked

Colin.

"I wanted us to go to the funfair. They said they had to spend the weekend gardening." Right: fucking bastards. Except to Adrian, who listened to our denunciations, but rarely joined in. And yet, it seemed to us, he had more cause than most. His mother had walked out years before, leaving his dad to cope with Adrian and his sister. This was long before the term "single-parent family" came into use; back then it was "a broken home", and Adrian was the only person we knew who came from one. This ought to have given him a whole storetank of existential rage, but somehow it didn't; he said he loved his mother and respected his father. Privately, the three of us examined his case and came up with a theory: that the key to a happy family life was for there not to be a family—or at least, not one living together. Having made this analysis, we envied Adrian the more.

In those days, we imagined ourselves as being kept in some kind of holding pen, waiting to be released into our lives. And when that moment came, our lives—and time itself—would speed up.

How were we to know that our lives had in any case begun, that some advantage had already been gained, some damage already inflicted? Also, that our release would only be into a larger holding pen, whose boundaries would be at first undiscernible. In the meantime, we were book-hungry, sex-hungry, meritocratic, anarchistic. All political and social systems appeared to us corrupt, yet we declined to consider an alternative other than hedonistic chaos. Adrian, however, pushed us to believe in the application of thought to life, in the notion that principles should guide actions. Previously, Alex had been regarded as the philosopher among us. He had read stuff the other two hadn't, and might, for instance, suddenly declare, "Whereof we cannot speak, thereof must we remain silent." Colin and I would consider this idea in silence for a while, then grin and carry on talking. But now Adrian's arrival dislodged Alex from his position—or rather, gave us another choice of philosopher. If Alex had read Russell and Wittgenstein, Adrian had read Camus and Nietzsche. I had read George Orwell and Aldous Huxley; Colin had read Baudelaire and Dostoevsky. This is only a slight caricature.

Yes, of course we were pretentious—what else is youth for? We used terms like "*Weltanschauung*" and "*Sturm und Drang*", enjoyed saying "That's philosophically selfevident", and assured one another that the imagination's first duty was to be transgressive. Our parents saw things differently, picturing their children as innocents suddenly exposed to noxious influence. So Colin's mother referred to me as his "dark angel"; my father blamed Alex when he found me reading *The Communist Manifesto*; Colin was fingered by Alex's parents when they caught him with a hard-boiled American crime novel. And so on. It was the same with sex. Our parents thought we might be corrupted by one another into becoming whatever it was they most feared: an incorrigible masturbator, a winsome homosexual, a recklessly impregnatory libertine. On our behalf they dreaded the closeness of adolescent friendship, the predatory behaviour of strangers on trains, the lure of the wrong kind of girl. How far their anxieties outran our experience.

One afternoon Old Joe Hunt, as if picking up Adrian's earlier challenge, asked us to debate the origins of the First World War: specifically, the responsibility of Archduke Franz Ferdinand's assassin for starting the whole thing off. Back then, we were most of us absolutists. We liked Yes v No, Praise v Blame, Guilt v Innocence—or, in Marshall's case, Unrest v Great Unrest. We liked a game that ended in a win and loss, not a draw. And so for some, the Serbian gunman, whose name is long gone from my memory, had one hundred per cent individual responsibility: take him out of the equation, and the war would never have happened. Others preferred the one hundred per cent responsibility of historical forces, which had placed the antagonistic nations on an inevitable collision course: "Europe was a powder keg waiting to blow" and so on. The more anarchic, like Colin, argued that everything was down to chance, that the world existed in a state of perpetual chaos, and only some primitive storytelling instinct, itself doubtless a hangover from religion, retrospectively imposed meaning on what might or might not have happened.

Hunt gave a brief nod to Colin's attempt to undermine everything, as if morbid disbelief was a natural byproduct of adolescence, something to be grown out of. Masters and parents used to remind us irritatingly that they too had once been young, and so could speak with authority. It's just a phase, they would insist. You'll grow out of it; life will teach you reality and realism. But back then we declined to acknowledge that they had ever been anything like us, and we knew that we grasped life—and truth, and morality, and art—far more clearly than our compromised elders.

"Finn, you've been quiet. You started this ball rolling. You are, as it were, our Serbian gunman." Hunt paused to let the allusion take effect. "Would you care to give us the benefit of your thoughts?" "I don't know, sir." "What don't you know?" "Well, in one sense, I can't know what it is that I don't know. That's philosophically self-evident." He left one of those slight pauses in which we again wondered if he was engaged in subtle mockery or a high seriousness beyond the rest of us. "Indeed, isn't the whole business of ascribing responsibility a kind of cop-out? We want to blame an individual so that everyone else is exculpated. Or we blame a historical process as a way of exonerating individuals. Or it's all anarchic chaos, with the same consequence. It seems to me that there is—was—a chain of individual responsibilities, all of which were necessary, but not so long a chain that everybody can simply blame everyone else. But of course, my desire to ascribe responsibility might be more a reflection of my own cast of mind than a fair analysis of what happened. That's one of the central problems of history, isn't it, sir? The question of subjective versus objective interpretation, the fact that we need to know the history of the historian in order to understand the version that is being put in front of us." There was a silence. And no, he wasn't taking the piss, not in the slightest.

Old Joe Hunt looked at his watch and smiled. "Finn, I retire in five years. And I shall be happy to give you a reference if you care to take over." And he wasn't taking the piss either.

At assembly one morning, the headmaster, in the sombre voice he kept for expulsions and catastrophic sporting defeats, announced that he was the bearer of grievous news, namely that Robson of the Science Sixth had passed away during the weekend. Over a susurrus of awed mutterings, he told us that Robson had been cut down in the flower of youth, that his demise was a loss to the whole school, and that we would all be symbolically present at the funeral. Everything, in fact, except what we wanted to know: how, and why, and if it turned out to be murder, by whom.

"Eros and Thanatos," Adrian commented before the day's first lesson. "Thanatos wins again."
"Robson wasn't exactly Eros-and-Thanatos material," Alex told him. Colin and I nodded agreement. We knew because he'd been in our class for a couple of years: a steady, unimaginative boy, gravely uninterested in the arts, who had trundled along without offending anyone. Now he had offended us by making a name for himself with an early death. The flower of youth, indeed: the Robson we had known was vegetable matter.

There was no mention of disease, a bicycling accident or a gas explosion, and a few days later rumour (aka Brown of the Maths Sixth) supplied what the authorities couldn't, or wouldn't.

Robson had got his girlfriend pregnant, hanged himself in the attic, and not been found for two days.

"I'd never have thought he knew how to hang himself." "He was in the Science Sixth." "But you need a special sort of slip knot." "That's only in films. And proper executions. You can do it with an ordinary knot. Just takes longer to suffocate you." "What do we think his girlfriend's like?" We considered the options known to us: prim virgin (now ex-virgin), tarty shopgirl, experienced older woman, VD-riddled whore. We discussed this until Adrian redirected our interests.

"Camus said that suicide was the only true philosophical question." "Apart from ethics and politics and aesthetics and the nature of reality and all the other stuff." There was an edge to Alex's riposte.

"The only *true* one. The fundamental one on which all others depend." After a long analysis of Robson's suicide, we concluded that it could only be considered philosophical in an arithmetical sense of the term: he, being about to cause an increase of one in the human population, had decided it was his ethical duty to keep the planet's numbers constant. But in all other respects we judged that Robson had let us—and serious thinking—down. His action had been unphilosophical, self-indulgent and inartistic: in other words, wrong. As for his suicide note, which according to rumour (Brown again) read "Sorry, Mum", we felt that it had missed a powerful educative opportunity.

Perhaps we wouldn't have been so hard on Robson if it hadn't been for one central, unshiftable fact: Robson was our age, he was in our terms unexceptional, and yet he had not only conspired to find a girlfriend but also, incontestably, to have had sex with her. Fucking bastard! Why him and not us? Why had none of us even had the experience of failing to get a girlfriend? At least the humiliation of that would have added to our general wisdom, given us something to negatively boast about ("Actually, 'pustular berk with the charisma of a plimsole' were her exact words"). We knew from our reading of great literature that Love involved Suffering, and would happily have got in some practice at Suffering if there was an implicit, perhaps even logical, promise that Love might be on its way.

This was another of our fears: that Life wouldn't turn out to be like Literature. Look at our parents—were they the stuff of Literature? At best, they might aspire to the condition of onlookers and bystanders, part of a social backdrop against which real, true, important things could happen. Like what? The things Literature was all about: love, sex, morality, friendship, happiness, suffering, betrayal, adultery, good and evil, heroes and villains, guilt and innocence, ambition, power, justice, revolution, war, fathers and sons, mothers and daughters, the individual against society, success and failure, murder, suicide, death, God. And barn owls. Of course, there were other sorts of literature—theoretical, self-referential, lachrymosely autobiographical—but they were just dry wanks. Real literature was about psychological, emotional and social truth as demonstrated by the actions and reflections of its protagonists; the novel was about character developed over time. That's what Phil Dixon had told us anyway. And the only person—apart from Robson—whose life so far contained anything remotely novel-worthy was Adrian.

"Why did your mum leave your dad?" "I'm not sure." "Did your mum have another bloke?" "Was your father a cuckold?" "Did your dad have a mistress?" "I don't know. They said I'd understand when I was older." "That's what they always promise. How about explaining it now, that's what I say." Except that I never had said this. And our house, as far as I could tell, contained no mysteries, to my shame and disappointment.

"Maybe your mum has a young lover?" "How would I know. We never meet there. She always comes up to London." This was hopeless. In a novel, Adrian wouldn't just have accepted things as they were put to him. What was the point of having a situation worthy of fiction if the protagonist didn't behave as he would have done in a book? Adrian should have gone snooping, or saved up his pocket money and employed a private detective; perhaps all four of us should have gone off on a Quest to Discover the Truth. Or would that have been less like literature and too much like a kids' story? In our final history lesson of the year, Old Joe Hunt, who had guided his lethargic pupils through Tudors and Stuarts, Victorians and Edwardians, the Rise of Empire and its Subsequent Decline, invited us to look back over all those centuries and attempt to draw conclusions.

"We could start, perhaps, with the seemingly simple question, What is History? Any thoughts, Webster?" "History is the lies of the victors," I replied, a little too quickly. "Yes, I was rather afraid you'd say that. Well, as long as you remember that it is also the self-delusions of the defeated. Simpson?" Colin was more prepared than me. "History is a raw onion sandwich, sir." "For what reason?" "It just repeats, sir. It burps. We've seen it again and again this year. Same old story, same old oscillation between tyranny and rebellion, war and peace, prosperity and impoverishment. " "Rather a lot for a sandwich to contain, wouldn't you say?" We laughed far more than was required, with an end-of-term hysteria.

"Finn?" "History is that certainty produced at the point where the imperfections of memory meet the inadequacies of documentation. " "Is it, indeed? Where did you find that?" "Lagrange, sir. Patrick Lagrange. He's French. " "So one might have guessed. Would you care to give us an example?" "Robson's suicide, sir. " There was a perceptible intake of breath and some reckless headturning. But Hunt, like the other masters, allowed Adrian special status. When the rest of us tried provocation, it was dismissed as puerile cynicism—something else we would grow out of. Adrian's provocations were somehow welcomed as awkward searchings after truth.

"What has that to do with the matter?" "It's a historical event, sir, if a minor one. But recent. So it ought to be easily understood as history. We know that he's dead, we know that he had a girlfriend, we know that she's pregnant—or was. What else do we have? A single piece of documentation, a suicide note reading 'Sorry, Mum'—at least, according to Brown. Does that note still exist? Was it destroyed? Did Robson have any other motives or reasons beyond the obvious ones? What was his state of mind? Can we be sure the child was his? We can't know, sir, not even this soon afterwards. So how might anyone write Robson's story in fifty years' time, when his parents are dead and his girlfriend has disappeared and doesn't want to remember him anyway? You see the problem, sir?" We all looked at Hunt, wondering if Adrian had pushed it too far this time. That single word "pregnant" seemed to hover like chalk-dust. And as for the audacious suggestion of alternative paternity, of Robson the Schoolboy Cuckold...After a while, the master replied.

"I see the problem, Finn. But I think you underestimate history. And for that matter historians. Let us assume for the sake of argument that poor Robson were to prove of historical interest. "

Historians have always been faced with the lack of direct evidence for things. That's what they're used to. And don't forget that in the present case there would have been an inquest, and therefore a coroner's report. Robson may well have kept a diary, or written letters, made phone calls whose contents are remembered. His parents would have replied to the letters of condolence they received. And fifty years from now, given the current life expectancy, quite a few of his schoolfellows would still be available for interview. The problem might be less daunting than you imagine. "But nothing can make up for the absence of Robson's testimony, sir. " "In one way, no. But equally, historians need to treat a participant's own explanation of events with a certain scepticism. It is often the statement made with an eye to the future that is the most suspect. " "If you say so, sir. " "And mental states may often be inferred from actions. The tyrant rarely sends a handwritten note requesting the elimination of an enemy. " "If you say so, sir. " "Well, I do. " Was this their exact exchange? Almost certainly not. Still, it is my best memory of their exchange.

思考与讨论

（1）节选内容中存在着两种对立冲突的历史观，分别是什么？

（2）《终结的感觉》中记忆对个人历史的建构作用是如何体现的？

（3）托尼记忆中不确定的个人历史有哪些？

（4）如何看待小说中维罗妮卡这一女性形象？

（5）如何看待小说中托尼的悔恨？

（6）艾德里安为什么自杀？如何看待艾德里安的自杀？

 拓展阅读

［1］Callus, I. "There Is Great Unrest": Some Reflections on Emotion and Memory in Julian Barnes's *Nothing to Be Frightened of* and *The Sense of an Ending*. *Prague Journal of English Study*. Vol.1, No.1(2012), pp.55－77.

［2］Moseley, M. *Understanding Julian Barnes*. Columbia: University of South Carolina Press, 1997.

［3］Wei, T.A. Julian Barnes and the Subversion of *The Sense of an Ending*. *Narrative*. Vol.31, No.1,(2023), pp.1－14.

二、格雷厄姆·斯威夫特

（一）格雷厄姆·斯威夫特简介

格雷厄姆·斯威夫特是英国当代小说家，英国皇家文学会会员。1949 年斯威夫特出生于英国伦敦，1967 年进入剑桥大学英语系，以优异成绩获得剑桥大学王后学院文学学士和硕士学位，后在约克大学攻读博士学位，但未完成有关狄更斯的博士论文。斯威夫特从事过很多工作，他在精神病院上过班，也曾经做过保安、农场工人等，但大部分时间在伦敦继续教育学院讲授文学课程。1983 年，斯威夫特辞去职务成为全职作家。上述经历对他的文学创作有很大影响。

1980 年，斯威夫特出版了第一部长篇小说《糖果店主》（*The Sweet Shop Owner*），该作品通过描述主人公生命中最后一天的经历和他对自己一生的回忆，用内心独白的方式展现了社会底层小人物的命运。1981 年，他出版了《羽毛球》（*Shuttlecock*），获杰弗里·费伯纪念奖，这是他第一部具有历史元小说特征的作品。1983 年出版的《水之乡》（*Waterland*）入围布克奖，获得《卫报》小说奖，1992 年被美国著名导演斯蒂芬·吉伦豪尔（Stephen Gyllenhaal）改编成电影搬上银幕，深受观众喜爱。他又陆续出版了小说《世外桃源》（*Out of This World*，1988）、《从那以后》（*Ever After*，1992）等。他的第六部长篇小说《杯酒留痕》（*Last Orders*，1996）在出版当年获布克奖和詹姆斯·泰特·布莱克纪念奖（The James Tait

Black Memorial Prize),并于 2001 年改编为同名电影。之后斯威夫特又出版了《白日之光》(*The Light of Day*,2002)、《明天》(*Tomorrow*,2007)、《希望你在这里》(*Wish You Were Here*,2011)等作品。

斯威夫特是一位小说实验家,他的作品往往具有独特的叙事结构,擅长将多重时间框架的历史讲述和心理分析结合在一起,具有丰富的历史哲理和思想深度。

(二)《水之乡》简介

《水之乡》被公认为战后英国小说的杰出代表。小说共 52 章,以英格兰东部的沼泽地区芬斯为背景,融水乡风景描写、个人家庭和历史叙事于一体,追述了 1943 年 7 月的一系列事件,讲述了二战后主人公历史教师汤姆·克里克的人生遭遇。全书有三条叙事线索,其一是汤姆的父辈克里克家族和阿特金森家族的过往历史;其二是历史教师做出放弃课本知识给学生讲授家族活历史的决定,遭到校长反对,汤姆因此失去了教职;其三是玛丽在丧失生育能力后偷窃婴儿,该行动牵扯到多年前弗雷迪·帕尔的死亡事件。斯威夫特将芬斯的地方史和几代人的家族历史联系在一起,生动地描绘了当地人的生活风貌,揭示了过去和现在彼此交织的神秘运作方式。

再现真实历史是斯威夫特创作的核心,而这种真实性在《水之乡》中通过主人公不断的反问一次次引起读者的疑问,真实和虚构的悖论重复出现并影响了历史叙述的可靠性。小说以汤姆父亲用童话般的语言讲故事作为开篇,全文围绕叙述者汤姆的个人、家族和芬斯沼泽地一带数百年的发展历史展开,穿插着他个人对历史和回忆的反思,文中处处都体现出不同的人对同一历史事件的阐释和对其意义的探讨。故事发生的场所芬斯沼泽地位于水域和陆地的交界处,正如叙述者的视角在过去和现在之间不停切换,暗示了历史与现实之间存在某种神秘的联系。该叙事策略打破了时间和空间的界限,呈现出典型的历史元小说的特征。

历史循环、因果报应是《水之乡》的另一重要主题。小说运用对比手法,将阿特金森家族酿酒厂的兴起和衰落同拿破仑的成功和滑铁卢惨败相提并论,确证了历史发展的因果循环论——建立在阴谋和罪恶之上的帝国必然走向失败。阿特金森家族的疯狂始于托马斯①因嫉妒年轻貌美的妻子莎拉而动手伤人,这似乎预示了后来迪克②因嫉妒怒杀弗莱德③的结局,将个人的毁灭与家族的没落乃至世界战争带来的灾难联系在了一起。小说表达了斯威夫特对现代科技文明发展带来毁灭性后果的担忧,借汤姆之口说出文明所谓的向前发展,无论是在道德层面还是技术方面,最终总是伴随着衰退,因此人类的历史只是不断循环往复和原地踏步。

斯威夫特的小说善于在宏大的历史叙事中描写小人物的命运。在普通人的平凡人生和其所处的波澜壮阔的社会背景的对比中,斯威夫特运用了不同的叙事声音,探讨个人经历与重大历史事件之间的关系,强调了创造客观真实历史的不可能性。《水之乡》的每一章都有一个严肃而富有深意的主题,看似各

---

① 阿特金森家族靠乔赛亚·阿特金高超独特的酿酒技术以酿酒业崛起,乔赛亚只有一个儿子威廉,威廉也只有一个儿子托马斯。阿特金森家族自乔赛亚·阿特金森始以酿酒为生,代代相传。托马斯·阿特金森生了两个儿子——乔治和阿尔弗雷德。阿尔弗雷德没有儿子,乔治只有一个儿子亚瑟,亚瑟只生了一个儿子欧内斯特。欧内斯特·阿特金森是小说《水之乡》叙述汤姆的外祖父。托马斯是阿特金森家族酒业的第三代传人,是小说叙述人汤姆的外祖父的曾祖父。
② 迪克是小说叙述人汤姆同父异母的哥哥,是汤姆的母亲与外祖父欧内斯特·阿特金森乱伦生下的弱智男孩。
③ 弗莱德是小说叙述人汤姆、迪克、玛丽儿时的玩伴,发小。迪克喜欢女孩玛丽,玛丽却在孩子们的性游戏后意外怀孕。弱智的迪克认为是弗莱德导致玛丽怀孕而心生嫉妒和恨意,在一次一起游泳时把弗莱德按在水中溺死。

自独立,实际上又被斯威夫特独特的叙述手法串联在一起,在小说整体的叙事框架中相互照应,展示出斯威夫特小说创作的创新性。

(三) 作品选读:《水之乡》①

SOME SAY they were originally Fenmen. But if they were, they moved long ago, tired of wet boots and flat horizons, to the hills of Norfolk, to become simple shepherds. And it was on the hills of Norfolk (low and humble hills as hills go, but mountain ranges by Fen standards) that they got ideas—something the stick-in-the-mud Cricks rarely entertained.

Before Vermuyden came to the Fens and encountered the obstinacy of the Fen-dwellers, an Atkinson forefather, on his bleating hillside, conceived the idea of becoming a bailiff; and his son, a bailiff born, conceived the idea of becoming a farmer of substance; and one of the fourth, fifth or sixth generation of idea-conceiving Atkinsons, while land was being enclosed and the wool trade fluctuating, sold most of his sheep, hired ploughmen and sowed barley, which grew tall and fruitful in the chalky upland soil and which he sent to the maltster to be transformed into beer.

And that is another difference between the Cricks and the Atkinsons. That whereas the Cricks emerged from water, the Atkinsons emerged from beer.

Those acres of land he ploughed must have been special, and Josiah Atkinson must have known a thing or two, because word got around that the malt made from his barley was not only exceptional but there was magic in it.

The good—and exceedingly good-humoured—villagers of west Norfolk drank their ale with relish and, having nothing to compare it with, took for granted its excellence as only what true ale should be. But the brewers of the nearby towns, eager men with a flair, even then, for market research, sampled the village produce on foraging excursions and inquired whence came the malt. The maltster in his turn, a simple fellow, could not refrain while praise was being heaped on his malt from declaring the source of his barley. Thus it came about that in the year 1751 Josiah Atkinson, farmer of Wexingham, Norfolk, and George Jarvis, maltster of Sheverton, entered a contract, initiated by the former but to the advantage—so it appeared—of the latter, whereby they agreed to share the cost of purchase or hire of wagons, wagoners and teams of horses to convey their mutual product, for their mutual profit, to the brewers of Swaffham and Thetford.

This partnership of Jarvis and Atkinson thrived. But Josiah, who had already conceived another idea, did not deny himself in this agreement the right to send his barley, if he so wished, to be malted elsewhere. Atkinson's foresight told him that in his son's or his grandson's lifetime, if not in his own, the brewers in their market towns would find it expedient to operate their own malting houses, close at hand, and that Jarvis, who for the present believed Atkinson to be tied by their

---

① Swift, G. *Waterland*. London: Picador, 2008, pp. 69 - 91.

joint commitment to the brewers, would suffer.

So he did—or, rather, so did his successors. While across the Atlantic the first warning shots were being fired in what is known to you as the War of American Independence, William Atkinson, Josiah's son, began sending his barley direct to the brewers. Old George's son, John, perplexed, enraged but powerless, could only fall back on local trade. His malting business declined. In 1779, with the boldness of a man only pursuing an inevitable logic, William Atkinson offered to buy him out. Jarvis, humbled, broken, agreed. From that day the Jarvises became overseers of the Atkinson malting house.

William, nothing compunctious, had only to complete the well-laid stratagem of his father. On his sorrel horse, with his tricorn hat on his head, he went visiting the brewers of Swaffham and Thetford. He announced that as for his barley, there was none finer, as they well knew, in the region; nor was there any shortage of it (for was he not even now bringing more land under the plough?) but henceforth no brewer was to have it unless it was malted at the Atkinson maltings.

The brewers protested, arched their eyebrows, pushed back their carved oak chairs, snapped the stems of their clay pipes. What of their own malting houses, built at considerable expense and for the express convenience of proximity? William replied that, by all means, they should continue to use them—to produce an ale that their customers would surely judge inferior. That as for the question of proximity, had not his own wagons given reliable service in the past?

The brewers huffed, scowled, loosened their itching periwigs; and at length yielded to compromise. The early 1780s in Swaffham and Thetford witnessed a phenomenon as yet unheard of. Ale was, henceforth, no longer ale but a twin-headed creature, one face bearing the accustomed character of ale but costing a halfpenny more, the other, at the old price, unfamiliar and insipid.

William Atkinson rode away, well pleased, from further consultations with the brewers, at which he is to be imagined, perhaps, sitting in their tap-rooms, jovially clinking tankards. For William owed his success not merely to the prescience of his father, or his own acumen, but to infectious good cheer. It was that magical liquor, cupped in their hands, winking and beaming even as they spoke, which prevailed, as much as Will's wily brain. Good cheer: was not this the ultimate aim of his- and their-business? And was good cheer to be propagated by rancour and hard feelings? Could he not tell these begrudging brewers how once his father, old Josiah, had taken him out into the barley fields where the wind rustled like a thousand silk petticoats through the ripening ears, and, stooping low and cocking his head to one side, had said: "D'ye hear that? D'ye hear that now? That's the sound of loosening tongues, that's the sound of ale-house laughter—that's the sound of merriment."

William's wagons lumbered from Sheverton to Swaffham and from Sheverton to Thetford with their sacks of malt. In time, brewers from Fakenham and Norwich, who had tied up no capital in makings of their own, found it worth their while to send to Sheverton for their malt.

But William, who was growing old and already conferring much of his affairs on his son, Thomas, knew that success could not continue unthreatened. Other Norfolk barley-growers, showing the farming enterprise he and his father had shown, must compete for the brewers' favours. Besides, Will Atkinson was still having ideas. He dreamed that the Atkinsons would one day follow the wondrous barley-seed from its beginning to its end without its passing through the hand of a third party. That the former shepherds who now farmed and malted would one day brew, and in a style far surpassing the tin-pot brewers of Thetford and Swaffham.

Picture a scene not dissimilar from that in which Josiah and William once stood listening to what the barley had to say, but in which it is now William who, leaning on a stick, commands his son's attention and directs his gaze towards the west, to where the Fens lurk in the misty distance. To where the peaty soil, such as has been won back from water, albeit admirable for oats and wheat, will never yield malting barley like that nourished by the furrows on which they stand. Drawing his outstretched hand across the view, he explains to young Tom how the people of the Fens import their malt from the uplands of southern Cambridgeshire, Hertfordshire and Bedfordshire. Very good barley country too, and very good malt, except that the numerous tolls levied on it as it is brought in barges down the Cam and Ouse make it expensive; and the natural hazards of those same waterways, which have a troublesome habit of bursting their banks, changing their course and every so often becoming choked with silt, ensure that supplies are unreliable, sometimes unforthcoming and, when forthcoming, often in poor condition. In short, the Fenmen pay hard for irregular and indifferent ale. And, as if this was not enough, the Fens are such a backward and trackless wilderness, that few Fenmen can lay their hands on what ale is available.

Looking down from his hilltop in an expansive and prophetic manner (which perhaps explains how, when I tried to visualize that God whom Dad said had such a clear view, I would sometimes see a ruddy, apple-cheeked face, beneath a three-cornered hat, with snowy hair tied back in the eighteenth-century fashion), looking down from his Norfolk hills, William clasped his son's shoulder and said perhaps some such words as these: "We must help these poor besodden Fenlanders. They need a little cheer in their wretched swamps. They cannot survive on water."

Picture another scene, in the parlour of the red-brick farmhouse that Josiah built in 1760 (still standing in all its Georgian solidity on the outskirts of Wexingham) in which Will unfurls a map specially purchased from a Cambridge map-seller and points with a nut-brown index finger to the region of the Leem. He takes as a centre the little town of Gildsey near the confluence of the Leem and Ouse. He compares the distance, by way of the Leem, from their own farmland to Gildsey, with that by way of the Cam and Ouse from the barleyland of the south. He draws his son's attention, for which no map is necessary, to the hamlet of Kessling, but a few miles west of Wexingham—a run-down cluster of dwellings amidst rough heathland and pasture where the young Leem, after its journey from the hills, begins to slow and gather itself—from which most of the inhabitants have already departed to become Atkinson labourers. He taps the map with his pipe-stem. The man who builds a malting house at Kessling and has the keys of the river will bring wealth to a wasteland. And himself.

Thomas looks at the map and at his father. The keys of the river? He sees no river; only a series of meres, marshes and floodlands through which perhaps a watery artery is vaguely traceable. Whereupon William, pipe-stem back in the corner of his mouth, utters a word which falls strangely and perplexingly on the ears of a man who lives on top of a chalk hill: "Drainage".

So Thomas Atkinson, spurred by his father, who goes to his rest in Wexingham churchyard, year of our Lord 1785, begins to buy waterlogged land in the Leem catchment and discovers that Drainage is indeed a strange, even magical, word—as magical as the grains of his own barley. Because in five or six years' time he can sell the same land, with the water squeezed out of it, at a tenfold profit.

While on the continent the millennium arrives, while the Bastille tumbles, Jacobins oust Girondins and there is widespread draining away of blood, Thomas Atkinson studies the principles of land drainage, of river velocity and siltation. How the efficacy of artificial drainage is measured by the increased water dischargeable through the natural drain of a river. How the velocity of a river increases as a fraction of the increase of water but siltation decreases as a multiple of the increase of velocity. He applies these principles with palpable results. He consults and hires surveyors, engineers and labourers, none of whom complain of his ignorance or his impatience or his parsimony as an employer. And amongst those who come to work for him are the Cricks from across the Ouse.

Thomas learns it isn't easy. And it's never finished. Little by little. The obstinacy of water. The tenacity of ideas. Land reclamation.

But, lest it be thought that amidst these arduous toils Thomas has lost sight of his father's Good Cheer, his account books record the provision of regular supplies of ale, made with Atkinson malt, to be brought from Norfolk, at some cost and hardship, considering the problems of transport, for the refreshment of his Fenland workers. And when in 1799, grown rich from land-speculation, and appointing an agent to run his Norfolk farm, he moves from Wexingham to Kessling—where, to the astonishment of the handful of villagers, he has not only had a house built but drawn up plans for the digging of a basin in the River Leem and the construction beside it, in due course, of a malting house of large and most up-to-date pattern—it is to bring with him a young and spirited bride of eighteen. And the man-servant, maid-servant, cook and stableman who have followed him from Wexingham cannot refrain from exchanging nudges, winks and leers at the unmistakable sounds that emanate thereafter from their master's chamber. Thomas, with good eighteenth-century uninhibitedness, is begetting heirs.

Who was this frolicsome and—so it proved—fecund young bride? She was Sarah Turnbull, only surviving child of Matthew Turnbull, brewer, of no great fortune, of Gildsey, Cambridgeshire—to whom Thomas Atkinson had one day come with the astonishing proposition that if he, Matthew, were to sell him, Thomas, one full half of his business, he, Matthew, would one day be a rich man. Whereupon Matthew had reflected deeply, paced several times around the sparsely furnished brewery office, and Thomas had spied, through the window, in the brewery yard below, the brewer's comely, light-stepping daughter, and, after discreet inquiries as to the health of the brewer's family, evolved a means of securing his aims in Gildsey more effective than any buying up of shares.

By the year of Trafalgar, Thomas had drained twelve thousand acres along the margins of the Leem; dykes had been dug by the score; some sixty or so wind-pumps were in operation; and tenant farmers were paying the lucrative rents and drainage levies that went with equally lucrative soil. From Kessling, where by now almost every villager received Atkinson wages, to Apton—a distance, by water, of nine miles—the river had been embanked and sluices and staunches built to control the flow.

But the remaining section between Apton and the Ouse proved difficult. Thomas suffered the fate of all men of initiative whose single-handed ventures pay off: he came up against a wall of rivalry, vested interests and parliamentary machination. For fifteen years he had waged war on water, mud and winter weather, but he encountered no enemy more stubborn than the elders of Gildsey and their elected representatives when they perceived that the navigation of the Leem was indeed feasible and land prices were rocketing. While Napoleon made his lightning marches against Austrians, Prussians and Russians, Thomas Atkinson got bogged down in protracted litigation and labyrinthine wrangles over navigation rights, land tenure and the constitution of drainage boards.

A lesser man would have been dissuaded. A lesser man would have cut his losses and returned to the dry and stable vantage point of his Norfolk hills. But in 1809, at long last, the Leem Navigation is officially, if grudgingly, ceded to him. Simultaneously, he gains the chairmanship—albeit over a divided and unruly board—of the Leem Drainage Commission.

He sets to work once more. The new banks of the river progress westward. Where he cannot buy land he buys cooperation. The Hockwell Lode is dug to assist the drainage of the particularly intractable region north of the lower Leem. A location is fixed, two miles from the junction with the Ouse, for the construction of a combined sluice and navigation lock, to control the entrance to the river. The barge-pool at Kessling is completed and a site on the west bank of the Ouse on the northern outskirts of Gildsey purchased for development as wharves. Though no boat has yet made the auspicious journey between Kessling and Gildsey, numerous craft are already plying their way with materials and waste between Kessling and Apton, Apton and Gildsey, and overtures have been made to the boat-builders in Ely and Lynn regarding the construction of a permanent fleet of lighters.

In 1813, while Napoleon, whose army once advanced so proudly in the opposite direction, retreats from Leipzig to the Rhine, Thomas Atkinson begins building the makings at Kessling. He is now in his fifty-ninth year.

In his fifty-ninth year he is still a hale and hearty—and a merry—man; a man who would claim no affinity with the vainglorious Emperor of the French. With his young wife (who now affects the loose gowns and coal-scuttle bonnets made familiar to us through pictures of Lady Hamilton and the mistresses of Byron), he strolls round the barge-pool at Kessling and inspects progress on the works. Is it merely coincidence that it is in the year 1815 that the large and lofty building is completed and christened, by inevitable choice, the Waterloo Maltings? Is it merely coincidence that at the outset of that year his father-in-law, the brewer of Gildsey, falls ill and is declared by his doctor to be not long for the world? Is it coincidence alone that the dignitaries of Gildsey, amidst the flush of national rejoicing, decide to forget their differences with this Norfolk upstart and to welcome him instead as one of their own, the bringer of prosperity to their town and a living emblem of the spirit of Albion? And is it no more than a sop to the times—or a sign of personal exultation, or a mark of willingness to be turned into a symbol—that when on a September day in 1815, amidst cheering and the fluttering of red, white and blue bunting, a little gang of four newly built lighters enters the Leem from the direction of Gildsey and, linked to a be-ribboned draught-horse, passes through the newly completed Atkinson Lock, the foremost of this gang—the flagship, as it were—should bear on its bows, beside the bright red stem-post and the device, soon to be familiar, of two crossed yellow barley-ears above a double wavy blue line, the name *Annus Mirabilis*?

Children, there is a theory of history which may be called—to borrow a word from the ancient Greeks—the theory of hubris. This doctrine provides that there can be no success with impunity, no great achievement without accompanying loss; that no Napoleon can go carving up the map of Europe without getting his comeuppance.

You sneer. Who administers this grand and rough justice? The gods? Some supernatural power? This is getting all too much like fairy-tales again. Very well. But even nature teaches us that nothing is given without something being taken away. Consider water, which, however much you coax it, this way and that, will return, at the slightest opportunity, to its former equilibrium. Or consider the handsome wife of Thomas Atkinson, formerly Sarah Turnbull, of Gildsey. Between the years 1800 and 1815 she bears Thomas three sons, two of whom live and one of whom dies; and a daughter, who lives, but only till her sixth year. For the techniques of land-drainage may have improved considerably but medical science is still in its infancy.

Sarah watches, on the arm of her lauded husband, the lighters passing into the River Leem, but tempers the pleasure in her lovely face with due signs of decorum and restraint. For it is only three weeks since her father—who never saw, save in his daughter's good fortune, the riches Thomas Atkinson promised him—went to his grave. And watching also, perhaps, somewhere along the banks of the Leem, are the Cricks—the father William and the brothers Francis and Joseph. But they do not cheer as heartily as the other spectators. Too much enthusiasm never went with their phlegmatic natures. And though they draw pride from their part in the making of this newly navigable, brightly gleaming river, they know that what water makes, it also unmakes. Nothing moves far in this world. And whatever moves forwards will also move back. A law of the natural world; and a law, too, of the human heart.

The townsfolk cheer. They drink ale (but not Atkinson Ale, for the town brewery remains as yet in the name of Turnbull and it would not do to dishonour the dead). There is jubilation and merriment. But just for a moment, perhaps, Thomas Atkinson wonders if this is the sort of merriment he wants—the merriment that goes with grand openings and speeches and toasts to the hook-nosed vanquisher of Bonaparte.

In the winter of 1815 to 1816 rain swells the River Leem which bursts its banks between Apton and Hockwell and floods six thousand acres of newly ploughed farmland. A grievous but sufferable disaster: Atkinson resourcefulness takes care of it and within three months the damage is repaired. In 1816 the price of wheat doubles and those same tenant farmers whom Thomas had provided with rich farmland can no longer pay either their rents or their labourers. Napoleon is beaten: the poor starve. In Ely a mob runs riot and sabre-waving dragoons who but a year before held the field at Waterloo are summoned to crush their own countrymen. Jubilation? Merriment?

Thomas surveys the stricken Fenlands. But this too he can bear. Because he is a rich man—and a barley-man, not a wheat-man to boot—he can be accommodating to his tenant farmers. He hands out shillings and finds food for the hungry (his dear wife herself does not shirk from ladling gruel beside the maltings at Kessling). And it is only because of these charitable acts and because in these hard times he continues to provide employment, as he has in the past, that no mob runs loose in Gildsey and storms, as it surely would have done, the local Bastille of the town brewery.

In 1818—when violence has ceased but there is no less hardship—Thomas fits out the ground floor of his house in Kessling as offices for his maltings and makes the second move of his life, from Kessling to Gildsey, to a grand residence, Cable House (which still stands), north of the market square, but a minute's walk from the brewery, with a view down the narrow lane, which was known then and is still known, though it is a wide thoroughfare now with a Boots and a Woolworths, as Water Street. The brewery is enlarged and ceases to bear the name it has borne for three respectful years, of Turnbull. The townsfolk taste, for the first time under its proper title, the inimitable flavour of Atkinson Ale made with Atkinson malt from Atkinson barley. The landlords of the Gildsey inns, whose names reflect the watery world which surrounds them—the Swan, the Dog and Duck, the Jolly Bargeman, the Pike and Eel—regale their indigent yet thirsty customers.

Does it soften their grievances—a dose or two of tawny Merriment? Does it soften old Tom's? For something is happening to Thomas, now a still robust sixty-three. He is becoming a monument.

Man of Enterprise, Man of Good Works, Man of Civic Honour. The portrait painted of him in this same year shows a countenance of undoubted character, but it does not have the twinkle of his father's eye or the soft creases of his father's mouth—nor will his two sons, George and Alfred, revive these features of their grandfather. Thomas is becoming aloof. He can no longer stand by one of his new drains and clap the shoulder of the man who has helped dig it. The labourers who once worked beside him—the Cricks perhaps among them-now touch forelocks, venerate him, regard him as a sort of god. And when, with the express purpose of showing he is not aloof, he enters the tap-room of the Swan or the Bargeman and orders a pint for every man, a silence descends on these haunts of mirth, like the hush inside a church.

He does not wish it—he cannot help it—but he feels himself measured up and fitted out for the stiff and cumbersome garments of legend. How he made the River Leem from a swamp. How he brought Norfolk beer to the Fens. How he fed the hungry by the barge-pool, became a pillar of... And, deep inside, he thinks, perhaps, how better and brighter things were that day in the old house at Wexingham, when the summer breezes blew through the window the sound of whispering barley and his father uttered the curious password: Drainage.

But even this he could bear, even this would be all right—for, God knows, Thomas Atkinson never believed in heaven on earth—if it were not for the matter of his wife. In 1819 she is thirty-seven. The playful, girlish looks which once won his fancy (and suited his business ends) have been transformed by the years into something richer and mellower. Mrs Atkinson is beautiful; with a beauty which is apt to remind Mr Atkinson of the beauty of an actress—as if his wife occupies some strongly lit stage and he, for all his public eminence, watches from a lowly distance. It seems to him that he has worked hard and achieved much and yet failed to give due attention to this wonderful creature with whom, once, he bounced so casually through the rituals of procreation.

In short, Sarah Atkinson is in her prime; and her husband is growing old and doting—and jealous.

In his sixty-fifth year attacks of gout confine Thomas within doors and disturb his usually even temper. He cannot accompany his wife on their accustomed walks, drives and visits. From the window of the house in Market Street, he watches her step into waiting carriages and be whisked away, and the constant paperwork before him, which concerns plans for the modernization and further enlargement of the brewery, the extension of the Ouse wharves and the conveyance of Atkinson Ale by river or road to ever more numerous points of consumption, cannot stop his thoughts, while she is gone, returning repeatedly to her.

Several men fall under his suspicion. His own brewery manager; a King's Lynn corn merchant; the younger members of the Drainage Commission; the very doctor who calls to treat his gout. And none of them can explain, for fear of imputing to the Great Man of Gildsey a slander which he has not openly voiced, that Mrs Atkinson is innocent, innocent, and has nothing but loyalty and devotion for her husband, whom everyone knows she adores.

One night in January, 1820, an incident occurs for which no first-hand account exists yet which is indelibly recorded in innumerable versions in the annals of Gildsey. That January night Sarah returned from an evening spent, so it happened, in the irreproachable company of the rector of St Gunnhilda's, his good wife and assembled guests, to a Thomas more than usually plagued by the pains of gout. It is not known exactly what passed between them, only that—according to what was unavoidably overheard by the servants and what Atkinson himself later gave out as confession— Thomas was gruff, grew surly, angry, and, whilst giving vent to the most unwarranted accusations and abuse, rose up from his chair and struck his wife hard on the face.

Doubtless, even if this action had not had the terrible consequences it did, it would have been regretted infinitely. Yet Thomas had indeed cause for infinite regret. For, having been struck, Sarah not only fell but in falling knocked her head against the corner of a walnut writing-table with such violence that though, after several hours, she recovered consciousness, she never again recovered her wits.

Whether it was the knock against the writing-table or the original blow which caused the dreadful damage, whether it was neither of these things but the moral shock of this sudden fury of her husband's, whether, as some have claimed, the knock against the writing-table was only an invention to hide the true extent of Thomas's violence—is immaterial. In a distraction of remorse over the motionless body, Thomas calls his sons and in a voice heard by the whole house announces: "I have killed my wife! I have killed my darling Sarah!" Horror. Confusion. Plenty of Here and Now. The sons, inclined at first, at what they see, to believe their father's bald summary of the case, send for the doctor—the selfsame doctor whose innocent attentions have contributed to this terrible scene—who is obliged not only to tend the stricken wife but to administer copious draughts of laudanum to the husband.

On that night in 1820 Thomas Atkinson is supposed to have lost completely all the symptoms of gout. At least, he no longer took heed of them. Far worse torments awaited him. All through the next day and on into the next night he must watch by the bedside, praying for those sublime eyes to open and those dear lips to move. He must experience the rushing relief and joy of seeing, indeed, the lips part, the mouth flutter, only to suffer the redoubled agony of knowing that though the eyes open they do not see him, or if they do, do not recognize him. And though those lips move they will never again utter to Thomas Atkinson a single word.

Sarah Atkinson is thirty-seven. Fate has decreed that, knocks on the head or no, she will live a long life. She will not go to her rest till her ninety-third year. For fifty-four years she will sit on a blue velvet chair before the window in an upper room (not the room once shared by her husband but a room to be known simply as Mistress Sarah's room), staring now straight before her down the cluttered thorough-fare of Water Street to the Ouse, now to her left over the rooftops to where, in

1849, the tall chimney of the New Brewery, on its site by the Ouse wharves, will rise.

But it is doubtful whether she will see these things. She will retain the paradoxical pose of one who keeps watch—but over nothing. She will not lose her beauty. Her upright, forward-looking posture will convey an undeniable grace. Even in old age when her flesh has shrunk but the firm mould of her bones remains (for in such a state her portrait will be painted, in a black dress with a diamond necklace, at the instigation of her sons—and what a perfect sitter she will make!), she will preserve the sadly imperious demeanour of an exiled princess.

At regular times servants will come, with meals on a tray, to comb her hair, light the fire, prepare their mistress for bed, or merely to sit beside her at the window, through bright mornings or sombre twilights, offering unanswered comment on the activity in the street below. And so too will come Thomas, to sit by his wife, often for hours on end, to clasp and wring his hands, to utter God knows what entreaties—but Sarah will never make the barest sign that she knows who he is.

All this he must endure. But first he must watch the doctor come daily, for prolonged visits. He must watch him look grave, thoughtful, shake his head and finally decide that he can do no more and the advice of specialists must be sought. Thomas will arrange, at great expense, for eminent physicians to come from Cambridge to examine his wife. He will conduct Sarah like some rare exhibit round the consulting-rooms of that learned city. He will take her to London to be examined, tapped, probed and considered by still more eminent men of medicine, and will donate to St Bartholomew's Hospital the sum of £500 for "the Further Investigation and Better Relief of Maladies of the Brain".

He will offer a fortune to the man who will give him back his wife; but no man will claim it. He will return to Gildsey, to the silent unrelenting enmity of his sons and the judgement of a whole town. For will they not, considering all he has done for them, his works and undertakings, the prosperity he has brought them, forgive him this one act of human weakness? No, it seems not. There are even those few, yet die-hard disciples of Temperance who add to the existing rumours the embellishment that when Thomas struck Sarah he was blind drunk from his own fine ale—and does this not prove the truth of the old saying that (far from spreading good cheer) brewers are the cousins of brawlers?

And if others have it in them to forgive Thomas, Thomas will not wish to be forgiven, not wishing to forgive himself. In the Jolly Bargeman and the Pike and Eel, where Temperance does not enter, they still smack their lips over Atkinson Ale, for its flavour remains ever true, ever conducive to the forgetting of troubles; and besides, the Atkinson business is now in the hands of young George and Alfred—long may they thrive. But as for old Tom, they preserve a dour brevity of comment or shake their heads, as once the doctor did over his poor wife.

The times cannot be numbered when Thomas Atkinson will ask, Why? Why? And again Why? (For heartache, too, inspires its own sad curiosity.) Not content with the verdict of physicians, he will embark, himself, on the study of the brain and the nervous system. To his library in Cable House he will add volumes in which are contained what human knowledge, in the 1820s, has to offer on the mystery of the human mind. Where once he pored over the topography of the Fens and the innumerable complexities of drainage, flood control and pumping systems, he will pore over the even more intricate topography of the medulla and the cerebellum, which have, so he discovers, their own networks of channels and ducts and their own dependence on the constant distribution of fluids.

But this is an internal land which cannot be redeemed cannot be reclaimed, once it is lost.

Abandoning science, he will turn to religion. The good church-goers of Gildsey who have hitherto observed Thomas alongside his wife and his two sons, uttering his Amens with the calm air of a man who regards the Sunday service as a wholesome if unabsorbing social duty, now witness the bent and furrowed brow, the forever restless lips of the sinner wrapped in penitential prayer.

He no longer attends to the expanding affairs of Atkinson and Sons. He no longer reads his newspaper (Castlereagh has cut his throat; Canning takes his place). History has stopped for him. He has entered the realms of superstition. It is even said that when God did not answer him, when God, even with his clear view, could not explain Why, Thomas sent out into the undrained Fen, for the services of one of those ancestors of Bill Clay, whose potions and charms were still regarded with respect. And that the reply of the wizened occultist (who had no cause to help Atkinson whose drainage schemes spelt the doom of his kind) drove the last rivet of grief into old Tom's soul: that Thomas Atkinson, as Thomas himself well knew, was only receiving the punishment he merited, and that, as for his wife, no magic in the world could bring her out of the state which she herself— had not Thomas looked closely enough into her eyes? —wished to remain in.

For two, three, four years, Thomas will look closely into his wife's eyes. For four years he will continue to sit with her in the upper room, wringing her hand and his own heart. And then in December 1825—story has it that it was in this selfsame upper room, in his wife's presence, that death occurred, and that the two were discovered, the one stone dead, the other not batting an eyelid—this once vigorous and hearty man, who a decade ago, though sixty then, would have been credited with another twenty or thirty years, worn out with remorse, is released from his misery. He is buried with due dignity, ceremony and appreciation of his Works, but with what seems also a certain haste, in St Gunnhilda's churchyard, a little distance from the south transept, in a grave capped by a massive marble monument, its corners carved in high relief in the form of Ionic columns. An inscription on the south face gives Thomas's dates and a record in Latin of his deeds (*qui flumen Leemem navigabile fecit..*) but not his misdeed; and the whole is surmounted by an enormous, fluted, crateriform marble urn, half covered by a shroud of marble drapery on which, where it extends on to the flat surface of the monument, lie (an incongruous touch on such a classical edifice, but no visitor fails to be caught by it or to note the extraordinarily life-like rendering) two sorrily strewn ears of barley. In his last will and testament Thomas leaves it to God, Time, and the people of Gildsey, but, before all these, to Sarah herself—"whom Providence restore swiftly to that wholeness of mind so to pass judgement but long to await its execution"—to determine whether his dear wife shall one day, again, lie beside him.

And shall we leave it too—possessing though we do the gift of hindsight—to see what God, Time and the people will decide, and make no comment, as yet, on what, if anything, lies beside old Tom's grave in St Gunnhilda's churchyard; nor make any moralizing and wise-after-the-event comparisons between the simple headstone, which stands gathering moss and lichens in Wexingham, of William Atkinson who died content and the grand tomb of Thomas Atkinson who died wretched?

To Thomas's sons, George and Alfred, mere striplings of twenty-five and twenty-three, yet already fashioned by regret-table circumstances into brisk and earnest young men of business, it seems that the air is cleared, purified. Their debt of shame has been paid and now with renewed righteousness, with renewed purpose, they can start once more. History does not record whether the day of Thomas's funeral was one of those dazzling mid-winter Fenland days in which the sky seems to cleanse every outline and make light of distances and the two towers of Ely cathedral can not only be seen but their contrasting architecture plainly descried. Nor does it record whether the people of Gildsey, who so confidently scorned the genuine grief of Thomas for his wife, failed to notice the lack of grief of Thomas's sons for their father.

But such things would have been appropriate. For the town, no less than its two young champions, feels, as it enters, indeed, its heyday, this ever-recurring need to begin again, to wipe the slate, erase the past and look to the sparkling landmarks of the future.

Has not the shrewdness of old William been borne out? No Fenland brewer, dependent on barley from the south, can compete with Atkinson barley malted at the Atkinson maltings and brought down the Leem in Atkinson lighters without a single toll charge. Soon not only the people of Gildsey but the people of March, Wisbech, Ely and Lynn will appreciate the fine quality and fine price of Atkinson Ale. And if Atkinson lighters can carry Atkinson Ale to all these places, and beyond, why should they not carry other things? Why should the Atkinsons not avail themselves of their favourable position at the junction of Ouse and Leem, and of the general improvement of the waterways, to turn Gildsey into an *entrepot* of the eastern Fens? The Atkinson Water Transport Company along with the New Brewery is perhaps already a living creature in the minds of young George and Alfred as they drive away from their father's burial.

And what creature stirs in the mind of Sarah Atkinson? If anything stirs in the mind of Sarah Atkinson. Popular opinion will not entertain the possibility that Sarah Atkinson is stark mad. (Was it not her husband who was the mad one when he struck his wife for no cause at all?) Popular opinion learns scarcely anything of Sarah Atkinson, though it knows that she sits constantly in that upper room, surveying the town like a goddess. And it begins to tell stories. It tells, for example, how although Sarah Atkinson never uttered a word to her husband after that fatal day, nor ever gave him a single glance of recognition, such was not the case with her two sons. That to them indeed she imparted, perhaps in plain words, perhaps by some other mystical process of communication, wisdom and exhortation. That it was from her, and not from their father, that they got their zeal and their peculiar sense of mission. Not only this, but the success that came to the Atkinson brothers came to them not from their own sterling efforts but from this wronged Martyr.

In short, that blow to the head had bestowed on Sarah that gift which is so desired and feared— the gift to see and shape the future.

Thus it was she who so uncannily predicted the exact timing of the repeal of the Corn Laws; it was she who devised a cunning strategy to outface the Challenge of the Railways; it was she who divined, and even caused to be, the boom years of the mid-century and who envisaged, even as they stood by their father's grave, her George and Alfred, masters respectively of the Brewery and the Transport Company and jointly of the Leem Navigation and the Atkinson Agricultural Estates, as kings in their own country.

Yet some imaginative Gildsey souls went much further than this. For when that portrait of Sarah in her old age, in her black satin dress and diamonds, was painted, and donated by the brothers, in a gesture both poignant and magnanimous, to the town, to be hung in the lobby of the Town Hall, it became the object of no small local pilgrimage. And it was not long before someone asked: did not the gaunt yet angelic features of Sarah bear a striking resemblance to those of St Gunnhilda, in the precious Gunnhilda triptych (then still in the church of her name)—St Gunnhilda who looked out over the devil-ridden Fens and saw visions?

Whether any of this contains a grain of truth; whether the brothers themselves regarded their mother as oracle, priestess, protectress, or merely allowed these rumours to circulate as a means of securing the favour of the town, no one can tell.

But a further story, which supports the stark-mad theory, which has been handed down and repeated too often to be lightly dismissed, relates that, whatever the bonds between Sarah and her sons and whatever the true description—serene, dumb, inscrutable—of her long and stationary vigil in the upper room, she would be seized every so often by a singular form of animation.

It began with a trembling and twitching of her nostrils; then a wrinkling of her nose and an energetic and urgent sniffing. This would be followed by a darting of her eyes hither and thither in an alert fashion and a claw-like tightening of her hands. Then her lips would rub furiously at themselves and while her face contorted and her body wriggled and bounced so violently in her chair that its oak legs sometimes lifted from the floor, she would utter the only words specifically attributed to her in all the years following her husband's dreadful fit of rage. Namely: "Smoke!, Fire!, Burning!", in infinite permutations.

The servants—and this bespeaks their devotion—would exert themselves to calm her. The butler would undertake a tour of the house, checking every fireplace and chimney. A maid would look from the window and affirm that neither smoke nor fire were visible—unless one included the fumes wafting from the brewery chimney, which were nothing but a good sign, or unless the wind was blowing from the direction of Peter Cutlack's smoking-house at the far end of Water Street, where Peter Cutlack turned slithery olive-green Ouse eels into crooked copper-brown walking-sticks. Another maid would be dispatched to the kitchen to ensure that whatever assailed their mistress's nostrils was not a portent that dinner was ruined. A boy would even be sent to inquire in the streets.

But all these steps were to no avail. Sarah would go on sniffing and wriggling and popping her eyes and hollering "Smoke!" and "Burning!" till exhaustion overcame her.

These fits, it is claimed, grew more frequent, and it is a fact not without irony, if entirely coincidental, that in 1841 the Atkinsons, amongst others, were responsible for bringing to Gildsey its first custom-built fire-engine.

More frequent and more distressing—and more embarrassing too. It is even suggested—though here skepticism must step in, for the principal evidence is that of one of the Atkinson servants dismissed for being in a shameless state of pregnancy and thus having a motive to invent malicious lies—that the spasms grew so severe and convulsive that, far from continuing to adore and sanctify their mother, the brothers packed her off to an Institution; though, for the sake of the townsfolk, they continued to preserve the legend (for example, by having a certain picture painted of Sarah in black dress and diamonds when in fact she was trussed up in a strait-jacket) that their Guardian Angel still watched over them.

All this, it is true, was much later, in the 1870s—Sarah, indeed, was a long time dying—when the brothers themselves were past their peak and young Arthur, Sarah's grandson, George's son, was already the driving force of the Atkinson machine. Yet even in 1820, the year of the shocking event, it was put about by certain omen-loving and sourly witty parties that when Thomas Atkinson devised his company emblem, so neatly denoting both his Brewery and Navigation interests, of the crossed barley ears over a symbolic representation of water, and cast about for a motto to go with it, he chose unwisely. For the motto which he chose—Ex Aqua Fermentum—which was once engraved in huge arched capitals over the main entrance to the New Brewery and which appeared on the label of every bottle of Atkinson beer, does indeed mean, simply, Out of Water, Ale, and can even be construed, as perhaps Thomas intended, Out of Water, Activity; but it can also be interpreted, as surely Thomas never meant: "Out of Water, Perturbation".

Children, you are right. There are times when we have to disentangle history from fairy-tale. There are times (they come round really quite often) when good dry textbook history takes a plunge into the old swamps of myth and has to be retrieved with empirical fishing lines. History, being an accredited sub-science, only wants to know the facts. History, if it is to keep on constructing its road into the future, must do so on solid ground. At all costs let us avoid mystery making and speculation, secrets and idle gossip. And, for God's sake, nothing supernatural. And above all, let us not tell stories. Otherwise, how will the future be possible and how will anything get done? So let us get back to that clear and purified air and old Tom tucked up in his new white grave. Let us get back to solid ground…

 思考与讨论

（1）节选内容中描写阿特金森家族的两对父子间的对话有何用意？体现了汤姆怎样的历史观？

（2）节选内容中关于莎拉的传说是怎样构建起来的？她的形象为何在不同人的印象中截然不同？

（3）节选内容中欧洲大陆的历史是怎么与阿特金森家族的历史联系起来的？

（4）小说中多次对芬斯沼泽地环境的描写有何作用？

（5）如何看待小说中玛丽的窃婴行为？

（6）如何看待小说中以普莱斯为代表的学生们对于历史的理解？

 拓展阅读

［1］ Acheson, J. Historia and Guilt: Graham Swift's *Waterland*. *Critique Studies in Contemporary Fiction*, Vol. 47, No. 1(2005), pp. 90 – 100.

［2］ Astrid, B. "Man Is the Story-Telling Animal": Graham Swift's *Waterland*, Ecocriticism and Narratology. *Isle Interdisciplinary Studies in Literature & Environment*, Vol. 25, No. 2(2018), pp. 220 – 237.

［3］ Reed, R. "Telling It Unabridged": Graham Swift's Revision of "*Waterland*". *Studies in Bibliography*, Vol. 57, No. 1(2005), pp. 289 – 298.

三、希拉里·曼特尔

（一）希拉里·曼特尔简介

希拉里·曼特尔出生于英格兰德比郡小镇格洛索普。因父母离异，曼特尔跟随母亲到柴郡的罗米利镇生活。曼特尔于1973年在谢菲尔德大学获得法学学士学位。毕业后，曾在一家老年医院工作，还为英国一些报纸和杂志撰写评论文章。出于对写作的浓厚兴趣，曼特尔开始从事小说创作，《狼厅》和《提堂》(*Bring up the Bodies*，2012)分别赢得2009年和2012年布克奖。《狼厅》是她的代表作。

希拉里·曼特尔的文学创作包括短篇小说、长篇小说和回忆录。曼特尔的长篇小说中历史小说最具特色，其中"克伦威尔三部曲"——《狼厅》《提堂》和《镜与光》(*The Mirror and the Light*，2020)最为著名。短篇小说集有《学说话》(*Learning to Talk*，2003)和《暗杀玛格丽特·撒切尔》(*The Assassination of Margaret Thatcher*，2014)。回忆录《放弃幽灵》(*Giving up the Ghost*，2003)讲述了曼特尔的童年生活。

希拉里·曼特尔的创作生涯始于 20 世纪 70 年代,其早期作品并未获得评论家太多的关注。1974 年,曼特尔开始她的创作生涯。曼特尔创作的第一部小说《一个更安全的地方》(*A Place of Greater Safety*,1992)重现了法国大革命的恢宏场面以及与之相关的历史事件,该小说直到 1992 年才得以出版,并获得了 1992 年的《周日快报》年度小说奖。曼特尔的另一部历史小说《巨人奥布莱恩》(*The Giant, O'Brien*,1998)讲述了 18 世纪的高个子爱尔兰人查尔斯·布莱恩在伦敦演出的故事,阐释了资本主义工业文明导致的人类异化问题。

希拉里·曼特尔的作品题材丰富,有以英格兰为背景的《黑暗至上》(*Beyond Black*,2005),还有以中东为背景的《加沙大街上的八个月》(*Eight Months on Ghazzah Street*,1988),《弗拉德》(*Fludd*,1989)的故事发生在英国北方磨坊小镇。《每天都是母亲节》(*Every Day is Mother's Day*,1985)是一部以现代生活为题材的长篇小说,这部作品的续集是《空白财产》(*Vacant Possession*,1986)。

希拉里·曼特尔的"克伦威尔三部曲"以历史为主线,虚实相间再现了错综复杂的都铎王朝历史。BBC 将《狼厅》和《提堂》改编成电视剧。《镜与光》写的是克伦威尔生命最后四年的岁月,该小说被改编成戏剧,由皇家莎士比亚剧团出演。"克伦威尔三部曲"的三部小说有相似之处,也有诸多不同,它们都在英国历史小说的舞台上展示出独特的魅力。

(二)《狼厅》简介

从托马斯·克伦威尔的视角出发,《狼厅》讲述了都铎王朝期间,英格兰国王亨利八世与第一任王后凯瑟琳离婚,与安妮·博林再婚引发的宗教与政治权力的斗争。《狼厅》既讲述了英国的历史,又讲述了克伦威尔的个人史。《狼厅》的现在时叙事,带给读者沉浸式的阅读体验,以当代的叙述方式讲述历史故事,语言风格细腻,篇幅宏大,人物角色众多,人物刻画栩栩如生。

作品开篇发生在 1500 年的帕特尼,年少的托马斯·克伦威尔遭父亲毒打而离家出走。1527 年,克伦威尔已是红衣主教托马斯·沃尔西身边的一名亲信,同样为红衣主教服务的还有史蒂芬·加迪纳。他们二人彼此争斗,都想得到红衣主教的偏爱。红衣主教与克伦威尔的谈话中提及亨利八世与凯瑟琳的事情,以及过去的一些回忆。后来红衣主教倒台,克伦威尔不离不弃,彰显了其有情有义的品质。在红衣主教亦师亦父的关照下,克伦威尔迅速成长可以独当一面。红衣主教的未竟之事是帮助亨利八世与凯瑟琳顺利离婚,这正是克伦威尔需要去完成的。虽困难重重,但克伦威尔没有退缩。亨利八世相信安妮·博林会为他带来一位男性继承人,所以他必须与凯瑟琳离婚。克伦威尔最后不辱使命,为亨利八世扫清障碍,实现了他的计划。《狼厅》的故事结束于 1535 年 7 月,此时克伦威尔正处于事业巅峰,深受亨利八世的信任,故事戛然而止使读者对"克伦威尔三部曲"后续的两部充满期待。

《狼厅》中人物众多,真实的历史人物在曼特尔的塑造下独具色彩,其中塑造最为成功的角色当属托马斯·克伦威尔。托马斯·克伦威尔在历史上确实是铁匠之子,而后成为英国历史上最重要的政治家之一,先后当过财政大臣、掌玺大臣、首席国务大臣,并被封为埃塞克斯伯爵。托马斯·克伦威尔力促议会通过一系列法案,推行宗教改革,解散修道院,进行政治改革,为英国后续的发展奠定了良好的基础。但对克伦威尔的历史记载不够详细,存在许多空白之处。曼特尔在《狼厅》中巧妙地填补了这一空白,把克伦威尔塑造成有血有肉有情有义的正面形象。《狼厅》之前的文学作品往往对托马斯·克伦威尔采取单一的妖魔化处理，常是邪恶自私的配角，而《狼厅》中的克伦威尔有政治远见、富有同情心、重视亲情友情、勤勉敬业。曼特尔对托马斯·克伦威尔的形象塑造颠覆传统，精细入微的刻画受到了读者的青睐。尽管克伦威尔因其出身经常被朝臣贵族耻笑，但这也恰恰证明了克伦威尔的能力超群。克伦威尔的崛起恰逢英国复兴，个人命运与国家命运紧密联系在一起，小说中克伦威尔既受限于历史，又能创造历史。《狼厅》作为"克伦威尔三部曲"中的第一部小说，是最具独特性，值得深入研究。

（三）作品选读：《狼厅》①

They are taking apart the cardinal's house. Room by room, the king's men are stripping York Place of its owner. They are bundling up parchments and scrolls, missals and memoranda and the volumes of his personal accounts; they are taking even the ink and the quills. They are prising from the walls the boards on which the cardinal's coat of arms is painted.

They arrived on a Sunday, two vengeful grandees: the Duke of Norfolk a bright-eyed hawk, the Duke of Suffolk just as keen. They told the cardinal he was dismissed as Lord Chancellor, and demanded he hand over the Great Seal of England. He, Cromwell, touched the cardinal's arm. A hurried conference. The cardinal turned back to them, gracious: it appears a written request from the king is necessary; have you one? Oh: careless of you. It requires a lot of face to keep so calm; but then the cardinal has face.

"You want us to ride back to Windsor?" Charles Brandon is incredulous. "For a piece of paper? When the situation's plain?"

That's like Suffolk; to think the letter of the law is some kind of luxury. He whispers to the cardinal again, and the cardinal says, "No, I think we'd better tell them, Thomas... not prolong the matter beyond its natural life... My lords, my lawyer here says I can't give you the Seal, written request or not. He says that properly speaking I should only hand it to the Master of the Rolls. So you'd better bring him with you."

He says, lightly, "Be glad we told you, my lords. Otherwise it would have been three trips, wouldn't it?"

Norfolk grins. He likes a scrap. "Am obliged, master," he says.

When they go Wolsey turns and hugs him, his face gleeful. Though it is the last of their victories and they know it, it is important to show ingenuity; twenty-four hours is worth buying, when the king is so changeable. Besides, they enjoyed it. "Master of the Rolls," Wolsey says. "Did you know that, or did you make it up?"

Monday morning the dukes are back. Their instructions are to turn out the occupants this very day, because the king wants to send in his own builders and furnishers and get the palace ready to

---

① Mantel, H. *Wolf Hall*. New York: Henry Holt & Company, 2009, pp. 45-62.

hand over to the Lady Anne, who needs a London house of her own.

He's prepared to stand and argue the point: have I missed something? This palace belongs to the archdiocese of York. When was Lady Anne made an archbishop?

But the tide of men flooding in by the water stairs is sweeping them away. The two dukes have made themselves scarce, and there's nobody to argue with. What a terrible sight, someone says: Master Cromwell baulked of a fight. And now the cardinal's ready to go, but where? Over his customary scarlet, he is wearing a travelling cloak that belongs to someone else; they are confiscating his wardrobe piece by piece, so he has to grab what he can. It is autumn, and though he is a big man he feels the cold.

They are overturning chests and tipping out their contents. They scatter across the floor, letters from Popes, letters from the scholars of Europe: from Utrecht, from Paris, from San Diego de Compostela; from Erfurt, from Strassburg, from Rome. They are packing his gospels and taking them for the king's libraries. The texts are heavy to hold in the arms, and awkward as if they breathed; their pages are made of slunk vellum from stillborn calves, reveined by the illuminator in tints of lapis and leaf-green.

They take down the tapestries and leave the bare blank walls. They are rolled up, the woollen monarchs, Solomon and Sheba; as they are brought into coiled proximity, their eyes are filled by each other, and their tiny lungs breathe in the fibre of bellies and thighs. Down come the cardinal's hunting scenes, the scenes of secular pleasure: the sportive peasants splashing in ponds, the stags at bay, the hounds in cry, the spaniels held on leashes of silk and the mastiffs with their collars of spikes: the huntsmen with their studded belts and knives, the ladies on horseback with jaunty caps, the rush-fringed pond, the mild sheep at pasture, and the bluish feathered treetops, running away into a long plumed distance, to a scene of chalky bluffs and a white sailing sky.

The cardinal looks at the scavengers as they go about their work. "Have we refreshments for our visitors?"

In the two great rooms that adjoin the gallery they have set up trestle tables. Each trestle is twenty feet long and they are bringing up more. In the Gilt Chamber they have laid out the cardinal's gold plate, his jewels and precious stones, and they are deciphering his inventories and calling out the weight of the plate. In the Council Chamber they are stacking his silver and parcel-gilt. Because everything is listed, down to the last dented pan from the kitchens, they have put baskets under the tables so they can throw in any item unlikely to catch the eye of the king. Sir William Gascoigne, the cardinal's treasurer, is moving constantly between the rooms, preoccupied, talking, directing the attention of the commissioners to any corner, any press and chest that he thinks they may have overlooked.

Behind him trots George Cavendish, the cardinal's gentleman usher; his face is raw and open with dismay. They bring out the cardinal's vestments, his copes. Stiff with embroidery, strewn with pearls, encrusted with gemstones, they seem to stand by themselves. The raiders knock down each one as if they are knocking down Thomas Becket. They itemise it, and having reduced it to its knees and broken its spine, they toss it into their travelling crates. Cavendish flinches: "For God's sake, gentlemen, line those chests with a double thickness of cambric. Would you shred the fine work that has taken nuns a lifetime?" He turns: "Master Cromwell, do you think we can get these people out before dark?"

"Only if we help them. If it's got to be done, we can make sure they do it properly." This is an indecent spectacle: the man who has ruled England, reduced. They have brought out bolts of fine holland, velvets and grosgrain, sarcenet and taffeta, scarlet by the yard: the scarlet silk in which he braves the summer heat of London, the crimson brocades that keep his blood warm when snow falls on Westminster and whisks in sleety eddies over the Thames. In public the cardinal wears red, just red, but in various weights, various weaves, various degrees of pigment and dye, but all of them the best of their kind, the best reds to be got for money. There have been days when, swaggering out, he would say, "Right, Master Cromwell, price me by the yard!"

And he would say, "Let me see," and walk slowly around the cardinal; and saying "May I?" he would pinch a sleeve between an expert forefinger and thumb; and standing back, he would view him, to estimate his girth—year on year, the cardinal expands—and so come up with a figure. The cardinal would clap his hands, delighted. "Let the begrudgers behold us! On, on, on." His procession would form up, his silver crosses, his sergeants-at-arms with their axes of gilt: for the cardinal went nowhere, in public, without a procession.

So day by day, at his request and to amuse him, he would put a value on his master. Now the king has sent an army of clerks to do it. But he would like to take away their pens by force and write across their inventories: Thomas Wolsey is a man beyond price.

"Now, Thomas," the cardinal says, patting him. "Everything I have, I have from the king. The king gave it to me, and if it pleases him to take York Place fully furnished, I am sure we own other houses, we have other roofs to shelter under. This is not Putney, you know." The cardinal holds on to him. "So I forbid you to hit anyone." He affects to be pressing his arms by his sides, in smiling restraint. The cardinal's fingers tremble.

The treasurer Gascoigne comes in and says, "I hear Your Grace is to go straight to the Tower."

"Do you?" he says. "Where did you hear that?"

"Sir William Gascoigne," the cardinal says, measuring out his name, "what do you suppose I have done that would make the king want to send me to the Tower?"

"It's like you," he says to Gascoigne, "to spread every story you're told. Is that all the comfort you've got to offer—walk in here with evil rumours? Nobody's going to the Tower. We're going— and the household waits, breath held, as he improvises—to Esher. And your job," he can't help giving Gascoigne a little shove in the chest, "is to keep an eye on all these strangers and see that everything that's taken out of here gets where it's meant to go, and that nothing goes missing by the way, because if it does you'll be beating on the gates of the Tower and begging them to take you in, to get away from me."

Various noises: mainly, from the back of the room, a sort of stifled cheer. It's hard to escape the feeling that this is a play, and the cardinal is in it: the Cardinal and his Attendants. And that it is a tragedy. Cavendish tugs at him, anxious, sweating. "But Master Cromwell, the house at Esher is an empty house, we haven't a pot, we haven't a knife or a spit, where will my lord cardinal sleep, I doubt we have a bed aired, we have neither linen nor firewood nor... and how are we going to get there?"

"Sir William," the cardinal says to Gascoigne, "take no offence from Master Cromwell, who is, upon the occasion, blunt to a fault; but take what is said to heart. Since everything I have proceeds from the king, everything must be delivered back in good order." He turns away, his lips twitching. Except when he teased the dukes yesterday, he hasn't smiled in a month. "Tom," he says, "I've spent years teaching you not to talk like that."

Cavendish says to him, "They haven't seized my lord cardinal's barge yet. Nor his horses."

"No?" He lays a hand on Cavendish's shoulder: "We go upriver, as many as the barge will take. Horses can meet us at—at Putney, in fact—and then we will... borrow things. Come on, George Cavendish, exercise some ingenuity, we've done more difficult things in these last years than get the household to Esher."

Is this true? He's never taken much notice of Cavendish, a sensitive sort of man who talks a lot about table napkins. But he's trying to think of a way to put some military backbone into him, and the best way lies in suggesting that they are brothers from some old campaign.

"Yes, yes," Cavendish says, "we'll order up the barge."

Good, he says, and the cardinal says, Putney? and he tries to laugh. He says, well, Thomas, you told Gascoigne, you did; there's something about that man I never have liked, and he says, why did you keep him then? and the cardinal says, oh, well, one does, and again the cardinal says, Putney, eh?

He says, "Whatever we face at journey's end, we shall not forget how nine years ago, for the meeting of two kings, Your Grace created a golden city in some sad damp fields in Picardy. Since then, Your Grace has only increased in wisdom and the king's esteem."

He is speaking for everyone to hear; and he thinks, that occasion was about peace, notionally, whereas this occasion, we don't know what this is, it is the first day of a long or a short campaign; we had better dig in and hope our supply lines hold. "I think we will manage to find some fire irons and soup kettles and whatever else George Cavendish thinks we can't do without. When I remember that Your Grace provisioned the king's great armies, that went to fight in France."

"Yes," the cardinal says, "and we all know what you thought about our campaigns, Thomas."

Cavendish says, "What?" and the cardinal says, "George, don't you call to mind what my man Cromwell said in the House of Commons, was it five years past, when we wanted a subsidy for the new war?"

"But he spoke against Your Grace!"

Gascoigne—who hangs doggedly to this conversation—says, "You didn't advance yourself there, master, speaking against the king and my lord cardinal, because I do remember your speech, and I assure you so will others, and you bought yourself no favours there, Cromwell."

He shrugs. "I didn't mean to buy favour. We're not all like you, Gascoigne. I wanted the Commons to take some lessons from the last time. To cast their minds back."

"You said we'd lose."

"I said we'd be bankrupted. But I tell you, all our wars would have ended much worse without my lord cardinal to supply them."

"In the year 1523—" Gascoigne says.

"Must we refight this now?" says the cardinal.

"—the Duke of Suffolk was only fifty miles from Paris."

"Yes," he says, "and do you know what fifty miles is, to a half starved infantryman in winter, when he sleeps on wet ground and wakes up cold? Do you know what fifty miles is to a baggage train, with carts up to the axles in mud? And as for the glories of 1513—God defend us."

"Tournai! Thérouanne!" Gascoigne shouts. "Are you blind to what occurred? Two French towns taken! The king so valiant in the field!"

If we were in the field now, he thinks, I'd spit at your feet. "If you like the king so much, go and work for him. Or do you already?"

The cardinal clears his throat softly. "We all do," Cavendish says, and the cardinal says, "Thomas, we are the works of his hand."

When they get out to the cardinal's barge his flags are flying: the Tudor rose, the Cornish choughs. Cavendish says, wide-eyed, "Look at all these little boats, waffeting up and down." For a moment, the cardinal thinks the Londoners have turned out to wish him well. But as he enters the barge, there are sounds of hooting and booing from the boats; spectators crowd the bank, and though the cardinal's men keep them back, their intent is clear enough. When the oars begin to row upstream, and not downstream to the Tower, there are groans and shouted threats.

It is then that the cardinal collapses, falling into his seat, beginning to talk, and talks, talks, talks, all the way to Putney. "Do they hate me so much? What have I done but promote their trades and show them my goodwill? Have I sown hatred? No. Persecuted none. Sought remedies every year when wheat was scarce. When the apprentices rioted, begged the king on my knees with tears in my eyes to spare the offenders, while they stood garlanded with the nooses that were to hang them."

"The multitude," Cavendish says, "is always desirous of a change. They never see a great man set up but they must pull him down—for the novelty of the thing."

"Fifteen years Chancellor. Twenty in his service. His father's before that. Never spared myself...rising early, watching late..."

"There, you see," Cavendish says, "what it is to serve a prince! We should be wary of their vacillations of temper."

"Princes are not obliged to consistency," he says. He thinks, I may forget myself, lean across and push you overboard.

The cardinal has not forgotten himself, far from it; he is looking back, back twenty years to the young king's accession. "Put him to work, said some. But I said, no, he is a young man. Let him hunt, joust, and fly his hawks and falcons..."

"Play instruments," Cavendish says. "Always plucking at something or other. And singing."

"You make him sound like Nero."

"Nero?" Cavendish jumps. "I never said so."

"The gentlest, wisest prince in Christendom," says the cardinal. "I will not hear a word against him from any man."

"Nor shall you," he says.

"But what I would do for him! Cross the Channel as lightly as a man might step across a stream of piss in the street." The cardinal shakes his head. "Waking and sleeping, on horseback or at my beads...twenty years..."

"Is it something to do with the English?" Cavendish asks earnestly. He's still thinking of the uproar back there when they embarked; and even now, people are running along the banks, making obscene signs and whistling. "Tell us, Master Cromwell, you've been abroad. Are they particularly an ungrateful nation? It seems to me that they like change for the sake of it."

"I don't think it's the English. I think it's just people. They always hope there may be something better."

"But what do they get by the change?" Cavendish persists. "One dog sated with meat is replaced by a hungrier dog who bites nearer the bone. Out goes the man grown fat with honour, and in comes a hungry and a lean man."

He closes his eyes. The river shifts beneath them, dim figures in an allegory of Fortune. Decayed Magnificence sits in the centre. Cavendish, leaning at his right like a Virtuous Councillor, mutters words of superfluous and belated advice, to which the sorry magnate inclines his head; he, like a Tempter, is seated on the left, and the cardinal's great hand, with its knuckles of garnet and tourmaline, grips his own hand painfully. George would certainly go in the river, except that what he's saying, despite the platitudes, makes a bleak sense. And why? Stephen Gardiner, he thinks. It may not be proper to call the cardinal a dog grown fat, but Stephen is definitely hungry and lean, and has been promoted by the king to a place as his own private secretary. It is not unusual for the cardinal's staff to transfer in this way, after careful nurture in the Wolsey school of craft and diligence; but still, this places Stephen as the man who—if he manages his duties properly—may be closer than anyone to the king, except perhaps for the gentleman who attends him at his close-stool and hands him a diaper cloth. I wouldn't so much mind, he thinks, if Stephen got that job.

The cardinal closes his eyes. Tears are seeping from beneath his lids. "For it is a truth," says Cavendish, "that fortune is inconstant, fickle and mutable..."

All he has to do is to make a strangling motion, quickly, while the cardinal has his eyes shut. Cavendish, putting a hand to his throat, takes the point. And then they look at each other, sheepish. One of them has said too much; one of them has felt too much. It is not easy to know where the balance rests. His eyes scan the banks of the Thames. Still, the cardinal weeps and grips his hand.

As they move upriver, the littoral ceases to alarm. It is not because, in Putney, Englishmen are less fickle. It's just that they haven't heard yet.

The horses are waiting. The cardinal, in his capacity as a churchman, has always ridden a large strong mule; though, since he has hunted with kings for twenty years, his stable is the envy of every nobleman. Here the beast stands, twitching long ears, in its usual scarlet trappings, and by him Master Sexton, the cardinal's fool.

"What in God's name is he doing here?" he asks Cavendish.

Sexton comes forward and says something in the cardinal's ear; the cardinal laughs. "Very good, Patch. Now, help me mount, there's a good fellow."

But Patch—Master Sexton—is not up to the job. The cardinal seems weakened; he seems to feel the weight of his flesh hanging on his bones. He, Cromwell, slides from his saddle, nods to three of the stouter servants. "Master Patch, hold Christopher's head." When Patch pretends not to know that Christopher is the mule, and puts a headlock on the man next to him, he says, oh for Jesus' sake, Sexton, get out of the way, or I'll stuff you in a sack and drown you.

The man who's nearly had his head pulled off stands up, rubs his neck; says, thanks Master Cromwell, and hobbles forward to hold the bridle. He, Cromwell, with two others, hauls the cardinal into the saddle. The cardinal looks shamefaced. "Thank you, Tom." He laughs shakily. "That's you told, Patch."

They are ready to ride. Cavendish looks up. "Saints protect us!" A single horseman is heading downhill at a gallop. "An arrest!" "By one man?"

"An outrider," says Cavendish, and he says, Putney's rough but you don't have to send out scouts. Then someone shouts, "It's Harry Norris." Harry throws himself from his mount. Whatever he's come to do, he's in a lather about it. Harry Norris is one of the king's closest friends; he is, to be exact, the Groom of the Stool, the man who hands the diaper cloth.

Wolsey sees, immediately, that the king wouldn't send Norris to take him into custody. "Now, Sir Henry, get your breath back. What can be so urgent?"

Norris says, beg pardon, my lord, my lord cardinal, sweeps off his feathered cap, wipes his face with his arm, smiles in his most engaging fashion. He speaks to the cardinal gracefully: the king has commanded him to ride after His Grace and overtake him, and speak words of comfort to him and give him this ring, which he knows well—a ring which he holds out, in the palm of his glove.

The cardinal scrambles from his mule and falls to the ground. He takes the ring and presses it to his lips. He's praying. Praying, thanking Norris, calling for blessings on his sovereign. "I have nothing to send him. Nothing of value to send to the king." He looks around him, as if his eye might light on something he can send; a tree? Norris tries to get him on his feet, ends up kneeling beside him, kneeling—this neat and charming man—in the Putney mud. The message he's giving the cardinal, it seems, is that the king only appears displeased, but is not really displeased; that he knows the cardinal has enemies; that he himself, Henricus Rex, is not one of them; that this show of force is only to satisfy those enemies; that he is able to recompense the cardinal with twice as much as has been taken from him.

The cardinal begins to cry. It's starting to rain, and the wind blows the rain across their faces. The cardinal speaks to Norris fast, in a low voice, and then he takes a chain from around his neck and tries to hang it around Norris's neck, and it gets tangled up in the fastenings of his riding cape and several people rush forward to help and fail, and Norris gets up and begins to brush himself down with one glove while clutching the chain in the other. "Wear it," the cardinal begs him, "and when you look at it think of me, and commend me to the king."

Cavendish jolts up, riding knee-to-knee. "His reliquary!" George is upset, astonished. "To part with it like this! It is a piece of the true Cross!"

"We'll get him another. I know a man in Pisa makes them ten for five florins and a round dozen for cash up front. And you get a certificate with St Peter's thumbprint, to say they're genuine."

"For shame!" Cavendish says, and twitches his horse away.

Now Norris is backing away too, his message delivered, and they are trying to get the cardinal back on his mule. This time, four big men step forward, as if it were routine. The play has turned into some kind of low comic interlude; that, he thinks, is why Patch is here. He rides over and says, looking down from the saddle, "Norris, can we have all this in writing?"

Norris smiles, says, "Hardly, Master Cromwell; it's a confidential message to my lord cardinal. My master's words were meant only for him."

"So what about this recompense you mention?"

Norris laughs—as he always does, to disarm hostility—and whispers,

"I think it might be figurative." "I think it might be, too." Double the cardinal's worth? Not on Henry's income. "Give us back what's been taken. We don't ask double."

Norris's hand goes to the chain, now slung about his neck. "But it all proceeds from the king. You can't call it theft."

"I didn't call it theft."

Norris nods, thoughtful. "No more did you."

"They shouldn't have taken the vestments. They belong to my lord as churchman. What will they have next? His benefices?"

"Esher—which is where you are going, are you not? —is of course one of the houses which my lord cardinal holds as Bishop of Winchester."

"And?"

"He remains for the while in that estate and title, but. . .shall we say. . .it must come under the king's consideration? You know my lord cardinal is indicted under the statutes of praemunire, for asserting a foreign jurisdiction in the land."

"Don't teach me the law."

Norris inclines his head.

He thinks, since last spring, when things began to go wrong, I should have persuaded my lord cardinal to let me manage his revenues, and put some money away abroad where they can't get it; but then he would never admit that anything was wrong. Why did I let him rest so cheerful?

Norris's hand is on his horse's bridle. "I was ever a person who admired your master," he says, "and I hope that in his adversity he will remember that."

"I thought he wasn't in adversity? According to you."

How simple it would be, if he were allowed to reach down and shake some straight answers out of Norris. But it's not simple; this is what the world and the cardinal conspire to teach him.

"Christ", he thinks, "by my age I ought to know. You don't get on by being original. You don't get on by being bright. You don't get on by being strong. You get on by being a subtle crook; somehow he thinks that's what Norris is, and he feels an irrational dislike taking root, and he tries to dismiss it, because he prefers his dislikes rational, but after all, these circumstances are extreme, the cardinal in the mud, the humiliating tussle to get him back in the saddle, the talking, talking on the barge, and worse, the talking, talking on his knees, as if Wolsey's unravelling, in a great unweaving of scarlet thread that might lead you back into a scarlet labyrinth, with a dying monster at its heart."

"Master Cromwell?" Norris says.

He can hardly say what he's thinking; so he looks down at Norris, his expression softened, and says, "Thanks for this much comfort." "Well, take my lord cardinal out of the rain. I'll tell the king how I found him."

"Tell him how you knelt in the mud together. He might be amused."

"Yes." Norris looks sad. "You never know what will do it."

It is at this point that Patch starts screaming. The cardinal, it seems—casting around for a gift—has given him to the king. Patch, he has often said, is worth a thousand pounds. He is to go with Norris, no time like the present; and it takes four more of the cardinal's men to subdue him to the purpose. He fights. He bites. He lashes out with fists and feet. Till he is thrown on to a baggage mule, stripped of its baggage; till he begins to cry, hiccupping, his ribs heaving, his stupid feet dangling, his coat torn and the feather in his hat broken off to a stub.

"But Patch," the cardinal says, "my dear fellow. You shall see me often, once the king and I understand each other again. My dear Patch, I will write you a letter, a letter of your own. I shall write it tonight," he promises, "and put my big seal on it. The king will cherish you; he is the kindest soul in Christendom."

Patch wails on a single thin note, like someone taken by the Turks and impaled.

There, he says to Cavendish, he's more than one kind of fool. He shouldn't have drawn attention to himself, should he.

Esher: the cardinal dismounts under the shadow of old Bishop Wayneflete's keep, surmounted by octagonal towers. The gateway is set into a defensive wall topped with a walkway; stern enough at first sight, but the whole thing is built of brick, ornamented and prettily inlaid. "You couldn't fortify it," he says. Cavendish is silent. "George, you're supposed to say, 'But the need could never arise.'"

The cardinal's not used the place since he built Hampton Court. They've sent messages ahead, but has anything been done? Make my lord comfortable, he says, and goes straight down to the kitchens. At Hampton Court, the kitchens have running water; here, nothing's running but the cooks' noses. Cavendish is right. In fact it is worse than he thinks. The larders are impoverished and such supplies as they have show signs of ill-keeping and plunder. There are weevils in the flour. There are mouse droppings where the pastry should be rolled. It is nearly Martinmas, and they have not even thought of salting their beef. The batterie de cuisine is an insult, and the stockpot is mildewed. There are a number of small boys sitting by the hearth, and, for cash down, they can be induced into scouring and scrubbing; children take readily to novelty, and the idea of cleaning, it seems, is novel to them.

"My lord", he says, "needs to eat and drink now; and he needs to eat and drink for...how long we don't know. This kitchen must be put in order for the winter ahead. He finds someone who can write, and dictates his orders. His eyes are fixed on the kitchen clerk. On his left hand he counts off the items: you do this, then this, then thirdly this. With his right hand, he breaks eggs into a basin, each one with a hard professional tap, and between his fingers the white drips, sticky and slow, from the yolk. "How old is this egg? Change your supplier. I want a nutmeg. Nutmeg? Saffron?" They look at him as if he's speaking Greek. Patch's thin scream is still hurting his ears. Dusty angels look down on him as he pounds back to the hall.

It is late before they get the cardinal into any sort of bed worthy of the name. Where is his household steward? Where is his comptroller? By this time, he feels it is true that he and Cavendish are old survivors of a campaign. He stays up with Cavendish—not that there are beds, if they wanted them—working out what they need to keep the cardinal in reasonable comfort; they need plate, unless my lord's going to dine off dented pewter, they need bedsheets, table linen, firewood. "I will send some people," he says, "to sort out the kitchens. They will be Italian. It will be violent at first, but then after three weeks it will work."

Three weeks? He wants to set those children cleaning the copper. "Can we get lemons?" he asks, just as Cavendish says, "So who will be Chancellor now?"

"I wonder," he thinks, "are there rats down there?" Cavendish says, "Recall His Grace of Canterbury?"

Recall him—fifteen years after the cardinal chivvied him out of that office? "No, Warham's too old." And too stubborn, too unaccommodating to the king's wishes. "And not the Duke of Suffolk"—because in his view Charles Brandon is no brighter than Christopher the mule, though better at fighting and fashion and generally showing off—"not Suffolk, because the Duke of Norfolk won't have him."

"And vice versa." Cavendish nods. "Bishop Tunstall?"

"No. Thomas More."

"But, a layman and a commoner? And when he's so opposed in the matter of the king's marriage suit."

He nods, yes, yes, it will be More. The king is known for putting out his conscience to high bidders. Perhaps he hopes to be saved from himself.

"If the king offers it—and I see that, as a gesture, he might—surely Thomas More won't accept?"

"He will."

"Bet?" says Cavendish.

They agree the terms and shake hands on it. It takes their mind off the urgent problem, which is the rats, and the cold; which is the question of how they can pack a household staff of several hundred, retained at Westminster, into the much smaller space at Esher. The cardinal's staff, if you include his principal houses, and count them up from priests, law clerks, down to floor-sweepers and laundresses, is about six hundred souls. They expect three hundred following them immediately. "As things stand, we'll have to break up the household," Cavendish says. "But we've no ready money for wages."

"I'm damned if they're going unpaid," he says, and Cavendish says, "I think you are anyway. After what you said about the relic."

He catches George's eye. They start to laugh. At least they've got something worthwhile to drink; the cellars are full, which is lucky, Cavendish says, because we'll need a drink over the next weeks. "What do you think Norris meant?" George says. "How can the king be in two minds? How can my lord cardinal be dismissed if he doesn't want to dismiss him? How can the king give way to my lord's enemies? Isn't the king master, over all the enemies?"

"You would think so."

"Or is it her? It must be. He's frightened of her, you know. She's a witch."

He says, don't be childish. George says, she is so a witch: the Duke of Norfolk says she is, and he's her uncle, he should know.

It's two o'clock, then it's three; sometimes it's freeing, to think you don't have to go to bed because there isn't a bed. He doesn't need to think of going home; there's no home to go to, he's got no family left. He'd rather be here drinking with Cavendish, huddled in a corner of the great chamber at Esher, cold and tired and frightened of the future, than think about his family and what he's lost. "Tomorrow," he says, "I'll get my clerks down from London and we'll try and make sense of what my lord still has by way of assets, which won't be easy as they've taken all the paperwork. His creditors won't be inclined to pay up when they know what's happened. But the French king pays him a pension, and if I remember it's always in arrears... Maybe he'd like to send a bag of gold, pending my lord's return to favour. And you—you can go looting."

Cavendish is hollow-faced and hollow-eyed when he throws him on to a fresh horse at first light. "Call in some favours. There's hardly a gentleman in the realm that doesn't owe my lord cardinal something."

It's late October, the sun a coin barely flipped above the horizon. "Keep him cheerful," Cavendish says. "Keep him talking. Keep him talking about what Harry Norris said..."

"Off you go. If you should see the coals on which St Lawrence was roasted, we could make good use of them here." "Oh, don't," Cavendish begs. He has come far since yesterday, and is able to make jokes about holy martyrs; but he drank too much last night, and it hurts him to laugh. But not to laugh is painful too. George's head droops, the horse stirs beneath him, his eyes are full of bafflement. "How did it come to this?" he asks. "My lord cardinal kneeling in the dirt. How could it happen? How in the world could it?"

He says, "Saffron. Raisins. Apples. And cats, get cats, huge starving ones. I don't know, George, where do cats come from? Oh, wait! Do you think we can get partridges?"

If we can get partridges we can slice the breasts, and braise them at the table. Whatever we can do that way, we will; and so, if we can help it, my lord won't be poisoned.

 思考与讨论

(1) 节选中作者如何看待英国民众性格,体现在哪些地方?

（2）节选体现了怎样的写作特点,这一写作特点有何功能?

（3）如何看待《狼厅》中托马斯·克伦威尔的形象?

（4）小说中红衣主教和克伦威尔的关系如何?

（5）如何理解小说中示巴女王挂毯这一意象?

（6）如何看待小说中塞克斯顿这一弄臣角色?

 拓展阅读

［1］ Arnold, L. *Reading Hilary Mantel: Haunted Decades*. London: Bloomsbury Academic, 2020.

［2］ David, K. The Human Pared Away: Hilary Mantel's Thomas Cromwell as an Archetype of Legal Pragmatism. *Literature*. Vol. 34, No. 1(2022), pp. 109 - 139.

［3］ Pollard, E. *Origin and Ellipsis in the Writing of Hilary Mantel*. New York: Routledge Talyor & Francis Group, 2019.